Triangle
The Complete Series

SUSANN JULIEVA

& ROMELLE ENGEL

"Triangle - Book 1: Triangle" and "Triangle - Book 2: Redefinitions"
Copyright 2002-2010 Susann Julieva.

"Triangle - Book 3: Recast" and "Triangle - Book 4: Retribution"
Copyright 2004-2010 Susann Julieva and Romelle Engel.

All rights reserved.

This is a work of fiction. Names, characters, places, and incidents either are the products of the authors' imagination or are used fictitiously, and any resemblance to actual persons, living or dead, business establishments, events or locales is entirely coincidental.

ISBN: 1489556311
ISBN-13: 978-1489556318

A NOTE FROM THE AUTHORS

A heartfelt thank you to everyone who sent us feedback over the years, cheering us on and caring so much about our characters.
This is for you.
Much love,
Susann & Romelle

Susann
writes the point of views of
James Foley, Casey Mills, and Danny Rizzo

Romelle
writes the point of view of
Nick Keller

For more information and other publications
by Susann Julieva, please visit
www.susannjulieva.com

Book 1
Triangle

SUSANN JULIEVA

1 AZURE

JAMES: Azure. Vast and cloudless. High above, out of reach. And still, when you're lying on your back and you stare at the sky for long enough, you can't help feeling its weight pressing down on you. But maybe that's just me. I'm not really the beach kind of person. I'm sure one of those annoying sea gulls cruising above will shit on me sooner or later.

What am I doing here anyway? I have a paper due on Monday that's waiting to be finished. Not to forget the six other pressing things that I'll somehow have to tackle before the weekend is over. Yet here I am, doing nothing more demanding than lying on the sand and breathing.

Shocking as it may be, I do like to study. I love the fact that no-one can ever know everything. Woodhaven's campus with its exquisite libraries and neoclassical buildings is a sub-universe dedicated to knowledge and truth. Or at least it's supposed to be, despite all the arrogance and ignorance that you find wherever smart people gather. But still, university is my refuge. Home is where the lies are, hidden beneath a shadow veil. Home is where the ghost of Simon lives on, haunting every step that I take.

Clearly, I need an afternoon off like a hole in the head. But Casey insisted, and I can never say no to him. Casey Mills is one of the two people on Earth whose company I actually enjoy, and ergo my best friend. Or more precisely, he'd be my best friend if I had more than one friend to choose from. Which is fine. I never gave a damn about popularity, and vice versa popularity never gave a damn about me.

But sure enough, this friendship can't be all laid back and easy, because my life just doesn't work that way. The whole point of being friends is to be just friends. So naturally, it's just my luck to have a secret crush on him.

I think I've been doing fairly well in hiding it from him so far, and I have no intention of changing that strategy anytime soon. Take it from the reigning king of introverts, it's wrong that some things are better left unsaid. In fact, most are.

The afternoon is drowsy, listless, and I swear I can feel my brain cells slowly getting fried in the heat. The sun is mercilessly bright, and Rizzo stole my sunglasses when I wasn't paying attention. Sneaky son of a bitch. Casey invited him to come along, and I knew that was a mistake. I'm not sure exactly how today's setup came about. How do you invite someone on a trip that you can only make if they give you a ride in their stupid shiny Porsche?

As may be derived from my using the word stupid in connection with a freaking dream of a car like that, Danny Rizzo is definitely not one of the two people on Earth whose company I enjoy. I won't deny that I can't stand most people, because most people are idiots. But him I just loathe. Rizzo is the kind of guy who gets away with anything. He's the only person I've ever met who always gets what he wants, no matter how unlikely and absurd it may be. He treats people like toys, replaceable like bubble gum. You chew on it for a while, and when it's lost its taste, you spit it out. That's Rizzo. And can you believe it, they all love him for it. And for one reason only: Because he is drop dead gorgeous.

"You wanna get some ice cream?" Casey's slender form casts a deep shadow on me when he sits up beside me and draws his legs up.

"You buying?" Rizzo lazily lifts his head. He is lying sprawled in the sand crosswise in front of us like a huge bug that's been squashed under a boot. Damn the bastard, he's getting a tan already.

Casey smiles, and for a brief moment his blue eyes wander over the perfectly muscled body at our feet. Then he notices that I'm watching him, and quickly averts his gaze. He laughs softly. "Uh... okay."

His baggy shorts slide down a bit as he gets up, revealing a crack of the soft, white skin of his butt, but he pulls them back up immediately. Rizzo and I exchange a glance as he walks away, his steps slow and heavy on the sand. Damn. Suntan boy chuckles and rolls back onto his back, shielding his eyes from the bright sunlight with his arm for a moment before dropping it with a deep sigh. How about using my sunglasses?

"You're turning lobster-red."

Gee, thanks for stating the obvious. I'm fully aware of the fact that I don't tan. I just burn. And yes, I'm sure Casey would prefer a perfect tan to perfect lobster-red anytime. Especially with a flawless Adonis body like that. "Eat me, Rizzo."

He just laughs, sizing me up with his admittedly beautiful dark eyes. "Geez, Foley, relax. There'll be enough time to be that stiff when you're dead." He grabs something and lifts his hand, waving a small tube. "Want some sunblock?"

"Who'd you steal that from?"

Rizzo cracks one of his infamous sly smiles and shrugs nonchalantly. Before I can say anything he gets up and flops down next to me. Far too close for my liking. His leg brushes against mine, and the bastard watches my face for the tiniest trace of reaction. Which I won't give him, of course. I stare back at him coolly, and know instantly that that was a mistake. Our eyes lock, and sure enough, neither of us will grant the other the satisfaction of looking away first.

"You know," Rizzo begins with that pleasant voice of his, and it feels like a silk scarf drawn across my body. I briefly wonder if the heat has fried my brains already, and left me with nothing but the raging hormones of my tender age. I'm supposed to be immune to this guy.

He opens the tube, and squeezes some sunblock onto his palm. I don't even care what he's saying. All I really hear is that voice. "People with light skin have a higher risk of getting skin cancer."

"Wow. A decade ago that piece of information would've been shocking news to me." I actually manage to sound as disinterested and bored as I'd like to be. I force myself to look away and not stare at Rizzo's lean fingers spreading the white creme on his hands. I realize my mistake when he doesn't use the sunblock on himself, but without prior warning puts his hands on my chest. I jump, naturally. But he starts to rub the sunblock in anyway, as if it were the most natural thing on earth. The tiniest trace of an amused smile is dancing on his lips. Bastard.

"Relax, James." Barely a whisper, and still a command. Rizzo's hands slide over my body, his fingers hot on my skin. It's electrifying, and sexy, and the fact that I don't want it to be makes me want to hit him. God do I hate this guy. He's not irresistible. Nobody is. With some difficulty, I take a deep breath and, for lack of better alternatives, return to staring at the annoying sea gulls in the sky.

Azure. Casey's eyes make the sky look pale in comparison as he sits down next to me and hands me a cone of ice cream.

"Hey guys. Where did you get the sunblock?"

Rizzo and I exchange a glance. He's got a grin on his face as he takes the ice cream Casey is handing him. He's still looking at me when he licks at it. Then he lifts his eyes to Casey, and the grin broadens. Sneaky son of a bitch. I know what you're gonna say.

"Want some?"

Sometimes I really hate to be right.

2 TAKING SHAPE

CASEY: For painting the light is best in September, mild and golden, but summer remains my favorite time of year. If spring is the allegory for hope, then fall must be reflection, winter recreation, and summer the time for dreams.

Outside Cafe Plato, the sun burns down onto the small white tables as I watch people walking by in the distance. Everything has a bluish touch in this harsh light. I lean back in my chair, surveying the grounds, the tall maple trees and the old, impressive brick buildings in the background. Except for a few students sitting together on the lawn, campus is deserted, which isn't unusual at this time of day. The sun falling through the wide branches throws a playful pattern of shade and light onto the group. I recognize some faces, all of them part of the acknowledged in-crowd. They're teasing each other and laughing, absolutely at ease and carefree, and the beauty of the scene suddenly strikes me. Automatically I reach for my sketchbook and pencil. I take a long moment to take in my motif and carefully measure the proportions. As my hand begins to swiftly move across the paper, I try to chase away all thoughts and concentrate on shape only. It's hard in the heat of this afternoon, but I work calmly and undisturbed for a while. According to Professor Wickham, you can't draw when you're thinking, and you can't think when you're drawing. I'll never get why it is so incredibly hard not to think.

A motion on my left catches my eye. Someone is coming down the straight path that leads past the cafe, crossing a couple of other paths on its way. When the two slim figures approach, I recognize Danny, who is talking to a girl I don't know. They stop at a crossroad and say their good-byes. He doesn't even take the cigarette out of his mouth when she kisses his cheek. The brunette turns around twice to look back at him as she slowly walks away, but he's already moved on. My stomach squirms a little as he gets closer. It's still somewhat surreal.

You go mostly unnoticed all of your school days, you have your little group of friends, and you know that you're nowhere near to popular, but you're good. But looking back to it, I was a typical ghost at high school. Not part of any of the cliched groups, just someone that got along with everyone. Simply too average, too ordinary to be remembered after graduation. Interchangeable, forgettable.

And then one day at university, he's suddenly there, Danny Rizzo. Everybody knows him. You can't not notice Danny. He's never talked to you before, but he knows exactly who you are. He knows that you helped design the set last year for the drama department's production of An Ideal Husband. He didn't look at you once at the time, but he was so brilliant as Lord Goring that you didn't mind. But he sees you now. And him acknowledging your existence seems to be all it takes for complete strangers to suddenly know your name and greet you everywhere you go. All of a sudden you're not invisible anymore.

There's magic in being noticed. When I look in the mirror, I see myself as this funny little blur, unfinished, like a formless shape that can't decide what it wants to be. Like the outlines of a sketch, just a few hurried lines on a piece of paper. Why is it so important to be seen just to know who we are?

Danny's friends catch his attention and wave him over, and I watch as he joins his crew. Ever since I first saw him, I've been wanting to paint him. The naturally curly brown hair, the dark, expressive eyes, the features of his face so perfectly regular that you could put it in the textbook as an example of what to the human eye is beauty. But there's something about him that goes beyond that. A nonchalant charisma, and a mysterious confidence that I've always wished I could have. He stands out in a crowd, impossible to overlook.

James doesn't like him. But James is next to impossible to please, let alone impress. He makes a point of despising what everybody likes. And I have to admit, I actually like that about him. I like that he doesn't take crap from people, and doesn't follow the masses. I know I can be easy to influence sometimes, but I've always struggled not to be. It's hard to resist the yearning to belong.

Giving up on the not thinking, I put my sketchbook aside with a small sigh. I'm not happy with the way the drawing is turning out, and I doubt that I'll finish it later. I have tons of unfinished drawings. I'm better at painting from my imagination.

"You should do this professionally," James said to me when I finally dared to show him my portfolio of fairytale illustrations. He took his time to look at each individual page, his grayish-blue eyes wandering over the pictures with wonderment and awe. Knowing the ruthless critic that he is, it really meant a lot to me. And for the first time I considered the possibility myself.

I met James when I was applying for the school paper. We're the same age but he's a year above me. He skipped a year at high school. He was already an editor, much younger than the others. Everyone of us newbies had heard that he was scary, and hoped they wouldn't be assigned to him during our tryout period. Well, I was the lucky one. At first, we didn't get along at all. He was bossy and ridiculously demanding, and I was pretty much lost all the time. I considered quitting on the second day. It was really hard on me that he so obviously seemed to dislike me. I didn't know how to handle that. But then I realized that James was the only one of the editors who actually let their applicant work on articles, while the others were just used as errand boys. So when Sam, the editor in chief, told me that James thought I had potential and had recommended me, I was pretty shocked. But it changed the entire way I saw him. I began to see James as someone who dared people to like him in spite of how unfriendly he was. I don't know why, but I found that fascinating, and strangely endearing. I never met anyone who cared less about what others thought of them. Granted, it still took forever for him to open up to me. But now he lets me see the side of him that he hides from everyone else. It makes me feel like there's nothing I couldn't share with him. And so we became friends.

I no longer work for the school paper. James talked me into using the time I'd devoted to it for taking art classes.

"I don't give a shit about what your parents say. You can't be a teacher, Casey," he said. "You're an artist."

So now when people ask me, "How can you like Foley? He's an asshole," I do as James would do. I don't try to defend him, because defending means admitting that there's a point to an accusation. I just shake my head and smile, and pass on Wittgenstein's words that James so sarcastically quoted to me on the day we met: *Whereof one cannot speak, thereof one must be silent.*

3 OF ANTS AND ARROGANCE

JAMES: People and ants have a lot more in common than you might think. We like to pretend that we're independent, unique individuals, and ours is a free will to soar in the liberal Western society that's shaped according to our beliefs. What a bunch of crap. The objectives of the human society are exactly the same as those of the ant society - survival, security, reproduction, defense, stability, and naturally, perpetuation of the system.

University, like all parts of the educational system, does a pretty good job at teaching people what really matters in life: success. Generously, it also shows you how to achieve that - by playing by the rules. *Parero ergo sum.* You don't need a totalitarian regime to oppress people. Nowadays we have peer pressure and MTV.

There are always hip people, sporty people, smart people, freaks and losers, no matter where you go. All the neat little social groups that you can never get out of. It's interesting that the geeks hate the popular crowd for being superficial and fake, but they're still dreaming of belonging. I never got the immanent logic in that, assuming that there is one.

Rizzo, though, Rizzo seems to defy all cliches, creating his own, and doesn't fully belong to any of them, and yet to them all. I guess you have that kind of freedom when you're beautiful. Beauty gives people a certain power, if they have the brains to use it to their advantage instead of getting used. Sadly, Rizzo is not a complete bimbo.

I pretend not to notice as he saunters over. His motions are smooth, like a big cat approaching certain prey. It looks like walking, but instead is a highly advanced art form. I force myself to look the other way. I wonder, for the thousandth time, why does someone like him hang out with Casey and me?

"Foley. Got a smoke?" He sits down on the back of the bench beside me. Enthroned above me, all hail the king of the world. Typical. As if I didn't feel common and ugly enough in comparison anyway.

"I don't smoke. You should know that by now."

The tiniest of smiles flashes across his lips, but he just shrugs. In this light his eyes are so black you can't see the pupils. Dark chocolate. I wonder what that mouth tastes like. "You waiting for Mills?"

"What makes you think so?"

"Don't you always?"

Great. He's known me all of five minutes and thinks he's already figured me out? Only that, judging by the tone of his voice - Christ. I glance at him through narrow eyes. All alarms go off, and I freeze inwardly. Does he *know*? Has he actually somehow, miraculously picked up on my feelings for Casey?

Rizzo cracks a sly smile that can probably get him laid anytime, anywhere, but I choose to ignore it. I know it drives him nuts not to get any reaction. "What? It's true, isn't it?"

"It's also none of your business."

"You're hopeless, Foley. Bordering pathetic. What's the plan? To pine away forever? Why don't you two just get it over and done with?"

Okay. I think we can safely say that he *knows*. God help me. My heart sinks, and my mind begins to race. What are the options? I could either try to deny it, or simply kill him. Both would confirm his suspicion, the only difference being that the latter would give him less time to enjoy it. Now that's just great. I glance at him icily. "You don't know what you're talking about."

"If you say so."

"I do say so. I'd be happy to repeat it if you need to hear it again."

He looks at me with undisguised amusement. "I'm not much for repetition."

"No kidding. Stay the hell out of my affairs."

"Or what?"

"Or else."

"I'm terrified, Foley."

"As you should be."

He chuckles, but there's a dark flicker in his eyes. "You're one arrogant ass, Foley, you know that?"

"And what are you then, Mother Theresa?"

"As long as precious Casey thinks I am."

Cheeky bastard. This is just another one of the twisted little games he likes to play, isn't it? Why would he reveal to me that he's figured out what I feel for Casey if not to deliberately make me suffer? Like a cat, he loves to play with the mouse before he finishes it off. I wonder what Rizzo is waiting for, because as much as it hurts to admit, I think Casey is lying beneath his paws already. There is nothing I can do but stand on the sidelines and watch. And he knows, and he wants me to know that he does. That's the only reason he's even talking to me.

Rizzo doesn't talk about doing things. He just does them. It's different with Casey and me. We have meaningful conversations, and do nothing. I look into his eyes and he looks away, and then he looks into my eyes and I look away. There are moments when my mind tricks me into believing that there is some definite subtext in our friendship. But those moments pass, and I'm back to thinking that I must be crazy to even consider the possibility. Tragically, it is an urban myth that all straight guys are potentially gay. And yet, ever since Rizzo appeared on the scene, lines get blurred, and everything seems possible. For him. Not me. And that hurts. He seems to trigger something in Casey that I never could. And that is nothing short of a catastrophe. Casey is the first one to make me feel like I'm worth something, or even special. And people like Rizzo have made me feel like worthless shit for way longer than I want to remember.

Our eyes meet, he smiles at me, and for the first time it seems completely genuine. In this moment he is so damn beautiful it's almost hard to bear. I frown deeply. The amused little smirk returns to his lips. Irritatingly, but undeniably inviting.

Well, color me stunned and pin a "kick me!" sign to my back. I suddenly have a sneaking suspicion that Rizzo likes arrogant asses every now and then. And right now, that arrogant ass would appear to be me.

4 TRUTH BE DARED

JAMES: It's too loud. Voices and music, thundering bass and raw guitars, all blending together until it becomes nothing but a mess of undistinguishable noise. I hate when it's loud. I don't like parties, because I don't like being in crowds. Did I mention that it was Rizzo's stupid idea to come?

I lean back in the shabby old armchair I somehow managed to get hold of, and sigh deeply. The upholstery stinks of cold cigarette smoke and something disgusting I don't recognize. Holding on to my beer, I survey the room, watching people come and go, wondering why they can never stand still. I'm a bit dizzy, but not quite drunk enough to not care. Casey is nearby, talking to a perky red-head with funny freckles. He knows her from one of his classes. She's not his type.

I'm mesmerized by the way his lips move when he speaks. I once overheard two chicks talking about him, saying how kissable he is. Kissable. I don't think that is even a word. But it's true all the same.

Rizzo is on the other side of the room, surrounded by the usual cluster of fangirls. Pathetic. Do they have no pride at all? That brunette there is all over him. Come on, girl. Subtlety is your friend. Even I know that Rizzo loves a challenge. He is only interested in what he can't have.

Suddenly he looks over, directly at me, and cracks one of those killer smiles of his. I just give him a look and roll my eyes. *Is that all you got?*

He grins, and for a brief moment I wonder if he just read my mind. I sniff and take a gulp of beer, and decide that he hasn't, because that would freak me out. I've had more logical moments, I think. But then I wasn't stuck in a room full of horny adolescents with nothing to do but drink. The air is so thick with the penetrating smell of cannabis that I get that familiar warm, heavy feeling just breathing normally. I stare at the ceiling, and imagine being in a cartoon movie. I could simply wipe out all the people around me with a giant eraser, until only Casey and I remain. I try to erase Rizzo as well, but he keeps popping back up. Most annoying.

Sometimes I wonder how it was possible for Casey to even slip under my guard like that. He's far too deep under my skin. Dangerously deep. I'd promised myself to never let that happen again. But kindness, the kind of genuine kindness that he possesses, is powerfully disarming. I like how his eyes focus on my face when he talks to me. I like how he smiles so warmly, sometimes a little shyly, and how he gestures with his hands. I like the way he really listens, and how he always takes a moment to think before he answers. I like the way he scratches his nose when he isn't sure how to react to something, and how he always runs his fingers through his short, blond hair when he's nervous. I like the way I know him thoroughly, and how he still manages to surprise me sometimes. I don't think there's anything I don't like about him. Except for that unhealthy infatuation with Rizzo, of course.

As if he had heard my silent call for him to rescue me from feeling isolated and out of place, Casey joins me and sits down on my armrest. Close enough for me to feel the warmth emanating from his very being.

"Hey, James." Kind eyes, beautiful smile. Makes me feel all warm and mushy inside. Makes me whole.

"Hey, Case."

A sympathetic smile softens the brilliant blue of his eyes. "You don't look very happy."

"Oh, we're alright." I show him my beer, and he chuckles.

"If you wanna leave..."

"No, no, I'm fine. This is..." I trail off and can't help grinning. "Okay, this is so not my idea of fun."

Casey laughs, and I'm feeling better already. Must be the alcohol, messing with my head. Or maybe I'm high. No idea how he does it, but he reduces me to a love-sick puppy, filled with the urge to write bad, sappy poetry. How sad have I become? It's very tragic. Casey moves back on the armrest until he can lean his back against the back of the chair beside me. We're practically sharing the seat now, and gravity pulls him downwards, towards me, until the left side of his body is pressed against me. Can't say that I mind. He smiles as he takes the beer from my hand and takes a sip, lets his right leg dangle as he looks around. He seems more relaxed now that he is beside me, and I guess that's mutual. Well, in a way. I ache to touch him, painfully, frighteningly. Sometimes I would really like to know what he sees when he looks at me. I wish I could see myself through his eyes, just once. I wish I could crawl beneath his skin, and see what the world looks like through Casey Mills' eyes. But could I cope with what I'd see, I wonder?

"Anybody up for a round of truth or dare?"

I look up with a small frown, and am surprised to find that a large group of people has sneakily assembled on the floor around us. Where did they suddenly come from? Casey sits up straight and shifts a bit, uncomfortably. Truth or dare? What is this, kindergarten? No way in hell. I'm not gonna hop around the room on one leg or do anything even more degrading. Why am I not surprised to see Rizzo join the circle with his entourage? He sits down directly opposite of us with an insidious grin curling his lips. Count me out of this. I glance at Casey, ready to get up and leave, the question in my eyes. But he just shrugs. Now that Rizzo is here, he wants to stay, come hell or high water. Which translates to me not going anywhere either. Great.

"Bring it on, baby." Rizzo winks at the tall blonde who suggested playing the game, and she laughs too loudly. She is wearing too much makeup, I can smell her cheap, flowery perfume from over here. What on earth leads girls to believe that guys like that kind of stench?

"Okay, I go first then." Blondie bats her eyelashes and giggles. Man, she is pissed. She leans a bit forward as she turns to Rizzo, the neck of her tight top giving everyone a great view at what she has to offer. "Truth or dare, Danny."

Rizzo takes a long drag on his cigarette, and exhales the smoke slowly. "Your choice."

Bimbo Blonde giggles. "Okay. I pick..." Dramatic pause.

"Truth."

Cheers from the crowd welcome the choice. I bet she'll ask if he could spend a night with anyone in the world, who would it be. Go, me. She really does. How lame.

"You want the truth then, do you?" The dark eyes sparkle mischievously as everyone cheers. You have to hand it to him, he's got them all wrapped around his finger. I don't even listen to his answer. I'm distracted by the way Casey is watching him with a little smile. Jealousy stirs inside of me. I snap to attention when I hear Rizzo saying his name.

"Casey. Truth or dare?"

"Truth."

Rizzo has a satisfied smirk on his face. "Ever kissed a guy?"

Roaring laughter, and Casey blushes furiously. But I'm relieved. That's not so bad. I know the answer to that, luckily. No reason to worry there.

"No. No, I never kissed a guy." Casey shrugs and laughs. He turns to me and quickly gives me an easy, safe question, because I pick truth, naturally. "Which three things would you like to have with you if you were stranded on an island?"

Let me pretend to think hard. You, rubbers, lube. How would you like that? I don't say that aloud. Instead, I do what everybody does when they play truth or dare: I lie. D'uh.

Round two starts, and far too soon it is Rizzo's turn again. I've got a bad feeling about this. And, as expected, Rizzo looks right at Casey without a moment's hesitation. I knew he wasn't finished with him yet. It was too easy. "Casey, truth or dare?"

Fearing no evil, Casey smiles, flattered to be chosen again. "Um... dare this time, I guess."

Oh no. Not good. I can see the trap closing, and now he's got him. Rizzo's eyes sparkle triumphantly. "Well, there's really just one thing I could dare you to do now."

Someone actually gasps, and two girls start to giggle madly. That wicked grin on his lips doesn't bode too well, but I refuse to believe he is seriously gonna do that until he speaks again.

"I dare you to kiss..." He pauses, looks around, searching for a victim or volunteer. I feel sick to my stomach. Man, this whole situation is so high school. Did I mention that I hated high school with a passion? Rizzo's gaze comes to rest on me. "Kiss Foley. Until I tell you to stop."

Son of a bitch. I don't even flinch. I stay perfectly calm and unimpressed on the outside. Life has taught me well to wear this mask. But Casey gasps, half-laughing, but the laughter dies in his throat. He shakes his head unbelievingly. "Are you serious?"

Rizzo only smiles and takes a drag on his cigarette. He leans back, waiting to be entertained. I get a strong urge to decorate the walls with his entrails. I can handle him trying to expose me, but does he have to do this to Casey?

Casey looks at me, and it makes my heart ache. It means so much to him to be liked by someone as popular as Rizzo, which leaves him with little choice in this awkward situation. Unless I just get up and leave. Everybody thinks that I'm the killjoy of killjoys anyhow, and I couldn't care less. But before I get a chance, Casey makes up his mind and regains his sense of humor.

"Um.. okay. Sorry, James."

Our audience laughs. I get nauseous. Then everything happens very quickly. Casey swallows and moves closer to me on the armchair, bends down. His breath is warm on my face, then his lips brush against mine uncertainly. Very softly, tender like a feather. We both shiver at the touch. Everything goes quiet around us. And then he starts to really kiss me. I hold my breath, and carefully kiss him back. I'm dimly aware of hearing cheering, but I shut it out. My head is spinning, and I lose my ability to think coherently. My mind ends in a loop, wrapped around the sensation of how very soft his lips are. He tastes a little like my beer, and indescribably good.

Suddenly he breaks the kiss and pulls back, and I realize that Rizzo must have told him to stop. There's applause, and shouting, and more cheering, and the girl sitting in front of us whispers to her girlfriend, "Why don't I ever get kissed like that?"

* * *

I catch him outside later, when the game is long over and the players have scattered. Stepping out of the house, I shiver in the chilly night air and rub my bare arms. Rizzo is alone in the darkness, propped against a wall, half-hidden in the shadow of a tall tree. I watch him for a moment as he stands there unaware of me with his head leaned back in his neck, gazing at the stars. It's quiet here, except for the muffled noise of the party coming from a half-open window. Thundering bass guitar, the song distorted, unrecognizable. Waves of laughter are tumbling outside through the crack. Rizzo turns his head my way as I approach him, his eyes black in the darkness. The air is rich and fragrant with the smell of earth and dried grass, the scent of summer nights.

"You owe me, Foley. I got you want you wanted, didn't I?" The soft tone of his voice doesn't quite match the cheeky words. He clears his throat.

I look at him coldly for a moment, then I shake my head. "You know nothing about what I want, Rizzo."

His eyes are fathomless. Cool, black jade. "Maybe. But I'm pretty sure I know what you need. Probably better than you do."

We stare at each other, another silent power play. But something is off about this. Something in his eyes that suddenly soften. Just like that. For once, he lets me win our little staring contest. And allows me a brief glimpse behind his superficial facade. Just enough to make me wonder why.

Abruptly, he pushes himself away from the wall, looks at me for one last time and grins to himself. Then he walks away, leaving me puzzled.

* * *

"James?" Casey calls me softly from the door. He has his shoulders pulled up and his arms crossed in front of his chest, shivering. "Damn, I can't find my jacket. You wanna go home?"

I walk over to him, my hands buried in my pockets. "Sure."

We don't look at each other as we step onto the pavement and slowly head towards the dorm. Thankful for it being so dark. My skin tingles, just knowing that he is walking along beside me. Close, and still completely out of reach. The streets are deserted. It smells like dawn. Silently we walk along, in step with each other, like we always do. We don't even notice it anymore, it just happens. Always has. I know that we'll never talk about the kiss, or even mention it. But still, it will always be there.

5 SKIN-DEEP

CASEY: I had a dream last night that was so vivid that I still remembered most of it when I woke up. It was my birthday and we were celebrating with family and friends. I got very strange presents; a stuffed weasel and a box full of snakes. I was very uncomfortable with that. Then I was standing under the mistletoe with James and he said he couldn't kiss me now because he had an important meeting. I think he was a professor, he was wearing glasses, and his dark hair was longer than he wears it. It made him look oddly rebellious and stern at the same time. But I just grabbed him and kissed him, and it was the most incredible feeling. But when I broke the kiss, I realized that I had been kissing Danny, and that James had already left, and I didn't care at all. It made me feel horrible and awkward when I woke up and sat up in bed. Like I had betrayed James somehow. But what was even more unsettling was the realization that I'd been dreaming about kissing men, and so loving it that I could still feel it dancing in my stomach, hot and exciting.

* * *

"Can I ask you a personal question?" I glance at James who is scribbling in his notebook, his hand moving swiftly across the paper. We're sitting in the second to last row of the empty auditorium, watching the dress rehearsal of a new German drama group initiated by the language students. James is here to write a critique for the school paper, and I don't understand a word they're saying.

"Sure." He finishes writing down his sentence before he looks back up to the stage and then at me.

I smile a little, suddenly insecure. It seems silly to ask this. "I know this is completely out of the blue and totally random."

"I'm sure I won't die of shock."

"Okay then, here goes: How did your mom react when you told her you were gay?

He arches an eyebrow and grins. "You're right. That was pretty random."

"You didn't die though."

"I'm a bastard to kill."

I have to smile, and he shifts in his seat, getting serious. "I never had to tell her, actually. She just knew. She says she could tell even when I was a little boy."

"And she doesn't mind?"

"Why would she? There's nothing she can do about it anyway. She just wants me to be happy, that's what she says."

I nod. "You were lucky. I mean, compared to other guys."

James' expression changes immediately and a painful frown appears on his handsome forehead, like a shadow falling over his soul. It makes him seem very different from the person he was just a second ago.

"Lucky, no." He voice is cold when he speaks, very quietly. He stares down at his notebook. "I was never lucky."

I feel bad immediately, and sympathize more with him than I'm letting on, because James hates sympathy. I know he doesn't like to talk about his past, and very rarely does. His real father died in a car crash before he was born. And then tragedy struck again when James was sixteen, when his stepfather lost his life. All I know about Simon Foley is that he was a firefighter, and that he died in an accident. I can only imagine how hard that must have been.

"Did Simon know, too?" I ask softly, carefully.

James stares at me for a long moment. His gray eyes get strangely blank of emotion, and a look so jaded appears on his face that it spooks me. "Oh yes, he knew."

I swallow, something in his voice giving me the creeps. I know that this is the end of this conversation, and he won't give away another word. I'm not sure I'd even want to know more, and that makes me feel bad again. There is a kind of darkness inside of James that I've sensed from the beginning of our friendship. It only ever flares up momentarily. But after all this time I still don't know how to deal with it.

I turn my head back towards the stage, trying my best to quickly come up with a safer topic. "So how's the show?"

A sarcastic little smile curls his lips, and he is back to his usual self in less than two seconds. "Oh, definitely the one thing the world needs. On top of atomic weapons, global warming, and AIDS."

"Ouch. That good, huh?"

"It makes me want to rinse my eyes and ears with acid."

I laugh, and he glances at his watch. "Let's get out of here."

"You're gonna miss the grand finale."

"I'm sure I'll get over it. Oh look, I already am."

* * *

James and I are sitting opposite of each other at one of the large tables in the big library. It is early evening. Flipping through pages and taking notes in peaceful silence, working on different projects for different classes. It is always refreshingly cool in these long halls. The smell of dust, wood, and books is in the air. I let my gaze wander through the room, and spot Leo's flaming red hair as she steps out of the dark line of shelves, her arm full of heavy books. She sees me and waves happily. I smile at her and wave back. Then I look over at James, who has that rapt, highly concentrated look on his face that always touches me. I never met anyone who was able to lose themselves with such enthusiasm in their school work. I wonder if I look anything like that when I'm drawing.

There is beauty that's just skin-deep, and there are people like James that you have to take the time to really get to know before you can see their beauty. But once you see it, they shine. I'm strangely moved all of a sudden, watching him. I remember how his lips felt on mine, and my heart starts to beat madly. I can feel myself blush, and quickly stare down on my open book. I never considered the possibility of being with a man. I never fancied men. I wonder what it feels like to James, to know with absolute certainty that he is gay. I wonder if kissing a man feels exactly the same to James as kissing Amber felt to me back in high school.

And I wonder what it felt like to James to kiss me at that party. But more than anything, I wonder what it is about Danny Rizzo that attracts me so much that I keep having these dreams of making out with him. It turns me on, and that makes me feel strangely ashamed of myself.

6 FANCY

JAMES: The sun hangs low in the sky, the light is mild and golden, but the air is still warm. It is one of those rare evenings when everything seems quiet and calm, and the world is perfect. Casey and I are sitting outside of Starbucks, opposite of the movie theater, wasting time until the film starts. Not a lot of people would be delighted to go see a foreign low-budget movie with subtitles. It is one of the things I appreciate about him. He cares about quality, not quantity. I lean back in my chair, watching him. Content just to exist and live this moment, with the smell of coffee in my nostrils from the steaming cappuccino in my large paper cup. But Casey is restless today. He pokes around in his cup with a Starbucks stick as if he were trying to stab the poor coffee grounds.

"Have you seen Danny? I thought he wanted to come."

Danny. I hate how he always calls him by his first name. He never says Rizzo, like everyone else. I hate how soft the name sounds, coming from his lips. I shrug, naturally not giving a damn. "You know Rizzo. He says things he doesn't mean all the time."

Casey looks at me silently for a while. "What exactly is it that you don't like about him, James? Tell me."

It is a simple question, so the answer should be easy enough. I think about it for a minute, and realize that everything I could say would probably make me sound like the jealous drama queen from hell. Which I like to believe I'm not, thank you. But someone has to at least try and wave a warning sign before he heads any further down catastrophe lane. I might as well cut to the chase. "Listen, Casey. I know you fancy him and all. But I just don't think he's good for you."

Casey blinks slowly, like he can't believe I actually just said that. He blushes noticeably, and how cute is that. "I didn't know you were aware of that," he smiles, speaking softly, and long lashes hide his eyes as he stares down at the table. "I think I didn't want to believe it myself."

"Does it throw you off that much, fancying guys?"

"No! God, no, don't think that. I mean, you are... and I'd never..."

I smile. "It's okay."

"It's just not like I generally fancy guys."

"Ah. So you fancy selectively."

He glances up briefly. "You're making fun of me."

"Why yes, I am."

He laughs, his blush deepening, but his eyes are warm when he looks at me. "Thank you."

"For making fun of you?"

"Nope. For understanding."

Who says I do, I want to say, but I stop myself. I really don't get why someone as smart as Casey can honestly fall for such a jerk.

Casey looks pensively into the distance, and the sinking sun makes his skin shimmer with a golden touch. Sigh.

"Don't you sometimes wish you could be free from all those fears and uncertainties? That you could just take this mess that is your life, and turn it into something special?"

I smile to myself. "You know, you're really one of a kind."

He turns towards me with a little frown. "And you're not half the jaded cynic you'd like to be. I know you wish for it too."

"Maybe you're right. But maybe you don't know me quite as well as you think."

"Really?" He smiles. "Is there something you wanna tell me?"

There's too much, Casey. Far too much, and there aren't nearly enough words in the world.

"Yeah," I reply lightly, deliberately ending our little heart-to-heart. I glance at the clock over the entrance of the movie theater. "Movie's starting any minute. Let's go inside."

***

The movie is about three guys who steal a car and drive across country, meeting some really bizarre people on the way. One of them is gay, and he falls in love with his best friend. I wish I'd known about that particular bit before. The film takes an unexpected turn from comedy to drama when one of the main characters dies. I don't know why, but something about the way the two remaining guys talk to each other, trying to deal, touches me. Something about their pain, their loss, the tragedy of life and death, and how nothing good ever lasts forever. Casey seems to feel the same way about it, he sighs softly beside me. I glance at him, and he looks at me with a strange expression on his face. I can't read it in the semi-darkness of the theater. He gives me a little pat on the arm, and turns back to the screen. I do the same. Then he looks at me again, and suddenly he reaches over and puts his hand on mine.

I freeze. Completely. Can't think. Can't act. Feel the warmth of his palm, his fingers on my skin. I think I'm in shock. Then my mind starts to race. God, what does this mean? Has he finally added up two and two and realized that I'm like that guy on the screen? That I'm crazy about him? I bite my lower lip; bite down hard, until I taste my own salty blood. Fighting the agony inside by inflicting physical pain onto myself doesn't help. Not this time. A minute passes slowly, his hand is still on mine. There is no air in this goddamned theater, and I can't breathe.

"I gotta take a leak." Too abruptly, I pull my hand away and get up. Hurry through the rows, glad it's so empty, trip and almost fall over, feel stupid, and hurry outside. I lean against the wall, and exhale.

Superb, Foley. How extremely mature. But in spite of my attempts at sarcasm, I hurt inside. Far more than I think is justified for once more making a fool of myself. I close my eyes, and the images flare up.

Pain. Pain and blackness. An all too familiar combination that my body remembers, and automatically replays. I get a flashback so vivid that it makes me feel nauseous. Small. Defenseless. Simon's voice, close to my ear. Hissing, spitting in my face.

"Not so clever now, are you? You faggot, you little piece of shit."

My fists clench on their own account. I fight the memory

down, push it to the back of my mind.

I'm not sure why, but somehow it is all Rizzo's fault. Things weren't so bad before he came along. I had Casey to myself. I had my little mantra about how he was straight as a railroad track, and I was completely out of the picture. And now this, his hand on mine. Why the hell did he do that? Suddenly there's this *maybe* that starts to grow in my head.

I think it is about time Rizzo and I cut the small talk and got down to business. I want to know what he is up to. Now more than ever, I'll be damned if I let that bastard have Casey. Not without one hell of a fight.

7 STRICTLY BUSINESS

JAMES: I've only been there twice, and always with Casey, but I know the way to Rizzo's dorm room like I've walked it a million times. It is always noisy on his floor: music plays loudly and people argue through open doors from room to room. For some reason the corridor leading to his room seems to be the messiest of the place. Fits perfectly. If you're out to hunt a rat, you gotta follow the breadcrumbs. Okay, here we are. Number 91, that's seven times thirteen. I'm not even gonna comment on that. I'm about to knock when the door opens all by itself. The slutty blonde I remember well from the Truth or Dare party struts past, not even deigning to look at me. Slightly amused, I shake my head and look after her, then to Rizzo who stands in the half-open door.

"You'd do anything on two legs, wouldn't you?"

He grins and shrugs nonchalantly. "She's pretty supple."

Thank you. Too much information. Opening the door wide, Rizzo steps aside to let me in. He is wearing a pair of jeans, and apart from that, a lot of nothing. His fly is still half-open. Oh, please. I feel like I've wandered onto a porno set. The air in the room is heavy with the appalling stench of cold cigarette smoke.

"Foley, what can I do for you?"

Sure enough, he lights a cigarette. He does it with a fluid, well-practiced gesture, exactly the way people in movies do. If I tried to do that, it would without a doubt look remarkably stupid.

I look at him with a frown, not bothering to hide my annoyance. "You can mind your own business and stop messing with Casey."

He coughs softly in an attempt not to laugh, puffing out smoke through his nostrils like the damn magic dragon in that song. "What are you, his mother?"

"Is he even your type?"

"Can't say that I have one."

"Big surprise. Does your dick do all the thinking, or is there a brain somewhere in there?"

He nods to my crotch. "Is there a dick somewhere in there, or does your brain have to compensate?"

I smile weakly. "Please. The only compensating I have to do is for the stunning lack of intelligence around me."

He seizes me up with a sly half-smile, cigarette in hand, looking cool, untouchable, and clearly amused. My fists clench. I glare at him. "*Why* are you doing this?"

"Because I can."

Damn the bastard, I know he is right. And it makes me feel so powerless. There isn't much in the world that I hate more than this feeling. God, I want to punch him. Real hard. Hard enough to see some blood.

He takes a step closer to me, his eyes on my face. "Why exactly are you here, Foley?"

"Do I mumble? Talk in a strange tongue? Stay away from Casey!"

"Make me."

Another step closer, invading my personal space. I don't move an inch, but I'm seething. I'm not going to let him provoke me. I'm not going to lose my temper. I'm not going to let him see how furious his nonchalance makes me, because that's exactly what he wants. Oh, screw that.

I grab him and slam him against the wall, but he just laughs. Laughs as I pin him to it with my left hand, right arm across his chest, close to his throat.

"I've really had enough of your shit."

His laughter dies as I lean in closer and stare into his eyes with cold, barely controlled rage. "What you gonna do now? Beat me up? Way to display your superior intelligence."

"Shut up."

"I'm gonna fuck your precious Casey, Foley. I'm gonna ride him hard until he comes screaming my name. How you gonna stop me? How far are you willing to go?"

I'm this close to snapping completely, and when he realizes, something flickers in his dark orbs. His breath is fast and hot on my face, and his tongue darts out to wet his lips. He lets his cigarette fall, and puts it out without looking down. It's there in his eyes, no mistake. Raw, undisguised lust. Bad boy, you like it rough, don't you? You're such a slut. I can see it, but it still takes a moment to fully register that he's turned on by what I'm doing. Turned on by *me*. Taken aback, I let him go.

We stare into each other's eyes. Rizzo is panting softly. Then, with a sudden movement, he takes a step and grabs me, pulls me to him. Crushing his lips against mine, he buries his tongue in my mouth. And I let him. Like an idiot, I'm overwhelmed by the sensation.

Something inside of me springs to life and I slam him back against the wall. He breaks the kiss for long enough for a low moan to escape his mouth. He tastes bitter, like cold smoke. I don't like it, but his tongue slides across mine, and that's all it takes to make me hard.

Rizzo, Rizzo for Christ's sake, wants me. He slides his hand under my shirt. Warm fingers claw into my back. Relentlessly. He's in control, and still he moans something that sounds like my name. Sounds like James, not Foley. Sounds damn needy. He opens my zipper, slides his hand in, and I let out a heated gasp. Wanting him to touch me and at the same time wanting him to pull back. Rizzo's eyes are black with desire as he steers me towards the bed. I only struggle for a moment, then I allow myself to be pushed onto it. The last few months have been a nightmare, when even tossing off could never really release the tension, because Casey was still out of reach. I shut my eyes. I just lie there, and as he takes me into his mouth, I don't want this to happen, and yet it feels amazing. *Don't stop.* He makes me whimper like a small, wounded animal. Oh god, so incredibly good.

* * *

I'm dizzy afterwards, flushed, and wonderfully drowsy. I could fall asleep on the spot. Rizzo flops down beside me, still panting a little. I notice the bulge in his jeans. My eyes wander over his chest, up to his face. Fine pearls of sweat glisten above his perfectly curved mouth and on his forehead. I would sell my grandmother's soul to touch him right now. But I won't. I never asked for a freaking blow-job. I owe him zip and zero. Rizzo turns his head towards me and grins to himself.

"What?" I growl.

"You and your freaking pride, Foley."

"Eat me. I hope your dick rots and falls off."

"Mmm. I love it when you get all mushy, baby." In spite of his sarcasm, Rizzo's eyes are surprisingly warm. Abruptly, he reaches over and cups my face with his hand, pulls me towards him. He leans in and kisses me. I don't return the kiss, but I let him go ahead anyway. I'm not sure why. His hand slides down my cheek, mimicking something that could almost be called a caress. There is a strange sparkle his eyes.

"You know you'll be back for more. Next time you won't get around it. I'm not the Salvation Army."

I chuckle softly. "Next time? And what do you dream of at night?"

"Things far beyond your imagination, Foley."

I sit up, stretch, and swing my legs over the side of the bed. Rising slowly, I pull my trousers up. I glance back at the bulge in his jeans, then at his face. "Have fun, you two."

Rizzo just grins, knowingly. "You *will* be back. You know it."

I resist the urge to look back at him as I walk to the door. I close it firmly behind me. Outside I sink against the wall and exhale deeply. I knock my head softly against the cool stone, as if that could make his words go away. Or the glorious image of him lying there on the bed, just dying to be touched by me. Damn. Of course I'll be back for more. And I hate myself for it already.

8 ENTRAPMENT

CASEY: I guess I don't really know what I want, only that I don't want to wake up thirty years down the line and be my dad. I mean, I love my dad. He's the best. And it's a kind of family tradition. Grandpa was an English teacher, he is an English teacher, and he jokes that all men in our family are fated to have that job. I'm not sure if I want to believe in fate. I was brought up to believe that dreams are important. But if your dreams are too far out of reach, maybe there's an alternative within your grasp. And if there is, then you should go for that.

You would think that James, being the snarling cynic that he is, would completely agree. But he is the only one who's ever truly understood what my art means to me. How it owns my soul. How that is *me*.

So when I was home this spring break, I nervously waited for the right moment for days. And then I finally confessed to Mom that I wanted to illustrate children's books rather than being a teacher. She said: "That's great, sweetie, but that's not a job, that's a hobby. You want a job that can provide for a family, just keep that in mind."

In that moment, I really wanted to be James and tell her to go to hell.

* * *

"You should come," Danny says, and smiles at me. "You can bring Foley."

It's late afternoon on Tuesday and we're sitting in the sun on the steps to his dorm. They're still warm, but the shadow of the building is growing longer at our backs. Friends of his are having a barbecue on Thursday. I've seen them around, but haven't met any of them. They're all seniors.

"Sure, I'll ask if he wants to come."

I'm pretty sure the answer will include mentions of razorblades rather being swallowed, but I'll try anyway. The fact that James is a vegetarian doesn't make him any more likely to attend. He has always been wary of anything that Danny suggests, but now he seems determined to even avoid breathing the same air. I don't know what brought that about. I've tried to carefully find out, but he got that dark look on his face, and changed the subject.

"I bet you twenty that he won't."

"You'll win that bet, I fear."

I'm intrigued by how warm Danny's eyes can get when he smiles. It's like the light is enamored with him. I feel special when he looks at me. I find myself daydreaming about being closer. He is such a laid-back person, but his strong confidence is intimidating. I feel self-conscious around him, but I jump at any chance to be with him. I want him to like me, and can never say if he does.

Back in high school I was completely in love with Amber. At least I thought I was. When we started dating, I was happy as can be. She felt like home to me. But she never captivated me in such a way. I feel bad about it, but it's true. But look at me now. My hands are sweating and I never know where to put them, where to look, what to do with myself. Everything's intense. I feel alive.

Danny looks at me thoughtfully for such a long moment that I get embarrassed. I stare down at my feet. One of my shoelaces is untied, and I'm glad for the chance to avoid his gaze. I bend down and tie it.

"Shame. I guess then you're not coming either."

As I straighten, I notice a strange gleam in his eyes. "Why would you think that?"

"Forget it."

"No, tell me."

"Sure you wanna know?"

"Yeah," I answer cautiously. "Should I brace myself?"

"I can hold your hand if you want," he grins.

Oh dear. I would honestly love that, and in my mind I can see James wincing at the romantic fool this probably makes me.

Danny tilts his head, looking at me intently. "They call you the Twins, did you know that? You're Twin and he's Evil Twin."

I'm baffled, and taken aback. But I try to laugh about it, and not let it show. I've never liked being sensitive. It makes a lot of things pretty hard. "Who's calling us that?"

"Oh, you know. People."

I look away. I feel hurt, more on James' behalf than on my own. I didn't have the slightest clue people were talking behind our backs. "You mean your friends do."

He shrugs unconcernedly. "Hey, who cares? They're jerks."

"They're your *friends*."

He laughs and shakes his head. "They're just people I hang out with, Casey."

"Is that how you see them?" I'm kind of shocked. I'd never talk about my friends like that, even if they were jerks. On second thought, if they were, I wouldn't be friends with them to begin with. "Is that how you see friendship?"

He smiles a little, but there is a fleeting sad, if not resigned look on his face. It is the first glimpse of vulnerability I've seen in him, and I feel cruel for having said that. But at the same time I'm fascinated. My heart is beating madly. Yes. This is the real you, Danny Rizzo. Right there. That is what I need to, what I absolutely *have* to get a chance to paint. But it's gone in a flash, and he's teasing me again.

"I'm offended. Twin."

"Shut up."

I can't help but laugh with him. He gets up and gives me a smile that makes me yearn for more. "See you on Thursday, Casey."

"I'll be there." I stay where I am and watch him saunter away, and I wonder how he's such a mystery. It takes me a moment to realize that in some roundabout way, he's completely tricked me into going to that barbecue. Because he is right. I wouldn't have gone otherwise, not without James. I feel a sudden sting as I grasp the truth in those people calling us the Twins. And I catch myself pondering if I should even ask James if he wants to come.

9 STIGMATIZED

JAMES: There's a spot up the green hill on the edge of Shriner's Park where I like to go when I need to think. Firstly, because you can overlook the whole campus from there. The voyeur in me loves that. Secondly, because of the trees. Old, gnarled willows with their branches hanging low like strands of hair. The perfect hiding place.

Today I got an awful lot to think about. But the truth is, it all boils down to one question that's on endless repeat in my mind: What the hell have I done? Part of me still can't believe what happened with Rizzo. I mean, I was physically present. I know damn well what went down in his room. When I close my eyes I can still feel him. Everywhere. And I know that Casey would never forgive me if he ever found out.

I exhale slowly, and let myself sink back onto the soft grass, stretching arms and legs out at my sides. Like a dead man. The dead man I would sometimes like to be. A ceiling of branches sways softly in the breeze above me. I close my eyes and just listen to the rustling of the leaves, sounding like the surf, far away. It reminds me of that afternoon we spent by the sea. Of the heat, and of Rizzo's hands on me. Stop. Stop thinking about it, damn it. Bad, bad, bad.

I sense a presence before I hear someone approaching on the grass, long before a shadow falls over me. Pretending not to notice, I keep my eyes shut, hiding a smile. I know who it is. I know because my skin starts to prickle and something inside starts to flutter like a flock of birds taking to the wind.

He sits down beside me and I can almost feel him smiling as he looks at my face. He rips out a blade of grass and playfully brushes the soft tip across my nose. It tickles, and I can't help grinning, but I still don't open my eyes. Maybe if I keep them closed I can pretend that things are different between us. That he knows what I feel for him, and doesn't mind. Casey traces my eyes, my eyebrows, runs it along my cheek like a paintbrush. He stops for a moment before he traces my lips, very slowly. I hold my breath. My heart is beating madly when I open my eyes. There is something thoughtful, tender in the brilliant blue orbs that look down at me. This sense of closeness between us. Closeness and trust.

"Gotcha." Casey smiles. "Don't think you can hide from me, James Foley."

"Far be it from me to even try."

"I've been looking everywhere for you." There's a trace of reproach in the words the way he says them, making me smile. It gives me warm feelings how he enjoys my company. That he misses me when I'm not there. Hell, that he even notices is more than enough to give me sweet dreams for weeks.

"Yeah? Why?"

"Well..." Casey flops down beside me. "Because."

"Okay then. If that's so, all is clear to me."

He turns his head to look at me with a charming smile. "You missed study group. Anna gave us quite the lecture about how it doesn't make sense to form a study group when nobody shows up." He winks at me. "Personally, I think she was just mad because without you being there, she actually had to do some thinking for herself."

I chuckle. He's probably right. What can I say, I'm brilliant. I'm that pathetic smart kid that used to get pushed around at school, until they realized that it was handy cribbing from someone who knew what he was doing. But I'm not someone you can push around without having to pay eventually. In this case, literally. I let them copy my homework, then blackmailed them for it. By senior year it had turned into a profitable way to increase my non-existent allowance. I have a long history of making deals with devils that has secured me a ticket to hell very early on. I never believed in salvation. But there's something about Casey that makes me want to be a better person. You look at him, you know: Here is someone true. He has miraculously kept a trace of innocence, like only someone with a happy childhood, a happy home can do. It makes me want to protect him. And it makes me scared that the callous bastard in me might rub off on him somehow.

"James?" Casey asks softly.

"Yeah?"

"You know when you said that you thought Danny wouldn't be good for me?"

I nod, hating to be reminded of Rizzo when I had just successfully banished him from my mind.

"The other day... Oh, I don't know." He trails off and stares up to the curtain of branches that hides us from the world.

"The other day what?"

He sighs a little. "It's weird. Sometimes I don't feel like myself when I'm around him." Lost in thought, he chews on the blade of grass. It's nodding in front of his face like a whip. I watch it unblinkingly. "Go on."

He glances at me. "It's hard to describe. It's like I change somehow. And I'm not sure I like what I become."

Oh my gosh. And eureka, and all that. Has he finally realized how manipulative that son of a bitch can be?

He smiles to himself with a trace of melancholy. "There was this girl in junior high. Amy Lee Wellman. She was my first big crush, you know."

"Really? I thought Amber was."

"No. No, she wasn't." He looks into the distance as if he can see his past there.

"Amy was... she was amazing. She was smart, and popular, and god, so beautiful. Everyone was a little in love with her. I wanted to marry her." He chuckles softly. "But I never worked up the nerve to approach her." He looks at me. "I wish I would have, you know. Sometimes I still wonder what would have happened."

"That was a long time ago, Case."

"Yeah. I'm pretty sad, huh? Point is, I don't want to make the same mistake again. What I feel for him is... I just really want him to like me. I want to know."

"To know what?"

"What it feels like. To be with someone who is so... To be

with someone like him."

I sit up abruptly, a dark frown on my face. "I'll tell you what it feels like. People like that, they make you feel like you're not good enough. You try to please someone, it makes you feel like shit. It makes you feel worthless."

He looks at me with a confused smile. "Woah, hold on! Why are you so upset?"

"I'm not upset, I'm pissed off. Can't you see what he's like? What *they* are like? Damn it, Casey. Why would you want to be with someone that superficial?"

"How can you be so sure that he is?"

"How can you be so sure that he isn't?"

We stare at each other heatedly, and realize what we're doing. I look away. "Look, I'm sorry. I just don't want for you to get hurt."

His eyes soften. "Yeah, I know."

An uncomfortable moment of silence passes. I can see him getting lost in his thoughts, and I have no idea what's on his mind.

"Have you ever thought about what it is you look for in a relationship?" he finally asks pensively.

I shrug. "Not really."

"I mean, it's easy to come up with a list of qualities you want your respective other to have. But that's not the same thing."

"So what are you looking for?"

"I'm not sure. Maybe... someone who can see me. Who can see who I really am. And it'd have to be someone kind."

Right. Because Rizzo is kind, gentle Mary, Mother of God. I mean, seriously, the hell?

"And you?"

"I don't have a lot of expectations, really."

"That's kinda sad."

"I like to call it realistic."

Casey smiles to himself, and slowly sits up. "You're kinder than you know, James. You're kind to me."

Kind. The word hovers in the air, can't sink in, can't connect with me. I don't know what to think of it, what to do. Do I dare hope...?

He pats my shoulder. "And you're a great friend."

Friend. Right. I'm inwardly screaming: For god's sake, turn your head, look at me! I'm right here, right beside you. Mere inches away. I'm someone, too. I *see* you. I don't want to be your friend. I want to be everything to you.

I keep a straight face and force myself to smile at him. "Why thanks."

"*De rien.*" Casey looks over the green meadows, down to campus. "Before I forget, I'm going home for the weekend. It's my dad's birthday this Saturday."

The intimacy of the moment is broken, flies open wide like a web and gets blown away by the breeze.

"Okay. Tell him happy birthday for me."

"Will do." He carelessly throws the blade of grass away. "Listen, I'd better get going. I gotta pack some stuff for tomorrow. See you later?"

"Sure."

I watch as he climbs to his feet and slowly descends the hill. Watch until he becomes one tiny spot among all the other tiny spots in the distance. So much for hoping against hope. Unfortunately, the thing with hope is that you can't just switch it on or off. It's not something you can decide to have. It decides to have you.

We fall so easily for what we'd like to be. Catholics have their saints to admire. They made them up to build a stairway to heaven, so that those who believed hard enough knew that it was possible to reach. But all it did was show them how great the distance really was. I may not know much about kindness, and even less about transcendence. But this I know for certain: The concept of all things unreachable is not to ever reach them, but to aspire to.

10 RECIPROCITY

CASEY: It's eight a.m. on Saturday and I'm on a Greyhound, wishing I had thought to bring something containing caffeine. The sky is dim as a frown. The landscape sailing past the window hovers with the little bumps in the road. The book on my lap has been lying there unopened for fifteen minutes. A man in the back is snoring softly. A couple of rows in front of me a mother is peeling an orange for her little girl and the fruity smell is in the air.

I think about the barbecue, being among all those hip strangers and feeling awkward. Wishing I had dragged my Twin along. And Danny, always at the center of attention, seeming so at ease. I don't know why he asked me to come. We barely got a chance to talk all evening. I left early, feeling sad.

I think about what James said about trying to please people, and the truth of it stings. Why am I doing this? Is Danny Rizzo, is anyone worth me changing for them to like me? But how can I be myself when I don't really know what it means to be me?

Sometimes when James looks at me, I feel like there is something... Like I mean much more to him than just a friend. But how could I ever be sure? He is so hard to read. There is something about James, a kind of frosty dignity that says: I stand alone. I need nothing and no-one in this world.

But I need him somehow, and that worries me. He makes me feel real, solid. Like an anchor in my life, rooting me in reality. Maybe subconsciously I'm trying to get away, to loosen the chain. Maybe Danny isn't the cause, but a symptom. One thing's for sure: If my friendship with James should ever end, it would be the cruelest blow. It would shatter a huge part of my life. But James, he would simply move on. Nothing can disappoint you if you have no expectations. It saddens me that he feels this way about the world, about life. I want to prove to him that he has got it all wrong. That there is beauty everywhere. If I could only get through to him like he gets through to me. But there's a line with James that you just can't cross. I wonder, for the first time, if he is afraid. But of what? Of me?

What if James... No, what am I thinking? No, that's crazy. But okay, just theoretically and for fun. What if he did have feelings for me? How would I feel about it? My pulse immediately accelerates.

James. James with the lonely eyes. James who makes a cupboard seem emotional in comparison, and firmly keeps the secrets of his past.

James with the dry wit and the sharp intellect. Who quotes Nietzsche, and listens to Pink Floyd. James who doesn't even believe in friendship, and still has never let me down.

Janie has a huge crush on him. It's the cutest thing to see my smarty pants kid sister blush and fall silent when he's visiting. And he's so lovely with her. He never makes his usual sarcastic remarks. He's such an amazing human being, and he doesn't even know.

The kiss steals back into my mind, and I try to remember the sensation of his lips on mine. Soft, gentle, sensitive. He didn't kiss me like someone who had been made to at a party. And I didn't kiss him like that either.

I get goosebumps, and swallow as I stare out the window. Wow.

11 SINNER

JAMES: Gently but steadily the raindrops are rapping against the glass of my window, and the world outside disappears in shades of gray. I watch as they slide down in small trickles. Mom used to tell me that when it rains, the angels cry. Sometimes because they're sad, and sometimes because they're happy. I was five and not so sure angels even existed.

So let's recapitulate, shall we? Casey wants Rizzo, not me. I want Casey, not Rizzo. And Rizzo... well, shags anything that hasn't run away screaming at the count of three. Which would appear to include me. I could kick myself for my stupidity. I completely fell for his trap. He's using me to get to Casey. He knows the moment I'm out of the picture, he'll have his way. And what would be a better way to get rid of me than to make me do something to hurt Casey? Damn that bastard, that is exactly what I've already done. All he needs to do now is to tell Casey about it, and I'm screwed.

There's a knock on the door, and I jump slightly. Who the hell is that? I don't get visitors. And Casey's not here over the weekend. Twenty-seven miserable, lonely, pathetic hours to go until I get to see his face again.

"Come in, if you must."

Well, kick my ass and call me a believer! I couldn't have been more surprised if it had been Santa Claus stepping into my room. It's Rizzo. For a moment I'm completely floored. He's never been to my place before. How does he even know where I live? "What do *you* want here?"

"I guess I should come by more often, just to get such a warm welcome," he grins and quickly crosses the distance between us with a few confident strides.

"What do you want?" I repeat, my expression blank of emotion as I stare up at his handsome face. He seems taller than I remember, but then again, I'm sitting at my desk and he's standing close before me.

"Do I need a reason? Or maybe you want me to make an appointment beforehand next time?" Rizzo chuckles, and his hand automatically slides into his pocket to produce a pack of cigarettes.

"Don't even think about it."

He rolls his eyes, but stuffs them back in without so much as a snide remark, and that surprises me.

"So, you have no reason to be here, but you still are," I analyze dryly.

"Ten points to the guy in the tasteless Spider-Man shirt."

I frown, then look down at my chest and realize that I'm wearing the shirt my mom gave me years ago. It was about two sizes to large then. Fits perfectly now. "Hey, you don't insult Spider-Man around here."

"And the geekiness just keeps on coming."

Giving him a look I raise an eyebrow. "Does this conversation have a purpose that I fail to see, or did you just come by to annoy me?"

"Foley, I'm telling you, even my grandma wasn't as uptight as you."

"I bet your grandma was a stripper."

His mouth widens to a grin, then he laughs, and I like the sound of that. Rizzo crosses his arms in front of his chest and turns around to lean against the desk beside me. His eyes sparkle mischievously as he looks down at me. "You know, you're really not that bad, Foley."

I blink slowly. Was that supposed to be some kind of compliment? Noticing the look on my face, Rizzo laughs again, and for some reason, he almost seems a little embarrassed. But it can't be, because he never is. He fumbles for his cigarettes again, but lets his hand drop limply at his side when he remembers, and it brushes against my bare arm unintentionally. I get goosebumps, and I pray he doesn't notice. Could he please not stand so close to me?

"Rizzo, if you think you can come by for a quickie in between your previous groupie and the next, I've only got one thing to say to you: There is a reason god gave you hands."

"Oh yeah? And would that be to do this?" Before I can react, Rizzo takes me by the arms and pulls me up from my chair, pulls me close to him. He looks deeply into my eyes, suddenly serious, almost pensive, like I've never seen him before.

"Don't..." I begin to say, but my throat goes dry and the words just disappear, are blown away. There is something incredibly intense about this moment, and I can feel my heart racing madly in my chest.

"Don't what?" Rizzo asks softly and runs a light finger along my cheek. To which my cheek reacts a lot less than my cock. "What are you afraid of, James? That you could actually start to like me?"

I swallow, and hate myself for blushing as I stare into his eyes. I don't know how to handle this new Rizzo that I don't recognize at all. Look at the rabbit, paralyzed by the cobra. "Hell, man. Do you think I don't know you're only messing with me to get to Casey?"

"Casey?" Rizzo arches an eyebrow and moves back a bit in surprise, then shakes his head with a smile. "You've got it all wrong, Jimmy. I'm only messing with Casey to get to you."

Okay. That sure hit home. I step back abruptly, freeing myself of his grip, and he raises his hands in a defensive gesture. I feel like I've just been slapped in the face.

"The hell?"

"For being such a smartass you catch on pretty slow sometimes."

"Oh, come *on*!" This guy is unbelievable! What's he gonna pull out of his hat next?

"What? Don't tell me you didn't notice. Geez, James..." Rizzo laughs softly. Shakes his head, and his eyes are smiling. "Forget Casey! It's never been about Casey."

"Yeah, right. That's why you always..."

"Well, I got your attention, didn't I?"

My jaw just drops. I don't know what to say, what to think, what to do. I just stand there, and a million voices in my head are buzzing like a beehive. I can't believe that asshole is looking me straight into the eye, taking the piss out of me. This is just another sick game of his. I know it. But damn, what a performance.

"You're so full of shit, Rizzo. I've just about had it with your crap."

"Yeah? The thing is, I don't think so, Foley." He pauses, and a tiny smile curls his lips. "You wanna know what your problem is?"

"You tell me, if you know so much about me."

"Your problem is that you want to be with Casey, but sleep with me."

I laugh dryly, feeling strangely numb. "Yeah, right."

"You know it's true." Rizzo moves closer and nonchalantly puts his hand on my neck, pulls me towards him with unexpected determination. Instinctively my eyelids flutter closed even before his lips press against mine, and his tongue slides into my mouth, wet and possessively. I want to have him. I want to take him now, hard and fast. I want him to bleed, god, how I want it. Instead, I push him away, so violently he staggers, almost falls.

We're both panting, our eyes dark as we stare at each other. There is a long moment of silence. Sobering. The sound of rain falling outside fills the room entirely. I feel like being locked in an outsized aquarium. Rizzo wipes across his mouth with the back of his hand, wincing like I hit him there.

"You're making a mistake, James." His soft voice is very calm now, and serious. Is he threatening me? No. For some reason I don't believe that. For once, he sounds honest.

What if he really told the truth? The thought rips through my anger and fills me with doubt.

"I'm not the Salvation Army, I told you that." He takes a deep breath, still recovering from my fierce reaction to his kiss that he clearly didn't expect. "So what is it you want?"

Alright then, you asked for it, you bastard. To think that for one moment, I almost believed you... "I want you to get the hell outta my place."

Rizzo nods, and smiles flatly. For the split of a second, there's something in his eyes... Hurt. It's gone when he steps closer and stares at me with a smug grin.

"I think Casey and I should have a little chat real soon."

I let him have his cliffhanger exit, but the moment the door closes behind him I sink onto the bed.

Damn. I'm done for. He's gonna tell Casey. I know he will. And it's all my own fault.

12 PROSTRATION

JAMES: I never thought I would be grateful for a party, but tonight it means that the whole dorm's deserted, and that is a good thing. They're all out, noisily having a good time at the annual "School's (almost) out for Summer" bash that traditionally takes place two weeks before the end of semester. It's basically a huge booze-up, disguised as a barbecue, with local bands playing so loudly you can't even hear yourself talking. But who needs to talk on such occasions anyway? All the cool people get to be incredibly cool, and all the losers get to feel left out, when in fact everybody is just trying to get laid. Naturally this is the event the whole campus is looking forward to all year. Thanks, but I'll pass.

I feel unreal as I slowly walk down the corridor to my room. A hell of a frozen lump in my stomach has been growing all day like a swelling inside. It's like reality is collapsing on me, or maybe I haven't been living in reality these past few months and now I'm suddenly being tossed back without a place to land. Casey and I have never fought before. Sure, we have our quarrels. Everybody does. He gets all grumpy when he is mad at me. It's kinda cute. But what happened this morning was different. Painfully real. And final. Like something important was broken that can never be mended.

"Is it true?" he asked when he came into my room, and I knew what he meant the moment I saw his face, even before he continued. "Is it true what Danny says? That you slept with him?"

Damn that bastard Rizzo. I knew he would do this. Just like he'd been planning it all along. Casey looked so hurt. I swallowed hard, trying to speak but unable to for a long, awkward moment. "What exactly did he tell you?"

"He says that you came to his room last week. And that you'd been trying to hit on him all semester."

"That lying son of a bitch," I hissed through clenched teeth, more to myself. But Casey heard, and he came closer.

"It's not true then? I didn't want to believe it, but..." He trailed off and a small, embarrassed smile hovered on his lips. As he looked at me, the smile faded. "James? There was nothing between Danny and you, was there? Nothing at all?"

I should have lied. I know I should have. But I couldn't. I just stood there with hanging arms, and the expression on my face must have said it all.

Casey inhaled sharply. He turned his head away quickly. "You should have said something. You should have told me, James." No argument, no accusations. Nothing. He just stood there, clearly shocked, and still far too composed. As though it hadn't quite hit him yet. Then he glanced at me, and I could see tears in his eyes.

It hurt like hell to see him like this. I wanted to tell him I was sorry. That I was an idiot and he had every right to hate me. But all I got out was a very lame "Casey..."

"So that's why you said Danny wouldn't be good for me. I get it now." Casey shook his head, and that painful, bitter smile felt like a kick in the gut. "God, you must think I'm so stupid."

"What? No! No, Casey, listen..."

"It's okay. You don't have to pretend anymore." He had this incredible dignity about him as he simply turned around and walked to the door.

"Casey, wait!" I followed quickly and pushed the half-open door shut again. I needed him to know, to understand... "There's something I need to tell you. Something important."

Casey stopped, his hand still on the door-handle. All the warmth had left his kind face. "Well, that's too bad, James, 'cause I don't wanna hear it."

He opened the door again and stepped out of the room, slamming the door shut in my face. I could still hear the icy, hollow sound minutes later.

* * *

So, yeah, I guess I screwed up good and proper. I don't blame Casey for hating me. I don't even blame Rizzo. Well, I okay, I do, but mostly I don't have the energy to. It's shattering to know with absolute clarity that things will never be the same again. How can we be friends now? I've destroyed everything. You don't sleep with your best friend's love interest. You just don't. Ever.

It hurts too much to think about it, and so I do what I always do when the pain comes. I morph into good old James, the Invisible. Hollow, numb, and blissfully blank of emotion. It's a simple technique of curling up in that place inside where they can't reach you. There was a time when being able to do that was a life-saver.

I've almost reached my door when Anna storms out of her room and nearly runs into me. Damn. With a bit of luck she might even have knocked me out.

"Shit, Foley! What the hell you doing up here?" she barks. Anna always barks, she doesn't just talk like normal people. But then again, you can hardly call a militant feminist with a pink-dyed Mohican and three lip-piercings normal.

"I live here," I answer dryly and am about to walk on when she grabs me by the arm and firmly holds me back.

"No, you don't. Get your sad ass down to the party. It's like the one night of the year when even a hopeless case like you is allowed to have fun!"

"Thanks, but I'd rather not."

"Right then, let's go!" she decides.

"Anna!" I hiss sharply as she begins to drag me back up the corridor. "I'm not going anywhere."

To my surprise she really stops, and glares at me. That's when I notice a deep hurt in her eyes that can't possibly come from my reaction. Has she been crying?

"What the hell's your problem? You can brood and mope down there just fine if you absolutely have to!" she snaps.

"It just so happens that I'd rather mope alone."

"Julie dumped me," she blurts out with no prior warning. "Bitch dumped me for Jenny. Jenny! Can you believe that?"

I have no idea who Jenny is, and to be honest, I couldn't care less. And still, something inside of me spontaneously sympathizes with her hurt. Great. Am I growing soft in my old age?

"But you know what?" Anna continues with almost scary determination, "I don't care. Whatever. I mean, if she doesn't want me, it's her loss. And you know what I'm gonna do tonight?"

I just hope she isn't planning to switch sides and explore uncharted sexual territories or anything, not as long as she's this close to me anyway.

"Get completely pissed," she smiles wryly. "And you're gonna keep me company." Ignoring my unwilling little snarl, Anna puts her iron arm around my waist and gives me an encouraging squeeze. "Come on, Foley, you look like that's just what you need yourself tonight."

Not sure why, but between excessive amounts of alcohol and being alone with myself, somehow the first sounds like the more healthy option. With a deep sigh I finally give in and let myself be dragged away.

* * *

I have no idea where Anna got the booze, but I swear I can literally feel my brain cells getting fried one by one while I take large gulps of it. Gah, it still tastes awful as hell now that we've emptied three quarters of the bottle. Anna watches me wince with a small, amused grin.

"You know, I never got why he likes you, but even you have your cute moments."

"Wuh? Anna, I'm trying to kill myself here with something that could be motor-oil from the taste of it. Don't make me think. Who're you talking about?"

Completely unmotivated she breaks into a giggle and rolls around on the soft, lush lawn that we're lying on - lawn you're not supposed to walk across- a bit apart from the crowd. Yep, she's definitely getting where I want to be. I don't really expect an answer anymore when she lifts her head and groans: "Casey, of course, you dickhead." She giggles again.

"Dickhead?" I start to laugh too, in spite of myself. "Shut up, you SCUM-reading dyke. What do you know anyway? Casey hates me."

"Yeah, right." Anna's head lands on my shoulder and bangs against my cheek, and we both moan pitifully. "You should hear him talk about you. James this, James that, James everything!"

"Ha. You're lying. He doesn't do that."

"Does too. And you're an idiot."

We're both silent for a moment. I stare up to the night sky above, trying to get my brain to process what she said. The party lights are too bright to see the stars tonight. Maybe it's overcast anyway. I thought I heard a roll of thunder rumbling in the distance earlier. The air is so thick you could cut it.

"And even if he did talk about me so much - which he doesn't," I glare at her. "That doesn't prove a thing."

"You're both idiots," is her meaningful reply.

"So what's he say about me?"

"Who?"

"Casey," I snarl impatiently.

"It's not what he's saying, stupid, it's the *way* he's saying it. Foley, how blind can you be?" Anna shakes her head, banging it against my chin again in the process and not giving a damn.

"Oww," I protest.

"I don't get you. It's like you actually enjoy being miserable!"

"Apparently," I say quietly, more to myself, and the tragic part about it is that I know she's probably right.

"He hates me now, anyway."

"What did you do?"

"Something unforgivable," I mumble.

"Nothing's unforgivable, stupid."

"Would you forgive... what's her face?"

"Julie? Never ever. Ever!" she replies darkly, and far too loudly. "That bitch can rot in hell!"

"Why, thanks. You fill me with hope."

Abruptly I sit up, ignoring Anna protesting loudly and slapping my arm. I thought I'd just spotted Casey at the edge of the crowd, not far from us. I was right. And he's not alone. Rizzo's with him. A sudden wave of hatred with the rage of a thousand hellfires grips me. I don't want to see this. I don't want to feel. I get a dark foreboding, making the palms of my hands sweat. They're talking. Standing close to each other. Very close. Sharing a beer, apparently. The intimacy is sickening. Something inside my stomach starts to spin, and in my current state, that is a very bad thing. I don't get this! He can hang out with Rizzo, but not with me? Why isn't he mad with him too? That's completely not fair in my book.

"Anna, gimme the bottle." I hold out my open hand and she slaps the bottle into it with a low grunt as she struggles to sit up beside me.

"What is it?" She follows my stare and glances at me when she's noticed Casey and Rizzo. "Uh-oh."

I put the booze to my mouth and just let it flow into me, but killjoy-Anna snatches it from my hand, spilling half of it on my clothes.

"Woah! Easy, big boy. I don't want you to hurl all over me!"
"Piss off."

Great, now they've seen us. Both Casey and Rizzo stare over to us for a long moment. I wish I knew what they're thinking right now. On second thought, no, I'd rather not. I can imagine what a remarkably pathetic picture the two of us fighting over a bottle of cheap booze must be. Rizzo frowns slightly, and makes a motion that looks like he's gonna come over, but then he decides not to. Instead, he flashes one of his killer smiles at Casey. And Casey returns the smile. He turns away from me like I'm some sort of lower being not even worth despising. But I can't stop staring at them. I know that Casey is fully aware of me watching as he puts his hand on Rizzo's hip and leans in to whisper something in his ear. They smile at each other, and Rizzo lifts his hand to cup Casey's face. And then they kiss.

I'm on my feet and over there so fast neither of them sees it coming, but at the same time everything seems to happen in slow motion. Sharp pain shoots through my fist as it connects with Rizzo's face, and he stumbles backwards, loses balance, hits the ground. I kick him in the guts, kick hard, and he howls in agony. It sounds like a symphony to my ears. "You keep your hands off him, you son of a bitch!"

Someone violently grabs me by the arms and pulls me back. "Are you crazy? Get off him!" Casey's voice sounds strangely distorted, like from far away through my haze. He pushes me out of Rizzo's reach, stares at me in complete shock. "James! What do you think you're doing?"

With my heart beating madly from the adrenaline rush, I stare back for a long, sobering moment, unaware of the sensation-hungry crowd around us watching. My gaze drops to Rizzo on the ground, who's got his hands pressed to his abdomen, blood dripping from his lower lip. Still he doesn't seem to be aware of it, he doesn't seem to feel any pain at all as the tiniest trace of a smile curls his lips in some kind of twisted satisfaction. There are no words to describe how much I hate him right now.

Without taking his eyes off me, Casey walks over to Rizzo and helps him back to his feet. What he is feeling, thinking, I can't tell. All I know is that I've never seen him this upset.

"Come on, let's go," he addresses Rizzo softly, but he's still looking at me as he says it.

I can't avert my eyes as Casey takes Rizzo's hand and they turn around, disappear in the crowd, headed for somewhere that isn't really hard to guess. But I would know where, wouldn't I? I chuckle at the irony, but it turns into something sounding more like a suppressed sob. A small, painful, surreal noise. I don't think I can move. Ever again. I just want to die right now, on the spot. A lightning strike might make for a good exit, but of course I'm not that lucky.

I'm suddenly aware of Anna standing beside me, but don't notice that I'm trembling before she puts an arm around me.

"Hey," she says softer than I ever thought her capable of. "You know, sometimes people do stupid, irrational things when they're hurt. Things they don't really mean."

I nod, but don't really listen to the words. Something wet hits me on the cheek. Then again on my arm. My hand. My hair. It's starting to rain. Within seconds, the raindrops come down fast and heavy, and the crowd scatters screaming in front of us, seeking shelter. I don't move. Neither does Anna. She looks up and welcomes the rain pouring down on her face like a cold, refreshing shower. We both stand still until we're completely soaked. It's cold, my clothes sticking to my body, but I can't bring myself to care. Finally Anna stirs beside me.

"Come on, Foley, let's get you inside before you catch your death and they sue me," she grins wryly and starts to lead me back to the dorm. I follow like a zombie, feeling dead inside.

13 MAKING SENSE

CASEY: I wake up in my own bed, and the first thing I do today is let out a deep sigh. I'm not sure if it's a sigh of relief, or one of the other, sadder kinds. Maybe it's a mixture of both. I sigh again, for good measure. When did everything get so complicated, and why does nothing make sense anymore?
It's a beautiful day. The air is clean, fresh and alive. I inhale deeply as I stare out the half-open window. Lush, green meadows glistening with a million tiny drops of water in mild morning light, like an ocean of pearls. We had one hell of a thunderstorm last night. In many ways, I guess. The image of James hitting Danny comes to mind, and I try to shut it out. But I can't forget the look on his face.

"What did you do?" I whispered, breaking the kiss as Danny and I stepped into his room.

"What?"

"To James. What did you do to James?"

He looked at me with an amused little smile, and pressed me against the door. That smile did things to me I don't even have words for. Then he kissed me again, and I couldn't help moaning softly. Felt so good. Felt so incredible. His tongue in my mouth, pure magic, sensual, slow. And my brain kept saying: *God, this is Rizzo. This is Danny Rizzo you're kissing. In his room.* But my brain hadn't shut down enough for me to forget what I wanted to know.

"Answer my question?"

"What makes you think I did something to him?" His grin broadened, his breath softly ghosting over my face. He's so beautiful, flawless, and doesn't he know it. There was a sparkle in his eyes that made me catch my breath. I think I was trembling slightly, not in the least bit prepared for what was happening here. He kissed me again. Then his hand slid into my pants, and I let out a gasp.

"Oh god." My fingers seemed to claw into his back on their own account. I had dreamed of this, I had been dying for this, but this was incomparably better. The pleasure shot through my body like a fever. I had never been touched like this before. And for him to be the one... I closed my eyes and desperately leaned into his touch. He knew exactly what to do to make the pleasure unbearably intense... Christ. I was turned on like never before in my life. Wide-eyed, only half able to believe what was happening between us. I was panting softly, every inch of my body dying for the sensation. And then he just pulled his hand away. I stared at him in surprise, only to find him laughing softly.

"Beg," he said with that incredible voice.

"Danny..."

"Beg," he repeated. "Beg for it."

"Please..."

"Please what?"

I tried to kiss him, but he moved his head away, watching my reaction. I let out a frustrated moan. "*Please.*"

"Say it. I want to hear it."

I tugged him close by his T-shirt and whispered the words into his ear, words I had never thought I would say to anyone. I felt dirty saying them, and it felt right. "Sleep with me. Please sleep with me, Danny."

He stared into my eyes, and for one moment I thought he was about to kiss me again. But he hesitated. His dark eyes were fathomless. Then he stepped away. Still panting, I stared at him unbelievingly. "What are you doing?"

He nonchalantly lit a cigarette, as though nothing had just happened between us. Nothing at all. "Well, what does it look like?"

"But... I don't understand," I said quietly.

"I bet you don't, Millsie."

It was hard to calm down again. My pulse was still racing, my body dying for his touch. "What's going on?" I took a step closer. "I thought... you wanted it too." My voice sounded small.

He snorted. "You're breaking my heart."

"What's the matter with you? You find this amusing?"

"Actually, yeah, I do." He laughed and looked at me with those beautiful eyes. Beautiful and, right now, so very cold. There he was once more, Danny Rizzo, all cool and aloof, out of reach. I had no idea what was going through his mind. He was impossible to read.

"Why did you bring me here if not to..."

"...screw you?" Rizzo finished my sentence, and there was a dangerous undertone in his voice. "'Cause that's what I'm all about? That's what you think."

"No. God, no, it isn't."

"Then what am I all about, tell me."

I shrugged helplessly. "I don't know. I mean, you barely gave me a chance to get to know you so far."

He rolled his eyes.

"I would like to paint you," I blurted out, and had no idea why I said that. God, I felt stupid. For reasons unknown, he wasn't flattered. No, instead he was looking rather annoyed with me.

"How can you be such a wuss, Mills? I mean, if you were at least a bit of competition. But this?" He gestured at me. "Geez."

My head was spinning. "I have no idea what you're talking about, but that wasn't very nice."

He laughed, but there was something in his eyes, like some kind of hurt shimmering through from deep down. "Well, hell. I'm not *nice*, Mills." He exhaled smoke through his nostrils. "I'm anything but."

"That's what you like to think," I replied stubbornly.

His dark eyes were resting on me with a mixture of amusement and disbelief. I just wanted to kiss him again. I just... wanted. Whatever it was he was trying to tell me, I didn't want to hear. His expression changed to something distant and cold. Danny took a step closer, and there was something threatening about it.

"You wanted to know what I did to James. But your question should be, what did I do to *you*?"

I stared at him, trying to make sense of his words. It was the look in his eyes, that merciless stare, that finally made me understand. And the penny finally dropped. It hit me hard, hard like a kick in the guts. The realization that he didn't really want me was harsh, but at the same time, I wasn't even that surprised. "You played me, didn't you?"

He tilted his head to the side and blew smoke into my face, waiting for me to say more.

"You got me to like you. You tricked me into thinking that you liked me too."

"And why did I do that, Casey dearest?"

The feeling of hurt and humiliation was so intense that I didn't think I could say another word. But I did. "Is this about James?"

He smiled one of those killer smiles of his, but his eyes remained cold. "For god's sake, Mills, you're slow. Now think again, and tell me why I brought you here."

I don't know where it came from, but the anger that came over me was so sudden and so frighteningly deep. I took a step towards him, and now we were only inches apart. I was positively seething. "You! You tried to drive us apart! *You* like James, that's the reason behind it all!"

Danny was laughing. "Oh, this is too good. I wish I had a camera."

That's when my fist clenched and I took at swing at him, aiming for his face.

* * *

Well, I didn't manage to hit him. He was too quick for that. But still, I feel horrible. Ashamed. I hate violence. I don't hit people. I never hit anyone in my life. And he looked like he was going to beat my ass from here to eternity. Rizzo is taller than me and way better built. He could have beaten the crap out of me. But he never did. So why didn't he? If he hates me so much, why not take the opportunity? And he must hate me, mustn't he, to play me, to use me like that.

I can't believe I fell for it. That I fell for him. That he managed to get under my skin, he even made me question my sexual orientation. And now everything's more confusing and complicated than ever. James tried to warn me, but I didn't listen. Everything is my fault. I don't blame James anymore, not for one second, for sleeping with Rizzo - if he even did. It hurt, but it didn't hurt my feelings as much as it should have. And that's the odd part.

I roll out of bed, and rub my face with my hands as I step to the window. How could I let things get so messed up? I am a horrible person. I guess there is only one explanation for why Rizzo did what he did to me. He sees me as competition, isn't that what he said? But wouldn't that mean that he actually believes that James *likes me*?

Oh shit.

That look on James' face when he hit Rizzo last night. He told him to stay away from me. God. I guess I really am kind of slow when it comes to these things. James may not be interested in Rizzo after all. Whatever happened between them, that was Rizzo's doing. I can see it now. Now that I know what he's capable of. And the only reason Rizzo ever told me that something had happened between them was to get me to be mad at James. And I was. I was hurt. Because James, my James, would never do anything like that to me.

James. My James. My wonderful, strange, amazing James. Whom I know so well, and who knows me better than anyone. I get a warm feeling just thinking of him, and my heartbeat suddenly accelerates. Is it true? Is James actually *in love* with me? Was that nagging suspicion I've had all this time right after all? I can't believe it. All this time, there was someone who truly cared about me, who was always there for me. And I didn't see.

I close my eyes, and think of our truth-or-dare kiss. And once more, I get goosebumps at the thought. His lips so soft on mine. Careful and sweet, like you'd never think he would be. There's a yearning, a yearning to be near him. My heart beats even faster. Are my feelings for James perhaps deeper than I was aware of? Now my pulse is positively racing, and I'm feeling all flushed.

Oh my god. How could I have been so blind? How could I not realize what he really means to me? I love him for being my best friend, and I love him for being *James*. For all the things he is, and for all the things he isn't. I love him. And I am *in love* with him.

The sudden rush of excitement and happiness is overwhelming. My James. My wonderful James. There's no ignoring it anymore. Casey Mills, most clueless being of clueless beings, has seen the light. And now I know what I have to do.

14 AFTER THE RAIN

JAMES: Ouch. Ow ow ow. Double ow. Mental note: Never ever drink booze again. Least of all with Anna. I'm lying curled up in fetal position underneath the covers. Every inch and fiber of my body feels sore. The world's worst headache ever is pounding in my head. I carefully open my eyes and immediately squeeze them shut again. Ow. Even the frail sunlight breaking through the scattering clouds is murderous. There's a foul taste in my mouth. All in all I pretty much feel like I've been chewed, swallowed, choked on and spat out. No wonder. God knows I drank enough alcohol last night to send even Godzilla into a happy little coma. But wait, I dimly remember hanging over the toilet and puking my guts out at some point, which must have gotten most of that shit out of my system. Anna was here, I remember now. She made sure I got rid of my wet clothes and got into bed right away. She stayed for a while. I don't remember when she left. Awkward.

For a long time I can't bring myself to move, and when I finally sit up it takes all my willpower to do so. Maybe a brutally icy shower will help me feel like something resembling a human being again, and with much effort I decide to give it a shot.

* * *

I'm clad in nothing but a large, soft towel when I return to my room some fifteen minutes later. Cold water is dripping from my hair, running down my back in small trickles. My mind is still in a bit of a daze, and everything I do takes me about twice as long as usual. To sleep, perchance to dream... I have only just sunk down on my bed again, trying to decide whether to get dressed or maybe curl up underneath the covers again, when someone raps against my door. Anna?

"What?" I answer grumpily, and sigh deeply when the door opens and Rizzo steps inside. Sure. Who else would it be but the one person on this planet I really, really don't want to see?

A strange, small smile warms his features when he sees me sitting there like the picture of misery. I notice a dark spot of scab in the corner of his mouth where I hit him. I hope it still hurts. Isn't he going to say anything?

He leans against the door, closing it softly with the weight of his body. Continues to look at me in that strange, irritating way. He doesn't look like he is mad at me, which is odd.

"You always this cute in the morning?" he finally grins.

Okay, three giant question-marks and a very unbelieving "huh?" here. "Why don't you piss off and get hit by a truck or something," I reply weakly and raise my middle finger in an unmistakable gesture.

Rizzo chuckles. "Good. You're still your old warmhearted, endearing self. I was worried for a moment."

I just roll my eyes in response. Slowly he comes over to me and sits down on the bed beside me. Bit close for my taste. Our arms touch, and I would like to smack him if I could just find the energy.

For a long moment we sit in silence and he looks at my hands resting in my lap.

"There was nothing between Casey and me," he finally breaks the awkward silence. "We just made out a little."

Okay, stop, rewind. I think I'm finally awake. He is kidding, right?

"You mean you didn't...?" I ask tonelessly, still trying to process the information.

He makes a face, but laughs softly, and somehow it sounds relieved. Like he is the one who needs to be relieved about it.

Wow. I don't know what to say. Or what to think even. This is good news, right? "Geez." I look at Rizzo, frowning. Not sure if I should be happy... suspicious... amazed? "Why are you telling me this?"

The fathomless orbs are shockingly warm and serious when he looks at me. "Because I'm an idiot," he says quietly.

In that moment, I suddenly understand. It hits me with the subtlety of a freight train. I guess Rizzo couldn't do it. He couldn't go through with it. And I'm the reason for that, am I not?

Jesus. I don't even know what to think of it, but my heart starts to gallop in my chest. Screwed up. This is really, incredibly, totally screwed up. I open my mouth to speak twice, but can't find anything to say.

"I do believe you are," I finally say, a smile in my voice that I have no idea where it came from.

"Look, James..." He looks away. "What I did, I didn't mean to..."

"Wait - Are you about to apologize?"

He gives me a look.

"'Cause if you are, let me get a camcorder for this historical occasion."

He crosses his arms in front of his chest, but there's a smile tugging at his lips. There's that sparkle in his eyes again, that's so very hard to resist. "James..." he just says then, and there is so much emotion in that one little word, in the way he says my name, that there is really no need to continue.

He tried to tell me before, didn't he? And I wouldn't listen. All the time when I was sure that he was playing some really messed up game with me, he was being honest. I've never seen him so self-conscious before, so vulnerable. And I realize that this here is the real Danny Rizzo, this is the side of him he hides from the world. And I wonder how on earth I of all people get to be the one to see.

"Oh damn..."

Our eyes lock, and for a perfect moment, there is complete understanding. I really don't know why I dismissed it before, this special warm light in his eyes when he looks at me that's never there when he looks at anyone else. The realization comes naturally, unspectacularly, that I probably never hated him. My god. I just thought I did, because it was the obvious thing to do.

"You know what I really want, James? For you to get together with Mills and realize that he can't give you what you need." There is an honest passion in his words.

"And what do I need, in your valued opinion?" Out of habit, my words are dripping with sarcasm.

Instead of answering the question, Rizzo takes my left arm by the wrist and lifts it from my lap. Forcing me to look at the bizarre pattern of thin white lines on my forearm, old scars that cover my skin. Defiantly I stare into his eyes as he speaks again, almost angrily.

"What do you tell him when he asks about these? Was it all an 'accident'?"

I violently pull my arm out of his grip, my cheeks flushed from burning shame and humiliation. But Rizzo is only just getting started.

"Did he ever ask? Did he? Do you think he even wants to know if you did this to yourself, or if someone else did?" He shakes his head. "Damn, James. He doesn't even know who you are."

"But you do, right?" I ask bitterly, and unconsciously my hands turn to fists.

"I know enough to freak you out, don't I?" His eyes are filled with challenge as he stares at me. "Does it make you angry? Do you want to hit me again? Yeah? Come on! I'm right here."

I am that close to doing it, to smashing my fist into his face. But when I lift my hand, to my own surprise, I grab him and pull him close instead. Our lips meet fiercely and Rizzo gives a small moan of pain and pleasure when a trace of salty blood comes from his small wound and mingles on our tongues.

I close my eyes, my heart is beating madly. He kisses me deeply, holds me firmly, not about to let me go. And suddenly I want nothing more than for him to understand. And I know that I've reached a turning point. I did my best and uttermost to hide them, my dark secrets, all my life. But in this moment, I want him to know *everything*.

Rizzo seems to sense this somehow. Instead of gaining intensity, the kiss takes an unexpected turn, slows down, becomes playful, and finally... soft. Tender. And it breaks my heart.

It's Rizzo who finally breaks the kiss, and his fingers linger on my cheek for a moment as his amazingly warm eyes search mine for a clue, anything to hold on to or work with. Then he gently leans his forehead against mine.

"He'd never understand, not the way I do," he says softly, thoughtfully, and I nod.

"I know." But I still love Casey, Rizzo. I can't change that. I want him, and need you, you were right. You were right all along.

Rizzo almost smiles, as if he read my mind again. "God, I can't believe you're doing this to me."

We both laugh softly, and I shrug helplessly. I can't tear my eyes away from his beautiful face.

There's a knock on the door and we both turn our heads. Wow. This is unexpected. It's Casey. I know it from the way he knocks, two times short, two long. Just one of the many secret codes we have.

"Come in," I answer, and beside me Rizzo shifts uncomfortably, as if he wants to move away from my side, but can't.

When Casey steps into the room, his presence is like a breath of fresh air flooding in. He is wearing dark, tight denim and a simple black T-shirt, and his short hair is tousled, the way I like it. His eyes immediately focus on Rizzo, clear and alert.

"What are you doing here?" Casey asks with a cool authority that surprises me.

Rizzo shrugs nonchalantly and flashes a cheeky grin. "It's a free country."

"I asked you to leave us alone." There is a dangerous edge to his calm voice, and he takes a step closer to the bed.

Whoa, Casey! I stare at him, totally perplexed by the sudden confidence he seems to radiate. They stare at each other. If looks could kill, I swear they would both drop dead any moment.

Finally, Rizzo raises his hands in a nonchalant gesture. "Whatever." Glancing at me, he gets up, gives me a little mischievous smile and a wink. "See you later, Jimmy."

I can only nod, and watch as he saunters to the door, not without deliberately bumping against Casey with his shoulder as he passes him on the way out. Casey cringes slightly, but doesn't move an inch. The door closes, and we are alone.

15 ICARUS

JAMES: Casey just stands there for a long moment in the middle of my room, looking at me. My head lowered, I gaze up at him nervously, not knowing what to expect or think. If I had one wish right now, I guess I'd simply turn back time and make sure to never hurt him. I never wanted that. But somewhere along this crazy ride, I must have lost sight of what I wanted and what I didn't.

I know I should finally apologize, or try to explain, but I can't find anything to say. I just feel so tired. And homesick. So very, very homesick for that warm place of perfect love and happiness I've never known. Where I can be me and feel good about it. Where I can be me and be loved for it. I know that it's Rizzo's kiss that brought this about, and that confuses me more than anything. Somebody should say something.

"Can we talk?" Casey finally asks.

"I was worried you wouldn't even talk to me anymore."

"Don't be silly, James. You're the only one worth talking to."

That was unexpected. If I'm the only one worth talking to, surely things can't be as bad as I thought, right? Shit, I can almost feel my eyes starting to shine hopefully. I don't want to be hopeful. When the hell has being hopeful ever done me any good?

There is actually a trace of a smile on his lips. He comes over to me, his eyes fixed on my face. Casey looks at me in a strange, thoughtful way, and his gaze seems to go deeper, beneath my skin. Almost as if he sees me for the very first time, *really* sees me. I get goosebumps.

"Damn. There was so much I wanted to say to you, a million things," he half-smiles and sighs softly, sweetly amused. "But now I can't remember a thing."

A brief smile flashes across my lips. I'm mesmerized by that look in Casey's eyes, by that warm, caring glow. Casey watches me intently, as if trying to interpret every little move I make, every trace of a smile, every tiny frown.

"But anyway." Casey pauses, and comes a little closer still. He chews on his lower lip for a moment before he continues to speak, very softly. "Look, James, I guess it doesn't matter what each of us did, or how we hurt each other. All that matters to me is that I don't want to lose you."

I swallow audibly, and a shiver runs down my spine.

"I'm so sorry," he says, and his eyes are carefully hopeful as he waits for my reaction.

"Sorry," I repeat tonelessly. "*You* are sorry?"

He nods. "I am."

"You do realize that it was me who messed up, right?"

"Well, you probably did, a little. But I don't blame you. And I certainly screwed up too. I know what he's like now, Rizzo. But who cares about him anyway, right?" he smiles.

"Don't you?"

"I don't give a rat's ass, to be frank."

And I can't help but laugh.

Casey takes another step closer, and this is definitely too close for friends to be standing. My heart is beating like crazy. He chuckles softly. "Oh, James. Don't tell me you still don't understand."

I just stand there like an idiot, arms hanging at my sides, staring at him. Then I blink slowly. "But…"

"Don't talk now."

So we just stand there and look at each other, and his eyes are shining like the stars. I'm so overwhelmed I have a lump in my throat.

"I know it took me forever to realize, and I hope it's not too late," he whispers. "But I'm in love with you, James. Is that okay?"

"Okay?" I just gape at him, and start to laugh. "Are you out of your mind?"

I pull him so close I am sure it has got to hurt. He clings to me, his fingers warm on my naked back. He caresses my hair as I lean my head against his face, searching for the words to say that I feel the same for him, but somehow I am unable to speak. Casey's scent fills my nostrils and I inhale deeply. His body is warm and solid against mine... At last. Gently his fingers run along my cheek, and I have goosebumps all over. Casey leans back a little to look into my eyes. He makes a tiny, shy motion towards my mouth with his head, and I can hear him breathing softly. I feel like I'm about to die any moment now as I bend my head slightly to meet him. Our breath mingles, tenderly plays on our faces as we both lean in. And then our lips touch and we pull each other close into a long, deep kiss.

* * *

Casey's skin is velvet, smooth like silk against mine when I hold him afterwards, his even, rhythmical breaths warm on the curve of my neck. I didn't think it would be him taking the initiative, but when he loosened the towel on my hips and dropped it to the ground, there was no stopping anymore. And everything was unbelievably intense. He's lying half on my side, his left leg entangled with mine, his hand resting on my stomach. It feels like with this small gesture, he is claiming me as his. It makes me feel proud, and in a way... whole.

While all my thoughts seemed to be suppressed before by strong emotions, they are now singing a chaotic, unordered symphony in my head. But I don't really mind. I am content, and satisfied, and absurdly happy. Guessing from the little smile on Casey's face, so is he.

Softly I kiss his forehead and Casey lifts his chin off my chest and smiles at me with warm, thoughtful eyes. He kisses my lips with so much emotion. God, he tastes so good, I could just eat him up. Pensively he runs his fingers along my chest, then down my right arm. His gentle fingertips linger on a small, round scar the shape of a cigarette tip. Casey lifts his gaze and our eyes meet. He doesn't ask about it. He never asks. He just looks at me in that certain way, waiting for me to tell. And maybe someday I will. Maybe someday I'll be ready. But not today, not now. Right now I don't want to think about any of that shit. I'm still scared that once Casey gets to see all of me, the real me, he won't be able to cope.

I kiss a trail along Casey's collarbone, and his fingers playfully dig into my hair. I love him. I know I do. But how can it be that I still feel so inadequate? Like I am just not good enough to be with such a wonderful, caring person? I could chain him to the bed and tattoo my name across his skin, and I'd still not be able to believe that he is mine.

As I begin to caress his chest with playful licks and kisses, his intense eyes cloud with lust. As I work my way downwards, he still won't let himself be so overwhelmed by desire to break eye-contact. And I get so jealous of the man I'll never be. Because when Casey looks at me like that, like I'm his every fantasy come true, I know I don't deserve to be held up so high. I don't get how I can be so incredibly happy, and at the same time... almost sad. Maybe all that crap going through my mind is simply me being so surprised when it all happened so fast and I didn't expect it in the least. Maybe it is too much all at once, maybe I'm not ready. Maybe you just feel that way when a dream comes true, even more so when you don't believe in dreams to begin with. Or maybe Rizzo is right after all. It takes faith, I know that now. More than anything it takes faith to love and be loved. And I never had any faith in faith before. But I'll be damned if I don't even try.

16 SUPPOSED TO BE

CASEY: This is how it's supposed to be, I feel this way every time I wake up beside James. I practically live at his dorm now. Which isn't as easy as I thought, since I'm a bit of a slob and he is fanatical about keeping order. I once moved all his pencils an inch to the right while he was out of the room. I kid you not, it was the first thing he noticed when he came back in.

"I know, I know, I'm Adrian Monk," he said with a grin, apologetically.

"You're not. Although I always thought Monk was kinda cool."

"Yeah, but I'm not cool. It's just the way I was brought up."

He seemed really uncomfortable talking about it, so I let it go. But he doesn't realize that I love him for those things. I always have. It just feels different now. Maybe because he is mine, with all the weird little habits of his. And I love those weird little habits.

I sat up one morning, got out my pencil and paper, and drew him while he was fast asleep. I don't know why, but he looked so lonely. I was able to capture that look. It turned out really well, but I never showed that drawing to him. He wouldn't have liked to be seen like that.

* * *

"I guess I win," I say quietly, without triumph, just matter of fact, as Rizzo casually sits down beside me on the front steps to the art department.

He doesn't look at me, but smiles with that unmistakable edge that even a movie star couldn't easily copy. "We'll see."

"I wish you would just leave it be. But you never will, will you?"

He only grins in response. I look at him, gorgeous as ever in the warm sunlight. Statuesque perfection. Like he was created by ancient Greek gods for the sole purpose of being admired. I would still love to paint him some day, how weird is that? And I still get a little nervous when he's this close to me. How could you not be? He just has that effect on people. I should hate him for it, but somehow I don't. I'm not sure I've forgiven him for what he did to me, but then again I'm really not sure there's that much to forgive.

"You really like James, don't you?" I say quietly. "That's not like you."

He laughs softly. "Don't presume you know me, Mills, just because we made out once."

"No, I wouldn't know you because of that. You'd make out with anyone if it suited your plans."

He looks at me with a sly smile, not offended. But his expression changes when I continue. "I know you because you didn't hit me that time when I tried to hit you."

"And what does that tell you about me?"

"A lot." It makes perfect sense, now that I've had time to think about it. "For one thing, you knew James would never forgive you if you had."

"Go on, I do enjoy a good amateur psychoanalysis."

"And it shows just how controlled you are. You never let go, do you? You can't. You always seem so laid-back, but you've got to be in control, at all times." I look at him pensively. "No wonder you study acting. And you are one hell of an actor already."

He smiles, and the smile seems genuine. He studies me thoughtfully with those amazing dark eyes. Why does he never do what you expect him to? Shouldn't he be mad at me for saying that or something? Maybe he is right and I know nothing about him at all.

I feel self-conscious all of a sudden, and try to hide it behind a half-joking remark. "You could at least admit defeat, you know."

Rizzo laughs, and practically radiates that aloof, mysterious confidence of his that makes me feel like a mere school boy. "Oh, but I'm not defeated, Mills. This little game of ours, it's only just begun."

"I hate you," I sigh.

He grins. "Don't you wish you would?" He climbs to his feet, and as he stands there in the bright sunlight, he throws a deep shadow over me.

"See you around, Mills." Without looking at me, he saunters away, and I stare after him, a strange chill lingering in the air. I shudder.

17 INVINCIBLE

JAMES: Well, this is it. The semester is officially over. I don't know why the end of term always makes me feel down. Maybe because you can never be sure that when you return in a couple of months time things will be the same. Campus never changes, but people still do. I have a feeling that this time, it might be me doing the changing. Tomorrow morning, Casey, Rizzo and I will go our separate ways. Not for too long in Casey's and my case. He invited me to come and stay. His family has this awesome lodge by a small idyllic lake, not far from where he lives. And this year, he promised we would have it to ourselves. Two weeks of quality time with my Casey to look forward to definitely makes going back home easier to bear. My Casey. It still feels weird to think about him that way. I can't get over the fact how incredibly amazing he is.

I remember talking about this with him a while ago, about people never being able to hold on to happiness. And I recall him saying something that I thought sounded not like Casey at all at the time.

"Maybe happiness is not really a long-term thing. It's only moments. And maybe love isn't about eternal bliss either. It's all about finding someone who makes it easy for you to experience and share those rare moments of happiness. And that's all there is to it."

I remember his words so accurately because it surprised me that a hopeless romantic like him should believe something like that. But I think he was right.

Rizzo is not amused, that much I can tell. It's hard to think of him as *Rizzo* now, because the name just doesn't seem intimate enough. I tried to call him Danny once, but he just laughed and shook his handsome head, his brown eyes turning into sparkling gold in the sunlight. "I like the way you say 'Rizzo'. It's sexy."

So Rizzo it is. Maybe he needs that kind of distance. Maybe we both do. I think he has been avoiding me all week, and who can blame him. I'm always with Casey, and hell, couples that just got together are always annoying. But sometimes I catch him looking at Casey with the cool interest of a surgeon contemplating which organs would be most painful to remove. And Casey, on the other side, can be surprisingly possessive. I just want for them to get along. Because I'm a selfish bastard, and I want them both in my life. There, I said it. But damn it, it's the truth. I don't know how or when Rizzo became important to me, I just know that he is. It's like he's that one piece of the puzzle that doesn't quite fit, but you know you need to place it for everything to come together and take shape.

Okay, Foley, let's make a deal. You will stop thinking about crap like this right now. You will simply lean back and try to enjoy tonight. And pray that Casey and Rizzo won't kill each other. Ack. Suddenly celebrating the end of term together doesn't seem like such a good idea anymore.

* * *

We took Rizzo's car and drove down to that all-year fair by the sea where all the bars and cafes on the boardwalk have clearly seen better days. There's a trace of decay in the warm, humid night air, a dusty melancholy that I like. Always at the peak of summer, you can smell fall blowing in on a lazy breeze, waiting to paint the leaves rust and gold. I like fall better anyway, because it's a time of change. Change is something I can believe in. It's much harder to believe that things are going to last. Rizzo got a bottle of cheap red wine from somewhere. It's really bad and horribly sweet, and we drink from it in turns as we lean on the balustrade and lazily watch a wild party that's in full swing on the beach. There is a young couple in love walking close to the water, and every time the waves crash to the shore the chick runs away with a shrill giggle you can hear from over here. I smile when she does it again.

Casey moves a little closer to me and puts his hand on my back. His gentle touch heats the spot where his fingers are lying immediately, but despite it still being unbelievably hot so late this evening and my T-shirt sticking to my skin already, I can't say that I mind. Rizzo is on my other side, holding the bottle of wine in one hand, a smoke in the other, looking unusually pensive as he gazes at the mysterious dark waters in the distance. The evening has been lovely so far, and both Rizzo and Casey seem to be willing to bury the hatchet. Well, more or less. I feel exceptionally good tonight, almost peaceful. Maybe it's the wine. Maybe it's the two gorgeous men framing me.

Okay, it's the one million dollar question, James. If you could have sex with either of them right now, who would it be? Geez. What is it with sex and heat? I can't think of a more powerful aphrodisiac. Violently dragging myself out of thirteen-year-old-walking-hormone-me, I catch a bit of friendly banter between Casey and Rizzo, and wonder why both of them are suddenly grinning as I glance at each of them, one eyebrow arched because I have no idea what they are talking about.

"He's definitely Oscar."

"He's not."

"Who is? Which Oscar?" I ask, and have a feeling they are talking about me.

"You are," Rizzo answers promptly with a mischievous grin without further explanation.

"So who are you, then? Miss Piggy?" Casey grins and snatches the bottle of wine from his hand to take a swig.

"That's Muppets, dumbass."

"Wait a minute, I'm Oscar from Sesame Street?"

"Rizzo thinks you are, I don't."

"In Henson-verse, I'd rather be Pepe," I frown slightly, and they both laugh.

"You are Statler and Waldorf, combined in one person," Rizzo chuckles, his eyes warm and in sharp contrast to the cheeky words as he looks at me.

I smirk dryly. "Sadly, that's probably true."

He winks at me and with a quick motion reaches over and steals the wine back.

Casey looks at him with a small, cool grin. "I got it. You're Rizzo, the Rat."

"Ooh, clever. Did you come up with that all by yourself, Fozzie?"

I can't help laughing out loud. "Fozzie? He's not!"

"Well, who's he then? Beaker?"

"God, you're satanic."

Giving Rizzo a look, Casey simply leans in to kiss me, and I return the kiss with a smile. Well, this round goes to Casey. Sorry, Riz.

Music is carried over from the crammed bar behind us. They are endlessly playing Southside Johnny's greatest hits on repeat, but I don't mind. It's exuberant and at the same time bittersweet. Somehow it fits the moment perfectly. They just don't write songs like that anymore. Lost in my thoughts I listen, and take Casey's hand in mine, squeezing it gently. I can sense Rizzo looking at me, and our eyes meet.

Rizzo smiles, and looks away. "Okay, my turn with a question."

"I have a feeling this isn't gonna be about Muppets."

"You can bet your tight little ass on that."

We laugh, even Casey does.

"First time you had sex. Let's hear it."

Casey and I look at each other. "How about you start?"

"Sure. She was gorgeous, a friend of my mother's. I was fourteen."

I snort. "Yeah, right."

"Could you be any more of a cliché?" Casey grins.

Rizzo shrugs nonchalantly. "What can I do. Chicks love me. Your turn, Jimmy Boy."

I groan. "Fine. Justin McEvan. Captain of the baseball team."

"School team?" Casey asks.

"No. The team I was on."

Rizzo almost chokes on his wine. "Wait a minute - you were on a baseball team?"

I glare at him. "I was *made* to, alright?"

"I can't believe you were a jock!"

"I can't either," Casey admits.

"Moving on," I say, giving them both a look. "So, this guy Justin. He pretty much cornered me in the changing room after a match. I thought he was gonna beat me up."

Rizzo laughs, and claps his hands.

"Yeah, I'm glad you find my life so amusing."

"James, you really don't have to…" Casey starts, but I shrug. I don't really mind.

"Anyway, that was it. My first time. I was fifteen, and fool enough to believe it would change things. Like the team wasn't gonna give me hell anymore after that. Like Justin would start to treat me like a person. Well, he didn't. Next time he wanted some, I punched him in the face and told him that if he and his dick ever came near me again, I'd cut it off."

Rizzo is almost pissing himself laughing. Casey is smiling, too, but at least he's trying to hide it.

"I'm sorry. That must have really hurt you, to be treated like that."

"Not that much, no. He was a jerk."

Rizzo is still grinning. "Mills, your time to amuse us."

Casey actually blushes. "Oh well. My girlfriend in high school, she didn't believe in sex before marriage. So my first was actually…" He looks at me. "James."

I smile and lean over to give him a little kiss.

"I think I'm gonna heave," Rizzo grins.

"And I," Casey announces, "am gonna go and take a leak." He kisses me again and walks away, looking for a bar or place that doesn't look too shabby.

I watch him leave, then I turn to Rizzo. "Okay, you. The truth. What was your first time *really* like?"

He laughs softly, and his eyes are sparkling mischievously. "*Swear* that you won't tell."

"Cross my heart, et cetera."

"Fine. I'll tell you. It was at some garden party our parents had dragged us along to. I don't think I even knew her name. She was cute, a few years older than me. We were bored. So we did it in the bathroom."

"What was it like?"

He grimaces. "Oh you know, first time. Kinda awkward."

I laugh, but I know that my eyes are shining warmly when I look at him. Damn that boy and his devilish charm.

"So you never scored with your mom's friend."
"Oh, that did happen. Just wasn't my first time."
"And was that kinda awkward, too?"
"Far from it." He grins.
"You're impossible."
"And you like that about me."
"Well... maybe a little bit."
"A lot. Admit it."

We laugh, and I'm glad to get around an answer because Casey returns. He joins us and makes a little motion with his head towards the beach. "Let's get away from the crowd."

* * *

We don't have to walk far to reach a spot where the beach is completely deserted. After all the noise on the boardwalk, the night seems strangely quiet, the only sound being the rhythmical surf licking at the wet sand beside us as we stroll along.

Rizzo backs away from the dark water and beckons us to follow him up to the dunes. It's exhausting to walk on the soft sand, especially with it being so damn hot tonight. When we reach the top, Rizzo leads us through the rough, high grass and we flop down in a hollow between the dunes, panting softly from climbing up here. The heat makes me feel slightly dizzy, thoughts are slow, molasses-thick.

"Too hot," Casey moans and rolls onto his side to rest his head on my shoulder.

Rizzo holds out the bottle of wine to him, but he tiredly shakes his head. I grab it, and take a long swig. Not that it helps much, but at least it's something fluid. Rizzo props his back against a wall of cool sand and watches Casey and me lying there together, his eyes fathomless in the darkness. The tip of his cigarette glows brightly when he takes a drag, like a firefly under a sky sparkling with a billion stars.

"So what are you up to this summer?" I ask after a while when the silence gets uncomfortable.

Rizzo shrugs and flicks ash from the tip of his cigarette to the ground with a lazy, well-practiced motion. "Nothing you kids wanna know about," he grins.

I just arch an eyebrow. D'oh. I thought we were past the snide remarks, but apparently not. His eyes are smoldering darkly as they quickly drop to Casey at my side, then they get warmer as they come to rest on me again. "I think my folks are going to Europe, France or somewhere, so I'll have trouble-free digs."

"France... wow. Why aren't you going with them?"

"Hell," he chuckles. "James, are you mad? I'm glad I don't have to hang with those idiots and play family."

"Fair enough," I grin and hand him the wine. Our fingers touch when he takes the bottle, and he stares into my eyes for a second before he downs the rest of the rich, bittersweet fluid. Gah.

Casey stirs beside me and slowly sits up, wiping a few drops of sweat off his forehead. He slides his hand under his white cotton T-shirt absent-mindedly. "God, I'd sell my soul for a cold shower right now. I think any kind of clothes would be too warm tonight."

Rizzo and I look at each other, chuckling softly, and I have a feeling we're both thinking the same thing. There's a sparkle in Rizzo's dark eyes when he proposes matter-of-factly: "So take off your clothes, Mills."

Casey laughs, then pauses and stares at him, taken aback. I swallow, and Rizzo licks his lower lip. We all know that was not a joke. It was a dare. I mentally fan myself. All of a sudden it seems twice as hot as before. The air is thick, heavy with expectation, tension and... sex. I could feel this thunderstorm brewing on the horizon all evening, ever since we got into Rizzo's car, but it was still possible to ignore before he brought it up. I guess there is always sex in the air as soon as two of us get together, let alone all three of us. And now Rizzo has got that hungry, predatory look in his eyes. Oh Jesus. A threesome? Is he serious?

I can feel Casey's gaze on me and turn my head towards him. The question is in his eyes: Is that what you want?

"You don't have to," I whisper into his ear after quickly sitting up beside him. I know that this dangerous rivalry between him and Rizzo could make him do a hell of a lot of things he normally wouldn't. I don't think threesomes are really his thing.

But still... Shit, the mere thought of watching him with Rizzo... or even having them both... Skin, and sweat, and muscles flexing with every motion, and soft moans... The aching stirs, deep and red and fiery between my legs. Suddenly I'm very aware of Rizzo intently watching every move we make, and I have a flashback of the night he made us kiss in front of everyone. Oh heaven help me.

Casey's eyes soften. Does he understand? Does he know? He takes my face in his hand and pulls me close for a soft kiss. He still continues to look at me after we part. And then he smiles and simply takes off his shirt.

With a sly grin Rizzo effortlessly strips off his own shirt and crawls over to join us. God, his is a body to die for. Watching impatiently as Casey raises my arms and pulls my T-shirt over my head, Rizzo's fathomless eyes are black with lust. Looking at me, he gives Casey a good, unexpected push, and he falls over backwards, landing on his back on the cool sand. Rizzo's hand reaches out to Casey's jeans, still without turning his eyes from my face. The sharp sound of the zipper being opened rips through the electrified silence as Rizzo grabs me and passionately buries his tongue in my mouth. For a moment my mind goes totally blank, and I just *feel*. Feel him exploring me, the kiss deep and hungry, tasting like wine and cigarettes, but for once I don't mind.

Rizzo breaks the kiss with a smug grin, then he turns his attention back to Casey, who used our momentary distraction to get completely naked. Something in the way Rizzo's eyes wander over Casey's skin sends a hot shiver down my spine. Casey has been watching us with more than interest, I notice with pleasant surprise as my eyes drop to his crotch. He starts to sit up to join us, but with a quick motion Rizzo grabs him by the shoulders and pins him to the sandy ground.

"Oh no, you don't," he orders him to stay down and climbs on top of him. Now straddling Casey, he pins his arms to the ground at his sides with a grin. A small gasp escapes from Casey's lips.

"Well, who would have thought," Rizzo chuckles softly and glances at Casey's arousal. "Little Casey's a naughty boy after all."

Something dark flashes in his eyes as he bends down, his lips temptingly hovering above Casey's, never touching. "Do you like it? Would you like to see me and your boyfriend get it on?"

"Screw you," Casey squeezes out and there's a flash of a smile on his lips before he grabs the back of Rizzo's head, pulling him down for a kiss. Rizzo more allows it than welcomes it, looking at me all the while. Something in his eyes gives me goosebumps, and I'm hot all over. I can tell he'd much rather be kissing *me* right now. I don't know why that does such wild things to me.

Casey frees a hand, signaling for me to join them. He puts his right arm around me when I lay down by his side and his fingers play with my hair while he is kissing Rizzo. This is one of the moments you wish you could freeze time and pause to simply enjoy the sensation. I lean back a little to get a better view, and my heart is beating madly. God, what a picture. Their skin glistens in the silver moonlight with every move they make. Casey's scent fills my nostrils, and Rizzo's eyes are still fixed on me, dark with desire.

As soon as Rizzo begins to move downwards, kissing, licking a trail along his neck, Casey draws me close and lustfully slides his tongue into my mouth. His eyes are glazed over.

No words are spoken, but the night air is filled with the sounds of our breathing and soft moans, a song of passion. Instinctively Casey's fingers dig into my back as Rizzo's playful tongue and soft kisses reach his bellybutton and he stops for a moment before he continues to tease the soft, white skin, moving further down towards Casey's crotch. Casey's hips rock slightly in response, and he's practically begging for more. I can almost feel the yearning, his body radiating with a fire burning underneath as my fingers caress his chest. I look down to Rizzo in the exact moment he takes Casey into his mouth.

"Oh god shit," my boy moans, and instinctively his body curves up to meet the touch. His breathing accelerates rapidly as Rizzo begins to work his magic. Jesus, this is hot.

I'm now so painfully hard and so ready that I almost can't bear holding on without touching myself to ease the ache. Glorious... The word runs through my mind and I hold on to it as I watch Casey writhe with pleasure for minutes until he comes.

Glorious, and otherworldly, and the most beautiful thing I have ever seen in my life. Rizzo wipes his mouth with the back of his hand, and there's something predatory in the way he looks up at me that makes me shiver.

"Your turn," he commands with that soft, sensual voice, and climbs down from Casey, fishing for something in the back pocket of his jeans. Christ. Does he always carry lube, or did he speculate on something happening tonight? He's got condoms, too. Rizzo needs only one moment to get rid of his denim. Then he moves over to me, both of us on our knees. I glance at Casey, who gives me a small, exhausted but content smile. I'll take that as a yes then, alright? Because honestly, even if I wanted to stop now, with Rizzo looking at me like that before he grabs me and pulls me close, I don't really think I'd be able to.

Our lips meet with so much passion it's almost painful. His hands are everywhere, almost violent, needy, possessive, and something raw, animal springs to life inside of me. There's unmistakable devotion in his kiss... and something else, almost submissive, or burning for submission. A wildcat, begging to be tamed. I'm panting from an overload of desire. With a quick, fluid motion, I force Rizzo down on all fours. He allows it with a low, sensual moan. Never taking my hands off his back, I position myself behind him. God, the most gorgeous ass the world has ever seen, and no doubt about it. I bend down and teasingly lick at the silken, salty skin of his back, and he curses under his breath as a soft tremble runs over his body. Rizzo dying with desire for me to take him, that's definitely not something you get to see every day, and it turns me on more than I can say. I admiringly run my hand along his back and over his ass, and he makes a small, almost painful noise that gives away the full depth of his craving for my touch. I've never been with anyone this beautiful, and there's something amazing, almost surreal about it.

As I carefully prepare him, he makes another low noise in his throat.

"God, James, come on," he curses almost desperately.

Not that I really needed another invitation. Rizzo, as far as he's concerned, seems to almost glow with ecstasy even before I begin to move in him. Oh god, this is unbelievably good...

* * *

With a loud bang Rizzo closes the trunk of his car and flashes a sexy little smile at Casey and me. We are all dead tired the next morning, and for good reason. A grin steals onto my lips just thinking of it. Casey and I came down from my room to see Rizzo off, and now we are standing beside his shining red ride, arm in arm, and Casey has his hand in the back pocket of my jeans. His dad is going to pick him up in two hours, and I'm taking a bus home this afternoon. I get a cold, nervous ball in my stomach thinking about leaving here and what awaits me, but I push these thoughts to the back of my head.

"You know," Casey says spontaneously as Rizzo squeezes past us and opens the driver's door, "James and I are gonna go to my family's holiday lodge for some time in a week. Why don't you give us a call and come by some time?"

Rizzo arches an eyebrow and looks from him to me, a sly grin appearing on his lips. "Maybe I will." His eyes linger on my face for a moment. He looks like he is going to say something else, but then he just smiles and gets into the car. I think I understand anyway.

Rizzo starts the engine and Casey and I wave as he speeds away, raising a cloud of dust that encircles us completely. Slowly the feeling sinks in that he is really gone. It feels like he has left a wide gap. Casey and I exchange a look and he smiles a little.

"That was... interesting." Casey sounds both pensive and amused as we turn around and go back inside the building.

I'm not sure if he's taking about Rizzo's exit, last night, or maybe this whole semester, but he is definitely right. I laugh softly and pull him close for a long, tender kiss. When we part there's a trace of sadness in his eyes that surprises me.

"Do you think he'll really come by?" he asks quietly.

"Hey, this is Rizzo we're talking about. 'Course he will," I grin, trying to chase away the melancholy that seems to hang heavy in the air now.

Casey nods and smiles a little, his hands warm on my chest as they slide down to rest on my hips. He doesn't look at me when he speaks again, softly. "I knew you wanted him."

Startled, I just stare at him for a moment, then I vehemently shake my head, very serious now. "Casey, all I want is you, don't you know that?"

The blue eyes light up when he looks at me, and he smiles in a way that touches my heart. "Maybe, yeah. But it's okay, James. Because you're with *me*."

I swallow, and force myself to smile. "I sure am." God, I feel like such a creep. I knew it. Last night was a mistake. Somehow, instinctively, Casey now seems to sense that there's a part of me that needs Rizzo almost as much as I need him. I don't know why it is that way. It shouldn't be, because Casey is the one I love. But Rizzo... Man, it'll take more than a good lay to get him out of my system. Exorcism or rehab, either way, there's something I have to do about it.

"You kinda looked like you wanted him too," I tease him.

"Nooo," he lies with a grin.

We both laugh, and it's just a tiny bit awkward, but he looks so cute.

"Love ya," Casey says under his breath, once again knowing exactly what I need to hear right now. I close my eyes to drink in the words. I put my arms around him and just hold him tight for a moment. And it's then that I know somehow that everything is going to be okay. I don't know how or when, but I'll find a way.

Suddenly someone punches me on the shoulder, and I let go off Casey and turn around to see Anna grinning at me. "See you next semester, dickhead."

"Have a nice summer, you crazy dyke."

On her way out she nods to Casey. "See? Got what you wanted in the end!"

I watch as the door closes behind her, smiling to myself. Casey is smiling too. It makes me feel hopeful. They never show you what happens after the glorious happy end. They never show you that it takes a continuous effort to love and be loved. And I'm sure Rizzo will somehow manage to turn my whole world upside down again next time we meet. But you know, that's fine with me. This certainly isn't the end of this story, but only the beginning. So just let him come. Let them all come. I'm ready. For once, I know I really am.

Book 2
Redefinitions

SUSANN JULIEVA

1 PAVLOV'S DOG

DANNY: Alright, I admit it, I'm excited. He's here. I can't keep myself from checking out that delicious ass of his as he strolls past me, into the hall. He stops right in the middle, drops his bag and just gapes unbelievingly.

"Geez. You call this a house? It's a freakin' palace!"

Yeah, what can I say? I guess it is. I just shrug and give him my special grin that never seems to have the same effect on him it has on every other goddamned person on this planet. J, you're killing me.

I watch with a smile as he gazes around wide-eyed, moving carefully like a museum visitor in some exclusive art temple. Most people are a little intimidated when they come to my place the first time, but I think James is the only one who ever looked so lost. I can almost hear his brain working, planning a surprising escape the moment I turn my back. Oh no, Jimmy, you stay right where you are. This time, you're not getting away so easily.

Feels weird, him being here. The original plan was to follow Casey's invitation and pay them a little visit, but the days went by and I kept putting it off, and finally I realized that I probably wouldn't go at all. Not that I didn't want to see him... But then I would have had to share with Mills, and that little twit is just not good at sharing. Come to think of it, I may not be either. Not when it comes to James. That's really irritating. That wasn't supposed to happen.

Anyway, last week I decided that something had to be done to make him remember that I exist, and gave him a call. And what does James do? He tells me precious Casey is visiting some relatives down South with the family, which is why he is home and not with him. I can take a hint, especially when it's being made with a "Save me!" sign practically attached to it. He sounded so relieved to hear my voice, it actually made me want to get into my car and just snatch him away from whomever or whatever was making him so miserable. Still, even when I asked, I honestly never believed he would accept. But here he is.

James turns around to look at me, a little frown on his handsome forehead. "I had no idea your folks were that rich."

"It's my mom's dough. Come on, I'll give you a tour."

He nods, looking terribly uncomfortable as he follows me down the corridor to the big living room. Yeah, well. It's not like I really love this place either.

Suddenly he stops dead and points at the painting we just passed. "Christ, is that real? Is that a real Klee?"

"Better be," I smirk and wink at him.

James stares at me like I just revealed to him that Santa Claus actually exists, then turns his attention back to good old Paul's doodling, completely and totally amazed. I had no idea he was so into this stuff.

I step to his side and watch him as his pretty blue eyes take in the painting, a look of awe chasing the nervous frown from his handsome face.

"It's so beautiful." He pauses, takes a deep breath. When he continues to speak, he sounds thoughtful. "I like how he cuts these thin, colored lines into the dark background."

"Why do you think he does that?" I ask with a smile, more to catch his attention than out of actual interest.

He glances at me, smiles a little, still in his own world. "People usually use bright colors on dark backgrounds, but he does it the other way around, see? It's only when you cut through the dark layer on top that the beauty underneath is revealed."

God, I want to kiss him. Smash him against the wall and kiss him until he's moaning with pleasure, and... No, maybe just kiss him. Perhaps even hold him. Okay, that's weird. The hell?

J always looks like he's cold, I can't figure out why. Maybe because he hunches slightly. Like he's trying to hide from something disturbing only he can see. Don't tell me you see dead people, Jimmy. I can't hide a small grin. Shit, I know I shouldn't be joking about this. I've got my own theory about the origin of this dark cloud hanging over James, and it ain't a pretty one.

Why the hell I'm so attracted to this guy I'll probably never know. Well, apart from the obvious. James is gorgeous, and blissfully unaware of it. He's got the frosty dignity of someone who's been through it all and is still standing. And really, the most amazing, intense eyes. There's *something* about him, something I can't figure out. I don't know how he does it, but he's got this way of bringing out a side of me I normally don't let people see. And I don't mind him seeing it. Maybe I even want him to.

* * *

"So this is the inner sanctum."
"Yeah, that's my room."
James nods and stares at the bed in the center of the room for a moment, frozen on the doorstep, like there's an invisible barrier keeping him out. He's got that look on his face again, the same look he had when I picked him up at the train station. Curtains and shutters closed, no chance of guessing what's going on inside. Damn, he can drive me nuts.
"Where do I sleep?"
Well, hell. I'd hoped he wouldn't mention it, and we could just see what happens. But now I don't really have a choice but to put him up in a guestroom, do I? Clever bastard. I give him a look to let him know I didn't forget. Like I could, even if I tried. I can still hear his voice over the phone, calm, almost cold. "I'm with Casey, you know that. I'm not coming to visit for a screw."

Then why are you? I never asked him that. Shit, of course I want to have him, or for him to take me again like he did that night on the beach. Oh yeah, that night... God. I don't think that night ever ended, because I can always feel him now, underneath my skin. I try not to think about it, but I'm hooked, that's the way it is. I want more. I *need* more. Wow, and I think that's kinda pathetic.

But damn, not everything is about sex. This is less about sex than I expected it to be. I want to get to know this guy. I want to know everything about him. I want it all, all the dirty little secrets, all the big lies, and everything in-between.

Without a word I lead him to the guestrooms, and open a

random one, let him step inside.

James looks around, one eyebrow arched, and smiles that little sarcastic smile. "Nice."

Yeah, screw you too. But don't think you get to come here and pull that "aloof and unavailable" crap forever. We both know it won't work. I know you want me. I just wish you'd finally admit it.

He steps to the window and looks out. "Nice pool." Then he lifts his gaze to the darkening sky, heavy with clouds, and there's a bitter storm brewing in his sea-green eyes. "It's starting to rain again."

When he turns around to look at me leaning against the doorframe, for a moment there's something in his eyes and they seem to soften. "Look, Danny..." He stops, seemingly surprised to have called me by my first name, but heck, not half as surprised as I am. "Rizzo," he corrects himself. "I know this is weird for you. It's weird for me too."

Gently raindrops are rapping against the window glass, and I wish I could wipe away this awkward silence.

Does he do that? Does he call me Danny when he thinks of me? First time he called me that, I just said that I liked the way he said 'Rizzo'. I do. But what he doesn't know is that when he says 'Danny', I don't know what to make of it. I don't want to think about what it implies. Maybe I just don't want to make more of it than there really is. I don't know why it gets to me like that. I want that *more*, I need that more. But I'm never gonna ask for it unless I'm sure he wants it too. How could I ever be sure when he's got "I love Casey" practically stamped on his forehead?

"Maybe it wasn't such a good idea to come here after all," James continues with an insecure frown.

He doesn't have the slightest idea just how bad that idea really was, does he?

"You hungry?" I say, ignoring his comment, because otherwise I might toss words at him that are perhaps better left unsaid. When he shrugs I turn around. "Let's get you something to eat then."

* * *

He follows silently as I lead him back downstairs. He doesn't show much interest in the contents of the fridge when I open it. He just stands there, looking at me. I try to ignore it, but his gaze prickles on my skin. Finally I can't help it and turn around, forcing a mischievous smile. "What? You want me for dinner?"

A brief smile flashes across his lips that were so warm and deliciously soft against mine. "Thanks," he simply says, and I know he's not talking about dinner.

I want to cross the distance and pull him into a deep kiss, wondering why I let him do these things to me. Wondering why he even can. I don't get emotional. That's not really something you do in this house. But sometimes, like now, I wish he'd let me express myself without having to rely on words. Because what could I possibly say?

"You're welcome."

2 UNINVITED

JAMES: I used to always carry a razorblade in a small, flat case in my pocket. That was plan B, a safety net. An unusual one, yes. But at that time, it helped to know that there was a way out after all. Funny, but hard as I try, I don't remember what plan A was anymore.

The pale, greenish neon lights are humming lazily above me, water splashes nearby. A siren's lure, trying to call me back again, but I can't be tempted. The nauseating smell of chlorine is everywhere. It reminds me of high school, of gloating laughter and the sharp pain of my face connecting with the cold iron of a locker door. The pain doesn't set in until the dizziness passes, but the humiliation remains, always. Smell and emotion, directly connected in my brain. Even as the memory of their faces fades, the mixture of chlorine and the stench of that old locker room is as fresh as ever in my mind. I still get that sick feeling in my stomach, and the instinct to run and hide.

Exhale. Relax. It's only shadows. Still, sometimes I wonder, when you have too many shadows in your life, does there ever come a point where they get too deep, and it all turns to pitch black?

I open my eyes and look across the chemical azure of Rizzo's pool to the large front window. It's dark outside, but I can see the pouring rain in the light falling onto the perfect lawn of this freaking perfect palace. Who has a swimming pool in their basement and another one in the garden anyway?

Rizzo climbs out of the pool, water dripping from his shining body. His hair looks almost black when it's wet. I'll be damned, everyone looks stupid with their hair flat like that, but he still looks gorgeous as hell. Simply too beautiful to be for real. Mildly fascinated, I watch how his muscles flex and relax as he saunters over and sinks onto the sun bed beside me with a pleasant sigh.

His warm, nonchalant presence washes over me like a summer breeze, and lingers.

There's a mischievous sparkle in his eyes when he turns his head and looks at me. "You look bored."

Frowning slightly, I give him a half-smile. "I'm not, really. I was born with this expression."

He chuckles and grabs his glass. The ice cubes rattle when he lifts it to his lips. "Another drink?"

I watch how the dark fluid vanishes in his mouth, lick my lips in reflex, almost able to taste the alcohol myself. Bitter, sharp, with a trace of sweetness, clear but sticky.

"Naw, I'm good. Tipsy enough to feel all warm and fuzzy inside, but not drunk enough to be seduced by you."

I get a smirk for an answer that sets something in the pit of my stomach aflutter.

"Damn, there goes my evil scheme."

I can't hide a small grin. Our eyes meet. There's so much unexpected warmth in his deep brown orbs, somehow it just makes me ache. He's not supposed to be so nice to me. He's not supposed to understand things he doesn't even know about. Or does he? I shiver slightly.

Rizzo puts his empty glass down and gets up, nods to the exit. "Come on."

Slowly I sit up, eyes wandering over his slender, muscular body again. To. die. for. Bronze with a touch of gold, shimmering silkily, and how does he manage not to look like a drowned corpse in this light?

"Where are we going?"

"Some place warmer."

I'm not even sure I can take any more warmth tonight.

* * *

This is so cliched it feels surreal. We're lying on the enormous white couch in the living room, staring into crackling flames dancing in the fireplace. Well, I am. Rizzo's watching me instead. Whatever it is, I wish he would just say it.

I never thought that there are people actually living like this, because it looks like something from the movies, or in some really fashionable decor mag. I bet their interior designer cost twice as much as the furniture. Everything just looks so damn *expensive* that I hardly dare touch a thing. I guess it's true what Rizzo said earlier. These rooms aren't meant to be lived in, but to represent. Represent what? That you can spend incredible amounts of money on furnishing your home with beautiful but entirely useless things? And yet it all looks so empty, lonely somehow.

The aromatic smell of firewood and smoke fills my nostrils, heavy and real. The dancing flames in the fireplace are the only living thing here. And Rizzo. Rizzo with that unreadable, pensive look on his face as he watches me. A trace of a smile is always lingering in the corners of his mouth.

Suddenly Rizzo reaches over, and lean fingers cover the distance, invading my personal space. Even though I don't really mind, I can't help jumping slightly at his touch. He gently lifts my arm a little to let the firelight fall onto my skin. "You never told me where these are from."

He's talking about the scars, of course. At other times, with less alcohol coursing through my veins, I would have pulled back immediately. I would have said something harsh, bitten out fast and hard like a snake. Or maybe just told him to go to hell. Plan B. I almost smile. If things were that simple...

"What makes you think I would?"

"Because I'm asking. Because I want to know." His eyes are uncharacteristically honest and serious. Has he really been wondering about them all this time?

I don't reply. I just look at him laying there in the firelight, beautiful and perfect like a young Greek god. His skin so flawless, and in spite of what he's trying to make believe, a tiny trace of innocence still left in his eyes. And yet, tonight for the first time, I realize that Rizzo has his own wounds. And for some reason unknown to me, it touches me somehow.

I still don't pull back when he lifts his other hand and gently begins to trace the scars that cover my skin. I don't pull back when he moves closer. And I know that I probably *should* pull back when he starts to kiss the fine, white marks, but I don't.

I just sit there, watching him, feeling the soft, tender touch of his lips, and I swallow hard. Looking up, he notices the look on my face, and pulls himself up to a sitting position, close to me. There's no fake sympathy in his eyes, but something unmistakably sincere that makes me realize that he really cares. And that he won't judge me, or try to help me, or pity me, or any of that shit.

"His name was Simon," I whisper hoarsely, and exhale.

3 REBAPTISM

DANNY: I think it was me who started the kissing, but it doesn't really matter anyway. What I definitely know is that his lips parted willingly when I slid my tongue in, that his hand pulled me close like he was clinging to a lifeline.

James moaned in my ears, and my skin burned with desire. Thoughts rotated in my head, all the things he'd said turning into a blur of his secret pain and my anger.

Simon. J's stepfather, whose belt buckles, and other possessions abused as instruments of torture, left traces on him that go beneath the flesh. Simon, who turned this beautiful boy into a cynical mess of self-hate so intense that nothing and no one can get through that barrier. There are different kinds of scars on his body, and they can't all be Simon's doing. I've seen this before, I know what it looks like, and that's disturbing and creepy on a whole different level. I know that what I've heard tonight is but a fraction of James' story. He didn't even say that much, actually. But those few words were enough. Or maybe they were all that I could bear, because suddenly my lips were on his.

"Rizzo, we shouldn't..."

"Danny. Say it. Say my name."

"Danny." His eyes were holding mine, and I was hard like never before. Like in a fever, sore, bleeding deep inside. Just like him. How was this happening?

He likes it rough, that's obvious. Likes it when there's pain involved, but despises himself for it. We both know that the world isn't some happy little fairytale, and pleasure and pain go hand in hand. I'd gladly be the one he takes his rage out on anytime. But not tonight. There was enough pain already, and he just looks so *wounded*.

Fine pearls of sweat are glistening in the hollow between his neck and his collarbone, and I bend down to lick them off with the tip of my tongue. Salty and sweet, like teardrops.

"Danny," he says again, and his eyelids flutter closed when a small, aroused moan escapes his lips.

I move as gently as I can inside of him, wanting to give him nothing but pleasure. I dreamed of doing this, god, countless times. I never thought he'd let me. He doesn't open his eyes when I start to whisper words I thought I'd never say to anyone. My voice doesn't seem like my own, sounds husky, sounds too tender to belong to me.

Passion takes over, words get choppy. He opens his eyes and looks at me, his face a mask of pure ecstasy. He comes in waves, buckling slightly, and I finally let go myself, and Jesus Christ, it's too good, it's too *intense* to describe.

When I pull out of him, I tug him close immediately, and he curls up in my arms like a child. We look at each other, and I run my fingers down the side of his face. "You're so beautiful."

I didn't mean to say that aloud. I wince slightly, expecting a sarcastic reply, but it doesn't come. He just smiles a little. Like it's something he'd like to believe, if he only could. Whatever it was that just happened between us, it's clear that something's changed. And it's kind of scary. I'll be damned.

This time it's definitely him who kisses me first. I wish that I could sink into that kiss, sink into him completely. Shit, I'm such a whore for him. I don't even mind. I'll be whatever he wants me to be, if that's what it takes for him to let me in.

He breaks the kiss and licks his lips, watches me watching him. "Danny." Thoughtfully he lets my name roll over his tongue, smiles unbelievingly. "Fuck."

A broad grin steals onto my face, and I can't resist. "Gladly. Just give me a couple of minutes."

We both start to laugh, and it chases the vulnerable moment away. Thank god. His breath is soft and warm on my face, and there's a sparkle in his eyes that wasn't there before. And there's that strange craving again, stirring underneath my skin. He opens his mouth to speak, but closes it again. Smiles. Just a little, just enough for me to understand.

I nod, his smile mirrored by my own. If there's a VIP area

inside of James' heart, I guess I just got my member's card.

4 HOME IS WHERE THE HURT IS

JAMES: Sometimes I wonder if there are mistakes you simply have to make. Maybe when you look back to them some time later, you'll find they weren't mistakes at all. I don't know what suddenly makes me think of the day I pushed him against the wall in his dorm room, when the way he touched me seemed so wrong and felt so right. Now leaving seems like the only right thing to do, but it doesn't feel right at all.

"Stay," he pleads softly when I open the door, his hand reaching out to cup my face, his lips close. "Don't leave because of her."

I can't reply, I simply lean in for a kiss. Just one more moment. Just him and me.

Somehow I know that the look in his dark eyes will be haunting me. The sound of the door closing behind me is harsh, cruel even to my own ears. But I can't change it, I'm scared shitless. Scared of allowing him to get closer, and even more underneath my skin than he already is. The truth is, I don't think I want to get to know him that well. God knows what will happen if I do.

* * *

Fall is coming. I can smell it in the air when I step off of the bus and begin to walk down the old road to our house. It's the smell of decay, so distinctive that even the first colorful leaves, dancing in the mild breeze like drunken butterflies, can't cover it up. Two more weeks and it's back to school. It used to be a relief returning to Woodhaven, but I don't have that refuge anymore. No matter if I go back or stay, the same questions, the same problems will be lurking at the back of my mind. Things have gotten worse with Mom again, and there's nothing I can do for her. Sometimes I wake up in the middle of the night and want to scream at the top of my lungs, because the walls seem to be closing in, and I'm useless, helpless, worthless just like way back then.

Home again. As I slowly climb the three steps to the porch, the familiar lump of worry forms in my stomach and it's getting harder to breathe. Holding my bag in a sweaty hand, completely unaware of its weight, I just stand there for a moment, staring at the screen door. It doesn't help to know that Simon's gone, because nothing's changed. My senses still sharpen and my whole body tenses. It's ridiculous how well these learned automatisms work, even if they're no longer needed.

The key turns with a soft click, and the door springs open with a pitiful creak. Must remember to oil it before I go back to university.

"Jimmy, is that you?" Mom calls weakly from the battered couch in the living room. She hardly ever leaves it anymore. The TV is babbling dully in the background, too low to understand, its only purpose to keep her company and chase away the lonely silence. I sigh, put my bag down and enter, forcing a smile.

"Hey, Mom. I'm back."

She's a mess, which doesn't surprise me much. I bet she hasn't showered since I left. Pale and skinny, drowning in her shabby pajamas that she won't part with, despite them being two sizes too large. She puts out her cigarette and waves her hand to make the smoke go away. She knows I hate it when she smokes. Simon's favorite brand. I try not to inhale the cold, bitter stench that fills the room.

"Was it nice with Casey?"

"That was last month, Mom. I was in Boston, with another friend. I told you, remember?"

"Oh yes. Yes, of course." She smiles, but I know she doesn't have a clue what I'm talking about. She'll probably have forgotten this conversation by the time I go upstairs. I know the look in her eyes all too well, stuck somewhere between reality and her own world. I cross the room and open the window to let in some fresh air.

"Did you take your meds?"

"I've been a good girl all week. Well, I forgot on Tuesday, but I think I didn't..." She trails off, her eyes focusing on the flickering TV screen. Great. She didn't take them, otherwise she wouldn't be in this state. Without a word I go into the kitchen and bring her the pills and a glass of water.

She accepts them with a smile and strokes my arm when I bow down to her. "Thanks, sweetie. What would I do without my big boy?"

Honestly, I don't know. I don't even want to think about going back to Woodhaven and leaving her alone again. I place a little kiss on her cold cheek and try to look cheerful, when I'm really all but.

"Do you need anything else? Are you hungry?"

She smiles, and for some reason, it hurts to see. I remember what her smiles used to be like before she became so frail, a mere shadow of a human being. I feel awful for having left her alone all week.

"I'm fine, thank you."

Fine. Right. She's never been fine in her life. And things have never been right for us either. The more time passes and the worse things get with her, the harder it's getting to believe that they'll ever be.

* * *

I turn on the shower, close my eyes and try to relax as a gentle stream of warm water runs down my body. The images steal into my mind uninvited, but I close my eyes, allowing them to roam freely for a while.

I don't even remember how we got upstairs and into his bed last night, but that's where I woke up. Five in the morning, and it finally stopped raining a minute before dawn. The sun a pale ball of fire crawling up behind the hills. Long rays of light fell through cracks in the clouds like messages from some higher power above blessing the moist, satiated earth.

He was already awake, head propped up on his arm, watching me with a smile that widened when our eyes met. His kiss was slow and soft, provoking emotions I never expected.

"Good morning," he whispered, his smile audible in his voice, accompanied by a warm shimmer in his eyes. No morning had ever been so good.

* * *

I squeeze out a bit of shampoo onto the palm of my hand and spread it in my wet hair. It smells of cheap perfume. His shampoo smelled of luxury and a world where anything's possible. I can almost feel his kiss through the water running down my back, the motions of his hands sexy and slow as they explore my body...

Still waiting. I'm still waiting for regrets to come. I'm sure there has to come a moment when I will start to feel bad about what happened. When I will begin to wonder how on earth I could do this to Casey. It seems incredibly wrong to feel so good when I should be feeling guilty.

Maybe I'm too much of a bastard to care. But I know that's not true. My feelings for Casey are unchanged. And yet, everything's changed. Because Rizzo changed. Or maybe he just showed me who he's always been, deep inside. Whatever it is that he's done, suddenly he's become this completely amazing human being that makes me catch my breath just thinking of him. Heart skips a beat, something flutters inside. It feels amazing, and yet, bittersweet. Because now there's this craving, like I left a part of me with him. Does he feel the same?

Danny. Aka the Artist Formerly Known As Rizzo. He's not the same. I'm not the same. And none of this really makes sense to me. I can't even think straight. Right now, I just *feel*.

He was kissing me when she opened the door and walked in, nearly giving us both a heart attack.

"Jesus Christ!" Danny swore and sat up straight in bed. "Can't you knock?"

The woman crossed her arms in front of her chest and arched a fine eyebrow. "I don't see why I should knock in my own house."

Her voice was unusually deep, a husky, sexy drawl. Shocked

by her appearance, I could only stare at her stupidly. This was Danny's mom? Holy shit. I don't know what I'd expected, but man, she was gorgeous. Tall and beautiful, like a model. Long, blonde curls and dreamy gray eyes, perfect make-up, designer dress. Looking so young she could have been Danny's older sister. So that's where his larger-than-life presence came from.

He crossed his arms too and frowned. When he spoke there was a coldness in his voice I didn't recognize at all. "Damn it, Lilah. What the hell are you doing here anyway?"

"Where's Paula?" She simply ignored his question, and from the cool, businesslike sound of it, she might as well have been talking to an employee instead of her son.

"I gave her the week off."

"For Christ's sake, Daniel. Look at the state this place is in!"

"What's it to you? You were supposed to be in France."

There was an awkward silence in which they just stared at each other. I'd come out of my shock enough to be horribly embarrassed, not knowing where to look. Being caught in bed with a guy by his mother ranked pretty high on my top ten list of Things I Don't Ever Want to Happen.

"So why are you back already?" Danny seemed all but happy about his mother's unexpectedly early return, and clearly not only because she was interrupting.

She rolled her eyes and sighed a little, which made her appear less like a goddess and more like a human being. Well, slightly.

"You'll be pleased to hear that Frank and I had a terrible fight. I couldn't stand to see his face anymore."

The news was taken with a small, careless shrug. I thought I saw a small spark of triumph in his dark orbs. "Are you getting another divorce, then?"

"We'll see," she replied matter-of-factly. Then she looked at me for the first time, strangely enough in a casual way, as if I weren't lying naked under the covers with her son. This was so bizarre.

"So, Daniel. Aren't you going to introduce me to your friend?"

* * *

The sound of the phone ringing is shrill, far too loud. I forgot how annoying it was. It's not like we get a lot of calls around here. Mom surely won't get it, so I quickly step out of the shower and wrap a towel around my waist, and hurry downstairs as fast as I can. She won't mind if I leave puddles on the floor. She won't even notice.

"Hello?"

"Hello right back to you, Jimmy boy."

There's nothing I can do to stop a silly, happy smile from stealing onto my face. So good, so relieving to hear his voice. "Danny."

"The one and only. Hey, you know, I was just thinking that it's been ages since we talked." My smile deepens as I listen to his warm, soft voice.

I chuckle softly. "Yeah, it's almost been two hours, hasn't it?"

"I know. It's unforgivable. I should have called sooner."

I laugh softly, picturing the grin on his face and the mischievous sparkle in the beautiful dark eyes that surely accompanies his words.

When he continues to speak, he suddenly sounds thoughtful. "Seriously, though, there's something I'd like to ask you."

"Okay, go ahead."

"You didn't leave because of Lilah. You left because of me."

Oh damn. "Technically, that wasn't a question," I grin, trying to gain time before I answer. Which he knows, I'm sure. But damn... Honesty is highly overrated. I don't want to hurt him. Which is insane, considering that just a couple of months ago I would have jumped at the opportunity to strike a blow.

"Damn it, J. Just tell me. I want the truth."

"Do we have to do this?" I sigh and sink down on the chair beside the phone. "Can't we just... enjoy it?"

He laughs a little. "Hey, I'm all for it, but the whole you running out on me thing makes it kind of hard."

"I'm sorry." I rub my eyes and sigh again. Why is it so difficult to tell him what I feel, why I left?

"Don't apologize. I'm not Mills. I'm not asking you to analyze and interpret, or whatever it is the two of you do all day. I'd just like to know where I stand."

I nod, forgetting that he can't see through the receiver. I guess he deserves to know. "The truth. Okay. The truth is... I'm not sure if I'm ready for this kind of thing. Whatever it is."

There's a pause, and I nervously run my fingers through my wet hair.

Danny's voice is calm when he speaks, and yet I can hear his anger. "Don't think so much, James. Do what you want. So, do you *want* to see me, or not?"

I close my eyes, suddenly wishing I could simply reach through the line and pull him close for a kiss. The aching is running wild in the pit of my stomach, my heart is beating madly, and my skin tingles, needy for his presence. If he could see me right now, words wouldn't be necessary.

Telling him the truth would be a bad mistake. Because up until now I could have fooled myself, made believe it was a one time thing. I could have put the blame on him, because he started it. And still, the words leave my mouth like they have a mind of their own.

"I want to see you."

"I'm on my way."

5 MOTHERS

DANNY: The house isn't hard to spot with James sitting on the steps leading to the front porch, waiting for me as I pull into the driveway. I stare at the plain building through the windshield as I turn off the engine, wondering why it feels surreal to be here now. I don't know what I expected.

Maybe something with a bit more of a "Psycho" feel to it. Dark and rundown, somewhere on the outskirts of town, yeah, that would have been something. But this is almost disappointingly normal. Just your average suburban family home. Lower middleclass. Could use some work here and there, but there's nothing unusual about it.

As I get out of the car and walk towards the lonely figure on the porch, he frowns at me and raises a hand to shield his eyes from the sunlight. I guess it's still creepy, someone with a history like James growing up in a place like this. Could be anyone's neighbor, and you'd never notice. Could happen behind any of these ordinary doors lining the street.

He gets up when I reach him and I take off my dark glasses, blinking as my eyes adjust to the brighter light. Brilliant blue with a trace of green, James' eyes sparkle beautifully in the sunlight, revealing their true color.

"You could have saved yourself the trouble of coming if you hadn't hung up so soon."

I shrug and grin. "It's good to see you too, Jimmy boy."

A smile flashes across his lips, but he shakes his head, the frown deepening. He fidgets with the seam of his shirt absent-mindedly, avoiding my gaze. Haven't seen him so tense since before we first shagged. "What's up?"

"Mom isn't doing well. You shouldn't have come. Now's not a good time."

"Ah." I sit down on the steps beside where he stands, unable to hide a small smile.

James looks down at me, eyes blazing in the light, as he snaps irritably, "No need to get comfy. You're not staying. And what the hell are you grinning at anyway?"

My smile widens when I look up, taking him in as he stands there like some pissed off watchdog. I like those tight jeans, and the view from down here couldn't be better. Hello there - he looks good in his plain black T-shirt.

I like it when he's mad with me, I admit it. But damn, he's irresistible when he's seething under the surface. Or when he's just playing angry because he's scared, like now.

"Am I too much for you?" I ask amusedly, raising an eyebrow and crossing my arms in front of my chest to show that I'm not going anywhere anytime soon. Well, unless I'm invited upstairs to his room, that is.

"What? Damn it, Rizzo..." He trails off, seeming to notice that he fell back into his old habit of calling me that name. He lets out a deep sigh and finally sinks down on the steps beside me.

James stares at his shoes for a moment before he looks at me, and our eyes meet for the first time since I've arrived.

"Danny, I'm serious. I can't invite you in. You don't know what it's like... what she's like on days like this."

I can't hide a smirk. "Hey, you've met Lilah. How bad can it be? "

This time, he actually smiles. We look at each other for a long moment, and it feels good, him looking at me. I swear I can see his insecurity slowly melting away, the tenseness vanishing. But still he doesn't seem to fully relax. Hard to believe that he was still in my bed just a couple of hours ago, and now we have to start over again. Hi, I'm Danny. Mind if I kiss you?

"Do you really want me to leave?" I ask seriously, never taking my eyes off his face.

James shakes his head, but sighs again. He's been thinking, hasn't he? Probably about Mills, and this whole messed up situation. He wouldn't be James if he didn't worry. Yay for me, for giving the boy a brand-new reason to hate himself.

"It's just... weird, you being here, is all."

"How so?"

He doesn't answer, he just continues to look at me. I don't know why he seems so sad somehow. For a horrible second I can almost hear him telling me that this isn't working for him, and my heart sinks. Ouch. Boy, I'm deeper in this than I ever expected.

"What am I doing here, Danny? I gotta be out of my mind." J shakes his head in disbelief, frowning again. He gets up and takes two steps to the door, opens the screen. Pauses, and looks back over his shoulder, his voice sounding almost angry when he speaks again.

"Well, what are you waiting for?"

* * *

She looks younger in the framed family picture sitting on the side of the kitchen table, pretty, almost beautiful. Three smiles, two of them seeming a little too happy to be for real. And this, I guess, must be Simon, with his arms around Mrs. Foley and the pale, skinny boy who can't hide that he's not comfortable with the touch, or with playing happy family.

I stare at the face of the man in the middle, while James opens the fridge door and gets both of us a soda. Simon *seems* nice. He's a tall man with dark hair, not bad-looking either. A man's man, someone everybody respects and likes to call their buddy. Hardworking, taking care of his family, and usually out for a couple of beers with the boys on Saturday night. Sporty, probably into football. Or baseball. Of course! That's why James was on a baseball team. No wonder he doesn't like to talk about it. While Simon's smile seems genuine, there's a frosty authority in his eyes that sends a shiver down my spine.

My gaze wanders over to a small variety of pill bottles thoughtlessly left on the table. More out of boredom than out of actual interest, I take a closer look at some of them.

"Lorazepam... Remergil... Haloperidol?" Alarmed, I look at James as he comes over. This shit isn't aspirin, man.

"They're Mom's," he explains briskly and quickly puts them out of sight, along with a couple of other meds standing around.

I watch him opening his can and taking a big gulp, not touching mine. "Jesus, what did that bastard do to the two of you?"

Slowly James puts down his soda, his expression blank, only his eyes are alive. "Don't," is all he says, very quietly, but it's all it takes for me to understand.

So I don't speak, don't question him further. No matter how much I simply *need* to know, I just can't torture him like that. Instead, I cross the distance between us and simply kiss him. He stands still, almost stiff for a moment, but then he leans into the kiss and his hands are on my back, pulling me close.

When we stop, there's that haunted look on his face again, and I wish I knew what to do. But it's not like I have much experience in the field. I don't have much experience in any of the fields he's taking me to. And that's not something that happens to me often.

* * *

"You like my Jimmy, I can tell."

It's late in the afternoon, and Mrs. Foley and I are smoking in the kitchen while James is mowing the lawn behind the house. She was really out of it this morning, but she's behaving pretty normally now. "It's the meds," James explained. "She forgets to take them, and the withdrawal has all kinds of nasty side-effects." Oh yeah, baby, the happy pills strike back.

With her hair washed and some make-up on her pale face, J's mom is almost pretty, and I guess she's not nearly as old as she seemed when I arrived. They've got the same eyes, James and her. A kind of faded blue, like a sky full of rain clouds. She seems pretty straightforward and has the same dry sense of humor he does, which I like. I blow out a cloud of smoke before I speak, smiling at her.

"You're damn right about that, Mrs. Foley."

"You know about Casey?"

I nod and grimace, and she reacts with an amused little half-smile that looks familiar.

"Casey's a nice boy, really. Jimmy absolutely adores him." She pauses, takes a drag on her cigarette, and tiredly rubs her eyes when she exhales. "But that's not a good basis for a relationship."

Surprised, I arch an eyebrow. Not only is she cool with her son having a boyfriend, and me being here anyway, she's also questioning J's relationship with every mother's dream son-in-law. Guess the old lady's not as gone as James made it sound. Man, I like her.

"What's a good basis, then?"

"Honesty. Trust. What do you think is the most important thing?"

I shrug nonchalantly and give her a charming smile. "Enlighten me."

She smiles back at me, but doesn't answer for a long moment, just stares into the distance with thoughtful eyes. Just when I think she's forgotten me completely, she replies after all. "It's the ability to accept a person's flaws without wanting to change them. Most people don't have that."

"I think you're a very wise woman, Mrs. Foley."

"Don't think that flattery will help you pass my inspection," she teases, eyeing me from the other side of the kitchen table.

"How am I doing so far?" I grin.

She chuckles softly. "Hard to say. I'm not sure if you'd be exactly right for my boy, or a complete disaster. I think you have the possibility for both in you."

"You know, you're probably right again."

James' mom laughs, and her laugh reminds me of him. They're alike in many ways, maybe that's why we kinda seem to click. I know it's weird, but I almost envy them, J and her. The way they get along. They seem to know each other so well. Lilah and I never had anything like that.

Sometimes when my mother looks at me, I have a feeling all she sees is a reminder of my father's failures and her disappointment in him. After all these years, she's still bitter, unable to forgive. I can't help it, though. I'm my father's son. I always have been, and there was a time when she was crazy about both of us. She used to call me "Little Grazzo", because Grazzo's what everybody called my dad. The Great Graziano Rizzo. Back then Lilah couldn't resist him, but hey, no woman could. I was still a little kid, but I remember the way she looked at me back then. I remember her being happy. I've never seen her like that again, ever since the divorce.

Looking at Mrs. Foley I notice that she's still wearing her wedding ring, and I wonder if that's what she did. If she accepted Simon's flaws, and if she loved him, in spite of what he did to her and James. I think she'd have more reason not to forgive than Lilah does. But look who's talking. It's not like there's nothing in my life that I haven't forgiven.

There's the sound of footsteps in the hall and we look at each other when James enters the room. Without a word, we both reach for the ashtray and put out our cigarettes. I realize how strange this scene must look when I see the little smirk on James' face.

"You two seem to be getting along pretty well." He sounds astonished.

"We have a vice in common." I wink at her, and she smiles as she pushes her chair back and very slowly gets up, making it suddenly obvious that she's not as well as it seemed just a moment ago.

"We have more than that in common, I think," Mrs. Foley says mysteriously. Her eyes linger lovingly on her grown son for a moment before she turns around and leaves the room.

I nod to myself, smiling a little. Guess she's right about that, too.

6 CAUGHT IN THE MIDDLE

JAMES: Hell if I ever imagined anything like this. Danny "Freakin' Sex-god" Rizzo sprawled out on my old bed, flipping through a tattered comic book. That's just weird.

Right now, he's right in the middle of my past, in what used to be my sanctuary. Everything here is exactly the way I left it the day I went away for college. Hanging from the ceiling, there's the old airplane model I made when I was twelve, transporting a thick layer of dust. The classic Star Trek poster has clearly seen better days, as well as the huge celestial chart on the opposite wall that I've always loved. Beside it hangs the framed picture of Mickey Mouse, complete with a faded autograph, a treasured memory of the one time we went to Disneyland. I think I was five then, because it wasn't too long after Mom married Simon. The whole concept of having a dad was still new to me. I can still remember what it felt like. I'm pretty sure Simon really liked me back then. He let me ride on his shoulders and bought me ice-cream. That was before he discovered that I was a hopeless case.

I'm sure to Danny this is just a room, nothing more. But these four walls know everything about me. They've seen it all, heard it all. There's a tale behind every stain on the floor, behind every scratch in the furniture. It's true that most of my childhood wasn't all too happy. But there were good times too, and this ugly old room helps me remember.

I lean against the door and glance at my watch. "It's getting late."

"Your mom invited me to stay. Did I mention that I like her?" He grins at me, looking up briefly with that irresistible sparkle in his eyes. "You really have a thing for Spider-Man, don't you?"

"Danny... no. Just no. You and me in this house..." I shake my head, walk over, and sink down on the bed beside him. "I really don't think so."

He props his head up on his arm, and eyes me thoughtfully. "Suppose nothing happened."

I laugh out loud. "Yeah, right."

He pulls me down to him so that my head rests on his stomach, and tousles my hair. I slap his hand away and we grin at each other.

"Okay, so maybe it seems unlikely," he admits, still grinning. "But it *could* happen."

"In an alternate universe, some other time."

We laugh again and he groans loudly, and sinks back onto the pillow. "Oh you just don't trust me."

"Damn right." My amused smirk slides off my face when I notice the look in his eyes. "You're serious, aren't you?"

Slowly I roll off his stomach and lie down properly by his side. "What are you saying? You want to, like, just sleep here? Talk all night? Cuddle? Sing me a lullaby?"

"Fuck off," he says quietly, his voice a little hoarse. The brown eyes are laughing like they always do, but I know him well enough now to realize that I just hurt him. Wow. The Great, Untouchable Rizzo who doesn't care about anything or anyone. But he cares about me, and it makes him vulnerable. And that's a good thing, because otherwise he might get too close, and there'd be nothing I could do about it.

It suddenly hits me, lying here beside him, taking in his perfect face. The soft curves of his lips, the shape of his dark eyes, and the way they seem like windows to his soul. I'm in high danger of falling for this impossible guy. And that's just something that can never happen.

"I mean it, Danny. I appreciate you coming by. It was good to see you. But you can't stay tonight."

He smiles, and his breath washes over my face like a tender touch when he turns to me. "Hey, I know that, smartass. You tell me something thrice and I get it immediately."

I can't help but grin and take a deep breath in a futile attempt to make every fiber of my body stop screaming: Please stay.

* * *

I'd never have thought that it could take so much willpower to close the door behind the very person I used to hate with a passion not very long ago. It takes me five whole minutes to get Danny to leave the house, and I'm actually beginning to wonder if I should let him stay after all when he finally steps outside. I close the door so quickly that it's probably rude, but I'm really just trying to keep myself from following him.

I take a deep breath and start to turn around when he knocks again.

God, he's impossible. I open the door with a smile, shaking my head. "What?"

"Forgot something."

Before I can ask what it is, he pulls me close and kisses me deeply. And I'm done for. I wonder if that feeling I get every time he kisses me will ever fade away. It's like I'm trying to push him away and draw him near at the same time. Yeah, I'm one hell of a nutcase.

My fingers dig into Danny's shirt as I pull him close, inhaling his scent. His skin smells so good, it's driving me crazy. That mischievous grin of his is just damn irresistible.

"Knew I left it here."

"God, that was cheesy."

Danny winks at me. "And you totally dug it."

I laugh as he turns and walks down the driveway to his car, and I bet he knows how gorgeous his ass looks in those tight jeans. The sun hangs low in the sky, a ball of orange fire that casts long shadows across the lawn. It smells of freshly mowed grass and earth, spicy and relaxing.

"See ya, Jimmy boy."

I raise my hand in a semi-wave, hesitating for a second before I go back inside, closing the door firmly behind me. Somehow I don't want to watch as he drives away. It might make me feel even lonelier.

* * *

The house feels incredibly empty now that he's gone, and eerily silent. I can hear the monotone ticking of the large clock in the living room, the fridge hums lowly in the kitchen. A door closes upstairs and Mom slowly begins to descend the stairs. I don't want to see her right now, because she would ask about Danny. She'd want to talk, and I really have nothing to say that I'd want her to hear. Quickly I turn to my right, and I'm halfway in the kitchen when I hear a knock at the door again.

Oh thank god. I don't even try to hide my relief when I run to the door and tear it open. "What have you forgotten... now."

"Not you, James, that's for sure."

I don't know if the warm chuckle of the vision standing in front of me has anything to do with the completely dumbfounded look on my face, but my guess is, it does.

The sun is setting, illuminating his slender form like an aura, and in spite of the shadows on his face, his eyes are shining brightly.

"Hey, you," he says softly, stepping closer.

My moment of shock passes, and I can feel my face starting to beam. "Casey! You're back!"

He just grabs me and pulls me into a hug. When I feel his arms around me, him leaning into me, and our bodies seeming to fit like two pieces of a puzzle, I slowly exhale and close my eyes. For a few precious seconds the world stands still and everything is wonderful. It's him, he's here, and I'm home.

Then I remember what I did, and Danny, who is still so close that I'm sure you could smell his scent on me. And I feel like the biggest creep on the face of this earth.

"I missed you," Casey whispers and gives me a little kiss.

I swallow, but I know my eyes don't lie when I look at him, because my feelings are honest. "I missed you too, Case. I missed you too."

Book 3
Recast

Susann Julieva
& Romelle Engel

1 PORCELAIN

JAMES: I think by now we've successfully established that I'm a big old geek. Not surprisingly, I always look forward to going back to school after summer. But this semester, things have changed. It feels like I've brought more baggage with me than I meant to. Because someone here knows now. Because he knows.

What I told Danny about my stepfather is nothing but the tiniest fraction of a multivolume tale, and yet he seems to guess too much already. I don't believe in psychoanalysis. I think there's a reason why we suppress certain memories, and some things are just meant to *stay* buried. There's more than enough that I do remember as it is. And that's some good shit, man, take it and smoke it in your therapeutic pipe, or otherwise shove it up your ass and leave me and my oh so meaningful nightmares alone.

The truth is, I *loved* Simon, just as fiercely as I hated him. But maybe one lesson, the most important I need to learn, is to make peace with all of that and accept that it's in the past. And more than that, to finally let it go. If I can only get one step closer to it this semester, I may have learned more than in my entire school days combined. But they don't teach you about life in European Literature class, do they?

Outside my window, dawn is quiet and colorless, September gray. I've barely slept tonight and I've been up for an hour, but I can't concentrate on studying for the life of me. Casey's still asleep in my bed, breathing evenly - and there's peace. Deep and rich, and real. The words are endlessly rotating in my mind: How could I possibly leave him?

Of course, it's entirely Professor Kinderman's fault for telling me. Woodhaven has an exclusive student exchange program with the Free University in Berlin. Every two years, they're granting a full scholarship to the best applicant. Which means that you get to go to Germany to study there for one year, all expenses paid. And you get to travel Europe during semester break for cheaper than you imagine in your wildest dreams. Kinderman's on the selection board, and he's the one who talked me into applying last semester. Seriously, I never thought I'd actually have a shot. Good things happen to good people, and hell knows, I'm not one of them. So why should it happen to me?

And then the prof asks me to stay on after class yesterday, and he basically tells me that I'm short-listed. In other words, I might actually get this. They'll make their decision at the end of next month, and that leaves me about six more weeks to torture myself. Because I want this, more than *anything*. I'd get to learn about European politics first hand, and that's priceless for someone wanting to be a journalist. I'd get to live in a different culture, on another continent, where everything just oozes history. I'd be able to visit Paris, stroll down the Rue de Rivoli. Gaze at the Forum Romanum in Rome, at the steps where Caesar was murdered. Look at Rembrandt's paintings in Amsterdam. Take a boat trip on the water streets of Venice, and stare in amazement at palaces of mighty emperors and kings that died hundreds of years before I was born. I'd live in a city that was divided by a wall for forty years and has become a cultural boiling point of East and West, creating something fresh and exciting. This is the city Bowie and Iggy went to to come clean, and hell, if it worked for them, it sure can't hurt another screwed up wreck like me. I'd get to get away from it all, for once and for all. If I get the scholarship. If I go. But if I go... it means leaving everyone I care about behind. It means leaving Mom, who can barely take care of herself as it is. And it means leaving Casey, when I've only just found him. He doesn't even know about this yet. I never told a soul that I applied.

In any case, Berlin and the scholarship are still nine months away. But what are nine months when you're at school? It'll pass in the blink of an eye. And the entire Atlantic is no distance to be underestimated. There's no way I could ask Casey to wait for me.

This is the chance of a lifetime. But it's like I'm keeping my fingers crossed for something I fear to happen. Just the right kind of food for schizophrenic me.

I can sense that Casey is awake even before he begins to stir underneath the covers. Then he lies still for a moment, yawns, and looks at me, sitting fully dressed at my desk with my legs drawn up. The sight doesn't seem to surprise him. He smiles, and glances at the clock.

"Christ. What are you doing up at this hour?"

"Thinking."

"I'd be shocked to find you *not* thinking for once," he grins and groans a little when he sits up. His hair is standing up in every direction.

I wait for him to come to me, looking all too tempting in nothing but his shorts. His body is still wonderfully warm from bed when we kiss.

"What were you racking your brains over this time?"

"Nothing important."

"That wouldn't be the same nothing that always makes you toss and turn at night?"

"Geez, do I do that?"

Casey shrugs lightly, turns around and jumps onto the desk beside me. "Where do you think this is from?" Legs dangling, he shows me a small bluish bruise on his arm, and my eyes widen with shock, but he's smiling.

"Oh shit. Tell me I didn't give you that!"

"You didn't. You just tend to... move a lot in your sleep, is all. I just happened to be in the way."

"God, I'm sorry." I feel awful. What the hell is wrong with me? Well, okay, I *know* what's wrong with me, but this is just plain scary. You don't get a bruise like that easily. That must have been a pretty good whack.

"Don't be." He leans over and rests his head on my shoulder, yawns again. "I don't mind. I like sleeping here."

"Well, perhaps you shouldn't."

He smiles and places a little kiss on my neck. "Don't be a dick. I'm not made of porcelain."

Perhaps I should be reminded of that more often, because I still tend to treat him like he is. He's too precious to me to behave otherwise. I've always been different around him, but it feels like I'm even more so now that we're together.

There's so much he doesn't know about me. And that is a very good thing. Although it *would* help sometimes if he realized that not everyone's brought up in a happy home with a kid sister and a dog named Cookie, I prefer for him to not recognize me as the hopelessly twisted lunatic I probably am.

Right, gotta get back on the sleeping pills then. They used to knock me out with the tenderness of a sledgehammer, which might help in avoiding future domestic violence. Ah, the things you do to not involuntary give your boyfriend solid beatings at night.

Speaking of avoiding, I haven't seen Danny since the day he came to visit me over the summer and left mere minutes before Casey arrived. By the way, I still get a heart attack just thinking of how freaking close that was.

He called me on the phone several times, but I cleverly missed it all by simply never being home. Mom handed me a small bundle of messages one night and shook her head. "I took these *before* he came by later this afternoon. I had a hard time trying to convince him that you really weren't here. Remarkably persistent, this one."

"Tell me about it."

"You really should talk to him, Jimmy. Putting it off won't solve the problem."

As much as I love her, those words weren't exactly what I was keen to hear. And I know that Danny deserves at least an explanation. But that would involve me looking him in the face and resisting the irresistible. And what am I supposed to tell him anyway?

Luckily for me, even after one week back at Woodhaven Casey is still too consumed by the usual start of semester rush to take notice of me coming up with absurd excuses every time Danny appears on the horizon. But that won't work for much longer. I really might have to emigrate then.

Truth be told, I don't trust myself when it comes to Danny. Not even enough to go over and talk to him in a public place. The dilemma of dilemmas, when trying to avoid further damage might just have the opposite result.

Swear to god, I had no intention of sleeping with him when I went to visit. And I seem to remember having made that fact pretty clear to Danny, too. But you know what he's like. And I'm still not feeling the guilt I should be feeling. Because it was right that night, it was exactly what I needed. He was exactly what I needed, and he *knew*.

But how can I be sure that it won't happen again? I can't be sure, and so my only chance is to stay away. He doesn't make it easy for me, though. Everywhere I go, everywhere I turn, he seems to be there. Paranoid much, Foley?

He slid a message under my door once, just a piece of paper, folded in the middle. When I opened it, all it said was "Jimmy Boy". It gave me a pretty creepy *Fatal Attraction* moment that I so didn't need. But after the initial shock had passed, I recognized it for what it really was, and it made me smile. Because I could hear him say it, close to my ear, his voice mocking, but soft. And I could see his dark eyes twinkling at me, and that deadly "you know you want it" grin on his lips.

Good Lord, yes, I do want it. And much as I love his work, I disagree with Oscar Wilde. Yielding to temptation can't be the only way to get rid of it. There's clearly another option, however unpleasant, but without doubt effective: Castration.

* * *

Our little game of cat and mouse comes to an end when I leave after the school paper meeting on Friday afternoon. The sky behind the large windows is gray and tired, the light falling into the corridor only dim. And there he suddenly is. The familiar handsome figure is leaning against the wall just opposite the door, casting a shadow on me when I stop abruptly. Some blind idiot bumps into me and pushes me forward, closer to him.

"Hey," Danny says, drops his cigarette and grinds it out with his toe. It's a non-smoking building.

Too dumbfounded to even echo his smile, I stand there, holding on to my books. "Hey."

The brown eyes are mercilessly fixed on my face. He nods to his left, smiling a little. "The exit's that way, if you're going to make a run for it again."

"Look, I didn't..."

"What?" He pushes himself off the wall and is suddenly standing much closer than is good for me. "You didn't what, James? Get my messages? Ignore me? No?"

He arches an eyebrow when I don't answer. "I must have been imagining things then."

"Yeah, well. Don't feel too bad about it."

"You forgive me? For thinking so badly of you?" Danny's eyes are just twinkling as he dances undecided between angry and amused. You little brat prince, you're not used to this happening to you, are you?

For the first time since I've met him, he seems unsure about how to act, which road to take. I decide to give him a nudge into the direction I myself favor clearly.

"Sure, I forgive you, this one time. As long as it doesn't happen again."

"I promise it won't." Go me. Amused is clearly winning now, and a small grin curls his lips. He leans in closely until our bodies almost touch and whispers close to my ear, "You fucker."

I can't help laughing softly, and step back a little to look into his eyes. "I am. I'm sorry."

He tilts his head slightly to the side as if trying to decide whether to actually believe me, then he smiles mysteriously and steps past me. "Come on."

I knew it. I knew this would happen. Like a puppet on a string I follow as he saunters down the corridor. It freaks me out just how effortlessly he gets me to do things I don't want to. When I'm around him, none of that seems to matter anymore. There's some sort of connection, obviously, although I really don't get it. I don't think it's actually possible for two people to be less alike than him and me. And still. He gets to me in ways that I never thought anyone would.

But what on earth, I wonder, is it that draws *him* to me? Why did he choose me of all people, to be the one who gets to see the softer side of this bad boy?

* * *

The door of his dorm room closes behind me with a soft click. I'm such an idiot. The treacherous, needy fever that had taken over my body the minute I noticed where he was leading me must have melted my brain.

"I can't do this."

"I know."

We're standing side by side, leaning against the door, and the room is very quiet, holding its breath. Funny how I don't feel trapped at all. Au contraire. I feel alive now, wide awake, more than I have in weeks.

"Why," that voice of silk asks softly, "Why are you doing this to me?"

"You know why." I sound too hoarse, and the words get lost in the deep silence that follows.

A hand reaches out and cups my face, runs its thumb along my chin, over my lips. Instinctively I lean into it, and my eyelids flutter closed. Breathe.

"Tell me what you want me to do."

I swallow. Oh hell. I have a pretty good idea of how many people would *kill* just to hear him say these words.

"I might get that scholarship for Berlin."

Ack. Where did that come from? I didn't mean to say that at all! Smart move, dude. The atmosphere changes immediately. With a smooth motion Danny pushes himself off of the wall and looks at me with complete surprise. "For Berlin?"

I nod, frowning a little, still trying to figure out why I told him.

"Hell."

Yeah, I second that.

"I didn't know you wanted to get away from me so badly." He's grinning now, but there's a trace of a frown on his forehead when he sinks down on the bed.

"It's got nothing to do with *you*."

"You sure about that?"

"This might come as a shock, but my world doesn't revolve around you, Danny." My moving closer and sitting down next to him might slightly dampen the effect of the words.

He just looks at me and smiles mysteriously. "You tell

yourself that, Jimmy Boy."

"I do. And I very much agree with me."

"Then kindly inform yourself that you're on *my* bed right now."

"So what? We're just talking."

"We're never just talking, James. You know that."

How very true. It's foreplay. Anything that happens between us is foreplay. Unless we're already at it, of course.

With a small sigh I let myself fall back onto his soft mattress and stare up at the ceiling. "You told me to tell you what to do."

"I did."

"Anything at all?"

"Anything." He lies down beside me and props his head up on his arm to look down at me. Oh boy. That voice of his does wild things to the lower half of my body.

"Then let's just talk." Quickly I raise my hand in a defensive gesture to stop him when he moves closer. "Don't touch me."

He freezes in mid-motion, and a crooked smile curls the corner of his mouth. He looks baffled, but impressed. And then he starts to laugh, shaking his head to himself.

"What?" I ask, my wall of self-confidence beginning to crumble. Is he laughing at me?

"Nothing." He rolls onto his back, still smiling to himself. "I just can't believe that I'm actually gonna do this."

"You are?" Great. There was no need for me to sound *that* surprised. There is mental head-against-the-wall-banging.

He willingly holds out his hands to me, grinning a little. "Tie me up if you must. Or you could just trust me, for once."

I laugh softly. "I might get back to you on the tying up. But I think we can do without today."

To my utter surprise, I suddenly realize that I really do trust him. I dare myself to, but my heart is beating loudly. And a part of me secretly wishes that he'll let me down, just to feel his hands on me. God knows I'm positively bleeding for it. But somehow I *know* that he won't disappoint me.

"So tell me, why do you want to go to Germany?"

He's either a far finer actor than I already know him to be, or he's honestly interested in finding out. And just the possibility of it makes me burn on the inside. My fingers twitch on their own account. When I force my hand down to rest on the covers, it touches his by accident. And I leave it there.

It's just about two inches of my skin against his, but electricity flows between us. And I know he feels it too. The spot heats up, but neither of us pulls away. And I'm dying to grab his hand, but refuse to, as if it were the most obscene thing.

This is not about the chemistry between us. And yet the chemistry is in everything.

Nothing I could say or do could truly shock Danny, shatter his world, or drive him away. I don't have to be careful around him. I don't have to pretend. I can be me, and be real. And now I know that this is why I'm really here. It's why I need to be.

2 MISSING OUT

CASEY: The bench on the edge of Shriner's Park is really unusually uncomfortable. There's a tall statue of one of Woodhaven's benefactors standing next to it, his face serene. James refers to him as the "stoned dude". I smile to myself. Somehow I doubt that that's the expression they were going for. I'm feeling very calm, watching as a rusty leaf sails through the air, spirals, hovers for a moment in midair, then flutters weakly to the ground.

James is late, but I'm used to it, and don't mind. I always tell him that he's taking on too much. I honestly don't know how he manages to get grades like that with all the extra work. But it's just one of the things I admire about him, his determination and dedication. I wish I could be more like that.

Lost in thought, I watch a group of people leaving the building not far from me. Drama students, and automatically my eyes search for Danny Rizzo. They gather by the front steps. Oh, here he comes. Sure enough they were waiting for him. Someone hands him a cigarette and he leans in as they light it. There's a little smile on his lips that does funny things to me, and it seems to be doing even worse things to that girl.

They all hang around near the building for a while. Something Danny says is making them laugh so hard I can hear it from here. Now someone is giving a funny impression of someone - probably a teacher - and the group is roaring with laughter. I can't help but stare at Danny, looking so carefree and much younger when he's laughing. It just makes me ache somehow. Damn, I wish I really *could* hate him.

It was a lot easier before he gave me that completely, totally mind-blowing blowjob on the beach. I close my eyes and take a deep breath as the images come, and try hard to banish them from my mind. I still get aroused every time I think of it. It's horrible. I don't like the way it made me feel. Because it was wrong, and some things should just never happen.

I look away, to the other side, the direction James will be coming from. Something safe. Think of something safe.

Professor Wickham's assignment is giving me a headache and I think about it for a while. How am I supposed to portray *"fear"*? I can hardly draw him a picture of a big, hairy spider, can I? I'll have to ask Leo what she thinks. We're in a couple of classes together and she always has the best ideas. I'm slightly startled when I notice someone approaching from my other side.

"I'm waiting for my man..."

Danny's singing voice is almost as husky as Lou Reed's, but not as curiously off-key. Damn. It's absolutely beautiful, just like everything about him. This is so not fair. My eyes focus on the perfectly sun-tanned face with the laughing brown eyes as he sits down next to me uninvited, and I shrug with a sheepish smile.

"Well, at least I have a man to wait for."

He chuckles. "So, how was your summer, Mills? Monogamous and boring?"

"Monogamous and fun, thank you. We had a great time at our holiday lodge. Too bad you couldn't come."

His eyes have that amused sparkle in them. It makes me remember why it's simply impossible to not have a crush on him at some point, although he's clearly the worst person *ever* to fall for. Feeling the need to say something else, I smile a little.

"And how was your summer?"

A grin flashes across his lips, but for reasons unknown, he fights to suppress it. "You wouldn't want to know."

"That good?" I ask, one eyebrow arched, and he just looks at me with a secretive smile dancing on his lips.

"Better."

"Good for you. Did you go anywhere interesting?"

"You could say that." There's something about the tone of his voice that catches my attention.

"Where did you go, then?"

Our eyes meet, and Danny seems to be thinking about his answer for a moment. The topic apparently amuses him.

Before I can get a reply, a shadow falls over the bench and we both turn our heads to see James arrive.

"Hey." James smiles at me and I greet him with a kiss, while Danny watches with an unreadable expression. "Sorry I'm late, the meeting took longer."

"No problem."

"Have you been waiting long?"

"Not that long, no," I lie warmly.

"Hey, Riz." James barely looks at him.

"Hey, Jimmy." Danny takes a last drag on his cigarette, then he drops it to grind it out.

James' soulful eyes follow the cigarette on its way to the ground. He blows a strand of hair out of his eyes. "So what's up?"

"We were just talking about our summer."

"Oh really?" James' gaze sharply lingers on Danny for a moment. There seems to be a silent interchange between them. Did I miss something?

"Mills tells me you both missed me."

"Terribly. Almost as much as a third foot," James replies sincerely, making me laugh.

Danny smirks. "Are you sure you mean *foot*, and not that thing between your legs?"

James' eyes widen dramatically. "You mean that's *not* a foot?"

"I could be wrong, but it strikes me as somewhat different."

Laughing, I get up and pull James up with me. "I think that's our cue to leave."

"You're such a killjoy, Millsie," Danny grins, and gets up too.

The conversation ends with some friendly banter, then we part. But something in Danny's eyes as he looks at James before he turns around makes me feel uneasy. Again, I think of the threesome, this time of watching them together. It was the first time I detected the same kind of darkness in Danny that I can sometimes sense in James. I've been thinking about it often over the summer, and it worries me.

* * *

"It's good to be back, isn't it? I actually missed campus a little." I smile at James as we walk along.

"I thought I was supposed to be the nerd here."

I laugh softly, with a sudden rush of affection. "You're not a nerd. It's not your fault you have a brilliant mind that demands to be kept occupied."

"I like the way you put that." His eyes are smiling at me, and mine are twinkling right back at him.

"Anyway, I know you must be glad to be back."

"Yeah, but I have my reasons. You love to be home with your folks. I would too, if they were my family."

"They adore you, you know that, James. You're practically part of the family. Mom would adopt you in a flash."

"And feed me until I weigh a ton," he chuckles, and I laugh. Very true. She goes on and on about how he's too skinny. Well, in my humble opinion, he's gorgeous and absolutely perfect.

Reaching out to casually grab my hand, he smiles mischievously. "I'm so disappointed that Janie no longer wants to marry me, though."

I laugh, remembering how lovesick my kid sister used to be over him. Now that she's decorated every corner of her room with posters of boy bands, the good old days of her James crush seem to be officially over.

Every time I come home now, Janie has become less like a child and more like a woman. It's both beautiful and saddening to see. She's no longer the little girl who loved to ride on my shoulders when we were kids, that's for sure.

Everything's changed now. I look at my boyfriend for a long moment, thoughtfully, and squeeze his hand gently. "I really should tell them about us. I don't know why I'm such a chicken shit about it."

"Don't feel bad. It's sad but true, parents tend to be open-minded only as long as it doesn't involve their own son telling them that they'll never have grandchildren."

I smile at his cynical words, but nod. I guess he's right. "I will tell them, though. Promise. I just need a little more time."

"Don't stress out about it. I understand."

I wonder if he really does. Thing is, I always wanted to have children, a whole bunch, at least three. I wanted to get married and be a dad. It's so firmly set in my mind that it's hard to let go of this ideal. But I could never tell him that. I look at James thoughtfully. Why do things have to be so hard? It sucks that Danny has such a way with him. It's as if, instinctively, he understands him better than I ever could. I'm jealous of that strange bond they seem to share, I admit it. I'm jealous of both of them for different reasons, and it makes me feel bad.

I think of Professor Wickham's assignment again, and suddenly I know what I'm going to draw. It's something vague, something darker than night, something you can't define. Something just barely out of your reach, but always lurking in the background. No boogeyman, no big bad, just a feeling. That cold feeling inside that something is about to go horribly wrong. You don't know why, when or how. But you know it will happen eventually. Right now, that is what fear means to me.

3 THE USUAL GAME

DANNY: Cafe Plato is the only place on campus with decent coffee, and the need for caffeine knows no social barriers. Which is why even I have to enter Planet Geek every now and then. The place itself isn't too bad, they're going for the art nouveau / Viennese coffeehouse look and have works by former students decorating the walls. You can always find the philosophers in the niche opposite the door, enigmatizing amongst themselves. The writers prefer the window front where they spend hours people-watching and typing away on their laptops. The theater crowd completely owns the backroom, so I'm usually there when I come in.

Sure enough, I'm spotted immediately, and various people are waving for me to come over the moment I enter the cafe. Trey's at the counter, just about to fight his way back to the backroom with a steaming mug of coffee in his hand. When he sees me, he stops and points at his coffee with a question in his eyes. I nod, and he grins and returns to the counter to order one for me. Good boy. Suddenly someone grabs my hand and Daria kisses me hello on the cheek.

"Danny, have you heard? Rumor has it that Jeff wants to do Arthur Miller this semester!"

"Does he?" I arch an eyebrow and grin. "I had no idea Jeff was a necrophiliac."

She laughs and playfully slaps my arm. "Really! You're impossible." She begins to drag me towards the backroom, but then I see something that makes me let go off her hand and stop.

"Go ahead. I'll be there in a minute."

"God, you always say that. And then we don't see you for hours!" She shakes her head but smiles. "Don't be long. Everyone's waiting."

When she continues on her way without me, I return my

attention to what made me want to stay behind. Over there. James with Mills, at a small table on the side. I know he sees me, but he just looks right through me, his eyes glazed over. As though he doesn't know me at all. It stings, more than I'm willing to accept. We've avoided talking to each other when the little dick of a boyfriend is present so far, but come on. Even Mills can't be that thick to not find that at least a little strange. So I'm thinking, can't hurt to make my presence known. And I head on over there. I won't be ignored, that's for sure.

"Rizzo," Mills greets me with a smile. "I never see you around anymore. Are you trying to hide from your fans or something?"

"Maybe." My cryptic grin makes him shift uncomfortably in his seat as I grab a chair, but his smile lingers. I can see through the friendly mask, though. He's about as enthusiastic about being around me as about getting his toenails ripped out. Suits me fine. Because if Mills doesn't like me, it can only mean that James *does*. As hard as J is to read sometimes, as obvious is the facial expression of super-boyfriend.

James looks past me and frowns slightly when the chimes above the door announce another customer. "Were you hiding from that one there?"

I look over my shoulder to catch the intense gaze of blue, coal-rimmed eyes. The tall, black-clad boy is slender, almost thin, the short hair dyed black. Way too many silver piercings glisten in the pale face, as though he were rebelling against the beauty it nevertheless possesses. Ah, the Goth kid. I remember him. Nick... Keller or something. We were in a play together last semester. An Ideal Husband. Good show. Great fuck. It was a one time thing and I haven't talked to him since. But something in his eyes just now catches my attention. I smile a little, vaguely, and turn back to James.

"What makes you think I would?"

"Maybe because he looks kinda scary?" Mills laughs.

"Does he?" I lean in closer and look into his eyes with a small grin. "Takes a whole lot more to scare me."

He notices the underlying challenge in my voice, and swallows. "Right. Then why don't you prove it?"

Sweet. Little Casey thinks we're playing in the same league.

We haven't even started, kid, and you're wetting yourself already.

James glares at both of us. "Nobody needs to prove anything here, okay?" He stares at Goth as he makes his way through the crowd to the counter. Something dark seems to flash in J's eyes. Hold on. Does he somehow *know* I've had the kid? If he does, he doesn't seem too pleased, and I quite like that. It gives me a thrill to think that he might be jealous.

A small frown appears on Casey's forehead, and I realize that he's noticed the look in J's eyes as well. Interesting. Maybe Sweetheart isn't as thick as he lets on, after all.

"I was only joking", he is quick to defend himself. Lame-o.

I shrug nonchalantly. "Too bad. I wasn't."

"Guys?" James interferes with a tired sigh. "Cut it out. I thought all that shit's in the past."

"It is."

We nod simultaneously, and once again I'm astounded as to how skillfully James plays my emotions. I think of his mom, and the man in the photograph with the confident smile and the cold stare. I try to catch his eye, but he looks at Mills, and they smile at each other. And then Mills leans in for a brief kiss and I get the urge to heave. I hate that they absolutely look like they belong. They have their own small world that I'd never be able to understand, even if I wanted to. But J and I... what do we have? Other than mind-blowing sex and one amazing conversation every couple of weeks? And lately there's been a devastating lack of sex, too. But here's the big surprise: I thought that I'd mind more than I do. Man, I *crave* to be with him again, and yet... the moments when he's with me and we're just talking almost feel more intimate. I've never had anything like that before. I've just never bothered. What for? But with J, everything is different. I feel like I need to own him completely to figure this out. One thing's for sure: I won't be the *other guy* for him. It's not acceptable.

But alright, let's play nice, at least for now. I manage a pretty convincing smile as I look at super-boyfriend. "What? We're cool. Aren't we, Mills?"

"Sure." He smiles. "I mean, it's a weird situation for all of us, with everything that happened," he adds with a wry smile.

You mean that night on the beach, when I made you beg for more, and your boyfriend had me in front of your eyes and you totally dug it?

"But we're all adults, right?" Right. Funny how he can't seem to look at me. "It happened, we all had fun, no need to feel awkward now."

No shit. I can't hide an amused grin. "You're feeling awkward, Mills? Do I make you nervous?"

"You *wish*."

"Will you stop it, or I'm leaving *right now*." James looks like he really means it, and I know he's mad. I'm just not sure if he's mad at me, at Mills, or at both of us. Shit. Okay, I'll be the reasonable one then. They tend to look better. So I shake my head and get up. "No, you two stay. I'm leaving."

"Rizzo, wait." Casey sighs deeply, jumping on the reasonable bandwagon. "Can we at least try to get along?"

"Sure." I crack a charming smile and wink at him. "We can *try*."

When he's smiling back at me, unable to hold my eyes for long, I realize that there's something else there, unspoken. Is he blushing? His eyes dart up to my face again, briefly, and he swallows. Well, damn. I blink slowly. Are you sure you're completely over me, kid?

"See you two later." I don't wait for them to reply.

I make my way through the crowd to the counter, ending up exactly where I meant to, which is right next to Goth. I lean against the counter and look at him as I wait for Josephine, the barkeep, to make her way over. She'll bring me the coffee Trey ordered before. Our eyes meet and I give Keller my special grin. Yep, still pretty, this one. Wouldn't mind having him again. Doesn't seem like he'd mind being had either.

I know that James is watching. I also know that Mills is doing his best not to watch but can't help it. Not that I give a damn about Mills. But I'm about to make a point here, and I have no doubt that both of them will get their individual message. I'll make you realize what you truly want, Jimmy boy. I'll make you see what you need. I'll force you to if I have to. Whatever it takes, you know that I'm game.

4 THE LIVING DEAD

NICK KELLER: Shit. Oh, damn. This isn't my bed. My eyes aren't even open yet, and I can already tell. Where the hell am I? All right. First step: eyes open. Ow! Shit, it's bright in here. I'm blind! Wait. No, just adjusting to the sun. Okay, this room looks... female. I'm in a girl's room. I wonder if she's pretty. I wonder how I got here. I wonder if it's a bad thing that I don't remember it.

Ah, the answer to my question. One of them, at least. She *is* pretty. And also angry.

"God, I thought you'd never wake up! I poked you just about a million times! I was this close to calling an ambulance for you, I hope you know." She's talking too fast. And too loud. My head feels like it's going to explode. Why is she so loud? "You have to leave, you know. Some of us need to go to class."

Class. Right. What day is it?

"What day is it?" My voice sounds awful. I'm not that surprised. My mouth tastes awful too. What the hell was I doing last night?

"It's Thursday you idiot, now get out of bed. I have to get to class. Don't you?"

Probably, but I don't really care. Not like I'd be much good in class right now anyway. And why is she so pissed off at me in the first place? Didn't we...

"Did we fuck?"

She snorts and rolls her eyes. "Real classy, Romeo. And no. Never in a million years. You came back here with my lunatic of a roommate. She's been gone for hours, but like I said, we couldn't wake you up. But you're awake now. So get out."

Rude bitch. I manage to roll out of bed and somehow stand up. And the room is moving. And I'm naked. Right. Clothes.

"Oh! God, they're on the chair!"

I finally get out of the room while I'm still pulling my shirt on, and she's *still* bitching at me through the door. Like I really need that. She's definitely not making my head feel any better, that's for sure.

I can think of exactly four things that *would* make me feel better right now. My first choice - well, there's no chance of me getting my first choice this early in the day. Marc would kill me for even thinking of calling before noon. Even if he didn't kill me, he'd certainly never sell anything to me ever again. And I'm not sure which is the worse threat: death or sobriety. My second choice isn't going to work either, because if I remember correctly, I don't have a damn thing left to drink in my room. Third and fourth are a shower and some coffee. And they seem to be my best bet.

The only question now is: which one first?

A quick look around, and I realize exactly two things. According to the mirror in the hallway, I look about as good as I feel. Which is to say, like complete and utter shit. So a shower definitely needs to be first. Luckily, I also realize that I'm in my own building, and just a few floors from my room.

It's only a matter of minutes before I'm under hot water, washing something pretty disgusting out of my hair. I'm not sure what (or whose) it is, but the shampoo gets rid of it quick enough.

I think about giving myself a little personal attention in the shower, but I'm sort of afraid I might end up slipping, and I'm not sure I'd be able to stand back up in my current condition. And I do *not* want to spend another afternoon sitting naked on the floor of a dorm bathroom. So that idea is vetoed and I finish up my shower.

I get dressed slowly, still needing coffee. Badly. I'd *love* something stronger. But what is it they say? Beggars can't be choosers, or some crap like that. I guess this is what it means. So I'll settle for the coffee. And thank god that most of my clothes are black, because I'm not sure I'd be able to match colors right now.

Black jeans, black t-shirt, black shoes. My hand is surprisingly steady, so I take my chances with the eyeliner. I'm able to get it on without poking myself in the eye. Much.

There's a cafe on campus not too far from my dorm, and the coffee there is pretty good. Better than anywhere else around here at least. And don't ask me why there's only one place on this entire campus where you don't gag when you drink the coffee. It's a goddamn university! People are either hungover or studying. Either way, they need decent coffee.

I mean really!

Better than being at home though. There I have to make my own coffee. And by the time I get up, that automatic piece of crap coffee maker is set for the next day. And damn if I can figure out how to override the thing when I'm hungover. And it's not like anyone else in that house is going to stop in the kitchen while I'm there and show me how.

Bastards.

I finally put it on the list of "Things Nick Needs While He's Here." *Non*-automatic Mr. Coffee. That damn list is hit or miss, though. Sometimes I don't think anyone looks at it for weeks at a time, but two days later my Mr. Coffee showed up on the kitchen counter. Mom never said a damn thing about it. I doubt she's even the one that bought it.

Doesn't change the fact that I *still* currently need coffee. I feel like a freaking zombie. One of those that's missing a few body parts or something. You know, like an arm and half a brain.

I'm still half a block away from the place, but I can just see someone walking in through the door. Even from here I can immediately recognize him by the way he moves.

Because I *remember* the way he moves.

Rizzo. Best, hottest lay I've had in a long time. And it was last year, which says something that I can *still* remember it. It's like he got stuck in my head, or something like that. Not that it's important or anything. We had to work together because of that show, but I don't think we've said a word to each other since then. On or off stage.

Wouldn't really mind doing that again, though, and that's not something I usually go for. You start hanging around one person too much, things get complicated. And I don't need that.

It's pretty crowded inside when I push my way through the door, and whose bright idea was it to put bells on the damn door? I need bells right now about as much as I needed that bitch shouting at me earlier.

The cafe isn't big, but it isn't small either. But I can immediately tell where he is. It's like the whole place *adjusts* itself to him. I don't know how he does it. I wish I did.

Holy shit. He's actually looking at me. What the…? He hasn't done that since… And what the hell is wrong with that asshole at his table? What did I do to *him* that he looks about ready to shove his coffee mug down my throat? Back off, man. Not like I slept with your mom or anything.

At least I don't think so.

I've been pushing myself past people this whole time, and I'm finally at the counter. I can't remember what her name is, the girl behind the counter, but I think I might love her. She says she'll bring me my coffee. Hallelujah.

I risk a glance back over at the table across the cafe while I'm waiting, but no one's looking this way anymore. I'm not sure what that was all about before, but they're obviously past it now.

I can't bring myself to care too much, because coffee girl is back. And she's the best person in the world right now. Coffee. Lovely, black, and sweet. It's way too hot, which I find out only after taking that first big gulp. It comes down to weighing pain against caffeine, and caffeine obviously wins. It's nearly perfect. And it would *be* perfect if I had a smoke to go with it.

And suddenly, there is one. Only it belongs to Rizzo. Who has somehow managed to cross the cafe while I was trying to mainline my way-too-hot coffee. And damn if I didn't forget what being this close to him does to my body. My hangover's instantly gone and the hair is standing up on my arms and he's giving me that grin (that "screw you, I'll do what I *want* to" grin) that I can actually feel. He's close enough now that I can feel it when he exhales in my direction. I inhale, not sure if I'm breathing the smoke in, or him.

He's loose and relaxed, and he looks the way I feel when I'm performing on stage. A thought rams into my brain out of absolutely nowhere, and I realize that he *is* performing for someone. I follow my hunch and glance over his left shoulder, and sure enough, Rizzo's "friend" looks about ready to spit nails. I can't help but grin.

So *that's* what this is all about. Hell, I've played this game before, more than once. Nothing better to piss someone off than going to "that boy with all the piercings". I've gotten good at helping make people jealous, but even if I wasn't, there's no way in hell I'm going to say no to that look Rizzo's giving me. He doesn't even need to say a damn thing.

We just stand there for a minute, still not saying a word. I watch him smoke his cigarette until he looks back over at me and one corner of his mouth quirks up. Then he turns and walks to the door, and I'm burning the back of my throat on the last of my coffee and following after him. I throw a grin back over my shoulder as I push out the door and laugh to myself as I watch that guy's eyes darken.

And then I'm done laughing, because I'm back in the sun, and blinking at the light, cursing the fact that I was too out of it to grab my sunglasses. I feel like I'm waking up all over again, and have to stop myself from rubbing at my eyes and messing up the liner.

Somehow, stepping into the sun almost made me forget about Rizzo, but suddenly my vision clears and he's right there - closer than I thought he'd be, and still with that grin on his face. And damn does he look good.

I'm very aware that I'm not at my best at the moment, especially standing next to him. I'm hungover and waiting for the caffeine to fully kick in. I'd be worried, but he doesn't really seem to mind.

He starts walking and I follow until he takes a quick turn into one of the campus buildings. I don't even notice at first, and I take a few more steps before he leans the upper half of his body back out the door.

"Hey!" He's grinning even more at me when I turn around in surprise. He raises an eyebrow as I walk back towards him. I don't say anything, and I know he's laughing at me.

I vaguely recognize the building we're in. I think I might've had a class here last year that I went to just enough to not fail. Up one hallway and around a corner and I'm not quite sure where we're going when he grabs my arm and pulls me into the men's room.

We're barely through the door when I'm pulled to the side and my back is against a tiled wall. A split second later he's pressed up against me, and even just that feels so amazing. I have to close my eyes to keep myself from making some embarrassing sound, and when I open them again I realize that there's actually someone in here trying to take a piss. I laugh out loud at the look on his face. And I just can't help myself.

"You done, or are you planning on staying to watch?" I lean my head back against the wall, my eyes half-closed, and rock my hips forward against Rizzo's as I say this, and I'm not sure which is better: the heat in Rizzo's eyes or the complete terror in the other guy's.

I slide my hand to the front of Rizzo's jeans, start undoing the buttons of his fly, and the guy at the urinal zips up so fast I'm afraid he's going to get something vital caught in there. Rizzo laughs low and sexy in my ear as the guy sprints from the room.

Something that sounds a lot like "unbelievable" is laughed against my neck before there's teeth there and a mouth that's so. Hot. I'm pulling at his shirt and over the pounding in my ears I can vaguely hear myself breathing shallowly through my mouth and saying things like "please" and "now" and "Rizzo".

His body is so damn amazing, and I can't even describe the things he does with it. The last functioning part of my brain stops to wonder how I could've ever forgotten something like this. Then even that part of my brain shuts down and all I can do is feel.

As I slowly walk back to my dorm a while later, my knees aching just a little, all I can think about is Rizzo. It doesn't even occur to me to worry about that. All I want to know is when the next time will be.

But then I realize that it's Thursday night, and there are always some amazing parties on Thursday nights. This is turning out to be one *hell* of a great day.

5 MILD LIGHT

JAMES: It's early October and ridiculous Halloween decorations are popping up everywhere. Someone put up a singing plastic pumpkin in the hallway of our dorm, which in itself deserves the death penalty in my opinion, because every couple of minutes someone pushes its button in passing and the thing starts to wail like Tina Turner on speed. I have plans of sneaking down at night to - accidentally - completely and utterly destroy it. These plans are only complicated slightly by it being unexpectedly difficult to find a chainsaw on campus.

Other than that, though, I'm glad that summer is over and no one can deny that fall has begun. And what an amazing fall we're having this year. Shriner's Park looks stunning with leaf colors ranging from bright yellow to deep flaming red. The mornings are shrouded in mist and the earth smells rich and moist all day long. Groups of enormous crows have taken over the grounds and like to attack the freshmen trying to feed them.

I've barely had time to look around and fully appreciate it. No matter how late I stay up to study or how early I get up, there's always more to do. Sometimes I get too wrapped up in it all, and I know that Casey's been feeling neglected. But he knows what I'm like. It's not something I can simply switch off. He makes no secret of thinking that I'm taking on too much, but I need that. Keeping busy keeps me from thinking, and if he had to live in my brain for just one day, he'd be the first to agree that things are better this way.

I treasure the moments with him. I always do. I'm so far from home when he's around, miles from back then. It just breaks me, how he makes me want to be a better person. Someone who wouldn't go around seeing somebody else behind his back. Someone he'd deserve to be with. Someone not tainted, jaded, and worn out.

It's draining though, trying to be more positive and more open. But hell, if I can't stand myself the way I am, I gotta do *something*. And it's easier to try for him. Still, if Casey knew who I *really* was, what I have done... No, he must never know. I could never tell him, or anyone. And that's not because I had to swear not to.

* * *

The sky is so blue it's unreal, like it's pretending that it's spring already. But the typical fluffy fall clouds are lazily drifting by above us, and I have a hard time concentrating. What does the sky look like over Berlin? Yet another secret weighing on my shoulders. But what good would it do now, telling Casey that I applied for the scholarship? It might just cause a big fuss about nothing, after all. So why on earth did I tell Danny?

Casey follows my gloomy stare to the park bench not too far from where we are sitting with our books, trying to study. Danny's crew is fooling around, enjoying the mild weather. Andrea, that beautiful but cold brunette, is looking over at us. Rich girl, the dean's daughter. She nods shortly when she notices me. Just about as warm as a freezer, but out of that bunch of clowns, she's the only one with a personality of her own.

Danny's friends have, for reasons one can only suspect, started to greet me whenever we meet. I either ignore them or tell them to go to hell, it's that absurd. They've never so much as glanced at me before, and now I'm supposed to feel special, because they acknowledge my existence? Screw them all. This isn't high school, and you can shove your popularity right up your ass. If you want me to be impressed with who you are and what you do, win a Nobel prize.

I've given up trying to avoid Danny, and still I hardly see him on his own these days. He's always with his crowd, and if he's not, then that little punk from the cafe can't be far. Something about that guy irritates me. Enough for my fist to feel the violent urge to decorate his face with a nice black bruise every time he leaves with Danny. He reminds me of a dog, and I don't like dogs. They're all about dribbling and following orders, and they smell awful when they're wet. So there.

I mean, I never expected Danny to take a vow of chastity because of me, but there's no need for him to make it *that* obvious that he's having one hell of a great time.

I'm in a relationship, I have absolutely no right or reason to be jealous, that's why it makes me even angrier that I *am*. Why is it so unbearably hard to see him with someone else? Why do I feel like he's supposed to be mine? But that's just the thing with Rizzo, isn't it? He has a way of making you want him to be yours and yours alone. But I'm *not* going to fall for that anymore.

The thought of us just being friends is plain laughable. So what else could we be?

Nothing. There is nothing else.

I look at Casey, and he's still gazing over to their bench. When he notices me looking at him, he smiles quickly. But something about that smile isn't quite honest, it doesn't match the startled look in his eyes. As if he were feeling caught.

He nods to the bench and rolls his eyes in mild annoyance. Then he shuts the book on his lap. "Just what *is* it about Rizzo?"

I try to fight the uneasy feeling, the feeling that I ought to really be paying attention to what's happening here. "I hate to be the one to remind you, but you were completely smitten with him last semester."

Casey snorts. "I wasn't. At least not that much!"

I smile to myself and read the last few sentences on my page. Then I close my book as well and shift a little to turn towards him. The golden light seems to soften the features of his handsome face. He has his eyes half closed, squinting at the sun. Two small slits of sparkling blue. He's lost a bit of weight lately, but it looks good. More mature somehow.

"But you, James," he continues with a frown. "You never liked Rizzo or his crowd. And now..."

"What now?"

"I'm asking you. What changed your mind?"

I'm puzzled by the unexpected question. How am I supposed to answer that? "Well, he's... I dunno." Okay, that was lame. I wince inwardly.

"What? What is he?"

I shrug and longingly glance down at my book. "Interesting?"

"Intriguing. That's what you really mean." Casey sounds more thoughtful than hurt.

I'm quick to shake my head. "He'll never be you."

Whatever it was, it seems to fall off him like snow falls off the trees in spring, and he leans over to kiss me.

"I'm sorry, James. I don't know what's up with me lately. Maybe I'm stressed out because of that paper I have due next week." He throws a dark look into Danny's direction. "But when he's around..."

"You have nothing to worry about, okay?"

He draws in a deep breath and sighs. I watch him for a moment, watching Danny, and I wish I could read his mind. So much has happened between the three of us, and we're all pretending it hasn't. I guess Danny's not the only actor in our little group. I suddenly ask myself how convincing a performance Casey and I are giving. I for one am definitely hiding something, but for the first time I wonder, is he hiding things from me as well?

"But I do worry," Casey finally replies quietly. "I *know* Rizzo wants you, and I think he's used to getting what he wants. And that should worry both of us."

He pauses, and looks away. "Remember last semester? Remember how he played us off against each other? What if it would have worked?"

"He's not gonna do that anymore."

Casey sits up straight and crosses his arms in front of his chest. I can feel a brand-new distance between us that I don't understand. It almost hurts when he looks at me, his eyes dark with suspicion and something else that I can't read. "Isn't he? I think you're wrong to trust him."

"Who says I do?"

He just stares at me, completely serious. "You know you do. But he's not your friend, James. He's nobody's friend but his own."

I don't know why his words upset me, but they do. And I feel the need to defend Danny, although I know that'll be a bad mistake. "You don't know him."

Casey laughs dryly, and for a second I get a glimpse of how much my liking Danny really gets to him. He always pretended that he was okay with it, but now I see that I've been blind. But just how blind have I been? And why does it feel like the sting of his jealousy is not directed at Danny, but at *me*? What are we really talking about here?

Casey's words cut through the distance between us like a whip lashing out at me.

"You don't know him either, James. He's playing you, just like he did me. And what on earth do you think you know about him anyway?"

We sit in cold and uncomfortable silence for a long moment. That was harsh. There was no need for that. But then again, maybe there was. Maybe I deserved it. Am I being loyal to him? Is it enough not to touch, not to kiss, not to make out with someone else, when I still want them? Just where exactly does betrayal start? Does it start where I feel like Danny understands me better than Casey ever could? Or does it already start where I'm priding myself on knowing stuff about Danny Rizzo? Does it start where I feel like I have a right to know? Does it start where I *want* to know?

I look over to the other bench where it's sunny and bright, to the girl whispering something into Danny's ear, and then giggling loudly when a sly grin appears on his lips. It's a good question. What *do* I know about Rizzo?

The answer is easy enough, and nevertheless thoroughly devastating.

"Nothing. You're right. Absolutely nothing."

* * *

"How've you been, Jimmy boy?" Out of nowhere, Danny flops down on the chair next to mine the next afternoon when I'm finally taking a brief break to eat. Yes, even I have to do that occasionally. He snags two fries from my plate and I let him, watching as they disappear in his mouth.

I just shrug. I'm not in the best of moods today. And how does he always seem to know when I need to see him, even before I know myself? Most irritating.

With the large stained-glass windows and the arched ceiling, the cafeteria always reminds me of a chapel. The beams of light falling inside today are mild. Tiny specks of dust are slow-motion waltzing in them. Danny's short hair is shining like a halo around him, and I'm half-waiting for a white dove to come down from heaven and land on his shoulder.

"You not talking to me today?" he asks with that irresistibly charming smile.

I take a sip of my Evian, trying to buy time before I speak. The truth is that I don't know what to say. Casey's words are spinning in my head again. I'd never even realized how little I know about Danny. And I wonder what he would tell me if I asked. The truth? Or a polished version of the truth he tells the adoring public to build the legend of Rizzo? Whoever that is. Am I sitting next to a complete stranger?

"Who are you really?"

I'm aware that that's not the kind of question to start a cafeteria conversation with, but the words left my mouth before I could stop myself.

Danny just looks at me for a long moment, and I can almost see the thoughts behind his eyes. His expression changes from baffled to amused, but then he seems to realize that I'm serious, and his little smile disappears. And he just looks amazed now; his brown eyes are warm.

"That took a while," he finally says quietly.

"You mean, people usually ask this earlier on?" Damn that sarcastic voice of mine. Maybe I'm just surprised that my strange little question seems to actually mean something to him. It does to me, and that makes me feel awkward and vulnerable. I'm not a big fan of this feeling.

"Nobody's ever asked me that, James."

I really do wish he'd stop looking at me. Why didn't I just keep my mouth shut? Why did I have to ask? It feels like I've foolishly crossed a line that I wasn't meant to cross. Or maybe I was, and that's why I'm freaking. Thoughts are roller-coaster riding in my head. I should just get up and leave right now. Turn around and never look back, as long as I still can. In my mind's eye I see that cold, warning look from yesterday in Casey's gaze again, sending a shiver down my spine.

Uncomfortably I pick at my food for a bit, then I finally put my fork down and glance at Danny. I can't *not* ask. I'm sorry, Case.

"So what's your answer?"

Danny holds my eyes and there's a beautiful open smile on his lips. "You're welcome to find out any time."

His words make my heart beat treacherously fast in my chest. For a moment there seems to be a silent exchange between us, some kind of deeper understanding. The world around us fades away, the noise of scraping cutlery on plates and muttered conversations disappears in the background of my mind. I read another answer in his eyes, and that answer says: *You can have everything. You can have all of me.*

Holy shit. What have I begun? How do I get out of this? Do I even want to? What is he trying to tell me? Am I supposed to break up with Casey? Am I to be with him instead? To have an actual relationship with *Rizzo*?

He can't be serious. I'm reading him wrong. I'm imagining things.

"Are you alright?" he asks warmly, and for a moment it really does feel like an entirely different person talking to me.

"Sure. I'm fine. I'm great."

I *have* read him wrong. I must have. He didn't actually tell me that he wanted to be with me. All he did was invite me to get to know him better. And where's a padded cell when you need it?

Danny nods to my plate with a twinkle in his eyes. "Food's getting cold."

"Help yourself."

He moves closer, and we start to eat together. I watch him while I'm chewing, and suddenly I can't help but smile.

No, he's no stranger to me. I have no idea what he is to me, but one thing that the shock just now made me realize is that he means a lot more than I was aware of before. Because a tiny, completely irrational part of me actually *loved* the idea of being with him. And that part is super curious as to what that would be like. The rational part of me can't even imagine, though.

Has he ever actually been in a serious relationship? Is he even capable of it? How would that work when we have absolutely nothing in common?

Crap. This is absurd. I'm going to stop thinking about it right now. I force myself to look away, take another fork full of veggies, and let my gaze wander through the room. And then I absolutely freeze.

Casey is standing in the open door, looking at us from across the room. I have no idea how long he's been there, but my guess is for quite a while.

I slowly raise my hand and wave for him to come over. But he just stands there and looks at me, with a completely unreadable expression on his face. Then he turns around and leaves.

When I turn my head to look at Danny again, his eyes are narrowed slightly as he is looking past me. It takes me a second to realize he's staring at the spot where Casey had been standing. And that barely visible, victorious subzero smile on his lips gives me the creeps.

6 ADDICTIVE

NICK: The ceiling is still white. It was white an hour ago when I collapsed back on my bed, and it's still white as snow now. The only time that it might have been anything other than white were those few times I remember blinking. Otherwise it's been white the whole time.

I can hear people out in the hallway. Hell, I even recognize some of their voices. They could probably come in here if they wanted, I'm pretty sure the door isn't locked. Nothing I could do about it either if they did. I tried moving a few minutes ago I think, and my entire body is like a giant pile of lead. I couldn't even get my head off the bed. That's... sort of funny, really.

Oh, and I thought of something *really* damn funny a while ago. My parents sent me to a shrink back when I was eleven. They were just starting to go through their divorce and they wanted to make sure I got through it okay. Shitty thing to do to a kid, yeah.

He told me that I have an "addictive personality" - can you believe it? Eleven years old! With my parents sleeping in different beds and shouting at each other all the time. Like I cared about addictive personalities. God, that shrink was such an asshole. Three sessions and I refused to go back. I'll never go to another one again.

Guess he sort of knew what he was talking about though, cuz look at me now!

This all started back in high school. And I wouldn't even be thinking about these things if I wasn't high as a kite right now. Damn, that was some good shit I took. Anyway, yeah, been screwed up for a while now. It's never been a bad thing before.

But now, and here's the hilarious part - and if I was more together I'd be *crying* I'd be laughing so hard - I'm addicted to Rizzo.

Rizzo!

I manage to close my eyes at the thought of him, and suddenly it's earlier today and I'm back in his room, covered with sweat and his body.

* * *

We're screwing in his bed, and he's been teasing me for what seems like hours before finally pushing into me, his forehead pressed against my shoulder, breath panting across my skin and drying the sweat there. I can feel the shape of his lips, and that tiny little thing makes me even harder.

But something in the way he's touching me - the way it's different than it has been before... I realize (and it's like someone kicking me in the goddamn head) I'm not the one he's fucking right now.

I almost push him off me, I'm so angry. I don't care who he sleeps with - it's not like that with us. But he'd damn well better pay attention to me when we're doing this.

He's still moving though. And I still can't believe the things he does... I can feel my brain almost leaking out my ear it's so good. But in the second before I lose all capability to think, it's all clear. I know who I'm "playing understudy" for.

And then - oh hell - Rizzo's curving his body against mine, and I'm completely gone.

* * *

I flop back on the bed and turn my face half into the pillow when we're done, trying to breathe slower. I'm going to need to stay like this for a while before I'm able to get up. I have no bones and no muscles, but I really don't give a shit right now.

That's when he laughs at me, and I'm satisfied that the asshole sounds at least a little winded.

"You're taking up my whole bed, Keller. Move your scrawny ass over." I feel a jab in my ribs, but it isn't *that* hard, so I know he's not actually upset.

"Screw you, Rizzo. I'm not moving for a while." I laugh.

"Besides, I was under the impression that you enjoyed my scrawny ass." The memory of him thinking of someone else jumps back into my brain and I stop laughing.

I feel the bed shift and fingers on my skin before one of my earrings is tugged - almost too hard. I wince into the cotton of the pillowcase before he heaves himself up, making some soft comment about baby goths invading his bed. I manage to raise my arm enough to flip him off, my hand hovering in midair even after I've delivered my message.

There's a familiar sound that I can't quite place, and he laughs again on a breathy exhale. I realize he must've gone across the room because I can hear him coming back towards the bed now. I open my eyes to see him standing there in a pair of unbuttoned jeans, denim and skin, smoking a cigarette and making it look completely incredible. He takes another drag and reaches over to wrap my fingers around it. My skin gives a little shiver even at that contact, but I try not to show it. I lift that hand to my mouth, take a long, grateful drag, and blink. Looking past his legs I see my black jeans thrown over a chair, the corner of a pack sticking out of the front pocket.

"Asshole," I say, but there's no heat to it and he grins down at me. I finally let my arm fall and it drapes across my ribcage, the still-lit cigarette threatening to drop from my fingers. He takes it back before I do drop it, crossing back to his desk where he leans while he finishes it off. I can feel his gaze on me even when I look down to rub at a nipple piercing that got flipped around earlier when I yanked my shirt off. Done with that, I close my eyes again and sigh. I can still feel him watching me - it crawls against my skin. I swallow against the rising lump in my throat that I don't want to acknowledge.

"Riz-"

"You can't stay," he says, and I nod to myself. I knew it was going to be one of these days.

"I've got-"

"Plans. I know." You bastard. My voice doesn't shake, something I'm glad for, but it's colder than I'd meant it to be. I push myself up from the bed, ignoring the unsteady way the room turns. I don't know if it's from my change in position or from something else, and I don't particularly care. I spot my boxers on the floor a few feet away and begin the awkward process of re-collecting my clothing. I always hate it, and it doesn't put me in a good mood, no matter how amazing a lay Rizzo is.

"You always going to do that now?" I ask him when I'm dressed again. We don't talk much, not about anything serious at least, and I'm not sure what makes me ask this now. He pulls a shirt on to cover that damn beautiful body of his and raises an eyebrow at me.

"What?"

"Fucking him when you're balls deep inside of me."

He stops and looks at me - looks *through* me. I can't breathe when the bastard does that, and I'm sure he knows it. And does it for that reason. But I almost think he's actually going to talk to me about this...

Then his eyes, I don't know, they change or something. And he grins at me. He's done that before. He's *always* doing it. Grinning at me. Laughing at me. Like there's some huge joke that I'm not in on.

This time though... This time it feels different.

And not just him laughing at me, but this whole thing. Him. It feels different than anyone else I've slept with in the past few years. He's the only one that's been around more than a day or two - we've been doing this for weeks now, and I'm still saying 'yes' and jumping up to follow him every time he shows up.

Maybe that's it. Someone like Danny Rizzo is bothering to come find *me*, even if it is just for a quick screw before going on with the rest of his day. And I'm basking in the shit like it's sunshine.

Not only that, but when I *don't* see him now, there's that same pull in my brain - that pressure I get when I've been sober for too long. Apparently I've gone and become addicted to a person. He's in my blood like everything else I'm doing.

And I realize something he must've known for a while now. That it doesn't matter what his answer is. Or even if he answers at all. I'm not going anywhere anytime soon. I'm as dependent on him now as I am on what Marc sells me.

It makes me angry again, knowing I've let myself get to this point. I'm such an idiot. And I need to get out of here - get somewhere that I can disconnect and forget what a huge pussy I am.

I turn toward the door, my body doing its best to keep up with my brain. There's a weight on my arm and I look down to see a hand wrapped around it above the leather wrist cuff. I look over my shoulder just enough to see his dark eyes focused on me. Between his gaze and his grip, my skin goes hot and tight and I barely suppress a shiver.

"Tomorrow." There's not even a question in his voice. Only statement, like it's a sure thing. Like *I'm* a sure thing. And even though I know now that it's true, it still grates against the little pride I have left in this.

"Fuck you."

"Tomorrow." An echo of that grin again. Like this is a game for him.

"I'm not your whore, Rizzo." But I know that's a lie, and so does he. He takes a step and slides his body up against mine. I blink slowly enough that my eyes are still closed when his whisper slips hot and dark against my skin.

"Tomorrow."

I swallow and shudder at the feel of his mouth suddenly at the corner of mine. He's kissed me all of two or three times, and it was shocking and demanding each time. And there's no way he doesn't know that I love it.

"Tomorrow," I whisper back at him, and I can *feel* his smile against my lips. I lean in to close that last distance, but he's suddenly gone, the left side of my body chilled now without him there. By the time my brain catches up to me and I force my eyes open again, he's already back across the room, grabbing a towel and some clothes like I'm not even there.

I slam his door on my way out, like a child. Part of me is beginning to hate this whole thing.

But I'll be back tomorrow, that's for damn sure.

* * *

I blink my eyes back open and stare at my ceiling again. Maybe it wouldn't be so bad, if he weren't so wrapped up in that guy from the cafe. Who obviously already has a boyfriend. Or whatever. And Rizzo doesn't have the brain in his head to look around at anyone else.

Not that I'm jealous. I'm not, dammit! There's no ties holding Rizzo to me, and I'll be damned before I'll admit that there are ties holding me to him.

But shit. My skin crawls when I don't see him. The backs of my eyes itch and I get this pain in my chest. And the only word I have to describe this shit is 'withdrawal'. From a person!

Holy crap, the room is spinning again. God, does that stuff feel good. Like the whole world is turning. And turning right around me. Whatever Marc brought me was exactly what I needed. I can hardly feel my body at all.

I'd called him up when I got back to my room. Marc, not Rizzo. I don't need Rizzo any more. I don't. But if I don't have him… I'm realizing that I need something else to replace it. Him. Something strong.

"Take me somewhere, Marc," was all I'd needed to say, and that gravel-wrecked voice was laughing at me through the phone, promising to be over in ten.

Nine minutes later, he'd handed something to me with a grin. I paid him without even asking. I don't want to know what he brings me. It always works, so I don't need to know. And it's not like I need to worry about money. My parents never blink an eye when I need more. Like they're paying me off so that they can forget about me the rest of the time.

Marc made some comment about something screwing with me. I didn't need to hear it and kicked him out of my room. I'd already knocked back that handful of whatever he'd brought me and I was starting to spin. Couldn't get the door locked, but at least I got it closed and got to my bed.

I've been here ever since. Not sure how long. Doesn't matter, really. Not today.

* * *

I woke up about 30 minutes ago. At least I think so. I'm pretty sure. Sometime between the time I finally passed out and the time I woke up (and I have no clue how long it's been), I must've come to just enough to take my clothes off, because I'm only wearing my boxers now. Either that or someone did come into my room. To strip me down and leave me in bed. Yeah right.

Anyway, my head's mainly clear right now. I could probably eat something, but laying here is too nice to bother hauling my ass up for food. Only I'm pretty sure it's a Tuesday afternoon. And I think I've got one of Jeff's classes this afternoon. One of my actual drama classes. So I know I should get up. These are the important ones... And being a drama class, I might just see Rizzo around in the hallways or something.

Shit, I can't stop thinking about him. This is insane.

Rizzo with his skin. And those eyes. And that damn shit-eating grin of his. And his hands. And his body. The way he moves. His voice. The little sounds he makes and the way his breath catches when he's inside-

Damn! Now I've got morning wood and it's not even morning!

Screw this shit, I'm going to class!

* * *

I didn't have a lot of time to get dressed and get to class, and now I'm sitting here wishing I'd at least grabbed some coffee, because Jeff looks like he's ready to pop. And it's got to be something big to make him that excited.

He's waited until the end of class though. Now we're all gathered around and waiting for him to let us in on the little secret. Most of us are at least second years and have known him for a while. So it's pretty much silent when he starts to talk.

"Now I know a lot of you had heard rumors that we were going to be doing a Miller performance, but that was only my backup plan in case we needed it. But the original plan has been okayed by the University.

"I'm sure by now you've all seen the posters or heard about our Bicentennial celebration. Woodhaven was founded two hundred years ago, and to mark the occasion, the administration is planning a cycle of events throughout the year." I can hear some moron in back getting excited already, when Jeff hasn't even told us a damn thing yet that any of us didn't already know.

"The drama department is going to be part of the celebrations. Instead of having two small shows this year, there is just going to be one large show in the spring. Plus, we'll be combining with other departments - dance and music - to do a multi-departmental performance…"

He actually pauses for dramatic effect. "…of Hamlet."

I swear some bitch gasps in excitement. Really. If I weren't so wiped out, I'd roll my eyes.

Not that it isn't exciting. It's majorly exciting. And I need to get a part. I know that right now.

Everyone in the class has started whispering to people around them, and I can see Jeff smiling in satisfaction. Then he turns and sees me looking at him. He waves me over as he dismisses the rest of the class.

As I walk up to him, I hear someone start to talk about who should be cast in what parts. Someone mentions Rizzo as Hamlet. It figures. He's not even here and the world revolves around him.

"Nick…" People are still leaving the room, and Jeff talks only loud enough for me to hear. "You doing okay?"

I blink at him. What sort of question is that? Am I doing okay? Do I look like I'm *not* doing okay? I'm in the prime of my life, right?

"Yeah," I hear myself saying. "Fine. Why?"

He looks at me like I'm lying to him. Looks me over a few times. "Come on, Nick. Pull yourself together. You can get a good part in this production if you try. If you keep your act clean. If you can keep *yourself* clean. Drop that crap you're doing, whatever it is."

"I don't know what you're talking-"

"Don't even try it, Nick. I've seen a dozen students like you. The ones that clean themselves up go on to be amazing. The ones that don't… they fall off the radar. One way or another." He's got this intense look going, and I can't think of anything to say. So I just nod.

He looks at me a little more, and I just blink at him. He finally shakes his head and sighs.

"Go. Try to remember what I said. You could be one of the amazing ones, Nick."

And what the hell do you say to something like that? I start to walk out, but he calls after me.

"Auditions for the show are in a week, Nick. Don't disappoint me."

I nod. Don't disappoint him. Right.

7 BODY LANGUAGE

DANNY: Brains can be sexy. Trust me on this. Had nothing better to do, so I went to the large auditorium to check out random English celebrity prof's lecture, because I knew James would be there. The room's crammed-full, but I have no difficulty spotting J. Sometimes I go Every Breath You Take-ing, I just love to watch him when he isn't aware of it. I'm fascinated with his body language. More often than not it's the only clue to what he's feeling inside. He's a hard one to read, but I love the challenge.

Tea Time ends his lecture with a smug, superior smile. When he asks if there are any questions, you just know he doesn't actually expect any of us grunts to have understood a single word of his complex jargon. That's when J slowly raises his hand, and the entire room turns to look at him, whispering.

I can literally feel him tensing underneath his cool facade, but he sounds matter-of-fact when he speaks. He's sitting there in his shabby gray jacket that can only pass as vintage if you look at it with eyes of love, the epitome of geekiness. But something incredible happens when his calm voice fills the room. Suddenly he has a sharp, intellectual authority to him that makes everyone fall silent. And screw me like it's Friday night, he just about rips Tea Time's theory apart by showing a significant flaw with one brilliant little question.

The Brit's not amused, and quickly dismisses the crowd before dashing away to probably never be seen on this campus again. And I'm *turned on*.

"Congrats, Pulitzer." I grin at J as I waylay him on his way out.

"On what?" he frowns, then he does a slightly amused double take. "Hold on. What are *you* doing here?"

Three guesses, Jimmy Boy. I don't really give a shit about

Cross-cultural philosophy and comparative politics. "Just heard that you're the new editor in chief." Of the school paper, that is. "Thought I'd stop by."

J stops short. "Who the hell told you? No one's supposed to know that yet!"

I grin. "Sorry. Can't reveal my sources."

He gives me a look, but smiles, and we stroll down the hallway towards the building's exit side by side. It's really noisy in here. Everyone's discussing the lecture, and people are looking at James, not at me for a change as they walk past. And somehow that feels good.

"Let's go somewhere," I suggest.

"No way."

"To talk", I clarify and roll my eyes. Our eyes meet briefly and once again I wonder what's going on behind his gray eyes.

Still he hesitates, but then he sighs. "Alright."

It's one of those rare, bright fall days where you just have to love the season, and there's some kind of lazy, laid back feeling all over campus. On a whim I stop next to the only empty park bench on our way to the cafe. It's too beautiful to be inside, and I don't feel like sharing him right now. James shrugs when I nod towards the seat.

He looks pensive when we sit down, and then he smiles a little. "We sat here before."

"Have we?"

"Last semester. You told me I was pathetic to wait for Casey."

I laugh. I vaguely remember. I think it was one of the first times we spoke alone. "Did not."

"Did too. And you were right. I never should have hesitated that long. But I was scared."

"*You* were scared?" I smile to myself. The first time I saw him, I thought, what an arrogant ass. There's something incredibly aloof about the way he holds himself, and something almost cryptic. The way he hunches slightly just doesn't go with the hostile air of distance about him. Real aggression is extroverted, not introverted. You can't study acting, that's what Jeff says. You can study people. And I've been doing that my whole life. When I first met James, I felt that something was wrong with this picture. It sparked my interest. That, and the fact that in spite of his bad taste in clothes, J's damn hot, with those incredible lips and a small perfect ass that just makes my head spin. And the way he kept pushing me back just added to the fun of the chase. But damn, now it's me who's caught in the trap.

James looks at me with intense eyes. "You think that's funny?"

"You do know that *you're* the one who scares people 'round here, don't you?"

He arches an eyebrow, and I swear he has no clue how sexy that is. "I scare people?"

"You're terrifying, Jimmy Boy. That Brit's flawless career is ruined because of you."

"I'm sure he'll recover." His voice just drips with wonderful dry sarcasm.

I nonchalantly put my arm on the back of the bench behind him when I turn towards him. "People respect you, don't you know? There's no need to make yourself small."

He gazes at me with his usual frown, and I realize that he really isn't aware of the fact. Sometimes I wonder what it's like to live in James Land. How can you not notice something like that? Is that Simon's doing?

J decides it's time to change the subject. "Rumor has it that you're to play Hamlet in that huge production they're planning."

I grin. "I'm not supposed to talk to the press."

James smiles briefly, unimpressed. "So are you?"

"*Jeff* wants me to."

He leans back a little and looks at me like I'm tripping. "Hell, this is one of the most prestigious roles in theatre history and you're having second thoughts?"

I shrug. Can we go back to talking about him? "Not sure if I see myself playing a wimpy prince who can't get his act together."

For the first time today, James laughs, and his eyes soften a bit. "What would you have Hamlet do?"

"I dunno. Probably screw Claudius and afterwards tell the queen what a faithful new husband she has."

"Clever. I suppose she'd then heroically commit suicide. Which would lead to Claudius being killed by an angry mob."

"And Hamlet and Horatio can finally get it on."

J laughs. "Well, you never know. Shakespeare might have liked that!"

We grin at each other, and I wonder why it always takes me so long to get through to him.

"Seriously though, there are so many ways to play Hamlet, Danny. He can be played passionate too. You can bring the same intensity to the role you had last year as Lord Goring. The audience loved you."

"Did you?"

James shrugs with a small grin. "I'm hardly objective. I get a hard-on when I see you on stage. But yes, I did."

Okay, new rule: You don't mention hard-ons when you're sitting this close to me, Jimmy. You turn me on enough just being here. And if you were anyone else, there'd be no prisoners. But you're you, and I can't do that. You got me by the balls, squeezing real hard. One way or another, I'm gonna explode soon enough. And that moment's getting closer as we speak.

"They're going for a combination of traditional and modern with the costumes. Tina showed me an early sketch. All black and lots of leather."

J blinks and swallows. "That's it, you're doing this!"

I laugh. Yeah, suffer like me. I'm sick of substitutes. You're the real thing, you're what I really want, and you know it.

"You're gonna kill them." James says quietly, and I know he believes it. And that means a lot. Right now, it means everything.

"As long as I'm killing you, Jimmy Boy."

When he looks back at me, I know that he wants to have me right now. It's clear to him, it's clear to me, and this is so messed up I can't even say.

Keller has become my favorite stand-in to work off the frustration. He's perfect. He'll do anything. And still, it's never enough. It's delicious, and still it doesn't come close.

I look at J, and I don't mind him knowing what he's doing to me. I want him to know. I want him to read me like I've learned to read him.

"I gotta go," he mumbles, and shifts uncomfortably. He looks sad all of a sudden.

"There's got to be a better way to do this," I say quietly.

"What are you proposing?"

I shrug. "No more sneaking around. You, me, coffee, how does that sound?"

His eyes find mine, and he looks mildly terrified. "That sounds scarily like a date."

I grin. "Does it now?"

"Are you being serious?"

"No", I lie with a smile. "But I can tell you I'm not loving being treated like your dirty little secret. Mostly since it's not actually that dirty."

"Danny…"

"Yes?" I lean closer and he gives me a half-hearted frown.

"Damn it." He sighs helplessly. He thinks about it for a long moment. Then he nods like he's just made a really big decision. "I suppose if it weren't an actual date…"

I grin. Gotcha.

* * *

Two days later we're sitting outside Cafe Plato, having said coffee. And it's weird at first, but after a while, I can see that he's starting to relax and enjoy himself. He tells me about an art project he's writing about for the school paper, and somehow the conversation turns to the Louvre. I tell him that the Mona Lisa's tiny and overrated, and that it's too crowded to have a proper look at her anyway. But James has such a yearning in his eyes, and I can tell just how badly he wants to see for himself.

"I prefer the Musee d'Orsay anyway," I say, almost apologetically. Here we are, having an actual conversation. Hell will freeze over any minute now.

"They have some Van Goghs and Gaugins there, don't they?" When I nod, he thoughtfully looks into the distance. "I like the Impressionists too."

"You're gonna go there some day. You'll get that scholarship, and then you can see it all for yourself." I can't believe myself, saying shit like that, and meaning it.

He looks up and frowns slightly. "I hope so."

"Well, if all else fails, *I* can take you."

"You wanna be my sugar daddy?" James grins.

"Oh hell yeah." We laugh.

"Have you been to Italy? Spain?"

"Yeah."

"Son of a bitch. You've been everywhere!"

Pretty much. Everywhere you want to go, and probably to quite a few places you seriously don't.

"You have to tell me. You have to tell me everything." His eyes are shining with excitement. And right now, I honestly want him to get that damned Berlin scholarship, regardless of what how much that would suck for me. What's up with that?

"How much time have you got?" I ask with a grin.

"Well, I'll make the time."

Son of a bitch, I think my heart just skipped a beat. Nobody has ever done that to me. I look at him, and I just *ache*. How is he doing this to me? Things are getting so intense; I've never felt this way. I've never felt like this about anyone. Just sitting here, talking, listening to his voice, looking at him. I'm not even thinking of sex, and it's about the best thing ever. Hell if I know how that's possible. My head is spinning, and suddenly I have absolutely no idea what to say or do. Oh crap.

He tilts his head to the side and looks at me, a little smile dancing on his lips.

"What?" I clear my throat.

"Nothing. You just..." His smile deepens, and he seems embarrassed. "You just had the most beautiful look on your face." He frowns at his own words.

"Hold on. That was a compliment." My heart is beating like crazy.

"Nope. Just stating a fact."

I chuckle softly. "Well, don't. Facts are not welcome here. Just flattery."

"You'll never get that from me, Mister."

"In that case, we're through."

He laughs, and takes a sip of his cappuccino, eyeing me over the brim of the cup. His eyes are sparkling, and I swear he's never looked so pretty, it's ridiculous. I'm finding it way too hard to breathe for my liking.

"Are you sure this is not a date?" he asks jokingly.

I wink at him. "Are you?"

* * *

It's a couple of days later, and I light a smoke when I leave one of Jeff's totally important meetings. Keller tries to catch my eye as he pushes past me, and I give him a little grin. Later.

"Hey, Rizzo. You got a minute?" someone calls to me on my other side, and I see Mills coming towards me. Great. Just what I needed on my so far completely boring and James-less day.

"For you, Mills, I got two."

I let him lead me a bit down the corridor to the side. Bright, colorful posters advertising the big Halloween bash in two weeks are all around, looking cheap on the massive stone walls of the old building.

We stop near a window and I hop up on the broad sill. Casey seems to briefly contemplate doing the same, but decides against it. He's not happy about having to look up at me, and dude, that's the point. It's raining outside, and the drops are rapping against the glass; the light is dim and pale. With its arched ceilings and renaissance look, this place always reminds me of a monastery in Italy I visited once, but Woodhaven isn't nearly as old. It's a beautiful fake, and ain't most things? It's very quiet now that everyone else has left, and Mills' eyes are resting on me.

"Big production this year. I hear you're gonna be in that play."

I blow smoke into his direction. "You after an autograph?"

"Thanks, I'll pass. I need to talk to you."

We're thirty seconds into this conversation and I'm bored out of my head already. I suppress a sigh. "Fine. About what?"

"I think you'll be able to guess."

"Aww. Sorry, Mills, I already got a date for Halloween."

"Oh, shut up. I'd like to talk to you about James."

And here he does something I did not expect, because he

hops up beside me after all. The window glass is cool against my back, and I look at Mills with interest. He does have some backbone, even if it only shows every couple of light-years.

"Let's hear it then."

His gaze quickly drops to the tips of his shoes, then his eyes focus on the opposite wall. He's got a determined expression on his face. "I want you to back off."

I almost laugh out loud, but bite my tongue. I'm having such a deja-vu. "Back off yourself", I suggest with a grin.

I earn a dark glance. "Why should I? He's in love with me."

"Has he ever actually *told* you that he is?"

His eyes narrow at my comment, and I know I hit the mark. "So what? Has he told *you*? What makes you think you got a right to try and come between us?"

I smile. "I wouldn't be able to, if things were so perfect, would I?"

Casey takes a deep breath and sighs. It irritates me, getting all kinds of weird, contrary signals from him. Does he want to kick my ass, or sob in my lap? We sit in silence for a moment. When he speaks again, he sounds gloomy.

"Why does everything have to be so complicated? I *hate* this entire situation."

"I'm not loving it either," I admit, and that seems to surprise him.

He looks at me, then he reaches over and simply takes the cigarette from my hand to take a drag. I watch as the smoke curls in front of his mouth and vanishes in the air. He hands the butt back to me, and now it's him who's watching as I exhale. I stare into his eyes, and unconsciously he licks his lips. Pretty.

"It was a mistake, that night, wasn't it?" he asks quietly.

"Which one? The night we made out, or the night on the beach?"

"Both."

I tilt my head a little, amused. "You don't regret it, Mills. Cut the shit."

"I don't. That's why it was a mistake."

I knew it. So. Not. Over. Me. A content grin steals onto my face. How brilliant is that? And how useful? I realize that this just might be it. The opportunity I've been waiting for for months.

He clears his throat, then he jumps down from the window sill. "I gotta go. It's no use trying to talk to you anyway."

I follow quickly, and corner him, moving in close. I'm taller than him, which always works to my advantage. He looks up at me, and the anger is all too obvious now. Anger and confusion. He never knew what he wanted, that's his problem.

"What? Why can't you just leave us alone, Rizzo?"

"It's you who came to me. So what do you really want, Mills?"

He pulls himself up to his full height and manages to hold my eyes, something tortured and hurt flickering in them. "Who'd want to be with you, when you're such a player?"

Ouch. Now that's fifty points to Hufflepuff. Great. I realize that it's not about sex with him at all. He's not like that. And I've always been crap at handling these things. Everyone knows what they're getting into with me. I don't make false promises. Even Keller, who'd get addicted to chewing gum if it paid any attention to him, knows the deal, and doesn't expect me to get all warm and mushy with him. Don't mess with me if you can't take the heat. And you can't take it, Mills, you know you can't.

I step back to let him go, but he stays where he is, and as he looks at me, his expression softens. "Why do you have to be like this, Danny?"

I smile vaguely. "It's gotta be the genes."

When he moves forward, I'm relieved that he wants to leave, but to my complete surprise, he doesn't step past me, but closer to me. And before I have time to react, he softly presses his lips against mine.

Shit.

He pulls me towards him with gentle hands, and I'm really not sure why I let him. Something about his tenderness seems to render me unable to push him back, even though it's what I want to do. What the hell?

And then there's something in his kiss that makes me realize for the first time what James sees in the boy. Because I suddenly get that Casey's on a mission to save my soul. Does he believe that he can make me a better person? That's just so wrong, and sweet, and completely like him that I can't help feeling some sympathy.

I don't actively return the kiss, but all the same my lips part slightly and I let it happen. I look at him, with his eyes closed, so careful and emotional. I'd taint you, boy. I'd break you.

Casey steps back, and chews on his lower lip for a moment, a thousand questions in his eyes. You know you're at my mercy now, Mills. You knew before you kissed me.

I could turn on the spot to find James and tell him what you just did. This would also be a fitting moment to let you know that I slept with your boyfriend during summer break.

But I don't.

"I'm not sure why I did that," Casey says quietly, more confused now than before.

I should use this to my advantage. He's practically asking for it, right? This is the best shot I've had so far at driving them apart for once and for all. He wouldn't even try to deny it if I told James. J would never forgive him. But there's something in Casey's eyes... it gets to me. And the thought of how much hearing about this would hurt James doesn't help either. Hell, not at all.

Goddamn. Here I am, making a decision that I know I'll regret. It's gonna hurt, Mills, but it's for the best. For all of us. I look at him, and take a drag on my smoke.

"I don't give a shit about you, Mills. Never have, never will. You get that?"

He inhales sharply, staring at me. I don't know what he expected me to say or do, but this was definitely not it. He looks small, and lost, and so very wounded, and I almost can't bear the sight of it. For crying out loud, I hope those aren't actual tears clouding his eyes. Come on.

"Yes", he finally says quietly, beaten. "I get it."

I don't stay to watch the whole tragedy of his sad existence unfold, but turn around and leave him standing there. No way I'm letting him know that he got through to me.

It's got nothing to do with Mills. This is all about J. As I walk down the corridor towards the exit of the building, I realize that I don't want James to break up with Mills because of some shitty ass kiss. I want him to break up with Mills because he wants to be with me. I don't even do relationships. Period. Or so I thought up until now. But none of that seems to matter anymore. I just want to let myself feel the way I feel about him, no more holding back. I want to be with that strange, wonderful geek all the time, and be confused, and amazed. I want to get the sweaty hands and the stupid racing heartbeat, and feel like an idiot, but a happy idiot to be sure. I want to be with James. I have to be with James. Because I'm crazy about him. Because I am *in love*.

I gotta find Keller. And this'd better be one hell of a fuck to get this shit out of my system and help me think clearly again.

8 TOUCHED

NICK: I know I wasn't imagining things - I saw him smile at me earlier when were walking out of Jeff's meeting. And that smile can only mean one thing. Which is why I'm sitting on the steps outside the dorm, smoking a cigarette, studying my callback audition piece, and freezing because the steps are concrete and it just stopped raining, so they're damp and really cold. I don't care if the air has warmed up a little, the steps sure as hell haven't.

But I've been sitting here for close to twenty minutes now, and no sign of Rizzo. Has he decided that he's done with me? Screw that! And besides, if he has, what was that little grin about earlier?

What if he wasn't actually looking at me? I pull my knees up and hunch my shoulders, taking another drag on my smoke. Am I wasting my time here? He could be screwing someone else right now, and I'm sitting here like an idiot, waiting for him and freezing my balls off.

Fine. I'm *not* waiting for him. I'm just sitting here and studying my audition piece and not waiting for anyone. I'm doing it outside on the steps because I *want* to, dammit. And I'm working on this now because Jeff hasn't decided who he wants in what parts yet. Except for Hamlet. They're not even holding callbacks for Hamlet. Rizzo's got it. Obviously. Wherever he is right now.

Where the hell *is* he?

It doesn't matter. Focus, Nick. Horatio. It's the part I want. I can do it, too. I know I can. I just need to convince Jeff. It shouldn't be a problem. I already have this bit memorized, I just need to practice it some more to get it absolutely perfect.

I smooth the paper out again. I have an actual copy of Hamlet somewhere, but Jeff was handing these copies out at the meeting today, and I figured what the hell. Couldn't hurt to take one, right?

One hand holding my smoke, the other flat against the paper, and I realize they're both shaking. Well forget this, if Rizzo's not coming, I'm going to go and make good use of my time.

Maybe *I'll* find someone else to sleep with. I've done it before. Plenty of times. *All* the time before Rizzo came along.

I take my last drag and drop the butt on the ground, but before I can grind it out with my toe, someone else is stepping on it, their shadow blocking the tiny bit of sun breaking through the clouds, and making me shiver. I tip my head back, and hey, look who finally decided to show up.

"About time, you asshole." I'm practically growling at him, but I can't bring myself to care if he knows that I've been waiting this whole time. For his part, he just raises one of his perfect eyebrows at me.

"You want to come upstairs, Keller?" I squint up at him and frown. Is he asking me?

That's... different. I don't think he's ever really *asked* before.

I stare up at him, but he doesn't say anything else. After a few seconds I nod and stand.

"Yeah, alright then."

* * *

He gets his door open and pulls me through, but before I can even turn, he's reached past me to push it closed again, stepping in until I'm forced to move back. Two unsteady steps and I'm trapped with the door against my back and Rizzo all along my front. Before I lose track of everything else, I reach my hand back to relock his door from the inside. He grins at me and presses close, his eyes going darker when I grin back at him.

He ducks his head and leans in quickly, and the lips against my neck are hungry and hot, the hands pressing my hips into the wood of the door stronger than I remember, and my head drops back against the door harder than I'd intended. I wince, wondering if I'll have a bump there, but then I feel teeth scraping along my skin and I couldn't care less about a stupid bump on my head.

But then, before we really get anywhere, he pulls away. I open my eyes, my fist clinging to the front of his shirt, ready to complain, but I can't get the words to come out.

Because he's looking at me now. Really *looking* at me. Right there, almost too close for me to focus on him, but I can see him smile a little. Not that usual grin that I know means the bastard's laughing at me - this is new.

But before I can translate this new smile, his lips are back on my neck, and hell, the way they feel against my skin... it's different. And if he had always touched me like this, I would've been completely gone a long time ago.

Because I realize that I finally have his attention. All of it. And *that* is almost better than anything else he's ever done.

I'm already so lost in the feel of him that it takes me a second to realize that he's talking to me, mouthing the words against the side of my neck.

"We're not doing this against my door."

He's stepping back, and the words still haven't quite made it to my brain, because all I can do is whimper and wonder where he's going and why he's not touching me any more. He helps me out by hooking his fingers in the waistband of my jeans and yanking me away from the door before practically dragging me halfway across the room. I finally realize what he's said and follow him willingly over to the bed, where he's already sitting and waiting for me. He catches me by the hips when I get close, pulling me in and sliding his hands slowly up under my shirt. I try to be helpful and pull the shirt off, but then I just stare down at the way his lips are moving against the skin of my stomach. I blink a few times, trying to process what I'm seeing, what Rizzo's doing. He hasn't done anything for himself, not yet at least, and usually I'm on my knees by now. His whole attitude confuses me just enough that it takes a while before the thoughts sort themselves into words in my brain.

"Rizzo... what-" My voice cracks when he tugs the black denim down far enough to bite at the tattoo low on my hip, the fingers of his other hand pressing hard into my skin to steady me. I swallow hard - a few times - and try again.

"Riz - what're you doing?"

He smirks up at me. "Shut up, Nick."

Shut up. I nod. Shutting up sounds like a *very* good idea.

* * *

I'm still catching my breath, waiting for my legs to be strong enough to walk on, because while I'd love to lay here all day, it's usually not too long before he's kicking me out the door. There's a reflection of something moving across Rizzo's wall, and it sort of distracts me as I try not to look over at him. I'm not sure what he's doing - just laying there or something. I don't think he's asleep, but I'll be damned if I'm going to look over to find out.

I can't help wondering when this silence is going to break with the inevitable command for me to leave (and it's always a command, never doubt that), but after a few minutes he sits up and leans back against the headboard. I hear his lighter flare, and then the smoke drifts in front of the reflection I'm watching. It's actually really pretty, and I almost forget about who's laying next to me as I watch it.

"Callbacks later this week."

I blink in surprise at the words and look up at him. He takes a drag and raises his eyebrows. This feels like… is this the beginning of a conversation? What the hell?

"Yeah…" I'm real articulate, but how am I supposed to respond to this?

"Ready for them?"

I blink again. This isn't normal. Not for Rizzo. Maybe this *isn't* Rizzo. It looks like him. Feels like him when I touch his skin. But Rizzo's never voluntarily started a conversation between us. Especially after we've just fucked.

"Working on it, yeah. Fine tuning and stuff like that."

He nods and the side of his mouth quirks up into a more familiar, arrogant little smile. "Well who better to fine tune with than Hamlet himself?"

* * *

I wake up with my face pressed against skin and it takes me

nearly a full minute to backtrack and realize where I am. And whose skin this is. What's even more confusing is that I'm the first one awake. The few other times (very few) that I've actually stayed the night with Rizzo, he's been the first one to wake up.

This morning, though, Rizzo's still asleep, which means I can lay here for a while and wake up properly and get a chance to really look at him. And I realize something I should've known before. Rizzo seems like a completely different person when he's asleep. He doesn't have that annoying smirk he sometimes gets. He doesn't have that grin that makes half this goddamn school weak at the knees. Including me, I admit it. And he doesn't have that hard edge to him that I sometime see. He doesn't have any of that shit.

I can see my hand trembling where it's resting on his chest. And it's been a hell of a long time since I had that smoke on the stairs out front, and even longer since I had anything else.

And I need something after last night, and whatever the hell was going on. I know it's probably some new twisted game Rizzo's playing, but shit, it's working. I'm worse off now than before.

I don't know if it's the way I'm shaking now, or something else, but I can tell that Rizzo's starting to wake up. I don't want to see him change back into who he is when he's awake. I can't deal with it right now.

Because if it's *not* a game...

Hell, if it's not a game, then he really was paying attention to me, and I am in way over my head. I slip out of the bed, grab my clothes, and I'm out the door before he even opens his eyes.

* * *

I can just make out Jeff's face in the front row, watching all of us up on the stage.

We're all good actors. Every one of us up here is. We're so good, in fact, that not one of us looks nervous, but you can feel it in the air. We all know what this role means, the sorts of people that'll be at the show, what it could do for us, and every person on this stage wants it as much as the next one.

And why do *I* want it? Shit, that should be obvious... This is the one thing I have that I'm good at. And it has nothing to do with either one of my parents. It's the one thing where I can get up in front of people and *make* them watch me. I can say "screw you" to my parents and people love me for it. It's the best job I can imagine.

If I can only convince Jeff to give me the role. I wish I knew what he's looking for - what he's expecting of us and of the part. It would make this audition a whole lot easier.

Of course, that's why he hasn't dropped any hints at all. He wants to see what *we* come up with. Brilliant asshole.

At least my hands are steady, though. I had to tear my entire room apart this morning before my shower, but I managed to find a tiny emergency stash I'd hidden who knows how long ago. Lucky thing, because I seriously doubt that Horatio is supposed to be as twitchy as I was earlier.

Now though, now I'm loose and relaxed, except for that pit of nerves in my stomach that comes with every audition. Everything I talked about and practiced with Rizzo is right there in my brain...

* * *

"It's not there yet. You've got the lines but it doesn't sound right." I can feel the bed *almost* moving, so I tip my head back and follow the long line of his body up and see that he's shaking his head at me. I just blink at him and relax again, looking at the wall across the room.

We're lying on his bed, completely naked, talking about Shakespeare and auditions. He's still propped up against the headboard, my audition piece held loosely in one hand. I'm using his thigh as a pillow, lying with one foot hanging off the end of the bed.

"Come on, Keller, do you want this part or not?"

I don't look up at him, but I frown at the question. "Of course I do."

"Then *show me*. Your Horatio's boring. And I'm not going to let a boring Horatio on *my* stage." He sits up more, and I shift over to let him, turning myself so that I can watch him.

He takes just a second to look at me, then he's moving and suddenly on top of me, propped up on those amazing arms, and I've barely had time to blink. He grins.

"You need more passion. Intensity."

"I need more passion? Right. And what does the 'master actor' suggest I do to *get* this intensity?"

He laughs at me and shifts his hips, and I'm gasping and arching like the whore he makes me into. His voice is suddenly in my head and running along my body, all at the same time.

"Say the lines again, Nick."

And I do, while he keeps moving against me. I finish them with my fingers digging into Rizzo's shoulders, and I don't care that he's laughing, because the lines have feeling, and passion, and Rizzo's a goddamn genius.

…And now if I can only remember exactly how that felt, I can't go wrong with this audition.

I see Jeff raising his eyebrows at me, and apparently it's my turn. I grin at him and step forward, and he nods at me.

Here we go…

9 HALLOWEEN SON

JAMES: I hate Halloween. With a passion. Not because it's a Celtic holiday turned into a ridiculous marketing gag for candy companies, but because the day where everyone gets to dress up as cowboys, monsters, and fairytale princesses happens to be my birthday.

We had an unwritten law back home, and that law said that October 31 had to be made the most miserable day of the year for me. Something really shitty always happened, and I'm not talking about everyday *oh I just spilled my milk* shitty. Really shitty. *Can someone just put me out of my misery* shitty.

Even with Simon gone, this year looks quite promising for shitty things to happen. I can almost feel it, lurking in the background and snickering in a creepy, manic way. Next week I'm gonna be told whether I get to go to Berlin or not. Next week my entire life is gonna get changed around - or not. And like I need even more pressure, Casey has been acting *weird* lately.

I don't know, sometimes I miss the old times when we were "just friends". Everything seemed so much easier then. But then I remember how unbearable it was, not being able to have him. I'd prefer getting my toenails ripped out one by one to that torture.

And then I sometimes feel like I'm such a disappointment to him. It's not like I'm not trying to change and be more open. And with the new position as editor, improved social skills are much needed. I'll never get why they picked me. I'm crap at team work. And I'm even more crap at running this show without having everyone in tears by the end of the day. I'm the critic from hell that everybody fears. I tell people when their writing sucks. Unfortunately, it usually does. And when the writing doesn't suck, the research is an insult to journalism itself. Rhea told me that the freshmen are absolutely terrified of me. And they're not even allowed to write for the paper yet. Go figure.

There are days when I just feel so old. Like I've lived all of this twisted shit at least twice, and it's on endless loop. Don't dream. Don't hope. Reality will turn out to be a hell of a lot worse than you'd ever be able to imagine. Every good thing has its flaw. Nothing in this world is perfect or lasts forever.

What's happening to us? Why does it feel like Casey is slipping away? Every so often, it doesn't even feel like he's with me when he's with me anymore. And I wonder where he is, or with *whom*.

* * *

There's a full moon outside my window, looking in. Mountains of heavy black clouds are drifting past it like monsters from another dimension. In the pale light, most of the trees are standing bare like skeletons against the bitter sky. If it weren't way too early in the year, I'd say it looks like snow.

Happy birthday, Foley. The powerful bell of the old campus clock tower just struck twelve. I close my book to call it a night. The small reading lamp on my desk leaves everything but the desk itself in utter darkness. Witching hour. Witching hour on my birthday. That's like Friday the thirteenth squared. My stomach clenches like a nervous fist and my skin covers with goosebumps instantly.

There's someone in my room, some kind of presence, hidden in the shadows. Someone is watching me. I can almost feel the ghost of Simon hovering in the air behind my back, his breath pure ice on the naked skin of my neck. It's making all my hair stand on end.

"What did you expect, James?" a voice like metal scraping over glass whispers through the darkness behind me. *"Do you think you deserve more than this?"*

There's a knock on the door and I nearly jump out of my seat. Ripped out of my daze, my heart is beating like crazy. Adrenaline's pulsing through my veins when I get up from my chair and cross the room to answer. It's Casey. Oh god, I'm so relieved. So happy to see his face right now! He falls into the room and flings his arms around my neck.

"Happy birthday, James!"

I swing him around and laugh when he starts to cover my face with kisses, until our mouths meet and we come to a halt. I close my eyes and press myself up against him, and he kisses me deeply and pulls me close with such devotion that I feel like jumping for joy. I feel like I've just gotten back what I've been missing, without even knowing what it was.

When we part, we grin at each other and I tousle his hair. "I thought you were tired and had an early morning coming up!"

He laughs mischievously. "Well, I lied. I wanted to surprise you!"

"I daresay it worked."

"Here." He pulls something out of the back pocket of his jeans and hands it to me. "This is for you."

I glance at the present, then back at him, a warm feeling spreading through my body. "You know there's no need to..."

"There is need. I know we said it wasn't necessary, but I wanted to give you something. I hope it'll come in handy."

He's beaming at me, and I can't help but smile. The small, flat box is wrapped in pretty paper, and it's unexpectedly heavy for its size.

"Go on, open it!"

So I do, and I blink when I hold his present in my hand. It's a silver dictating machine. Damn! That's just way too cool.

"Thank you! That's... wow. That's just what I need."

"I'd hoped it would be." He's beaming even more now, and I pull him close for a kiss. He looks into my eyes with warmth when we part.

"Mr. Editor in Chief. I'm so proud of you, do you know that?"

I swallow, and pull him into a hug. His body is warm and solid against mine, and it feels so good. I could stay like this for a long time, but he pulls back and smiles at me.

"There was another present leaning outside your door, I wasn't sure if I should bring it in. Should I go get?"

"Sure." I can't hide a frown. Another present? What's this all about?

When Casey returns a minute later, he's carrying a relatively large, flat, heavy-looking thing inside and presents it to me. It's wrapped in elegant glossy paper. Astounded, I stand and stare at it without taking the thing, half-expecting it to explode any second. Since there's no suspicious ticking sound, I finally accept it, and it really is heavy. Could be a book, a huge one. Who'd get me something like this? Who'd get me anything at all? How bizarre.

"There's no card," Casey says, and curiously looks at me.

No card. Damn. I think I have a hunch who this is from, after all.

"Aren't you gonna open it?"

"Sure. I'll do it later." I quickly put it aside, as if it really were that unimportant. In actuality, I'm nearly dying from suspense. What is it? Is it really from whom I think it is? And why? Why would he get me anything for my birthday? Why would he even know that it's my birthday today?

"I'd rather celebrate with you right now."

Casey smiles knowingly, and crosses the short distance between us to kiss me. Something raw and hungry springs to life inside, and mingles with the love I'm feeling. I ache to feel him, want him, need him now. Hands fumbling, our tongues playing, we stumble towards the bed.

* * *

Afterwards, I lie awake and listen to the sound of his even breathing for a long time. I'm cold on the inside, frozen. Everything I've been suspecting, fearing for a while now has been proven true tonight. He doesn't belong to me anymore.

There was no real feeling in the sex, not from his side. I was making love to him, and he was allowing it. Without giving much back. Nothing true, nothing real. Nothing like real passion. Nothing like what it used to be. It was routine. It was quick like a hurried rush, and sobering as it passed. And the bitter aftertaste is still in my mouth.

I feel so wounded right now. The tears that I can't cry are

almost choking me. What's happening, Casey? Where are you? Who are you with? Who are you thinking of when we're together? Can't you either hide it better, or finally talk to me?

This isn't working. For the first time, I feel that it's the cold and bitter truth. I'm not finding what I need here. That's why I'm secretly seeking it with somebody else, even though I couldn't admit it until now. And you are too, Case. I know that now. And it hurts, because I love you still. I may never be able to say it, but I do.

Things will look brighter again in the morning. And I'll tell myself, it's not that bad. We can work it out. And I'll know that it's nonsense, but I'll cling to it. And so will you.

I can't lose you, Casey. I can't lose your kindness, and your friendship. I can't lose your belief that I'm a better person than I am. I can't lose your love. I can't lose you. I can't.

I swallow hard and carefully slip out of bed. The mystery present is still lying on my desk, shimmering in the bright moonlight. I stare at it for a long moment, feeling defeated. I will have to push these feelings back, suppress them, like I've learned to do. I will have to before the morning comes. And the new night, with that stupid Halloween party I've foolishly agreed to come along to with Casey. But it's not morning yet.

My fingers are trembling when I tear the expensive paper apart. I was right. There's only one person on this planet that this could be from. No card needed. I get a lump in my throat when I tenderly run my fingers over the glossy cover. It's an awesome, expensive illustrated book about Berlin.

* * *

It's still my birthday, and will be for two more hours. Just two hours, and how much worse can things get in so little time? Well, knowing me and my life, pretty much anything could happen.

We're at the big Halloween bash, and there's something here that makes me remember why I didn't want to come: People. There's people here. Tons of 'em. People in the most ridiculous costumes, just dancing, partying, shouting. I couldn't be forced to wear a costume when threatened with electroshock treatment, but Casey looks mighty fine in his Grease outfit, with the borrowed black leather jacket, the tight black denim, and a cigarette tugged behind his ear. He's doing an alright job with the attitude too, I think. I can't stop staring at him, but it hurts.

I got through most of my birthday okay, although it did start with me running into Anna wearing a wig and a dress that made her look like someone's aunt, barking at me that she was gonna be Simone de Beauvoir today. Scarred for life, I tell you.

Then my dear school paper colleagues thought I would enjoy having a surprise party bestowed upon me, and forced me to eat cake so disgustingly sweet my stomach's still recovering. But now, after having just spent a rather draining hour in Casey's room, deliberately not talking about the things we probably should be talking about, it's almost not completely bad being at the party. The punch really sucks, though.

Invisible fanfares announce the arrival of His Majesty the King, and everybody seems to stop talking for a few seconds. And sure enough, a minute later, Rizzo casually enters the room with his date. I only get a glimpse before they're immediately surrounded - like he's some kind of rock star.

I exchange a look with Casey, and his smile seems to carry a trace of sadness somehow.

"That's just the way he is, I guess," he says quietly, and I nod.

"Yeah, that's the way he is."

I let my gaze wander through the room, and frown when I notice someone staring at me darkly. Great. Look who's here: Danny's little "friend" from the cafe, aka the Tall Pale Nuisance that just doesn't seem to know his place. And wow, in such a brilliant disguise too, wearing a dark red shirt instead of the usual black one. Nearly unrecognizable, if it weren't for that familiar murderous look he's giving me. I'm not even gonna dignify this by staring back. I don't get a chance to anyway, because suddenly Danny steps to Casey and me, and I turn around to face him.

Tonight *he*'s dressed all in black, with a head scarf that gives him the air of a bandit. His ruffled shirt is unbuttoned all the way down to the last two, showing that amazing, perfectly tanned chest that just makes me want to whimper. I don't even *dare* to take a closer look at his costume. He has a sword, and a pistol too.

"Who're you supposed to be? Zorro?"

"Me? I'm a pirate, mate," Rizzo grins roguishly. Dude. He's got a fake gold tooth! And a golden earring, I notice now. Looks awesome. And he's sizzling as ever, maybe even more so tonight with that sparkle in his eyes. Casey's positively drooling, and I can't even blame him. Who wouldn't?

"And your date?" Casey asks with a glance at the girl in the pretentious period dress across the room.

"She's Scarlett. I was supposed to be Rhett, but the man has no sword, and I had to have a sword. So now she's that lass from Pirates of the Caribbean."

"Elizabeth," Casey helps quickly.

"Bless you, laddie, that's the name." Danny grins, doing a fine pirate accent, and nonchalantly leans on his shoulder. Casey seems to tense at the touch, and Danny's grin broadens when he leans in close to his face. "Where's the rum, boy?"

"Uh. They have punch over there."

"Punch." Rizzo arches his eyebrow only slightly, but there's something truly menacing to it, and once again I know exactly why he's the reigning star of the drama department. Then that irresistible roguish grin is on his lips again. "I think we can do better than that!"

He gives Casey a little push in my direction, winks at me, and disappears in the crowd. A minute later, I get a brief glance of a funny looking King Kong handing our pirate a small bottle with dark liquor, then the two of them are gone.

* * *

Okay, I've really had it now. With this messed up birthday, and this hellhole of a party. Everybody just keeps disappearing! Where the hell did he go? I can't see Casey anymore as I'm fighting my way back through the swaying masses with two brimful paper cups occupying my hands. Punch for him, mineral water for me, and I'm mincing like a ballerina, trying to avoid elbows and people abruptly stepping backwards for no apparent reason. It's all moving bodies and absolutely no air, and a wave of claustrophobia is just about ready to hit me. I manage to dodge an enthusiastically outstretched arm, when suddenly someone bumps into me really hard from behind. I get pushed into the next guy's back like it's a goddamned game of dominos, beautifully emptying the entire content of my cups on him.

"Hey, what the hell?!" the involuntarily showered one snaps angrily.

"Ah, for god's sake!" First I turn the other way and stare right into the yellow eyes of Dracula, who was apparently waltzing with a chick who's either supposed to be a mermaid or a really bizarre looking dragonfly.

"Forry," his fanged mouth opens to a wry smile. Before I even get a chance to inform this jerk that this is *not* the dance floor, I get an unexpected push from my other side. Irritated, I spin back around to stare into a pair of really pissed off eyes.

"Back off, asshole!" someone spits at me.

I push back automatically, before I even recognize Goth Boy. "What's your problem, man?"

With the black eyeliner smeared, his blue eyes seem all the more intense, virtually turning into fiery daggers as he gets even more worked up. "My *problem* is that I've got an arrogant little fucker spilling punch all over me!"

And it keeps getting better and better. Out of all of campus assembled, of course it had to be *him* Dracula pushed me into. Why am I even surprised? Trust good ol' Foley to find the most strained and worst possible moment to have his first face to face encounter with this son of a bitch. "Do I look like I did it on purpose?"

"Well, why else would you be spilling your crap all over me?"

Oh boy. This doesn't bode well for either one of us getting out of this little heart-to-heart without a couple of bruises. I take a deep breath and try to stay calm, and I say to him like I would to a little child: "Room full of people. Carrying punch does not seem to go with that." I guess I should also apologize, but then again, that jerk shoved me. And so I just glare at him instead.

"Right. And I'm supposed to believe that it's some huge coincidence that you spill it on me? I'm not buying it."

I roll my eyes. From the gigantic size of his widened pupils,

I'm prepared to encounter a bit of paranoia. "Well then, don't. Whatever."

"Don't give me your damn 'whatever'. Not when you're coming over here, ruining my shirt and pissing me off."

"Right, that's my purpose in life, pissing you off. All I do every day is wonder how to best piss off Rizzo's little lap dog."

Bingo. For this, I immediately earn another hard push, and my being impressed with his eloquent ways is growing by the minute. Real smooth. God, I really, really want to shove that bastard's pushing hands right down his throat. It's not like I'd be missing much of a conversation.

"Screw you! I don't even know what he sees in you!"

I don't blink when I stare into his eyes, and he's staring right back at me. "Someone not as messed up as you are, I'd say, you sad little punk."

The reaction to my calm words is unexpectedly rapid, and even more unexpectedly painful, because this time, the push is so damn hard, it rams me right into a table, loudly knocking all kinds of things off it; glass scatters on the floor. Oh hell! Everyone around us stops dead and gapes mindlessly.

"That's not too difficult, is it?" His thoughtless reply is pure hatred, and it takes him at least three seconds to realize what a clever thing he just said.

I smirk. "No, not really." Slowly I stand up straight again and stare into the pale boy's eyes. "What're you gonna do next, sophisticated? Hit me?"

Our audience starts to laugh, and I think I even hear some cheers, but I pay no attention to them. Right now, I'm locked in his gaze, as he is in mine. And I swear, I can tell that he wants to beat the living shit out of me, so much. But now he can't, and even in his current state, he gets it, and it infuriates him even more. I seriously doubt he'd manage to land a hit without tripping over his own feet if he tried. My fist is practically twitching to be sent straight into his face, but I will *not* start a fight on October 31. Never again. Not a chance in hell.

He's standing so close to me that I can feel his hot breath on my face. I'm trying to force myself to calm down, but I can't keep from glaring at him loathingly. All muscles underneath his white skin are alert with tension. His eyes drop to my lips, for a split second only. But that moment is very clear, and somewhat sobering. Then he frowns, and I frown with him.

Suddenly there's a strong hand on my arm, shoving me back a little, and him into the opposite direction.

"Hey you idiots, knock it off!"

Anna de Beauvoir hooks her arms under Goth Boy's from behind, and mercilessly pulls him the first few steps away from me. And you better believe that militant dyke has the strength to do it. She mumbles something about cavemen and there being no evolution for our sex, but I'm too busy continuing to stare at Goth through narrow eyes to really listen to her. He manages to free himself and angrily shakes off her hands. But he just throws me another dark look before he pushes through the crowd and disappears.

What the hell was *that* all about?

* * *

It's no use. I'm never gonna be able to find Casey in this insane crowd. God, I really hate my birthday. With a deep sigh I lean against a wall and immediately wince. Damn! My back hurts from my previous encounter with the edge of a table. What a miserable, completely messed up night this is. But what was I expecting?

The feeling of loss and of loneliness that I've been carrying around all day deepens. Standing still, all alone in the crowd, I'm watching the blur of happy faces passing me by. A nice strong drink would be a fine thing now, and I long for that familiar hot sting in my throat. But history has shown that it's never a good idea for me to get drunk and lose control on this particular day of the year.

"I thought you hated parties," Captain Danny Sparrow grins when he magically appears at my side, out of nowhere it seems. How does he always seem to be able to find me anywhere?

"I do." Hell, I can't even begin to say how good it feels to see his face right now. Forget the drink, this is way better. I even manage a very vague half-smile.

He tilts his head slightly, thoughtfully studying my face as though trying to read my mind. His small smile is teasing, but there's a warm sparkle in his eyes. "Then what are you doing here?"

"Well, it's Halloween. And Casey wanted to come." I have to almost shout to make myself heard over the noise. Danny steps closer to me, and if I weren't propped up against a wall already, I'd move backwards instinctively to keep the minimum safety distance.

"Yes, but what are *you* doing here?"

I get what he's trying to tell me with this, and it irritates me, because he's right. Yes, I'm only here because of Casey, because he really wanted to come. And Danny's also wrong, because there's nothing I wouldn't do to keep things with Casey working for just one more day. Always for one more day, for as long as I can.

"You'd never change for anyone, would you?"

"People don't change, Jimmy. You know that."

"All the same. Would you?"

The pirate smiles before he takes a sip of his beer, and I'd love to be that dark and bitter fluid right now, just to be swallowed like that. If he knew... if I could only talk about it all. To someone. To him. I wish he'd simply grab me and take me away, to a place where this freak show called my life is nothing but a bad dream.

Danny's expression becomes an interesting mixture of mischievous and pensive while he ponders my question. "Someone once told me: the most important thing in a relationship is the ability to accept the other's flaws without wanting to change them."

"Would you call sleeping around a flaw?" I ask ironically.

"Are we talking about you or me now?" he grins.

I laugh dryly, but the truth of it stings. "You seduced me."

"I could do it again. If it weren't for that flaw you got. That Mills guy, you know."

"Does that mean you could accept that he and I are together?"

"Have I done anything to make you think otherwise? Have I

even touched you since summer?"

Well, true. He hasn't. "But then again, we're not in a relationship, you and I. Ergo you don't need to accept my flaws."

Danny laughs, and it sounds like velvet and freedom. "You just reduced your own chastity to absurdity, Einstein!"

Hell, if not mine, then certainly his. If you can even make a connection between Rizzo and chastity without annihilating the entire existence of life on this planet. It's like bringing antimatter together with matter.

I'm still wrapped up in the poetry of this thought when he suddenly grabs my arm and just snatches me away from all the noise. Effortlessly he steers me through the crowd, out of the room and out the backdoor. I step into complete and utter darkness. It takes my pupils a long moment to adjust. It's freezing out here.

The night vibrates with screams and laughter from the distance, where bizarre masks and costumes are roaming and playing tricks on anyone so unlucky to cross their path. Garlands of toilet paper are decorating the trees of Shriner's Park.

Danny's hands are on me and he's pressed up against me in a moment, like a heat wave hitting me in the chill of the night. God, it's been so long, and is that why it's all it takes to make me so hard? I can't breathe when he slides his tongue inside my mouth, and my body goes completely rigid with desire so intense it causes physical pain. He whispers, breathes my name into my ear, and my fingers sharply claw into his back to bring him even closer to me. I want his hands on me, tighter, harder, I don't give a shit about the sharp pain shooting through my back at the touch. And suddenly there's clarity. There's another reason why things with Casey aren't working, one that I didn't want to see: He's that reason.

"Danny," I whisper his name. And he responds, with such heated passion it makes me feel dizzy and drunk.

His hands are all over me, my hands are all over him, and we're panting into the ecstasy of the kiss. It's like a hard drug being injected into my veins, pulsing through my body and completely blowing my mind. His scent alone is driving me over the edge.

This very moment is all that matters. There's nothing else. There's no past, no future, there's only right now. And this is the real thing. This is the real thing, and I realize that it's true. There's nothing else comes close.

Virtually unable to hold it back like a school boy, I violently come with such sweet, painful pleasure, and limply sink against him. And he catches me, and holds me.

He's so warm against me, and his arms feel good around my body. His cheek is soft against mine as he calmly breathes the rest of the tension away. His breath flutters like wings over my skin when he bends down to tenderly kiss my neck, and he seems to tremble a little. I'd completely lost all awareness of how freezing it was out here.

Something icy and wet gently touches my face. Slowly I lean back and look up at the sky, and a snowflake elegantly sails through the air and lands directly on the tip of my nose.

I don't believe it. The first snow this year, and the ground all around us is already covered with a thin layer of white fluff. Flakes are whirling through the air, and deep silence falls over campus, the kind of ethereal silence only snowfall can cause.

And we just stand there, in each other's arms, and watch in amazement. My heart is beating like it's gonna burst. I don't believe in signs, but this is one is so high-profile, it could make even me a believer.

Danny smiles at me, and with the head scarf gone and fallen to the ground, snowflakes in his dark hair, his skin seeming to glow somehow, he's the most beautiful thing I've seen in my life.

"Happy birthday," he whispers.

10 OUTSIDE

NICK: I wake up to the sound of my next-door neighbor screwing his girlfriend. No, I take that back. Not screwing her. Making love to her. At 7:30 in the morning. Now, I'm all for getting some in the morning, but it's usually wake up, do your thing, find your clothes, and run.

But not them. No, they've been at this for almost half an hour now. All "oh baby, I love you," and "yes, perfect, oooh," and "sweetheart," and so many other things. She lives out of state, so when they get together, they spend all their time declaring their undying love for each other. It makes me want to vomit.

So I do. Into my garbage can.

Okay, that might actually be from the hangover I have right now. Lately I haven't been getting them, and let's just pretend it's *not* because I haven't gotten sober enough to even have a hangover.

This morning though, it's there, and just as painful as ever. Like it's trying to make up for those mornings I was still drunk enough to not have one. Like I cheated it out of making me feel like shit, and this is its revenge.

And the greatest part is that there's absolutely nothing in my room to help me out. Unless you count aspirin and water. Which I don't. Obviously.

At this point I figure my day will get better. It has to, right?

It doesn't.

* * *

I skipped classes today, figuring that getting my head to stop pounding was more important. I've eaten, I've had a few drinks, put a call in to Marc to meet him later, and I'm on my way to see the posting of the parts for Hamlet.

I'm in a pretty good mood now, and who should be walking towards me but Rizzo. He's talking to someone I don't know, smiling and laughing. As he gets closer, he looks over at me. No, that's not right... he looks *through* me. Like I'm not even there.

"Hey," I say to him. Nothing too much. Like I would to anyone I knew. But there's nothing from him. Not a smile, not a wink. Not one goddamn flicker of one perfect eyelash.

What the hell?

I turn and watch him walk away from me now, my stomach trying to claw its way out of my body and follow after him. I don't understand what all that was about. Did I do something to piss him off? I can't remember anything...

The last thing I remember is our little "practice session" for my callback audition. And he definitely wasn't angry with me then. I saw him after the auditions, hanging around outside the theater and talking with some of the other drama kids he knows. But he wasn't angry then either. He even told me I had a good audition. So what's with the silent treatment now?

I'm totally confused, but I can hear the group of people ahead talking as they wait for the cast list to be posted. It suddenly goes up a notch, and I know the list is there.

Do I go after Rizzo, try to find out what his problem is? Or do I go look at the cast list? It shouldn't be that hard of a choice, right? Rizzo's just one person - acting is more important than one person.

So why is it so hard for me to turn and go toward the group of excited voices?

This thing with Rizzo will have to wait. I'll go find him later. Right now, I have a part to go claim.

* * *

I blink again, but the words on the paper don't change. Nick Keller. Marcellus.

I've been here so long that everyone else has gone now, and it's just me and this damn piece of paper taped to the wall. And those stupid damn words that aren't supposed to be there.

Marcellus! This has to be a mistake. I owned that audition, I know I did. And for me to have had that good of an audition and get Marcellus? Obviously a mistake!

Stupid shitty part. I could do this part drunk and high and it wouldn't make any difference at all. It doesn't require anything from the actor. Come on, say a few stupid-ass lines, then dick around backstage for the rest of the show.

Blink.

Nick Keller. Marcellus.

"Nick?" The voice is quiet, trained, and familiar. I finally turn away from that unchanging piece of paper and look at my traitor of a director. He doesn't say anything else, and when I figure out that he's waiting for *me* to say something, the words are dragged from my throat without me even thinking about them.

"Marcellus, Jeff? Why? My audition was better than that and we both know it." He opens his mouth to respond, but I cut him off. "You can't deny it, Jeff! I was better than that. I *am* better than that!" I'm yelling, but I can't stop myself. I have to make him see. I can't do this part. No one goes to Hamlet to see Marcellus. I'll get stuck in the back and no one will see me at all. "Jeff, please! You have to give me a better part! This isn't supposed to be my part!"

I can feel myself beginning to panic, but the only thing I see in Jeff's eyes is pity. And it stops me in my tracks. He's not going to give me a different part. All my arguments are gone, and all that's left is one question.

"Why? After that audition, why?" I choke the words past everything I'm feeling, but all I get is more pity from Jeff.

"It's not always all about the audition, Nick. I told you that you needed to clean yourself up. And you haven't. We can't afford a liability like that on this show, Nick. You know how big this is. For *everyone*. We can't have you playing with that shit while you're carrying a main part." He looks at me closely and shakes his head. "I'm sorry, Nick."

And he walks away. Leaves me standing there.

* * *

Alcohol, drugs, and people. Maybe something will help take my mind off of all this shit. I'm at some Halloween party that claims to be the biggest on campus. They're probably right, too. There's so many people here, most of them in costume, and all I can hope is that this will help fix my shitty day.

After I'd managed to finally leave the drama department after Jeff and I had our tender little moment, I found Marc and told him what a messed up day I was having. I started to, at least, before he said that he wasn't my therapist *or* my friend, and that he didn't want to hear my bitching. But he gave me a little something extra for my cash, so now I'm flying high and ready for this party. Screw what Jeff says, I can do what I want.

What I want right now is to forget everything that's gone wrong today. Which is hard to do since Rizzo's here. Of course. I wasn't able to find him earlier in the day when I was looking for him, but I knew the instant he walked in. It's like a shift in the air, a change in the tone of people's conversations, the way the hair on my arms stands on end. All because of him.

And he knows it. God, look at him standing there all in black with a scarf over his hair, and I don't know if it's an actual costume (it has to be, because he has a sword), but I don't care, because he makes it look so damn good. I can almost ignore the fact that he's talking to that ass he's always around and hasn't even looked my way.

Just like earlier today.

Fine, I can play that game too. I can find someone to go home with tonight.

But of course *that* doesn't even work tonight. Instead, I have to deal with Mister-"I'm better than you and Rizzo likes me more and are you going to hit me now?"-Asshole.

And god, I do want to hit him. I want to swing my fist and feel it connect with his face and see pain in those endless blue eyes of his and see blood on those damn *distracting* lips. But I can't, now, can I? Not after he's said that loud enough for everyone watching to hear. And not with the way the room is slowly spinning around me...

And then there's someone pulling me away, some girl I don't know, and people are laughing, and I'm being shoved out of the room. And I want to go back in there and hurt him as much as I can. Maybe find Rizzo and hurt him too - maybe because I hate him right now, and maybe because I just want to feel his body against mine.

But I don't do that. I don't do any of it. I leave the party instead.

I don't go far... I'm surprised I make it as far as I do - into the park. But when I start tripping more than walking, I figure it's time for me to stop for a while.

I'm still in sight of the house, I can see the squares of the windows, the shadows of people walking in front of them. They all look like they're vibrating, but maybe it's just me that's vibrating.

Or shivering.

I'm freezing my ass off out here, alone in the park, because as I was walking out the door, I couldn't remember if I brought a coat to the party, much less where it might have been. So I'm out here, wearing nothing but my shirt, and is this shirt even mine? I don't think I even own anything this color.

All I want right now is to go home so I can go to sleep and this whole day can be over, but I still can't get my legs to work. So I just stand here, lean against this huge tree, and watch and listen to the party going on without me.

I watch as two people rush out into the cold, looking as desperate to leave the party as I was - but for a completely different reason.

They're pressed so close together that I doubt even this cold can get between them. And this is just perfect, isn't it? Because that's Rizzo. And him... whatever his name is, I don't even know. And he called *me* Rizzo's lap dog, but look at *him* out here pressed up against Rizzo. He's just where I want to, need to be. And they're - damn - they're kissing. And moving against each other. And so hot.

Rizzo's hands are curving around arms, ribs, hips, holding tightly, soothingly, tipping a chin back for a closer kiss. Someone's shirt rides up, and the quick flash of pale skin shining in the moonlight is just too much for me to handle.

I tip my head back against the tree at the perfect angle so that

I can rest it there and still watch them. My hands slide inside my shirt, inside my boxers, and I can't help it, can I? Because they're amazing standing there like that. And it's so painful, but it's so damn good.

And maybe I drank a little too much or took a few too many pills tonight, because it's *not* a normal thing to be watching the guy you've been sleeping with as he's kissing some other guy. And it's definitely not normal to be getting off on it.

Just the thought is dirty enough to send a guilty pressure along my spine, and it makes me curl my cold, numb fingers around myself in my boxers. It's so messed up for me to be doing this, but I start to match them, moving my hand at the same pace they're moving against each other. I want to close my eyes and imagine it's Rizzo's fingers moving around me, but I can't tear my gaze away. It's all too much, the cold, the thoughts, the images of them, and as I see the guy's legs give out, I feel mine do the same. Only Rizzo isn't there to wrap his arms around me like he's doing for the guy clinging to him. Instead, I get the rough bark of the tree catching my shirt and scraping my back raw as I slide down to the ground.

They're standing there, breathing, outlined in the moonlight, and Rizzo still has his arms wrapped around that asshole. They're holding on to each other like there isn't anyone else around. Like I'm not even there.

I might as well not be. I could walk over there right now, and I *still* wouldn't be there. Not where it counts. I'm on the outside, and there's no one here to wrap their arms around me. Rizzo sure as hell isn't. And as I watch them kiss again, I know that Rizzo never will be.

I'm still sitting there after they finally leave, the snow falling on me now. I watch a flake land on my hand and it doesn't melt until I raise my shaky arm and blow a hot breath on it. A far-off corner of my brain tells me I should get inside, and I almost (*almost*) wonder why I should bother. I wonder how long it would take for someone to come looking for me if I just stayed here and let the snow fall on me.

But I pull myself back up against the tree, thinking that my back is going to look spectacular in the morning, and I get my sorry ass home. Alone.

11 TABULA RASA

JAMES: You can't choose who you fall in love with, or when. I realize this when Danny tears open the door to my room on Thursday afternoon, and his beaming presence immediately lights up my four gloomy walls like it's the coming of the freaking Fairy Godmother.

"You genius!" He laughs and pulls me into an exuberant hug. His dark eyes are sparkling when he lets me go to look at me. "Man! You're going to Berlin!"

I can't help but laugh as well. His joy is infectious. *He's* infectious. "I know. They told me this morning."

"And I have to wait to hear this from somebody else? Son of a bitch!"

I shrug and grin. "I wasn't sure if I should be happy or not."

"Are you crazy? It's your dream!"

"What's this all about?"

Casey's standing in the open door, watching the scene with a small, confused smile.

"Hey, Rizzo," his voice is softer than it used to be when he was talking to him. Danny barely acknowledges his presence with the smallest of nods. The clear blue eyes seem to darken as Casey looks from him to me and back.

Steve from two doors down has also stopped on his way past my room and is gawping at us curiously. "Yeah, man, what's the buzz?"

"None of your business," Danny replies calmly but sharply, and poor Steve is quick to hurry on, like a wet dog drawing in his tail.

Then Danny puts his arm around my shoulder and finally looks Casey in the face, an undoubtedly sly smile on his lips. "Your brilliant boyfriend got himself the Berlin scholarship."

Casey just stands still and stares, the complete and utter

surprise visible on his face. Oh damn. Guess we can safely say that the cat's out of the bag. Why did he tell him? This was my job. A job I completely suck at, admittedly. I throw Danny a dark glance that he shrugs off with an amused grin. Yeah, okay, so it's my own fault. And yeah, sometimes I need you to kick my sorry ass. But you know nothing about how fragile relationships can be. Or perhaps you do, and you just love to hurt him. But hurting Casey is the same as hurting me, won't you ever understand?

I think I notice a trace of cruelty and a silent challenge in the unfathomable eyes looking back at me. Like Danny's silently telling me, "Go ahead, James. Push me a little further. I've come this far with you, and this close to you. I'm not moving back an inch."

But nobody's moving back an inch anymore, are we? Positions have become scarily entrenched. In this moment I realize that everything that's been seething underneath the surface - within all three of us - is about to reach a peak. Perhaps because we finally know what we want. I for one know that I do.

That nonchalant grin is on Danny's lips again. "What do you say, Mills? Aren't you damn proud?"

Slowly Casey steps into my room. He looks pale. "Is that true, James? I didn't know you applied."

"I was gonna tell you. But then I thought it was better to wait till I had their answer..."

"What made you think you couldn't tell me this?"

Danny rolls his eyes. "And here comes another endless debate!" When he pulls his arm off of my shoulder, hidden from Casey's view he gently runs his fingertips along my back. A wave of excitement shivers through my body. "See ya later, Jimmy Boy."

"Okay."

"Bye." Casey's voice sounds small and beaten. The way that Danny ignores him, he might as well not be here at all. But Casey *is* here, and I can tell by the look in his eyes that he does mind being purposely overlooked like that.

We both watch as Danny saunters out the door, closing it behind himself, and the air in here seems cooler now that he's gone. Feeling strangely trapped, I get the urge to run after him. Anything to avoid what I know is coming now. I'm not a fan of confrontations, and don't you know it? Hell, how am I ever gonna explain the scholarship and my hiding the application? I have no explanation, save that I'm a pathetic loser of a chicken shit.

When Casey turns towards me again, there's an expression on his face I've never seen before. I'd almost think that he hates me right now, if I didn't know him well enough to know that isn't possible. I'm gripped by a sudden fear.

"Casey, listen, I'm sorry. I was gonna tell you, I was just about to..."

"It's not that," he cuts me off impatiently. He closes his eyes for a moment and exhales deeply. Then he almost seems to smile a little, bitterly. "I'm such an idiot."

"What? No..."

"No?" When he opens his eyes again, the deep blue orbs are shimmering with tears. But all the while he appears to be strangely composed. "I went through hell because of you, James. I couldn't bear to hurt you."

"What're you talking about?"

"Do you really not know?" There's pain in his voice now. Casey sinks down on my bed like he's in some kind of trance. His gaze is fixed on the floor when he speaks again. "I'm in love with him too."

* * *

Through the closed window, I can hear the distant noise of a wild snowball fight on the grounds below. Cheering, screaming, shouting, laughing. The world outside is having a party, unaware and uncaring for the drama unfolding inside these four walls of mine.

We're sitting here on the bed, side by side, and the silence is thick enough to be cut into pieces. I've kind of been in this situation before, haven't I? But everything was different then. And everything's even more messed up now. Who'd have ever thought this would be possible?

I'm feeling utterly lost, and horribly guilty, and goddamnit, so betrayed. And I don't know whether to laugh or cry. All the words that I could say are frozen in my throat, and they're choking me.

"I never meant to hurt you," Casey finally speaks.

"I never meant to hurt you either." That broken voice doesn't sound like my own.

He glances at me. "Look, James," and why does he have to be the strong one now? How can he be so composed and so beautiful with those heartbreaking tears quietly rolling down his cheeks? "Maybe you and I... were never meant to be together."

"How can you say that?" I manage only a raspy whisper.

"Because we're *friends*." He reaches out to grab my hand, but I pull it away before he can. No, don't be kind. Don't touch me now. But don't you let go. Don't say it's over. Please don't.

I bite down hard on my lower lip to keep the agony I'm feeling from spilling out of me. I'm such a creep. I'm worthless. I'm nothing. I'm less than nothing. I'm not even here. There's only blackness ahead, and the familiar mist is coming over me. And with it, the violent need to cut. Voices, whispering in my mind. Telling me that only the sight of my blood can save me now.

"You're not even worth a good beating, you piece of shit, you fucking queer," Simon grins maliciously, and lets his threatening hand fall down. Kicks me in the guts one last time, and I know my small, wounded whimper is music to his ears. I don't know for how long I stay like this after he's left, a ball of pain, everything hurting and throbbing. I want to crawl out of my skin, that ugly old skin covered with scars and tainted memories. I want to fly away and not be me anymore. I want to be gone.

I claw my fingernails into my legs, right through the fabric of my jeans. I feel no pain. I feel nothing. I apply more pressure, too much pressure, and then the taste of blood is suddenly in my mouth, and I blink slowly.

"James?" Casey strokes my cheek, then he pulls me close and holds me carefully. "It's okay. We're gonna work it out," he whispers close to my ear, and his voice is cracking a little. "I know we will. I'll always be your friend. I'm here for you."

I can feel myself nodding, but it takes a moment for his words to sink in. *How?* I want to say. How can we be friends now? After what I did, after how you lead me on? Were you ever really in love with me, or did you just think you were? Did you just pretend?

But at the same time I know that he didn't. He's not that kind of person. He must have thought it was real. But I'm not Danny Rizzo, I'm not the one he fell for to begin with. And if anyone knows about the things Danny can do to you, no matter if it's willingly or unknowingly, I do.

I think I have an epiphany, this very moment. I have no reason to feel hurt, or to be angry. I have no reason to forgive, or be forgiven. And it's no use blaming myself. And it's no use trying to search for answers. Because there are none. We can't chose who we fall in love with, or when. Maybe it's nobody's fault. Maybe these things just happen, and there's nothing anyone can do to stop them. In the end, it doesn't make the slightest difference how much you love someone. It happens all the same.

As much as it *hurts* to lose what we had, it doesn't hurt nearly as much as it would have done a few weeks ago. And maybe Casey is right? Maybe we are meant to be friends. Maybe that means more than I thought it did. And maybe, just maybe, it's gonna be alright. If I go and make it alright.

Maybe it's a bit late to do the right thing, but it's not *too* late. It's easy to see things from Casey's point of view, having been in a similar situation. How could I spend time with Danny now, knowing how it makes Casey feel to see us together? And damn, I know exactly how shitty that feels. It's pure misery. How could I knowingly put him through that? I have to stand by my best friend now. There is no other way.

I don't know for how long we sit like this before he lets me go and looks into my eyes. "God," he says with a crooked little smile. "I don't wanna lose you, you hear?" he mumbles close to my ear.

"You're not going to." We hold each other for a long moment before we both pull away.

"Well," Casey sighs softly. "We can't both have him. And he never wanted me."

I sit up straight and shake my head. Then I lift my hand and wipe away the last one of his subsiding tears. "Forget it. I'm not gonna do this to you anymore. I promise."

* * *

It's true that I suck at making decisions. But once I do make them, I stand by what I've decided. It seems ironic that now that I finally know what I want, I have to let it go.

A couple of hours have passed, but so much has changed this afternoon that it seems like forever. It's getting dusky already. That intense, pure blue you only see just before dark that makes all the lit windows appear bright yellow. The way to his dorm is much longer than I remember. The air is so cold it stings like needles on my face. Wish I'd put on a scarf. It's early November and clear that winter is here.

I don't really expect Danny to be home when I knock on his door, but he is. I can hear low voices inside. It takes a whole minute before he answers. Enough time for my hands to get sweaty and my stomach to turn into a frozen lump.

First thing I see when he opens are those beautiful laughing eyes, then his bare, drop-dead gorgeous chest. Heat spills out into the corridor. He must have flung on his trousers in a hurry. His broad smile is mirroring happy surprise.

"James!" He elegantly steps outside through the crack, managing to not even give me a glimpse of who's still inside, before the door snaps shut with a soft click.

"You're not alone," I state flatly.

He shrugs with a charming grin. "Want to come in? He'll be gone in a minute."

"No, don't bother. I'll be quick."

"Don't be," he says, and moves closer to me.

Oh boy. How am I ever gonna be able to do this? "I need to talk to you."

"It just so happens that I need to talk to you too, Jimmy Boy." That small smile on his lips is irresistible, even more so when I notice the tiniest flicker of nervousness in his eyes. Heart's beating madly. Danny Rizzo nervous? What does this mean? There's something in his dark orbs that seems to be speaking to me already, a kind of warmth that makes me feel hot all over and chases the chilly air still clinging to me away. I fight hard to not let it get to me and keep up my indifferent facade.

"About what?"

"About you and me."

Oh damn. "I'm here for that too."

"Fire away, I'm all yours."

Oh god and hell. I cannot do it. I can't. But I *have* to. I can't be weak. I can't mess this up.

Of all the things that Simon taught me, one thing has enabled me, and will always enable me to get through anything. And for that I owe the bastard. It's like a switch that I flick, and it turns off any kind of feelings. At all. I go completely blank on the emotional scale, and my rational side takes over completely. I flick this switch now, and seconds later I am ice.

Danny seems to sense this change immediately, because his smile fades, and his expression turns uncharacteristically serious. I know he's as ready as he'll ever be to hear what I have to say, and so I speak. "I can't go on seeing you anymore. This thing between you and me, it has to end."

He blinks slowly, and his usually pleasantly soft voice sounds a little hoarse. "What?"

"Whatever this was, it's over. That's all I have to say."

"What kind of crap is this?" He laughs unbelievingly, and just shakes his head.

"You want an explanation? There is none. None that you'd accept anyway."

"You're damn right!" He stares at me, trying to read me, but I know that in my current state, it's simply not possible. And I'm thankful for that.

My apparent cold seems to finally fully hit him now, and his eyes turn dark with defiance and hurt.

"This is bullshit! Is this Mills' doing?"

"It's my own decision. You heard what I said, Rizzo."

"Rizzo!" He laughs, but it sounds painful. "What's going on, James? Why are you doing this?"

"I'm gonna leave now," is all that I can answer.

"No!" His eyes are the most intense plea and his voice is soft again when he continues to speak. "No, James. Not like that. Talk to me."

Again, I just shake my head.

"Talk to me."

I feel the pull of my emotions wanting to spring back to life, but I can't allow them. And there really is nothing else to say. "Just let me go, Rizzo."

"Not without a very good reason."

He puts his hand on my arm, and that's just too much for me to bear. It's more instinct than conscious will, but I slap his hand off, perhaps harder than I meant to. My eyes are completely empty when I stare at him. They have to be.

"Don't touch me. Ever again. Stay out of my life."

But I can't turn away yet. I take in his handsome features one last time. To memorize him. To memorize the way he is when we're together. He's beautiful. He'll always be beautiful to me. And maybe some day, I'll be able to let him know. But not now, not for a very long time. And perhaps never.

Then I turn around and walk away, and he doesn't try to stop me anymore. I can feel him staring at my back for another long moment, then his door is opened, and I can hear his voice talking to someone. It's the coldest and most painful thing I've ever heard. Short, strict, devoid of all feeling.

"Out. Get out."

My turning round the corner and heading down the steps is the parting of our ways. As far as I'm concerned, from this moment on we'll be strangers, he and I. That's when the switch flicks back on its own account, and the feelings spring back to life.

Standing very still, I try to breathe, but I can't. The pain starting to flood me is too intense.

I'm vaguely aware of hurried footsteps coming towards me, then someone deliberately bumps into me, walking down the steps. He stops and briefly turns around, with blue eyes spitting fire. Goth Boy. I might have known it was him in Rizzo's room.

"What've you done now, you fucker?" he spits at me.

My eyes are still empty as I stare back at him. "Just grow up, kid" I hear myself answer tonelessly. Maybe the emotional void I still am for the most part spooks him somehow, I don't know. But he hurries on without another word, without looking back again.

I let the cold hit me when I step outside into a world of blue. The first stars are appearing in the darkening sky. There's nobody on the snow covered, winding path except for me. Even Goth Boy has vanished like a ghost.

It's done. I just told Danny that it's over. Press reset, and it's like we never knew each other at all. Tabula rasa. I'm on my own again. Casey and I've broken up. We're back to being friends, or at least back to trying to be friends once more. Casey's still Casey, Rizzo's still Rizzo, and I'm still the same old Jimmy Foley, whoever that is. We're all back to square one. Almost. But there were special moments, there was someone who made me feel like it was okay just to be me. There was pain, and there was beauty, and damnit, there was sex good enough to blow your mind for good. It wasn't all for nothing. Rizzo left his mark on me. I wonder, did I leave a mark on him as well? And if so, is he going to hate or cherish that mark?

I'm feeling so much older as night falls silently around me. I wonder where the decision I made is gonna lead me. And what he's doing now, but I quickly chase the thought away. If I can't forget, I'll force myself to. And if I can't stop feeling for him, I'll make myself feel nothing at all. And if I hurt him, I am sorry. For once in my life, I have to be a true friend. I have to do what is right.

12 AVALANCHE

NICK: Rehearsal's a joke. This whole play is a joke. And me? I'm a joke in it. With this shitty little part. At the back of the stage, where no one can see me at all. I'm meant to be up front, in the spotlight with the lead actors. But instead I'm stuck back here, where no one sees me, and no one pays attention to me, not even when I say my lines. They all look bored during my scenes, and I don't blame them. I'm bored too.

Because rehearsal isn't the escape it's supposed to be. Every time I walk through the doors, I can feel Jeff's eyes on me. Watching me, studying me, like he's looking for something specific. It makes me want to itch at my skin, because it's constant. I can feel it on me, and I can't get rid of it.

What makes things even worse is that he's the *only* one looking at me. Rizzo's barely even glanced my direction in days. Ever since he kicked me out of his room. I don't know what the hell that stupid asshole said to Rizzo, but I'd love to kick his face in. But I haven't even seen him since that day in the hall.

I've been calling Marc every few days now, spending a ton of money, just to make it through. I've pretty much quit going to classes, but I still come to every rehearsal. I can't let it go, even if it is a shitty little part. Sometimes, when I stop to think about it, I think it might be all that's keeping me alive.

* * *

Hot lights, a kickass costume, heavy makeup on my face, and I'm someone completely different. It's my first time on stage, and everyone's attention is on me. This is the easiest thing to do, and the best feeling in the world. I could do this forever.

The girl across the stage from me is usually one of those stuck up theater whores that I've had to deal with for the past few months. She was rude to me in rehearsal, ignored me in the hallways at school, but she's someone different now too. She's in love with me, and I'm in love with her, and everyone is in love with us. I think I might like to sleep with her after the show. And I'm pretty sure she'll let me.

* * *

It takes three people saying my name before I realize that I've completely missed a line. I don't even know what I was thinking about, but almost everyone's turned to stare in my direction: angry, annoyed, bored. Jeff's stare cuts through from the audience seats, pinning me to the stage. In his eyes, there's something else. There's that pity again.

I manage to choke out the line I missed (after a prompt from the girl that's sitting in the front row, feeding us lines), and the rehearsal goes on. But I can still feel Jeff's eyes.

* * *

"I saw you doing some work in class. You're good. I'm directing a show later this semester called 'An Ideal Husband.' I think you should audition."

I stare at this guy that's pulled me aside after class. He's not one of my teachers, but I've seen him around the department. The students that have been here at least a year call him Jeff and stop to talk to him whenever they get a chance. I've heard them saying that he directs the really good shows this department does, and that he hardly ever talks to first years.

"Yeah, I'll audition. Thanks, man."

* * *

I try to hurry out of rehearsal, but I don't move fast enough. Jeff catches me as I'm shoving my crap into my bag.

"Nick. We need to talk for a minute. Can you come back to my office?" I haven't been able to shake the feeling of him watching me through the whole rehearsal, and by the look on his face, I know that he hasn't suddenly changed his mind about giving me a better part.

I just nod my head, finish cramming everything into my bag,

and follow him to the office he keeps in a dingy little room backstage. The place is cluttered, every chair buried under books, show posters lining the walls, and when he shuts the door it feels like the walls are closing in on me.

He sits on the edge of his desk for lack of any other place to sit, and starts talking about responsibility. The responsibility of the actor, the director, the cast, the crew. He talks about maturity and regret. I try to follow his words, but I swear the walls are closer than they were just a second ago and I'm having a hard time catching my breath.

"...so I'm asking you to leave the cast."

He stops talking, and I think it's the silence that makes me focus. He's looking at me like he's waiting for a reaction, and I have to replay what I can remember of the last few minutes to see why.

"What?" My mouth is sticky, and I have a hard time swallowing.

"I'm asking you to leave the cast, Nick. I had hoped that giving you the role of Marcellus would make you realize that you needed to just focus a little more, to quit the drinking and the drugs, whatever it is you've been doing, but you've gone in completely the wrong direction. If you'd even asked me for help, this could've been different, but you've fallen so far from where you were last year at this time, and you're pulling us down with you. You're making us drag behind, and as the director I can't have that. You're no longer in this show."

I stare up at him. Nothing makes sense. He shakes his head and steps over to open the door. "You need to leave now, Nick."

I just nod numbly, grab my bag and walk home.

It doesn't hit me until I close the door to my own room behind me.

* * *

I'm at a party, trying to find something other than the watered down bowl of punch that's had everyone's leftover liquor dumped into it. Back home I knew who could hook me up with the stronger stuff, but I've only been on campus for about a month, and I haven't been able to find anyone reliable yet.

I see a guy in the corner with someone I know from one of my classes. He has greasy hair and flat looking eyes, hands shoved in pockets that look full of promise. They exchange money and something else that they keep mostly hidden from the rest of the room. I go over when they're done, hanging around and waiting for him to look over. When he does, I nod at him a little.

"Hey," I say. He looks me over and sort of grins at me. I know he knows why I'm here.

* * *

"Marc, it's Nick. I need you to help me out with something. It's important. Call me when you get this."

"Marc, it's Nick again. You answering today?"

"Marc?" It takes until the third call before he actually answers his phone.

"Yeah, Keller, it's me. Will you stop stalking my phone now? What do you need?" His rough voice cuts in and out on a bad connection. I can barely understand him, but the question is always the same. And the answer I give is the same as it has been since I met him at that first party.

"I need you to take me somewhere, Marc. Soon. It's really important." Because you never actually say what you want. Especially over a mobile phone.

"Yeah, okay," he replies, his attention half on something else. I can almost make out talking on the other end, and I know he's dealing with someone else while he's talking to me. I'm grateful he even answered the phone if he's that busy. "Five minutes, Keller. Where do you need me to be?"

I let him know I'm in my dorm, and he hangs up on me.

* * *

I've had one of those days where I can't stay in my room. I need to be somewhere with other people, so I find a party and start looking for someone to go home with. I'm not having any luck, but then he's suddenly there - Danny Rizzo. We've been rehearsing together for 'An Ideal Husband', but this is the first time I've seen him offstage. All dark eyes and glowing skin

and a sinful body. And shit, if I don't fall right at his feet.
"Pretty little Goth boy out all alone tonight?"
His voice curls around me like a living thing and makes everything else not matter. Nothing I ever drank, nothing I ever took made me feel like this. I exist, I'm real, I'm alive. And I need more. All he can give me.

I actually wake up in his bed the next morning. I pretend to be asleep when he starts to wake up, and I get my ass out of there as soon as he's left to go shower. I don't do mornings-after. It's not like there's anything for us to talk about. It was just one night.
One time.

* * *

I met Marc about an hour ago, and paid him more money than I ever have before. Everything's taken on a fuzzy haze, so I don't know how long I'm standing outside of Rizzo's door, just staring at it, before someone walks by, laughing.

"You need to knock if you want him to answer, idiot." The voice seems like it's coming from very far away, and I don't turn fast enough to see who it is. It's like trying to move through syrup, and by the time I'm able to look down the hall, the voice is long gone. I wonder if there was even anyone there at all, or if I'm hearing things now too.

The words echo in my head, and I realize that I *haven't* knocked. I watch as my hand raises itself slowly, rapping on the door.

I count my breaths as I wait for him to answer. I reach four and blink, and he's suddenly there, the door open enough for me to see the center of his body from head to toe. And even that limited view is beautiful. I can only stare at him as he stands there. I'm still counting my breaths for some reason, and I get to nine before he says something.

"What."

It wasn't the reception I was hoping for, but at this point, I'm willing to take anything. At least he's talking to me at all.

"I need…" I trail off. Why am I here again? What do I need? A fuck? A hug? Someone to talk to? I open my mouth to say something, but all the words stick on my tongue, and nothing comes out.

"You're messed up, Keller. Go home."

This breaks me out of whatever haze I'm in. I can't leave now. Not yet. Wasn't there something I wanted to tell him? Some reason I came here in the first place? Something that seemed so urgent as I was in my room, laying on my bed, waiting as whatever I'd bought from Marc worked its way into my brain.

Staring into Rizzo's dark eyes, I remember why I can't leave yet.

"No!" And I can tell I'm almost yelling, even though I don't think I meant to when I opened my mouth. But my own voice makes me remember what it was I wanted to say, and I push on even though the words still want to stay hidden behind my teeth. "No, I won't. I need to stay. And you need to listen. I'm so sick of you ignoring..." He's not even paying attention to me *now*. He's focusing on something over my shoulder. I slap my hand on the door, close to his face. "*Listen* to me! Pay attention to me for one goddamn minute!" His gaze lands on me again, but it's not what I want. It's not enough.

I step in closer to the opening of the door and reach out my hand to touch the T-shirt that covers his chest. He steps back just as my fingers brush the soft material, and I whine softly, like some sort of pathetic animal, wanting something to touch, something to feel. His eyes turn dark and cold, and I'm not sure if it's from anger or from something else that *might* be pain if this wasn't Rizzo.

"Rizzo, please..."

"No. I'm not your mother, Keller. Go. Don't come around again." And he steps back and closes the door, cutting me off. Locking me out. Just like that. And that's it.

I lay my hand flat against the wood, resting my forehead next to it and trying to breathe, but it's not easy. I can hear him moving on the other side of the door, doing whatever it is he does when he's in there alone. Every little sound is like a bullet in my head.

* * *

It's the last day of sixth grade, and the sun is still high in the sky when I use my key to open the door to the house. The sound of my bag hitting the floor echoes through the entryway and I call out into the silence.

I walk a giant circle through the house before I find the letter from mom on the kitchen counter, next to the blinking answering machine. The note tells me that she's gone out of town with her new boyfriend, and that dad will pick me up before dinner to stay at his place for the weekend. There's no phone number on the note.

I hit 'play' on the answering machine, and my dad's voice is there, telling my mom that something's come up and that he won't be able to pick me up. That he's been pulled out of town on some business and won't be back until Monday. He doesn't leave a phone number.

I look around again and wonder how such a big house can feel so much like it's trapping you when you're alone.

* * *

I don't go back to my room after I finally leave Rizzo's. Instead, I listen to the low thrumming of the drugs in my veins, telling me to find someone else to help me forget everything. I find a group of people with more alcohol than they can drink, help them finish it off, screw one of the girls that climbs into my lap, and pass out until the sun wakes me up the next day.

I have no clue what time it is, but the sun is high above me when I drag myself out of there. I get back to my prison of a dorm room and don't even bother to lock the door behind me. I don't really see the point. No one ever comes here anyway.

I think about going out and finding another party. Finding someone else to spend tonight with. But I'm feeling so transparent right now that I'm not sure anyone else would even be able to see me.

I lay on my bed, staring at the ceiling. Every time I think, every time I breathe in, every time I blink my eyes, it hurts so much I think I'm going to scream. But I know that screaming would hurt just as much. Or more.

I turn my head to look away from the ceiling, and my eyes land on the wonderful little pile of stuff I bought off Marc yesterday. It helped to numb things enough that they didn't hurt so fucking much, the memories of getting kicked out of the show, of Rizzo shutting the door in my face.

I grab the bag and tip the whole thing out onto my bed, a little avalanche of pills. I look at them, count them, wonder how many it'll take to make the memories stop hurting. I grab one of the bottles left near my bed and wash down as many I can with the warm sludge left at the bottom of it. It burns all the way down.

As things start to go fuzzy again, I wonder if it'll be enough to make the pain stop.

13 RIPCORD

DANNY: Rehearsals for the show are finally getting somewhere. More precisely, to the point where everybody seems to settle in, and the initial awkwardness passes. You can tell by those quietly working behind the scenes, building the set or sewing costumes stopping every so often to watch.

I'll let you in on a little secret. The only reason I got into acting was that it pisses Lilah off so bad. She'd planned for me to become Mr. Bigtime to impress her Country Club friends. Guess she's still trying to make up for the old faux pas, a.k.a. her marriage to my procreator. After divorce number one (which is the only one that counts for me) I figured that I had two options: to play along and grow up to be another bitter high-class zombie, or to never take shit seriously and do my own thing. Start my own game. Make my own rules. Yeah, I thought it was the cooler option too.

But that's just it, isn't it? For the very first time, my own thing's been snatched from my hands. And I'm left standing here, dumb-founded like some pathetic bastard, beaten at the game I created. Damn if I know how to deal with things now.

So I'm doing what anyone with the least bit of pride would do. I play pretend. I keep the show going. 'Cause hey, it just so happens that I'm an actor. And a damn brilliant one, too.

I don't sleep much, period. Grazzo's crazy genes. Lilah used to say it was abnormal, having all this energy and needing less than five hours of sleep. Back then, she said it with a wink and a smile. And dad would grin and reply, "Comes with the 'abnormally good-looking and talented' package. Deluxe version." With the split-up she lost her sense of humor like others lose a car key.

It can be a curse, though, being this restless. Every once in a while there are phases when I feel like running up my walls at night, under pressure like a steam engine. I just can't seem to lie still long enough to fall asleep.

With all this time on my hands, by now I know the entire play by heart. Not just my lines, pretty much everyone's. And Jeff is stunned by the intensity of my performance. I couldn't care less. I'm not doing this for him. I'm doing this because I need to. Hamlet, man, he's perfect. Being on stage is the only time I can relax. I can pour everything I feel into the role. Everything. Everything that I can't show in my own life. Because I'm Rizzo, right? And Rizzo doesn't get his heart broken.

I've been leading a saint's life of chastity since the day James walked out of my life. That's basically what he did, no matter how pathetic it may sound. This is a first, so cut me some slack. For some completely messed-up reason, even the thought of anyone touching me now fills me with disgust. I bear it on stage, or when I'm with the crew, and if I weren't so gifted at pretending, I'd be screaming out loud with anger and frustration every time it happens.

I quit smoking. Yeah, well. I didn't want to need that damn nicotine. I didn't want to need anything or anyone anymore. I've had enough of any of that needing shit. I'm finally past the point where I would kill for a smoke. It gets a little easier every day. Most days anyway.

I dug out some of Grazzo's old records, and I listen to them sometimes. There's no one that plays the sax quite like he does. I thought about giving him a call, but hell if I know what joint in which city he's playing tonight. He might not even be in the country. Sometimes I try to recall what it felt like when he was still around, when we were still a happy family. But the memory has faded to a strange mosaic of fractured bits and pieces.

Man, I loved being on the road, waking up in a different city every day. The circus of jazz, roaming from town to town. Constantly being on tour with his buddies. I was just a tiny little fart, but those were good times. The best. And then that bastard went and never even tried to get shared custody.

"You're so much like your father," Lilah always says. And that's no compliment, coming from her.

* * *

I could've asked why, but I didn't. Neither did anyone else. Jeff never made a big announcement. We have a new Marcellus, and nobody seems to notice. Or maybe it's that nobody cares. I gotta admit, it really doesn't make much of a difference who says the lines in the end.

"What happened to Keller?" I ask Trey quietly when we're leaving.

He gives me a completely blank look, kind of scared he might have missed something important. "To who?"

Is it important? Damn man, the kid was just one of the leads last year. But anyway. I can't be bothered to explain, so I just shrug. "Forget it."

It's just after five in the afternoon and it's dark already. The long, empty corridor echoes from our steps and low voices. The chill of winter hits us harshly as we step outside, and when I draw in a sharp breath, the icy air stings like needles in my lungs.

"Foggy again," Andrea mutters, winding her scarf around her neck twice before embracing her own shivering body. "God, I hate November!"

I don't know, I kind of like the dark months, but I don't say that aloud. Steph takes my arm and presses her freezing body against mine. I resist the urge to push her away.

"Where to?" Dave looks over for guidance as we step onto the misty path and start to leave the brighter area close to the building behind.

Andrea snorts. "Smart. Because today we clearly won't be going to where we've been going to for years after rehearsal!"

"To the cafe then?"

"Oh please."

I can't hide a small, quick grin. She walks on faster and rolls her eyes as she passes me by. Andie and I have known each other pretty much all our lives. I don't think Jeff had any clue on her practically being my sister when he gave her the role of Ophelia. He seems to believe that she's the yin to my yang. If there were anyone I'd be able to talk to about James, it'd probably be her. But I don't. Actually, if there were anyone I'd be able to talk to about James, it'd *be* James.

Were we ever really close, or was it something I imagined because I wanted it? Did he ever really trust me? Did I trust him? Were we pals? Friends, for Christ's sake?

I suddenly think of Nick the other day, of him shouting at me, desperately. "*Listen* to me! Pay attention to me for one goddamn minute!"

Pay attention. I wanted, I needed to have James' attention. I had to have all of him. I can still feel him now, pressed up against me. I can feel his breath trembling on my face, his hands on my back, pulling me close. The scent of his skin in my nostrils, his taste on my lips. It's that *craving* that's driving me insane.

Abruptly my feet seem to stop on their own account.

"Danny?" Steph looks at me with mild surprise. I can just make out Cafe Plato in the distance, like a beehive oozing light in this misty darkness. I don't answer when I free my arm from her tight grip and step away.

"Danny?" she repeats, sounding worried. Everyone else has stopped as well and stares. Attention. I have everyone's attention. Always.

Call it a gut feeling, but this uneasiness gnawing at my stomach is as bad as it gets. Something about Keller. Something about the other day. Something about that look on his face, in his eyes. Something about when I wouldn't, couldn't respond. Something alarming. All he asked for was... what the hell did he ask for anyway? Why was he there? Why did he come to me?

I turn around. Screw this. I'm heading for his dorm. Right now.

* * *

I sit down on the dorm's freezing front steps and watch as the ambulance pulls out of the driveway. It's completely dark now. Fog mysteriously wavers above the grounds. I can hear when the car leaves campus, that's when the siren starts to wail. It sounds more and more distorted until it eventually dies away in the distance. They're really moving fast.

The few people who've crowded at the entrance are staying on for a bit to gossip. Big scandal, right? Nobody asks me if I know anything about it, and no wonder. What would I have to do with some drug-addicted punk who got himself a ticket for a one way trip? Yeah, what would I?

Nick looked completely *dead*. And beautiful, in a bizarre way. White as snow. Perfect like a doll. Delicate skin in sharp contrast to the raven hair.

As the mad adrenaline rush starts to fade, I'm beginning to feel more and more exhausted. Like all energy is slowly draining from my body. And the thought crosses my mind that if I hadn't stopped by his room tonight, no one else might have. Maybe not for days. Come to think of it, I've never really seen Keller with anyone. He's got to have some friends, right? He's got to have *somebody*.

More and more people are crowding on the front steps now, the news is spreading fast. And from what I overhear, none of them seem to know Nick. Some vaguely remember "that guy who always wore black, you know, the one with all the piercings." "That jerk who always swore a lot?" Yeah, man, that's him alright. And apparently everybody knew that he'd had it coming. Assholes.

Thank god the door wasn't locked. Thank god he was still breathing, however shallowly. Thank god... thank god for what? It's not like things couldn't have been that much worse, is it? Because how much worse *could* things get?

I can't bear to be here and listen to these idiots talking and joking around me anymore. I rise to my feet to walk away.

In that same moment, James arrives, probably from a late class, and pushes through the crowd to get through to the entrance. He's wearing that ugly old coat, and he looks pale, but handsome as ever. Without seeming to notice, he's moving straight towards me, and I don't move an inch. And for a second there I'm hoping... I don't know what. That he'll stop to talk, and take this throbbing pain away. That he'll smile at me again, see me again, care again. That things will be just like they were between us. He looks up as he passes, and our eyes meet briefly. He doesn't even flinch, just moves on, and disappears inside.

I close my eyes and try to breathe it off. But the nausea keeps rising all the same, and there's cold sweat on my hands. I walk away quickly, until I reach the lonely darkness of the park. The fog and the black shadows of the trees swallow me.

White as snow. Perfect like a doll. Should I ever fall, who's gonna be there to catch me? Who'd even dare to tell me if I pushed things too far? Trey? Andrea? The thought makes me choke out a small, painful laugh.

After all this time, after everything that's happened, I don't know whether James would just watch until I hit the ground, cold and unmoved, or if he'd still care enough to pull the ripcord to save me in time.

White as snow, and perfectly still. Why did the kid have to go and pull some shit like that? Did he do it on purpose? Was it an accident?

Things with Nick were never supposed to be complicated. But I guess a lot of things weren't supposed to be. Why the hell did I have to be the one to find you, Keller? Why did you ever come to me? Don't you know that I'm crap at this kind of thing? No strings attached, you knew that from the start. It was supposed to be a one night, one time thing. I never gave you reason to hope for more than what it was. And you didn't, did you? Why would you have? You don't even *know* me! And I sure as hell don't know you.

I'm sick and tired of putting on a show. I'm sick of them all. Sick of the emptiness. Sick of being on my own.

And yet to me, what is this quintessence of dust?

There he is, wimpy prince Hamlet who can't get his act together, right in my head. And anything but wimpy now that I'm beginning to understand. What was I waiting for? What the hell was I waiting for?

Are you gonna live, Keller? Was I too late?

My stomach starts to turn, and I lean against a tree, coughing painfully. Violently fighting down the urge to heave. The effort seems to drain me of all energy, leaves me small and sore. The icy air stings in my lungs again. Everything around me momentarily fades to pitch black. White as snow, and images of angels and demons are spinning in my head. It feels like a dance of death for the prince of pretending.

Over there, I remember. Just over there is where I kissed him last. Just over there is where James finally seemed to be mine. Snow on Halloween night. How fitting is it, something as unlikely happening that very moment? How unlikely is it, Rizzo falling for someone like him?

There's only questions left, no answers. There's only might-have-beens and could-have-dones. And still, no regrets. It makes me calmer, realizing this. Have I been changed? Am I still the same self-centered bastard I once opted to be? Am I still playing games, or has the game begun to play me?

White as snow. Perfect like a doll. And a distant ripcord, dangling just above my reach. There's nothing left for me to do except wait. I'm standing still, feeling the rough bark beneath my fingertips, listening into the darkness. And so I wait.

Book 4
Retribution

Susann Julieva
& Romelle Engel

1 TIME OUT

NICK: Dark. Numb. Quiet. Hot, hard hands shaking shoulders. Dark eyes, familiar voice, worried (like it shouldn't be, never is). Not supposed to be here. Why now?

Fading. Dark again. Still. So still.

Angry voices. Loud. Too many. Beeps and lights, noises and hands. More hands. Fading in and out.

Moving. Cold. More lights, alien wail.

New pain. Throat, stomach, head. Twisting, aching, stabbing, tearing, turning inside out.

Cold. Freezing. Shiver. Hot. Shiver. Nauseous. Shake.

Talking. Screaming. Begging. Please, please, make it stop.

Stop.

* * *

I'm staring at a woman that's sitting in a chair near where I am, and I know that she's asked me a question. Or told me something important. I know that I'm supposed to know who she is. I know that the white coat she's wearing should be some clue. I know that I should probably remember where I am, too.

But I don't. I don't, because every time I try to grab onto a thought, it slips away again like sand, and there's nothing I can do about it. And really, it doesn't bother me. It doesn't matter. I don't care.

I don't care about anything.

I watch her lips move as she talks, and the words move around me like I'm not even there. "University, stress, friends, lifestyle, too much, common, drugs, attempt, help, medication, suicide, Nick." I know that last one, it's my name. I remember...

* * *

"Nick, come on. Sign the papers. They won't move you somewhere else without your consent, and they won't let me do anything unless you agree to it. I can't have you in County Hospital, and my lawyer says that unless you sign this, it's either that or jail. The neighbors would never stop talking if they found out. So sign the paper, and you'll be moved somewhere else... I should've made your father deal with you for once."

It fades again. I'm glad until I forget to be.

* * *

I wake up with the sun slanting across my ceiling and the hard edge of something pressing into my face. When I move my hand up, I realize that the edge belongs to a plastic bracelet that's around my wrist just tight enough that I can't pull it off.

There's a knock somewhere to my left, and when I turn my head, I realize that it came from the closed door there.

"Keller, you awake?" A large man pokes his head in the room, his dark skin a contrast to his clean light scrubs, and I just blink at him, wondering if I'm supposed to know who he is. The way he says my name makes me think that I should.

* * *

Cold floor under my chest. Bare. Shivering and sweating and why am I on the floor? Someone's yelling, crying. It stops when I take a breath, and I realize it's me. I clench my teeth together and it doesn't start again. Heavy weight on my back that shifts once I stop yelling.

"You done?" Deep voice. I nod and the weight is gone, dark arms picking me up to set me on my feet.

"You going to run again?" I didn't realize that I had been running, but I shake my head.

"Okay. Back to bed then."

* * *

He sees me looking back at him and gives me a smile that seems mostly friendly. "Yeah, Doc said you might be more with it today. You getting up for breakfast, or do I need to come in and haul you up?"

Terrified at the thought of this strange man coming in the room to "haul" me out of bed, I push back my covers and slide out, wincing when my bare feet hit the cold floor. The man leaves without another word, and I'm left to study this place.

The room around me seems familiar, even has a very few of my things in it, but at the same time, it's like it's the first time I'm seeing it. I try thinking harder, hoping that my brain will give me some answers, but all I get is some stupid fog, nothing in focus. Nothing that helps me any.

I step outside the door, bare feet on harsh carpeting, and look down the long hallway, a line of other doors just like the one I'm looking out of. I see a woman up the hall leave her room, shutting her door behind her, and walking in the opposite direction.

I have nothing better to do than to follow.

* * *

I end up in a sunny room where people are sitting down to eat breakfast. Mine ends up being a bowl of shitty oatmeal and a banana. I never eat bananas, and I hate oatmeal. But the nurse (or whatever the hell she is) who's there tells me that I've been eating it since I got here. I try to tell her that I don't even know where "here" is or how long I've been here, but she just smiles at me and walks away.

She comes back after about 20 minutes to check on me and looks at my still full bowl and uneaten banana. She frowns a little and writes something on a clipboard she's carrying, then points me in the direction of where other people are putting their trays.

* * *

I'm curled up on the floor of my room, shivering and sweating, and feeling like my insides are trying to crawl out. Like my skin is too small for my body. Like I need something to make it better. And if I don't get it, my skin is going to split right from the top of my head all the way down my spine. And then my skull will split open. And even then, it still won't be enough to make this feeling go away. My face is wet, and I can't tell if it's from the sweat or the tears that I can't seem to stop. I think it's about 3 in the morning, and even though I know someone has to be out there, no one comes when I scream. There's only the hollow echo of my own voice.

I look up at the door (the one that was locked when I tried to open it a few hours ago, the one that I pounded on until I could barely feel my hands any more), just in time to see someone peer in to check on me. Their face is framed in that little window that looks out into the hallway, and for a second I think that maybe they've finally come to help me. To finally give me something that will make me stop shaking and puking and feeling like I'm going to die.

But the face is gone almost instantly, and I'm left alone again. I try going to the door, crawling on my hands and knees, but I'm shaking so badly that I can only make it halfway there. I curl up on my side, still crying, still screaming, still begging for someone to come help me.

But no one does.

* * *

After breakfast, we're herded into a line in front of a single window in the hallway. When I get up to it, there's a guy sitting there with a tray of cups and a computer printout.

"Wrist," he says to me, like I'm supposed to understand what he's talking about. He's waiting for me to respond, but I can't seem to remember the right answer, if I ever even knew it. "Wrist?" he says again and points at me. I look down, trying to figure out what he's pointing at, and see my wrist that has the bracelet on it.

Oh.

I stick my hand out towards him, and he reads something off the bracelet. With a nod, he grabs one of the cups and holds it out for me. There're a couple of pills rolling around in the bottom of it, and I just stare at them until he holds out a larger cup, this one filled with water. He watches as I take it too, then just waits, staring at me.

I realize he's waiting for me to take them, so I tip them all into my mouth and use the water to wash them down. When I'm done, he asks me to open my mouth and looks inside, apparently making sure I've taken them all.

I feel like I'm in some bizarre new dimension, and I still can't figure out how I got here.

* * *

My first meeting with "Doc" is that afternoon. Or at least the first meeting with her that I remember. Another nurse comes to get me around 2 in the afternoon, and leads me to a door that looks like every other door here, only this one doesn't have a window in it. The nurse just tells me to go in, so I push the door open a little, not quite expecting what I see.

The room is filled with books, a couch, some chairs, stereotypical shrink's office. Which is what this is, I guess. There's a woman sitting behind a big desk, typing on a computer, which she stops when I poke my head in. She'd be hot if she weren't a few years past that, but she's still not bad. She's got dark blonde hair that's pulled up, and she's wearing a white coat that I guess means she's one of the people in charge here.

"Nick," she smiles a little when she sees me, "come on in. We'll see how you're doing today." Like everyone else, she talks to me like I should know who she is. Like she knows who *I* am.

* * *

"Yes, Mrs. Bancroft, we'll take good care of him. See if we can't get him back on the right track."

There's a long line of hard plastic chairs along one wall, and I'm sitting in one about halfway along. My mom is talking to this woman that I can't see very well because she's right in front of one of the huge windows, and the sunlight makes it nearly impossible to look at her. It's coming through and reflecting off her hair, and I try to see how long I can stare at the way it turns all shiny and sort of gold.

"Just fix it so that I don't have to deal with this again, and I'll be happy." That's my mom, her voice is familiar enough that I know it without even looking over. I hear her shoes clicking on the hard floor as she walks away.

The woman still standing next to me sighs, and I hear her talking before I realize she's talking to me.

"Let's get you to your room then, Nick." I look up at her again and end up staring into the sun.

"Okay."

* * *

I sit on Doc's couch as she tries to fill me in on some of the stuff I don't remember. Stuff like how long I've been here (17 days), that I was at County Hospital before this (3 days), that I've been on some serious meds since then (because of my "suicide attempt"), but not until after my body went through a massive withdrawal period (from what, no one's exactly certain, even me), that I'll be here for at least a month (possibly more), and that Doc's reduced my dosage of meds now because we need to talk about some stuff (and the meds make me too spaced out to do much more than sit and stare at people like a giant creep).

She finishes what she has to say and waits for me to start talking, but I don't want to. So we sit there for nearly 10 minutes without either of us saying anything. The truth is, I don't really feel like talking to her. I feel like yelling. Shouting at the top of my lungs for her to let me out of here. But I just don't have the energy for it. She seems fine with that though, so we just sit in silence.

I'm not used to silence. I've avoided it in the past. It's kind of hard to escape here though. My mind wanders as I stare at her wall, and for the first time in a long time I'm sober enough to follow it. Granted, I don't really like where my thoughts take me, but there's nothing here that I can use to escape them.

I look up a few times and nearly say something. Each time

Doc looks at me and raises her eyebrows, but each time I just shake my head and go back to thinking.

* * *

When we're done, Doc sends me back out into a main area where people are sitting and doing things like putting puzzles together and working on some sort of craft project, I guess. I don't have anything better to do, so I sort of wander around the room, watching them. Some of them look up when I walk by, but most of them ignore me. Like they're already used to me. I wonder if I'll ever catch up with everything I can't remember, or if I've lost that time forever.

I look at the tables they're all sitting at, the different colored paper, the glue, the bits of glitter and red and green. I look around the room and notice some lonely looking paper chains already hanging high up near the ceiling. On one wall, someone's hung up a giant paper tree covered in people's names and circular decorations. One of them has my name on it ("Nick K"), written in that familiar spiky handwriting that I've had since I learned to write.

I don't remember making it, but I can't ignore the proof that's hanging on the wall right there in front of me.

The way everything is arranged sparks something in my mind, and I try to add up the days through the fog that's starting to clear but still clinging to me. After a fight with my own brain, I finally remember something that Doc just told me. When everything comes together, it's the one thing that stays clear.

I'm in rehab for Christmas.

2 LONDON BOYS

DANNY: It's December, and I'm really not feeling up to ivy and mistletoe and all this shit. Lilah's idea of a perfect Christmas involves Aspen, après-ski, and excessive amounts of alcohol. It's always the same talk, the same people, the same routine, and I get bored off my head just thinking of it.
"Come to Europe then," Andrea says one afternoon after rehearsal when we're all settled at Cafe Plato. One of the many good things about Andie is that she seems to have an older brother or cousin in every city and country you could ever possibly want to visit.
"I might," I answer vaguely, but she shakes her pretty head.
"I'm not suggesting. It's set, you're coming with me."
"I am?" I smile a little, but I'm feeling exhausted and my heart isn't in the friendly banter. I know that she can tell.
"Yup. You might as well accept it, Danny. You have no choice."
Her deep green eyes focus on my face, and I look away. Andrea's family has been doing business with Lilah's for generations, or so it seems. Her mom and Lilah have always enjoyed pretending to be the best of friends. In truth, they never gave a shit, but that's high society reality for you.
I remember us kids sneaking around the house one day, and we peeked through a half-open door and found Walter, Andie's dad, making out with Lilah. Not long after the divorce, but Andrea's folks were still married then. We never threw a huge tantrum or anything. I think we just left and continued with whatever we were playing.
Later this evening, standing outside Andrea's dorm after she'd decided that I was to walk her home, she drops her cigarette and neatly puts it out with the tip of her shoe while looking at me.
"It's that boy, isn't it?" she asks calmly, in that voice that tells

me there's no getting around this conversation. "That Foley, that school paper guy?"

Damn. "Who?" I manage to sound bored, and she arches a fine, perfect eyebrow.

"That means yes, then."

"Andie, I really don't wanna..."

"...talk about it. I know. You never do." She studies my face for a long moment. "I just thought you'd like to know that there's some stupid talk going 'round. It's been noticed that you haven't exactly been... dating for a while."

That's a polite way of saying that I haven't been shagging my brains out. I half-smile to myself. "So what? Let them talk. It's not like I care."

"Yes, but maybe *I* do. Maybe I don't like it when people are talking behind my friend's back." She pauses. "Behind my oldest and probably *best* friend's back," she corrects herself solemnly. I can't help but smile.

"Andie..."

"Shush. You don't have to explain anything. But you're coming with me for the holidays. We're gonna spend Christmas with Aden in London, and New Year's in Paris with Nate. How does that sound?"

"Not bad at all."

"See? I know what's good for you. You're gonna be fine."

The way she says it, I'm willing to believe it. I'd really like to. I'm fed up with feeling like this. I don't even recognize myself anymore.

* * *

First stop: London, England.
It's snowing. Soft, gentle, massive snowflakes dancing through the air like in one of those completely overdone Christmas movies that I know would make James gag. I'd love to see that. Tie him to the bedposts and force him to watch "It's a Wonderful Life". Now that would be something. I'd have a good laugh.

James Foley. I'm trying to think of him in an objective way, as

I would of someone I don't really know. I don't think it's working all that well, because after all, this is has turned out to be a three person trip. Andie, and I, and him. He's here, not physically, but in my head, on my mind, all the time. He's in things that remind me of him, and he's in everything that doesn't. Fuck if I know how to handle this shit.

There are still odd moments when I could kill for a smoke, even though it's been weeks since I quit. And every so often I catch myself staring off into space, not thinking anything, just blank. I'm not doing anything else, so I let Andie drag me through one crowded store after another. There are no pantomimes on Leicester Square this time of year, and somehow I miss them as I stare out the window while we have our lunch at Pizza Hut.

Back outside, the streets are buzzing with Christmas shoppers and tourists. All the windows are decorated in red, white, silver, and green, and there's that special excitement of the holiday season in the frosty air.

Andie disappears in the changing room section of Selfridges, and I sit down beside a tired dad waiting for his wife and kid with at least five huge shopping bags huddled around his feet. A little girl is leaning against the wall opposite of me, chewing on her little fingers, and staring at me like I'm the most fascinating creature on earth. I crack a smile, and she giggles bashfully. Good to know that I haven't lost my touch with the ladies just yet.

Then we're on the move again, making our way down another one of the big shopping streets, snowflakes landing softly on our eyelashes, melting and leaving fake tears. Andie spontaneously decides to buy me a suede jacket that I really like, and I'm starting to feel a bit more with it as we stroll along.

She turns to stare after a hot young thing with an ass to die for that passes us somewhere on Regent Street. Noticing that I'm looking after him as well, she chuckles softly. "I swear, London has the highest percentage of pretty boys in the world!"

I grin. "You know I'm practically a Londoner, right?" If you believe Grazzo, thanks to a little sex accident, baby Rizzo was conceived in this city.

"Oh, you would have to be!" She laughs, shifts some shopping bags to the other side, and takes my hand in hers. It's just one of those moments when nothing big happens, but everything's perfect, and somehow you're feeling warm inside and whole.

We continue towards Piccadilly Circus, and suddenly stop at the same time. For a long moment, we just stare, because it doesn't feel real. There's a poster showing a guy with a sax who looks like my clone, only older by about twenty-five years. And my stomach just drops into my knees. "Shit."

"That's so totally not a coincidence. It's tonight." Andrea squeezes my hand as she takes a closer look at the ad. "Hey, do you wanna go?"

Apparently Grazzo's in London, for a concert in a legendary Blues club where I've seen him play before. Many years ago. Maybe too many.

Looks like we have it all: Christmas, snow, and a son the prodigal dad could return to. If only he wanted. If these things mattered to him.

* * *

"Dan, my man! Now that's a surprise!" Backstage after the show, Grazzo pulls me into a tight, warm bear hug, and doesn't let go for a while. His stubble's still so familiar against my cheek; he smells of expensive Whiskey and that same old aftershave. And for a moment, I'm a five-year-old again, absurdly happy to be home, because *home* is where dad is.

Over his shoulder, I can see Whitey grinning and winking at me. "Now if it ain't Little Grazzo! How's life been treating you, kid?"

"Not too bad, can't complain."

"Good, good. How's the old lady?"

"Married, or so she was when last I checked."

The old clarinet player laughs, his voice like gravel. "Goin' through them husbands quickly, ain't she, Graz?"

My dad pulls back and just shrugs with a grin. "What can I say, I'm hard to replace."

"*Impossible* to replace," a tall, anorexic blonde in a short dress purrs, and steps to Grazzo's side, her bony hands all over him. Another model he picked up after a show, no doubt. She's got to pinch him to be introduced.

"Danny, this is..." (short hesitation as he tries to recall her name) "...Nadja. - Nadja, my wayward son, who prefers acting to making use of his *real* talent, music." He says it with that grin, but I know he's only half-joking. He'll never stop bugging me about it, but I'd actually be disappointed if he did. It's the only time when he feels like a father to me, not just like any old buddy of mine.

"And oh my god, Andie? Geez, is that you?" He's finally spotted the one childhood friend I have that he could possibly remember. Andrea's leaning against the wall beside the door, unused to the chaos of an aftershow room full of crazy musicians.

"Look at you, all grown up, and what a beauty!"

This is the first time I've ever seen Andrea blush. The cold, removed goddess turned into a school girl - damn, it takes a lot. Grazzo's giving her his infamous grin, and seeing this, Anorexic Nadja turns on the spot and runs off slamming the door. Sadly for her, no one even looks up. You know my dad, you know lady drama.

I can see that Grazzo's unrivaled charisma is still doing the trick. I know what's coming next. He'll invite us to come along and hit the town. We're gonna have a blast with the old crew, we'll drink hard, we'll have a laugh, we'll drag out memories and all the old stories, and everything will be just like way back then.

And then, eventually, he'll just *disappear*. With some chick who's that much more interesting than the son he hasn't seen in years. Might even be Andrea getting lucky tonight. And he'll be gone just like that, without a word, without so much as a "see ya". He always does it. He's brilliant at completely leaving you behind.

All of a sudden I'm feeling sick to my stomach. There's not enough air in this buzzing, crowded room, as I realize that it's really me being the clone here, not him. I look at Grazzo, and I see myself, in twenty-five years. The Boy Who Wouldn't Grow

Up. Still the same, still messing around, always the same old tricks, never pausing to think, or care. A great buddy, but a horrible friend. And the worst father. Is this really who I'm bound to be?

Pathetic. But here we go again. Merry fucking Christmas, dad.

* * *

Next stop: Paris, France.
Paris is just as gray and ugly as any city in wintertime, but I don't mind. We're out for a walk on the boulevard along the Seine late at night, having left Grazzo and London behind with only a few minor scratches. There's no snow in Paris, and I think it seems more real without it.

"You need to get laid," Andrea states matter-of-factly, out of the blue, right after a half-hearted conversation about a new restaurant at the Champs Elysees.

"I do," I agree, and smile a little when she takes my arm and leads me down the steps to the riverbank. It's foggy, and freezing, but I don't mind the cold, because the scenery's pretty, and it's peaceful. I can just make out the shape of Notre-Dame in the distance, looming over the river like some dark, ancient creature. And for a moment, I feel like I'm out of time, hovering in the middle of eternity, and life below is small, and simple, and incredibly easy. For the first time in weeks, I can actually feel my body.

"You have to try and forget Foley," she says after a long moment of silence.

"D'uh." I give her a look. "Why do you think I'm here?"

"Fine, so stop your brooding. It's getting old."

"Hey, I don't *brood*, okay?" I grin vaguely.

"Alright, Mr. Touchy-Feely. Don't be offended."

I look at her for a moment. I'm not offended. I'm nothing, really. I know it's all I have been lately. And yes, it's high time to get over that.

"Andie? How about you shut up, fetch us a cab, and get me drunk quick?"

"Hallelujah!" She laughs with relief. I can tell that she's been dying for words like these, after having spent all this time dealing with that strange version of myself that's so different to who I used to be.

I grin at her. "I need a nice piece of ass tonight."

She laughs again. "With a head and a body attached?"

"Either way."

"You're such a slut," she states fondly.

* * *

And there he is, right in the heart of Paris. Clearly the nicest piece of ass this side of the Seine. We're in the city's trendiest club, it's New Year's Eve, and he's perfect. A friend of Nate's, French Boy whose name I forget, all dark hair and pouty lips, seriously pretty, and looking like he could be one hell of a shag. He calls me Dan*iel* in that thick French accent, and it sounds all wrong, but I don't care enough to let him know.

"You speak French very good," he tells me.

"Yeah," I grin. "And your English sucks."

He laughs and drags me onto the dance floor, and then I get swept away, and it's all perfume and sweat and bodies pressing against mine, and the DJ's a damn god.

And James is still there, behind my back, somewhere in the crowd, *stalking* me. All I want is to forget. I want to have him removed, erased from my memory. *Eternal Sunshine of the Spotless Mind*-me already. Because by now, I *hate* the bastard, and I miss him, and I hate him more for missing him. I'm still not feeling like myself, not like anyone else. I'm drifting, headed nowhere, and right now, I really just don't care.

The world can go screw itself. James can go screw himself. He can go cut himself, get some new scars, slit his wrists, he can bleed to death. I don't care. One of these days, I really won't give a shit anymore.

A couple of Caipirinhas later things get kind of blurry, the laughter gets louder, everyone gets wilder, talking is no longer necessary, and French Boy who completely abuses my name is all over me.

I'm actually having a good time, and surprisingly I don't mind being touched, for the first time since James... or Keller... Shit, man, for the first time in a while. When the hell did my life get so complicated? But the thought escapes me before I have time to ponder, because now there's hands, warm fingertips, gentle like feathers, teasing, tempting, sliding underneath my shirt...

French Boy takes a long drag on his cigarette, leans in and kisses me, giving me a taste of his smoke. And I find myself not minding at all. The kiss is slow and deep, and sexy, and his breathing accelerates as he presses up against me. I like the needy little sounds he makes, I like the way he tastes, bitter alcohol mingled with lime and something sweet, and I think I definitely want more of this.

Then it suddenly hits me, and I realize that I've got it all wrong. It won't make me exactly like Grazzo just to leave James behind. It's okay to do it. It's necessary to do it. There's no way around it, really, unless I want to spend the rest of my life in misery. All this time, I was walking away from god knows what. Not from James. Not really. I think I was walking away from myself, from who I really am. And suddenly I don't remember why I was doing that in the first place. Why I ever wanted to change. Why the hell would I need to change? I was fine before I met James. I was better than fine. I was *myself*. And even if being myself is being like Grazzo in some regards, so what? I am my father's son. And if that's seriously screwed-up, so be it. I don't need to justify myself. And if James can't handle the way I am, then screw that son of a bitch.

And before I even know what's happening, it's back just like that: my usual energy, flooding my body in a heartbeat. Like it had never left me, like it was merely taking a nap. And this is it. Here, right now. Live it. Love it. Do it. All I have to do is to let myself fall. All it really takes is for me to finally let go off all that bullshit that's been dragging me down. And then I simply do.

I can tell the difference immediately. I can tell from the submissive little moan escaping French Boy's lips as he gladly lets me take over. Hey there. I'm back. I'm here. I'm ready. Good ol' Danny Rizzo is back in the game.

Barely two minutes later, we're fucking in a narrow bathroom stall with a broken lock. It's got a French quote written on its

wall that makes me grin:
Mieux vaut faire, et se repentir,
que se repentir, et rien faire.
- It's better to do something, and regret it,
than to regret, and do nothing.

How about that? A perfect motto for the new year I think has just started. Literally, with one hell of a bang.

3 LOST AND FOUND

NICK: There is nothing more depressing than a bunch of addicts and crazies trying to make it through the holidays. Trust me.

The doctors and nurses tried to get people to make decorations and hang them up in the main room, but no matter how much they try, it still looks like a hospital. A hospital with pieces of sad paper on the walls. It would have been better if everyone just ignored that it was the end of December and let us go on with our lives.

But, like Doc told me one day when I was complaining about it, the point of being in here is to get us ready to go back "out there", or some shit like that, and if "out there" is having Christmas (or Chanukah, or Kwanza, or whatever the hell people are having), then we need to have it in here too.

Nevermind the fact that it's messing with everyone's heads. Because who wants to be stuck in the hospital for Christmas?

Not me, that's for sure. I don't want to be here no matter what day it is, but I don't have much of a choice. It doesn't matter if I want to be at some holiday party, drinking eggnog with everyone else. Or maybe just the liquor that goes in the eggnog. Finding a "present" from Marc and going off to share it with some pretty girl or guy. It doesn't even matter if I just want to be anywhere but here.

And as if the shitty decorations weren't enough, we're having a "holiday party" for families to come and visit. They can bring presents (as long as the nurses check them first for "contraband") and there's fruit punch and cookies, and everyone's trying to pretend like it's not messed up, like it makes sense to have a holiday party where half the guests can't wear shoes with laces and where doctors hover over everyone. Like it's normal.

But maybe it is normal. Because, just like normal, I'm sitting on the side watching everyone else have a good time. Alone, of course, because who would come visit me here? Certainly not my family. Not that I really blame them too much. Both Mom and Dad have their new families to be with.

"Nick."

I'm slouched down in my chair, arms crossed over my chest, trying to hide from the rest of the room, and I have to look way up to see Doc's concerned face looking down at me. Concerned. Great. Concerned usually means some sort of heartfelt discussion is in my near future.

She sits down next to me and watches the other guests with me for a while. There's a group in front of us that looks like they're having the best time in the world. Laughing and joking and hugging. It's the dad that's in here, and he annoys the hell out of me. He's here because he was driving drunk and hit someone. I guess the person's okay, but this was part of his court sentence.

The only thing is that he's all religious and shit, so he wants to save everyone else's soul. Like mine's even worth saving. But he's tried sitting me down three or four times in the two and a half weeks I can remember to tell me that "God loves me" and that I'll be able to leave all my problems behind if I just turn my soul over to "Him". Like that's really helped him out of his problems. The nurses have told him to stop preaching at people, but he still tries.

And now here he is with his family. His wife and his two perfect kids. And still annoying the hell out of me.

I've completely forgotten that Doc's sitting there until she clears her throat a little. She still looks concerned when I glance over at her, and I just cross my arms a little tighter.

"I sent invitations to both of your parents. I'm sure they're just running a little late..."

I can't help laughing at her. I know she's met Mom (I can sort of remember that if I try real hard), so I can't understand how she can keep thinking that my parents are just "running late". I shake my head at her and hear her sigh. I know she'll bring this up at our next meeting, but she's not going to talk about it in the middle of a party.

Some party this is turning out to be.

* * *

The first time Doc mentioned "family therapy" I knew it wasn't going to go over well, and the lack of an appearance at our holiday "party" just reinforced that. My mother is not a woman that appreciates being pulled away from her usual schedule. And my dad, well, he'd probably agree to come and then forget about it. I've seen it happen before. Not with therapy, but with enough other things that I guess I'm pretty much used to it by now.

Doc told me not to worry about it too much. That behind all the anger, parents just want their kids to be okay. I told her that she's never had to deal with *my* parents.

I was already warned, so it's not a total surprise when I walk into Doc's office and see my mother sitting there. Also not a surprise is the fact that she's talking on her cell phone. Doc's not here yet, and mom barely acknowledges I'm in the room, so I sit in my usual chair and wait.

Eventually mom finishes her call, closing the phone up with that little snap that I always hate. It's just plastic on plastic, but something about the sound gives me shivers. I should tell Doc about it. She'd probably think that it's "interesting."

Apparently I have super powers now, because just thinking about Doc brings her into the room. Pretty cool, especially since I was getting sort of twitchy just sitting here with mom ignoring me in favor of her PDA calendar.

"Mrs. Bancroft, thank you for coming today. Unfortunately, it seems that Mr. Kell-"

"Is a no-show. I'm not surprised. Remembering things about his family never was one of his strong points. I was always the one needing to rearrange *my* time. Speaking of, how long do you expect this to take? I need to pick up Daisy from her Kinderplay group in half an hour."

I have to smile a little, even given the situation. Doc looks completely stunned. I've seen mom do this before, fly in and take everything over without any thought for who's actually in charge.

She's a force of nature. I probably should've tried to warn Doc a little more, but then I wouldn't have the fun of seeing her look like someone smacked her with a board, and I have to get my kicks *somehow* in here.

"Mrs. Bancroft, I thought that I'd mentioned in our phone conversation that this is a slow and on-going process. We can't even begin to work on anything in less than half an hour. Nick needs-"

"Nick needs? Isn't that what I'm paying you for? To figure out what he needs and to fix him so that I don't have to do this again. Really, doctor, I'm very busy, and I just don't have the time in my day to drive down here and sit in a little room doing this. Why don't you do whatever it is you do, I'll pay for it, no one else will need to know we went through this, and we'll all be happy."

She gets up and starts putting on her coat. I can see Doc working on a protest, but I don't think it's going to do much good. I knew this wasn't going to work.

"Now, if you'll excuse me doctor, I need to go pick up my daughter, drop her off at the sitter, and then get back to work. I can't just sit here all day; I have better things to do."

"Oh that's right, mom. Run off and spend time with your perfect job and your perfect family and pretend I don't even exist."

It's the first time I've said anything since I walked into the room, and she finally turns and looks at me, almost surprised that I'm even here at all. To be honest, I'm a little surprised myself, that I finally decided to say something.

"Sometimes Nick, I wish you didn't."

No matter what I've been feeling myself, hearing her say it practically sucks the oxygen out of the room. It's a struggle to find the air to say anything else, and when I do, it comes out as a whisper.

"Well maybe if you wish hard enough, one of these days it'll come true." My breath catches in my throat the second I get the words out, and I wonder if maybe we wouldn't have all been better off if I'd ended up taking a little more that night. My ears are ringing and I can only partially hear that Doc's trying to say something. My vision is fine though, and I can see mom picking up her things and walking away.

On top of it all, I can feel that familiar nausea starting to build half way between my stomach and my throat.

"Nick, calm down. Mrs. Bancroft, really, if we could just talk..."

But mom's already out the door. I know she won't be back again. Doc will have to figure out some other way to fix me.

For now though, I have to go throw up and not think about what just happened.

Might be easier to forget if I had something around here to drink...

* * *

Our lights-out time is 10:30 every night, and even New Year's Eve isn't going to change that. So I'm laying in bed when I should be out getting wasted and partying like everyone else is tonight.

New Year's Eve.

A whole new year.

A whole new year with nothing that's going to change. It's going to be the same shit that the past however many years have been, and there's not a damn thing I can do about it.

Doc and I were talking about it a little after the whole fuckup session with my mom, and Doc was saying that I could make this year different if I tried. Like she wants me to, I don't know, get clean and stop screwing everything that moves, and go back to classes and apply myself or some shit like that.

She said it was a good time for me to be in here. That my resolutions can actually mean something this year, instead of just making them out of habit because it's what everyone always does. That it can be a new life instead of just a new year. I don't know what she's expecting from me, though.

So I'm laying here in bed, and I'm thinking how they say what you're doing at midnight on New Year's is going to set the tone for the rest of your year, and it just doesn't seem worth it. I never asked for this. I never asked to be trapped in here, forced to change everything I've become. What's the point of me changing if no one else around me is going to?

What's the point of anything?

* * *

I'm in the TV room. Visiting hours, yeah, but the people that don't get visitors get to watch TV during that time. It's where I always am during visiting hours. Sort of a consolation prize since no one loves me enough to come and visit me. Or something like that.

"Keller!"

It takes me a second to even realize someone's talking to me, because I don't expect anyone to come find me during visiting hours. It's Jerome, the on-duty nurse. He's probably my favorite nurse here, actually. I vaguely remember him tackling me one night right after I got here, but it's one of those memories I'm not quite sure of. He's pretty cool though, if you manage to redeem yourself after getting tackled. Which I think I'm maybe managing to do.

I must have just been staring at him, because I don't remember saying anything. It happens every once in a while, I guess. Doc says it's like I'm looking across the room at something, but my brain is completely gone. She says it's due to the meds, and it should stop eventually. I hope so.

"Keller, pull your head back to earth. You've got a visitor."

A visitor. Me. But I don't get visitors, and can't even think of who it might be. But Jerome doesn't lie about shit like that, so I heave myself out of the chair I've been in for the past hour and go out to the visitors' room.

And there he is. Rizzo. Beautiful as always. It makes me stop and stare for a few seconds, just like it always does. He even looks *comfortable* sitting there. Asshole fits everywhere, and makes me feel a little smaller in comparison.

It's a struggle to work up the courage, but I finally walk over and sit across the table from him. I don't really want him to see me like this, but I don't have a choice now. Refusing to see him would cause more trouble here than just going along with it. He looks at me, and it takes a few seconds for recognition to register.

"You look..."

I can tell he's searching for words, so I offer up a few.

"Like shit? Worse than usual? Like I need a bag to put over my head?"

He laughs. He's always laughing at me. "I was going to say 'different'."

Different. Yeah. I'm sure I don't look anything like he's used to. None of the black, none of the fishnet, none of the makeup, none of the piercings. None of the stuff that made me *me*. They took it all away from me, saying I'm more likely to recover if I leave behind the things that link me to my old lifestyle.

Right. All it does is make me feel worse most of the time. Or like I'm in some strange play that no one gave me the script to. And I think it might be a comedy, only no one's let me in on the punchlines. I'm beginning to think maybe *I'm* the punchline.

Even my hair's different. I haven't dyed it in a while, and they gave me a haircut last week, so most of the black is gone now, leaving the natural light brown behind. Not quite the "little goth boy" that Rizzo's come to expect. Plain jeans and a long-sleeved blue shirt. And slippers. Because it's always cold in here.

"Different. That's an awfully nice way for you to put it."

We sit in silence for a while. After about two seconds I can't look at him anymore, and can't stomach the thought of him looking at me like this, so I stare down at my hands instead. Pick at a scab from a scrape that I'm not sure how I got. Every instinct I have is telling me that I should just tell him to go, because I can't imagine why he's here in the first place. Rizzo always had better things to be doing.

Eventually I can't handle just sitting there anymore. I have to say something. "Why are you here, Rizzo?"

He tilts his head to the side, still looking at me intently, taking his time to fully study the different me in a way that makes me fidget in my seat. There's an almost thoughtful smile on his lips when he speaks. "You overdosed. I found you." There's no reproach in the words, nothing patronizing, just stating a fact. Like this should be answer enough.

It's not enough though. The information shocks me, even though somewhere in my mind, I had to know that someone found me. I guess I just didn't expect it to have been Rizzo. And it creates more questions than answers, especially with the way he'd been ignoring me at the time.

I can't even manage to hold eye contact as I try to come up with something else to say, running a hand awkwardly back through my hair, and wincing as I realize that probably only draws attention to how different I look now. I manage to get my voice under enough control that it doesn't falter when I finally think of something to say.

"Well. Sorry about that then, I guess. Huge downer on a booty call, right?" I force a laugh and shrug a little.

He grins, and it's confident, but it's not the go-screw-yourself grin I'm used to. "I hope you can handle the shock, Keller", he replies with a smile, "but it wasn't one."

Everything about this conversation so far is confusing, Rizzo's attitude, what he's saying, the fact that he's even here in the first place. It makes me even more nervous, and the way I'm fidgeting probably looks a lot like it used to when I'd start craving something. I try to cover it up by laughing again, but I can hear how flat it sounds.

"You don't exactly seem the type to stop by to borrow a cup of sugar or something. And I'm not really the type to *have* a cup of sugar to lend, so..." I don't know why else Rizzo would've been coming by. The only thing that comes to mind is something regarding the play, but that doesn't make sense either.

I can feel my fidgeting getting worse, twisting my fingers together to try to still them, and I actually force myself to start one of those breathing exercises Jeff was always teaching us to control our nerves onstage. I send up a quick prayer that Rizzo doesn't notice how hard it is for me to keep playing my usual part in all this.

He leans forward slowly, glancing at my hands before looking back up at my face. "For god's sake, Nick, relax", he says softly. "It's okay. Okay?"

Okay. I feel like laughing at that, actual real laughter, because things are so far from okay right now. I manage to untwist my fingers and reach up to rub at my eye, a nervous gesture I thought I'd trained myself out of when I started wearing eyeliner every day.

"What's the definition of 'okay' in your world, Rizzo? Because this?" I gesture around at the lounge. "This doesn't really qualify as 'okay' to me."

He arches an eyebrow, and something dark flickers in his eyes briefly, but it doesn't show in his voice. "I don't know, Nick. Given the fact that you almost died on me that night, I'd say this is pretty 'okay'."

I don't even know what the look in his eyes means, and I can't help shaking my head. "No. It's *not*. I'm trapped here, and I'm not even me anymore. Not that it was that great being me before, but it's even worse now because I have to *think* about it. And about how much of a screw-up I am."

I finally look right at him again, trying to find some answers there, but he's not Woodhaven's best actor for nothing. I try to match his don't-care attitude, but I know that I'm not anywhere near as good of an actor as he is. "And on top of everything else, now you're here. And I have no idea why you'd even want to come around. Because honestly, other than my family, you're probably the last person I expected to show up."

He thinks about this for a second, and seems to come to a decision. Then he leans forward in his chair and looks me straight in the eye, suddenly focused and serious. Suddenly real. Like a completely different person. It reminds me of the time I woke up in his bed before he did, of the way he looked then. It's unsettling to see, when I'm so used to the other Rizzo.

"I *really* didn't want to come", he admits with a nonchalant shrug. It's followed by a smile, though, a genuine one. "But I wanted to know how you were doing, and those assholes wouldn't say over the phone."

It's enough to startle me into staring at him for a bit. It *looks* like Rizzo, and it sounds like him. But the things he's saying... "You called?" I can feel the confused frown on my face. "Why would you call? Why would you want to know?" Why would he *care*? None of this makes sense. "You... know that being screwed up isn't contagious, right?"

He looks at me in a way that seems to say, *'god, you're a piece of work, aren't you?'*, but there's warmth in his eyes. "Yeah, and I sure hope that being *stupid* isn't either. I didn't know I wasn't supposed to care whether you live or die."

"Do you?" The words slip out before I can stop them, and I wince at how pathetic they sound. One of the things I've been trying to tell myself since I got here is if they ever let me out, I have to stop caring so much about what Rizzo thinks. But it's hard to remember that when he's sitting in front of me with that smile that, for once, doesn't seem to be mocking me. I try to get at least a little of my self respect back, but it's long gone, and everything comes out wrong. "Or is it just that you thought twice about losing an easy lay?"

I shake my head and wave off the question before he can even respond, looking down again so that I don't have to see whatever his reaction might be. "Damnit. That... It's not what I meant. Ignore that..."

There's a smile in his voice, just barely audible. "It's kinda hard to ignore that you seem to think I'm the world's biggest asshole." There's a pause before he adds: "Guess I deserve it."

I barely even want to look up at him, because this has quickly turned into the world's worst conversation, but I glance up anyway, shaking my head. "No. I'm just saying shit without thinking, as usual. Just ignore me, seriously." I try to push away the thought that it's what he's used to, clenching my teeth to keep from actually saying it.

"I don't think so. You've got something to say - just say it." The warmth seems to go out of Rizzo's voice a little, but it's more familiar now, more like what I'm used to.

"What, you really want me to talk about my feelings now, Rizzo? You never wanted to hear it before." I pause, wondering if I should continue, and the words slip out, quiet but sincere. "That wasn't ever the way we worked."

"Yeah. And you knew what you were getting into with me." He looks like there's more he wants to say on the matter, lots more, but he pauses to think about it for a moment. Then he leans back in his chair, giving me some space.

"Look, Keller. Whatever you wanted to see in me, I was

exactly that, apparently. That's why you kept coming back for more. And now you're sitting here, telling me that I treated you wrong, when you've been treating yourself like *shit* all this time." He looks into my eyes. "What do you expect me to say to that?"

I shake my head a bit and a sigh escapes. Why does he always have to be so frustrating? "I don't know *what* I expect you to say. If anything." My fingers twitch with want of a cigarette, but we're not allowed to smoke inside, even if I had any. "And I know that I was messed up. I still am, if you haven't noticed." I gesture again at our surroundings as I keep talking. "But you haven't exactly made it easy, either. And do you want to know why I kept coming back? Because you're hot and talented and actually paid attention to me for a while, and it felt *good.* And you can't lie and say that you didn't get off a little on our whole... arrangement."

A smile flashes across his lips. "I liked sleeping with you. And yeah, it was convenient." He tilts his head to the side. "What you did with the rest of your time wasn't my business, and vice versa. That *was* the arrangement."

He looks into the distance for a moment before his eyes focus on my face again. "I knew you were messed up. But I was too messed up myself at the time to care."

I'm a little surprised that he's even admitting to such a thing, but I have to smile a bit myself. "Well, you hid it pretty well most of the time. I have to give you that. No wonder you get the leads in all the plays." I go quiet for a bit as the thoughts move through my mind. "So. We're both screwed up. Glad we can admit that. What now?"

There's a sparkle in his eyes when he grins at me. "We each get our act together. 'Cause couples therapy is *not* an option."

His attitude is contagious now, something seeming lighter between the two of us than I can ever remember it being before. The laughter's hiding just under the surface of my words. "What's the matter, Rizzo? Don't want to sit here and listen to me talk about my feelings? I'm told it's what I'm supposed to do here. And I'm sure Doc would be happy to include you in our appointments."

He grins. "Sure. I can see that happening. We'll sob in each other's laps, and we'll *share,* and everything will be wonderful.

When do we start?"

Laughing with Rizzo is unfamiliar, but it feels good to joke with him. "Doc's been pushing for family therapy, but you're the closest thing to a family member that's actually shown up for more than two minutes. And I think I've said more to you than I have in a session since I got here. She'd probably pull you into her office right now if she knew you were here." I try not to wince at how pathetic parts of that sound, letting the laughter cover it.

He smiles, but he doesn't laugh. Just looks at me thoughtfully. "Yeah well, parents - can't live with them, can't kill them."

"I'd have to be able to find them first." The words slip out, just like they have been, without me thinking about them first. I realize how bad most of them probably sound, but I try to soften everything with a smile. "And then I'd probably have to schedule time to do it."

He winks at me, leans forward and lowers his voice to a whisper. "Say no more. It can be arranged."

I smile again at the return of the banter, and lean forward in my chair a little as well, dropping my voice to match his. "I'm not sure you're the 'Godfather' type, but thanks anyway."

He grins. "You ain't seen my 'Pacino' yet."

While my laughter comes easy in response, I'm surprised by the comfortable feeling behind it. It's something I've rarely felt with another person. In the moment, I'm able to forget our history and just enjoy sitting and talking with Rizzo.

"The anticipation is killing me."

* * *

It's cold outside, and gray like it gets in early January. I hate it, but there's really no escaping it. There's a steady stream of visitors coming in today, and even in my chair in the TV room, I can feel the draft that cuts across the floor from the constantly opening doors at the front of the building. There's nothing good on the TV, the weather channel murmuring out the 7-day forecast at me.

I can hear it when someone else comes into the room, but my

back's to the doorway, and I don't feel like turning around, so it's a surprise when whoever it is stops near my chair. I turn my head just enough to peer up at a familiar smile, shocked to see it again.

"You came back." My words slip out without my thinking, and Rizzo's smile widens just a little.

"I wasn't doing anything important today. Had the time."

The words alone might've hurt way too much at one time, but this time I catch the look in his eye, the lightness to his tone, and I grin back up at him. "Well thanks for stopping by again. Is this going to be a regular thing now? Because I can pencil you in on my calendar if it is."

I'm trying to match Rizzo's tone, but he just shrugs at me and smiles. "We'll see."

4 UNHAPPY NEW YEAR

JAMES: You know how things tend to go when you break up with someone you still love. How you say to each other: "I'll never stop caring about you. Let's always be friends!" And then you go and just drop off each other's radar completely. Well, big surprise: Things are no different with Casey and me.

It's January and the world is about as colorless and worn out as I feel. Christmas at home was draining, as per usual. Mom and I do our best to pretend that we're happy during the holidays, and we know that we're not, and it's all pretty messed up. We try not to think of Simon, and she feels compelled to tell me stories about my father from when I was too little to remember. I've heard them all a thousand times, but I like hearing them. I like the look she gets in her eyes when she talks about him and his family. We lost touch with them when she married again. "Your father would have been so proud of you", she always tells me. I'm fairly certain he wouldn't have.

It's weird to think that I don't really have any family besides her. Mom's parents are gone, Simon's folks hate my guts, and I don't blame them. As far as I know, the only relatives I have left on dad's side are my German grandmother whom Mom thinks moved back to Germany with dad's sister years ago. So I guess it's possible that I also have cousins across the Atlantic, somewhere. Mom says I should try to find them when I go to Berlin. I told her that over 82 million people live in that country, and I don't intend to ring on every door.

As far as Christmas gifts are concerned, I'm happy to report that this year she knitted me a sweater that actually fits. It's gray, which she knows I like. She gave me that look and said: "I don't know why you would like a color that isn't even a color." To which I replied: "Maybe I do because it isn't." I guess gray is less of a color than a state of mind. One that was tailor-made for me.

New Year's went by quietly, with us watching the Times Square celebration on TV, making snarky remarks, and clinking glasses with herbal tea at midnight, because she's not supposed to drink alcohol. I thought about giving Casey a call the next day to wish him a happy new year, as you do. I didn't though. Because I realized the one I really wanted to talk to was Rizzo.

Casey hangs out with his artsy people now, and he seems to be doing alright. He spends a lot of time with that red-head Leo who gazes at him like he's god's gift to womankind. It fills me with evil glee that she doesn't seem to know that he swings another way.

Casey and I aren't ignoring each other or anything. Our ways just mysteriously don't seem to cross much anymore. This would leave me all by my lonesome if Anna had not - for reasons unknown and better not questioned - decided to take me under her wing, and make me hang out with her scary dykes. On occasion I find myself almost enjoying their company. I don't even *want* to know what that says about me.

Anna is dating Rhea now, who happens to play the Queen in the *Hamlet* production. So it's just my luck that she keeps me well informed of how Rizzo is doing - regardless of how much I assure her that *I do not want to know*. According to her, the mourning period is definitely over. Which means in plain English: He's out there shagging his way through the one half of campus he hasn't had yet.

So yeah, Rizzo. I've taken to calling him that again, even in my head. It helps me be less of a mess about it all. At least that's what I tell myself. I know that I've screwed this one up for good, and I guess that's just what I'd meant to do. To break this beyond repair. To cancel out any possibility of anything ever happening between us again. What can I say, apparently I succeeded. When you tell someone that you're through, you can't expect them to not take that personal. Even more so when you treat them like thin air afterwards, which yes, I have done, and yes, it was necessary. If I hadn't, I would never have been able to go through with this.

I wonder how many times Rizzo has even been dumped before, if ever. And just when he'd started to open up, which is wow, probably as un-Rizzo as it gets, I do this shit to him. Why? Because my ex-boyfriend was so hung up on him that I couldn't bear the thought of breaking his heart like that. I don't even know how Casey feels about Rizzo now, since he seems to stay as far out of his way as I do. This is exactly why one should never try to do a noble thing. 'Cause now I'm both Casey-less and Rizzo-less. Go figure.

* * *

"That is *so* sad", Rhea says as we leave the building after Medieval European Literature class. She blows strands of dark hair out of her eyes, and looks at me like she wants to wrap me in a blanket and make me soup. "I can't believe you've never seen 'The Princess Bride'!"

"I know", is my sarcastic reply. "I feel seriously deprived."

"Oh, Foley, but you totally are, I swear." She shifts her books and moves to put her free arm around me, and I completely fail at slipping away in time.

"She's right, you know", Anna chimes in on my other side, and forcefully takes my arm. Her Mohawk has turned a dark shade of purple during the holidays, and compared to the previous pink, it makes her look slightly less aggressive. Very slightly, though. I feel like I'm being dragged off to prison.

Rhea tilts her head to the side as she looks at me. "We must change that."

"Tonight", Anna decides, and they beam at each other. We pass a window and I notice that it's snowing again. But the flakes are tiny, at the harsh wind's mercy that twirls and spins them in the air.

I shake my head sadly. "Tonight? Too bad. I'm busy."

"You're not. You left your personal organizer open at lunch."

"Geez, you ever heard of that thing called 'privacy'?"

They both grin. "Nope."

I roll my eyes. "What did I ever do to deserve this?"

Anna seems delighted at the opportunity to explain. "You've been a very naughty boy. Not quite as naughty as one would hope, but you get extra points for the effort."

"This is hell, right? I've died and gone straight to the Ninth Circle."

Rhea gives me a sweet smile. "Aww. Come on, Foley, it'll be fun. I promise."

I eye her warily. "You said that before, and then you made me watch 'Tipping the Velvet'."

But they just laugh and ignore all my efforts to slip out of their affectionate grip as we make our way towards the library. God, I am so doomed.

* * *

I turn up the collar on my coat and shiver as I step outside into the darkness. I'm on my way over to Rhea's dorm, because if I don't come freely, the dykes will turn up on my doorstep to get me. It might involve kicking and shouting, and I'd rather avoid that, thank you very much.

The snow that fell this afternoon has already turned into slush that makes smacking noises under my brisk steps. It isn't far to Kennedy House, so chances of me not freezing to death on my way there are reasonably high. At least until I stop dead in my tracks and stare in shock.

I've spotted Rizzo a small distance ahead. I can just make him out at the edge of the shadow of a building, but I'd recognize his tall, slender figure anywhere. That in itself is no cause for alarm, but he's talking to that scumbag of a dealer who always hangs around campus. I don't even know what to think for a moment, but my mind is racing, and my stomach feels like a tightening knot. *Please tell me he's not buying. Please.* Because if he is, I don't care what I did and what he thinks of me, swear to god I'm gonna stop him, by force if I have to.

But it looks like they're just talking. No, *arguing*. And I'll be damned - Rizzo looks pissed off. I've never seen him like that. What the hell? He doesn't raise his voice - doesn't have to - but there's something so sharp about his tone that it worries me. Whatever is going on over there, it's not just something minor. It's something that must really matter to him. I can't help it, I need to know what's going on, so I carefully move closer, leaving the safe shadows of the trees lining the path.

Scumbag seems to be trying to talk his way out of something, to calm Rizzo down, but it has the opposite effect. I'm not yet close enough to quite make out what they're saying, but Rizzo's voice is a subzero threat that makes me shudder, and *I'm* not even the one he's talking to.

Whatever Scumbag replies, it's exactly the wrong thing. What comes next is so fast and unexpected that it gives me a start; Rizzo punches the guy in the face, knocks him down with what seems like very little effort.

Blood is dripping from the dealer's nose, leaving a red trail on his face, and now I can hear what Rizzo is saying. Very slowly, calmly, and as icy as the North wind.

"You're going to *stay away* from him."

Scumbag stares up at him for a moment, wiping his nose with the back of his hand. Then he nods, looking defeated, and might I add, pretty pathetic, too.

I manage to slip back into the line of trees just in time before Rizzo turns around and steps onto the smaller path that leads right past where I'm hiding. My treacherous heartbeat is trying to give me away as he approaches. I can literally see him relaxing as he's passing through the mild light of a lamppost. The anger just rolls off of his handsome face. It's replaced by something that I know will haunt me for the rest of the night: a small frown and a fleeting sadness. He puts his hands in the pockets of his suede jacket as he saunters past me. I follow him with my eyes, everything inside of me just *aching*. Aching to talk to him, to find out what just happened here. To find out what's wrong, because so much seems to be. Because this isn't the Rizzo I know, the Rizzo everyone knows. This is Danny. And it just *hits* me how much I really miss him. And I want to tell him so badly.

What I do instead is wait until he's gone. Then I step back onto the path, my shoes soaking wet, my face freezing. And I continue on my way to watch some stupid fairytale movie that according to two crazy dykes is supposed to cheer me up forever. Well, good luck with that.

5 PHOENIX

NICK: Saturday afternoon means weekend visiting hours, and I'm actually in the main area, waiting again. I never thought I'd be one of the patients that waits for people to show up, but it's what I've become. Rizzo's still the only one that comes to see me in this hellhole, and he doesn't visit all the time, but he's been here enough now for it to be a regular thing.

We've been talking about stuff more, and last time he visited, he mentioned the play, and how rehearsals are going to start up again soon. I was surprised that it took him so long to say something about it, but I guess I'm learning that he does have the ability to be tactful when he wants. Him mentioning it got me thinking about it again though, and although *Hamlet* isn't the sort of reading you'd expect to find in the psych ward, I asked Doc to get a copy for me. She seemed a little surprised when she handed it over, like she didn't expect me to want to read it after everything that happened leading up to me landing in here. I don't blame her. Most of the times that she's tried to talk to me about the play, it's been like pulling teeth. It's not exactly an upbeat conversation topic for me.

And yeah, it's almost a little like torture to read it again, especially Horatio's lines, which I'd had just about memorized when Jeff gave me the part of Marcellus. It's something I need to do, though, for myself. The play's going to be all over campus if I ever get out of here, and I'll have to deal with it. So I guess this is just my way of forcing myself to get used to it now, when I can try to handle shit on my own terms. It's taking me a while to get through it, just because I keep setting it down to think about things, but I figured that waiting for Riz to show up would be as good a time as any to get through a little more of it.

Ophelia's breakdown keeps me occupied for a while, and I have to laugh to myself a little. I'd always thought she was just an annoying add-on character, someone that didn't even need to be there. But her confusion - the way her world breaks apart as Hamlet messes with her - well shit. Forget Horatio or Marcellus, because Jeff should've just cast me as Ophelia.

I suppose it's not the nicest comparison to make, and it's not like Rizzo killed my family or anything. I actually feel bad about the comparison, especially when a familiar figure eases comfortably down onto the other end of the couch. I finish the line and mark my place before tucking the book down between my leg and the cushion and looking over at him with a smile, pushing my previous thoughts away. "You're late today. Hot date keep you away?"

Rizzo leans back against the arm of the couch, body a long line of satisfaction that I can't help glancing down at for a second, and grins at me. "I wouldn't exactly call it a 'date'..." He tops it off with a wink, and I can only laugh at him, seeing the tease for what it is.

I gesture at his hand a little where I can see his knuckles are a little roughed up, still smiling. "Yeah, doesn't look like a very successful date, if it was. What's the matter, having to fight off all those groupies lately?" I've never even heard of Rizzo getting in a fight, but his hand looks pretty raw.

He shrugs, casual grin still firmly in place. "What can I say? Everyone loves a tortured prince." He gestures down at where I've tucked the book away, almost seeming interested that I have it here, and I'm actually a little embarrassed that he's caught me reading it, thinking back again about the comparison. I can feel the tips of my ears flush hot and pink, and I try to shrug as casually as he had.

"It passes the time," I reply to his unasked question, but my answer seems weak even to me, especially since there's a million other things I could be reading. I sigh and shake my head. "And if I ever get out of here... get back to campus... shit's not going away any time soon, right?" There's a pause that I'm starting to recognize as Rizzo thinking before he replies.

"Not even if you want it to, no." Rizzo's still smiling, his tone light, but I look over just in time to catch something else. I wouldn't even be able to name what it was, but it tells me that something isn't right.

"Do *you* want it to?" The question is out before I can stop it, and Rizzo glances over, seeming surprised. I'm not sure at what. Maybe that I'm not completely lost in my own head anymore, and can actually pick up on shit. He shakes his head though.

"Not the whole show. Just certain people in it." He laughs it off as a joke and changes the subject, but we both know he's acting even now.

* * *

The room's swimming, and I'm certain that I've misheard what Doc's just said. When I ask her to repeat it, though, it stays the same.

"We're releasing you next week, Nick. You've been here over a month, your mandatory time here's done, your school semester has started, and I don't want you missing any more classes than you absolutely have to. Plus, even though we both know that there's things you still have to work on, you've actually made a lot more progress than I expected."

I'm already shaking my head, ready to argue, but she talks over it. "Nick, the drugs are out of your system and you're responding well to the medication we've got you on. From what I can tell, from what you've told me, you're more stable now than you've been in years. I know you're scared. Everyone's scared to get back out there, especially after something like you've been through. But hiding in here isn't going to make it any easier. We'll set up appointments for you to come in, lots of them. We'll keep you healthy." She pauses and looks at me so seriously that I can feel my throat go tight at the unspoken *We'll keep you alive.*

She doesn't usually say shit like that, not with that tone. Even hinting that the overdose was more than just an accident, and that all the shit leading up to it wasn't accidental either. I've said it in sessions, we've talked a lot about self-destructive behavior and depression and coping, and there's shit about it in my official file, but damn if I hate admitting it when I don't have to.

Everything else she says washes over me, and eventually I head back out to the main lounge, trying to get my hands to stop shaking. The feeling is familiar, but this time it's not for the reasons I've been used to. I'm still sitting there when Rizzo shows up. I can tell that he's in a good mood when he comes in, an extra energy to his step that I can feel even though I don't look up. It stills, though, when he gets closer, and by the time he sits down, he's serious and quiet.

"Nick?"

I have to close my eyes to try to steady myself against how concerned his voice suddenly sounds. Now that I'm able to pay attention, I hear the worry and care that's hidden under everything else. I notice the little hints of vulnerability. It tugs at me in a strange way when he sounds like this, makes me wonder more about the parts of himself that he doesn't usually show, the things he doesn't usually say, the things I've always missed before and am finally starting to see now. On top of everything else that's just happened with Doc, it's so unsettling. My eyes are still closed when I take a breath to steady myself.

"They're releasing me... next week."

There's a stillness between us while I wait for a reply, but none comes. I finally open my eyes to look over at him, and he's smiling at me. Not laughing, not teasing, just smiling a little. Happy.

"Best news I've had all day," he says, voice warm enough to wrap around me. There's something under the words that I've never heard before from him, something relieved and relaxed and though I know I don't deserve it and never will, it makes me feel like maybe I can handle this.

* * *

Logically, I know it's been less than two months. Logically, I know that nothing's going to have changed. But it still feels strange when the cab pulls up to campus and everything looks the same. The buildings still stand where they always have, winter-bare trees filling the spaces in between. There's a fairly new blanket of snow making everything reflect clean and bright as I watch people hurry between buildings to get out of the cold. Just like they always have.

Everyone's bundled up in heavy jackets and scarves, covering their faces and hiding who they are. I wouldn't be able to recognize anyone out there even if I did know them. The fact that I don't makes it even worse. Like I'm a stranger on campus. I have to laugh, because it's basically the truth. The only one on campus that I can even claim to know at this point is Rizzo, and no matter that he came to visit me in the hospital, I know that being on campus is going to be completely different. I know that here he's *Rizzo*, and a messed-up Nick Keller doesn't have any place in the world of *Rizzo*.

The cab pulls up in front of one of the dorms, one I've never lived in before. Between Doc's recommendation and the University needing to shuffle people around at the semester break, I've been moved into a different room, a different building. I pay the cab driver from the cash that my mom had dropped off along with some more of my things, and head up to my new room. When I get there, I find all of my old things already there, thrown into haphazard boxes. I wonder who got to sort through it all. Cops? University administration? My family? I'm sure Rizzo would've said something by now if it'd been him.

Even though it's a different room, it still smells like a dorm. Like people and books and microwave food and a mixture of dirty and clean laundry floating in from the hallway. Other than the boxes and the standard dorm room furniture, the room is empty. I start with making the bed, putting on the clean, recently washed sheets that I find in the bag from mom. When it's done, I sort of want to just crawl in and never look back out, but I know that I shouldn't, that it'll be hard to get moving again if I stop. It doesn't make it any easier to ignore the temptation, though.

It takes me a few hours to unpack and sort through everything. Most of it I don't need. Most of it I don't even *want*. It's all just reminders of a person that I don't want to be any more. Someone that I can't be, if I want to actually have a second chance. There's a part of me that wants to be someone better than that guy, and even if I doubt most of the time that I can do it, even if I think that it's only a matter of time before everything goes totally ass-up again, I have to try. Even though I know that trying will just make it harder when I eventually fail again.

If. Not when. Shit, it's hard to think positive.

I have the clothes that my mom dropped off - jeans and soft shirts in soft colors, everything washed before she left it there, just like the sheets were, so that everything smelled like laundry and not the stores. I never saw her when she stopped by, probably just long enough to drop the bags and leave again, but I figure the fact that they didn't still have the tags on was a good sign, like she was putting at least some effort into it. Like maybe there's still hope there for us. Maybe with a few years I can start to fix that part of my life too.

But that's looking too far ahead. One step at a time, just like Doc told me.

I take a good bunch of my shit to the trash, dumping more black clothing and fishnet and eyeliner than I even realized I had. It's not easy, but it's therapeutic, and I can't help think that Doc might be proud of me for it. I'm a little proud of myself, to be honest. And I can breathe a little easier once it's gone. The room looks pretty empty, only a few things hanging in the closet for me to wear, but I've gotten used to the hospital and how clean it always was. So it's strangely comfortable. And as cheesy as it sounds, it looks like the room of a guy that I might like to be. A little boring still, it could maybe use something on the walls, but it's getting there.

It's getting there.

* * *

Going to class is interesting. It's... Well, it's a lot different when you're sober all the time. It's a lot different when you actually *go* all the time. Doing the reading and the homework helps too. Things make sense, and it's easier to follow the professor.

I'd better watch out. I might actually start to like school.

Well. Shit, if I'm being honest, though, there *is* a problem. I had to rearrange my schedule when I got back, because of last semester. I pretty much failed all my classes, and there's some other stuff I have to make up too. And when things got moved around, I lost my theater classes. So I'm stuck with core requirement classes, which is actual work, and I don't have anything in my major to off-set it.

And I'm obviously not in the play any more. I doubt that Jeff will ever let me be in a play at Woodhaven again.

I have a feeling it's going to make for a long semester, and a lot of work. Especially since the administration has put me on some sort of special academic probation. But if I can get through the next few months and pass all my classes, then I think I might just be able to eventually make it to graduation too.

* * *

I have no hobbies. This, I know, is tragic and sad. But it's true. I've been back for just a few days, been to all of my classes at least once. They take up a good chunk of my time, and studying and doing homework does too. But despite the fact that I've apparently become a huge school-dork in my quest to survive and not fail completely, there's still time left over that I'm having trouble filling. Doc said it'd probably be a problem, gave me all sorts of suggestions and shit, and that I should call her if it got too hard, but whatever. I'm trying to tell myself that I'm just bored.

But it's not just that. Because I also want a drink.

God, I want a drink so bad that I can almost taste it. I got home from class, and it's a Friday afternoon, and people are already starting to party for the weekend. And me? For the first time since I got back, I really want to be out there with them. Partying and hooking up, and shit, I haven't gotten laid in months. Not since Rizzo stopped asking last semester and started ignoring me, and we'll just ignore how pathetic *that* sounds. I think about calling him, but it's weird now that I'm back on campus. I've only seen him from afar, really, and I'm not quite sure what we are here. What I am sure of is that I can't call him about this. And I shouldn't have to. I *should* be able to get through this on my own.

But this is too much for me to handle today, and I don't know why it's so bad right now. I haven't had to do this yet, and I feel guilty about interrupting her Friday, but I call Doc's emergency number, apologizing even as she picks up the line, but she talks over me, telling me that it's alright and trying to get me to stop rambling at her.

Her voice makes it easier for me to breathe, and I'll never tell that to anyone because it sounds so stupid. But it's the truth.

"Get out of your room, Nick. You need a change of scenery, especially on the weekend." That's her advice. Which is great, but Woodhaven's not a huge campus, and to be honest, there's a limited number of things *to* do.

There's always the cafe though, and caffeine is one of my "allowable" addictions, so it seems like the best solution for the moment. I head out of the dorm, grabbing the latest edition of the school paper on the way. If nothing else, I can make fun of the articles in my head.

* * *

I never used to go into the cafe on a Friday night, always at some party or another, so I never realized that it's actually open on Friday nights. It's pretty full when I push my way through the door, school paper shoved into the pocket of my coat along with hands that I can barely feel because I didn't think to grab a stupid pair of gloves before I left my room.

The girl behind the counter looks at me like she's trying to figure out where she knows me from, but I just smile a little at her as I order my coffee. She says she'll bring it over to my table, so I slip an extra few dollars into the tip jar before I go to find a seat. There's one in the corner, and by the time the girl comes over with my coffee, I've already started in on reading the paper.

It's, surprisingly, not that bad. This is actually the third edition I've read since I've been back at school. I know, I know. Sad that *this* is what my life has come to these days. How far the mighty have fallen.

I have to admit though, sitting in the cafe, the school paper spread in front of me, even if it's on a Friday night when almost everyone else on campus is out partying - it's the best way I've found so far to pass the time that isn't going to class or doing homework. And really, they've found someone to write that doesn't suck, doesn't make you want to gouge your eyes out just to save yourself from the goddamn boredom of it all.

I've been checking too. Every article that's managed to keep my attention all the way through, I'll check to see who wrote it. Apparently this "James Foley" guy, he's a writer and the editor, and he's good. Name sounds familiar too, but hell if I know why, because I've never picked up the paper before. For all I know, I could've slept with him. I might know if I saw him. Might not.

Still. I wonder what it'd be like to talk to the guy. Hell, if he talks anything like he writes, I might even be able to have a conversation with him. Make my first friend. Maybe not, but I guess it doesn't matter either way. It's not like I'm going to go hunting him down. That's a little too stalker for my tastes, thanks. I'll keep reading the paper and if I somehow run into him that's cool.

Probably won't though. I figure writers for the paper are pretty out there. You know, in a social, party way. That's the way I remember it being in high school. And since avoiding the parties is why I'm reading the paper in the first place, my chances of running into the guy don't seem very high.

* * *

Is it pathetic to say that the cafe is becoming my home-away-from-dorm? Because it is. Getting through the weekend and into my second week back, I've been here almost every day. I'm pretty sure the people behind the counter are starting to know who I am, at least by order, because when I walked in earlier, the girl at the register just nodded at me and said she'd bring "it" to my table. And she did. A perfect coffee, just the way I like it.

I've also claimed a table as "mine", where I always try to sit when I'm here. It's back in the corner, out of the way of the people just there to socialize, big enough that I can spread out a book or two if I need to do some homework. It feels ridiculous to be so worried about school when I never was before, but it's what I've got going for me right now. It's maybe the one thing I can at least try to be good at this semester.

God knows I've got nothing else going for me right now.

I sure as hell don't have a social life going for me, that's for sure. And that's one of the things about coming to the cafe. My little table gives me the perfect spot to watch all the people that come in with their friends, and it's a nice, masochistic little reminder that no one's going to come sit by me.

Since I've started hanging out here, I've seen Rizzo come in with some of the theater kids, and I've seen that guy he used to hang out with come in and be all cozy with two girls. It's easy for people to ignore the table in the back corner though.

Especially when it's just a guy working on his homework most of the time. I keep my head down and the world moves around me. Even on a quiet night like this, when there's only a few other people in the place.

You'd think that the lack of people would make it obvious that someone's headed to my table, but I don't even notice it until a chair is pulled out and someone sits across from me. I'm more than a little surprised to look up and see that it's Rizzo smiling back at me.

"Long time, stranger. Haven't seen you since you got back." He smiles more as he says it, and I can't help smiling in return at the familiarity. "You been hiding from me?"

I shake my head as I set down my pen, and actually glance around the cafe, checking to see if anyone's watching us. It's a strange reflex, and I realize that I'm worried about people seeing us together for *his* sake.

"I've been right here. You've been busy." I'm not trying to make him feel bad, either. Not like I maybe once would've. It's just the truth: he's been busy. Classes and the show and friends. "There's only so many hours in the day. You've got shit to do." I quirk a smile at him. "Everyone on campus knows that."

He looks at me with that look I've gotten so used to. The one that says *You are a little stupid sometimes, aren't you?* He settles into his chair more comfortably, looking for all the world like he's going to be there a while, and grabs my coffee to take a drink of it. "So. How're you settling in?"

I get the feeling that he actually wants to know, and even though it still surprises the hell out of me, I close my book and start to talk.

6 DON'T TELL

JAMES: With a start I wake up from that nightmare, the one where I'm covered with blood and I'm in the shower trying to wash it off. I think it's *his* blood, and I'm filled with terror, shame and disgust. But no matter how much I scrub, it always reappears, and I start to panic. Then I realize that the blood is my own, it's coming out of my pores, but somehow I can't stop scrubbing. So I scrub and scrub until my skin turns translucent and I start to vanish, bit by bit. That's when I wake up, my heart beating madly in my chest, still trapped in so many layers of fear that I can't even breathe. It takes me agonizing minutes to calm down and find my way back into reality.

I let out a deep sigh and rub my face, hoping to shake off the broken feeling. Then I sit up and haul my sad ass out of bed. I know it's no use trying to go back to sleep; besides the gray hues of dawn are already creeping in through the window, throwing long shadows on the floor. The nightmare is still trapped inside of me, coming to life every time I close my eyes. My mind wanders back home, to how it used to be, to Simon, to all the years between then and now that never managed to bury *that day*. You can swear never to speak of something again, but nothing will keep it from haunting you.

There are things in my life that I'm not proud of, memories of when I failed to be a good son, a good friend, a good anything. But there is one moment, one defining moment that shattered everything about the person I'd always thought I was. Since that day, that one moment when I was sixteen, I've never really been the same. You may believe that I've always been this jaded asshole, but nobody starts out that way. When I look back to those days before everything changed, I cringe at how innocent I still was in many ways. I actually believed that one day, everything would be okay. That I would miraculously get

Mom to leave Simon, and we'd start a whole new life somewhere. I thought there wouldn't be a price to pay. I thought we'd already paid more than our share. I was so sick of wearing turtle necks and long-sleeved shirts every other day in summer. I was sick of pretending. They're usually careful to only hit you where you can hide it, but when Simon lost it, man he lost it big time. And that summer things were worse than ever. There were nights when I lay awake listening to the steady humming of cicadas outside, skin covered with brand-new bruises, wondering if I'd live to be seventeen. If it hadn't been for Mom, I would have run away years ago. But I couldn't leave her behind. I wonder how my life would have turned out had I had the courage and cold-bloodedness to just split. You don't know how often I wish I would have.

I rub my tired eyes as I sit down at my desk and hesitate a moment before I turn on the little lamp on it. As expected, it's way too bright when I do, and everything seems darker now outside the window. I grab a book and turn on my old laptop, because now that I'm more or less awake, I might as well work on my literature assignment. I glance around the room while the computer starts up. My eyes come to rest on Rizzo's illustrated book on Berlin, and my stomach tightens with a strange yearning. I have so many mixed emotions when it comes to leaving. I accepted the scholarship, but just between us, I still don't really see myself going. Logically, I know that it doesn't make much of a difference if I'm at Woodhaven or across the Atlantic; Mom would still be alone, with no-one to look after her but a detached, overworked social worker. It would be more expensive to give her the usual call every night to check if she's taken her meds, that's for sure. I know she really wants me to go and take this chance. She wouldn't be Mom if she didn't. But I just feel horrible about it all. I've been feeling so restless lately, like I'm waiting for something bad to happen any minute. And I'm not even the kind of person to buy into this whole foreboding shit. And then I sometimes ache for someone to tell me it's all bullshit, and Mom's gonna be fine, and I'm gonna be fine, and there's no point in worrying myself sick. And I ache for that person to be Rizzo, and then I have to hate myself for being majorly pathetic. Welcome to how my mind works at 5 am.

A little *ping* noise startles me and I stare at the computer screen. I exhale with relief and a sudden feeling of warmth spreads through me. A chat window has popped up - it's Casey.

"Hey there, Sleepless!"

I can't help but smile as I swiftly type a reply: "*You're one to talk, Awake-at-ungodly-hour.*"

"Art assignment. Just got back from lame attempt to take pictures of statues in dark park. Teeth still chattering. Status of ass: frozen off."

I chuckle to myself. "Now that's a shame. I liked that ass."

There's a little pause and I impatiently wait for a reply. I'm still mildly shocked when it comes. Just four little words, but they make me swallow hard. Repeatedly.

"I miss you, James."

* * *

Eleven hours later we sit at what used to be our "usual table" at Cafe Plato, and I'm happy to report that Casey's nice little ass is, in fact, still there. Hallelujah. The other good news is that we both look equally tired, so I don't have to feel too bad about my whole Dracula getup - pale face, dark shades underneath my eyes. Feeling strangely self-conscious, I stare at my hand resting beside my steaming coffee mug, noticing how the veins on the back of it are showing. I think I might have lost some weight.

"You look good, James," Casey smiles, studying me with kind eyes. "I like your hair a little longer."

I wince and look up at him from underneath some strands of hair. "I look terrible. And I really need to get it cut."

"Don't you dare."

He, on the other hand, is wearing his hair really short now. It makes him look more mature, and brings out the brilliant blue of his eyes more. I want to tell him, but somehow the words won't come. So I just sit there like an idiot, not knowing what to say or do. Awkward.

Just as the silence starts to get really uncomfortable, he suddenly reaches over and takes my hand in his. I'm taken by surprise by this move, but his fingers are warm and wonderfully familiar on mine, so I don't pull away.

"I'm sorry I haven't been around much lately. I feel like such an ass," he says softly.

"No, it's okay. Really. I've been pretty busy myself."

"Well," he clears his throat, "I wasn't *that* busy." He looks out the window for a moment before his gaze finds mine again. "I just... I needed that space, for a while. It was tough, getting over everything. Getting over you." He pauses briefly. "And I'm not saying that I completely am. Over you, that is. I guess this sort of thing just takes a little more time."

I swallow. "Guess so."

He takes a sip of his cappuccino, eyeing me over the brim of the cup. "But I miss our friendship, James. More than I can say. I don't think there's anyone who knows me better than you do. And I miss talking, and just hanging out. I miss all of it." He shrugs. "I don't know, even though things will probably continue to be a little weird between us for a while, I'd take 'weird with you' over being completely without you anytime. Does that make sense?"

"Strangely enough, it does." I try to smile, but it ends up rather crooked. I'm not sure how I feel about this. It's so very good to see him, but it still hurts somehow. I'm torn all over again. Part of me feels the same way - I never wanted to lose him as a friend. If I can just get over feeling so awkward, I know it would be awesome to hang out again. Because I've been missing him too, like crazy. I wish I could get myself to admit as much, but somehow I just can't. It takes me a moment to realize that there's also a part of me that's actually still mad with him. For ever getting me to give up Rizzo. Which was my idea and my choice, not his. He never asked me to do it. It was my doing, mine alone. So how can I be mad because of it? How schizo is that?

"What's on your mind?" He looks at me intently, and I may just be squirming a bit in my seat. "James, are you okay?"

"Yeah. Sure," is my quick reply. A little too quick, possibly. I sigh a little, trying to beat all the confused emotions into something that makes enough sense to talk about it. "I guess I just need to get used to this again, is all."

He nods, and he's looking a little insecure all of a sudden. "I understand. If you need more time, then I..."

I grab his arm instinctively as he already moves to get up. "No! No, stay."

The smile I get for that warms my heart somehow, and I'm starting to feel more relaxed as he sits back down.

"Thank you," he says softly.

"For what?"

"For bearing with me. Not just now - through it all."

I clear my throat uneasily, and smirk at him. "Well, yeah. You can be a bit of an idiot on occasion."

He laughs. "That makes two of us then."

I grin. "So it would seem."

He looks at me with sparkling eyes, then he reaches over. "Come here, you bastard." And he pulls me into a hug, and I let him. And then I hug him back. Because I love the scent of his skin, and the warmth, and it just feels like being... home. And something cold inside of me seems to vanish into thin air.

After that, we change the subject and start to talk about this and that like we always have, and suddenly the conversation comes easy. We tell each other about school projects, I get to be snarky about the lameness of some of my reporters, and he almost pisses himself laughing when I tell him about Anna kidnapping me for lesbian movie night. He mentions Leo a lot, I notice. They seem to be getting along pretty well when they work on art projects, and I'm surprised to be glad for him at last. The only subject we both carefully avoid for an hour is Rizzo.

That's when Andrea and his usual crew walk in, and we both know it won't be long before Rizzo shows up as well. Thursday. Vocal Production class must be over. I feel lame for having his schedule memorized.

I glance at my watch. "Shall we leave?"

Casey nods quickly. "Okay."

We're out of there faster than you can say "chicken shit", and naturally, it's just then started to snow again.

"Crap." I pull my coat tighter around me, and we both stand under the roof indecisively for a minute, staring into the big, dancing snowflakes. You almost can't make out the trees along the paths through them. The smell of snow fills the air. Wintertime can really kiss my ass. I'm so ready for spring. It's freezing, too.

Casey glances at me. "Where to?"

"Listen, I kinda still need to finish an assignment."

"Okay."

"But this was nice," I hear myself admitting before I can stop myself.

He smiles brightly. "Same time tomorrow then?"

"Sure."

There's a silence between us again for a minute, but this time it's not awkward. I used to love that, our comfortable silences.

"It was good to see you, James." He pulls me into a hug, and I pull him close.

"I'm not over him either," he whispers suddenly, close to my ear.

I can feel myself tense noticeably, but Casey doesn't let go. "You, my friend, need to go tell him, though."

"Tell him what?" I hate that my voice sounds all hoarse.

"That you want him back, of course, silly. Because if you don't, I will."

I pull back abruptly. "What? No, you won't!"

He shrugs, almost mischievously, his breath visible in the chilly air. "Someone has to do something."

"Yeah, and that involves staying the hell away from him!"

"And quietly moping for the rest of your life?"

"As if!" I snort. "Not the *entire* rest of my life," I add quietly, and Casey chuckles.

He looks at me with kind eyes. "I knew it. James, you're such an idiot. Let me talk to him."

"You try that, and I'll never speak to you again. I swear."

"You make a fine drama queen, did you know?"

"Casey, I'm serious. The thing with him… it's over. End of story."

He just gives me a look, and starts to walk towards the dorm. I follow him into the falling snow, my heart beating madly. "Swear you won't say a word to him. I mean it!"

But he just smiles to himself and falls into an easy jog, quickly disappearing behind a curtain of twirling snowflakes. His voice echoes along the pathway: "See you tomorrow, James!"

I stare after him, dumbfounded, a feeling of impending doom creeping over me. He didn't mean that, right? He's not actually gonna try to... is he?

Oh boy. I start to run after him. "Casey, wait up!"

But he's already gone.

7 SECOND CHANCES

NICK: Damn insomnia. I swear you don't know how sweet being able to sleep is until you can't do it anymore. Staring at the wall or the ceiling, thoughts going a million miles an hour, body being absolutely trashed with exhaustion, but not being able to sleep. It's a goddamn nightmare, if you'll excuse the pun. Ha-damn-ha.

Doc doesn't want to put me on sleeping pills yet, but I can't stand just laying there in my room, so I've settled into a cycle. I stay out at the cafe almost every night for as late as I can stand it, then head back to my room, dragging myself the entire way. Then I stay up even longer, usually dicking around on my computer, before hauling myself over to my bed, to hopefully pass out for a few hours.

It's not great, but it's the best I've got right now. Riz usually joins me at the cafe when he can. I get the feeling that he doesn't always sleep much either. I appreciate the company, so I haven't called him on the way he looks pretty exhausted sometimes too.

It's a night without him though, and the entire campus is dark by the time I make my way back from the cafe to my room. Even though it's more than a little creepy, I cut through the drama department, passing the doors to the large theater auditorium. They're closed, but there's piano music sneaking out around the cracks. I hesitate near one and listen. The sound is distorted a little through the door, but whoever it is, and it must be a music major, they're real good. I want to sneak inside to see who it is, maybe listen a little, but before I can decide if I should, the song stops. There isn't another to follow it, so I hurry down the hall before the person comes out and sees me listening at the doors like a creep.

* * *

The next night, when I take the same shortcut, one of the doors to the auditorium is cracked open, so I slip inside. The theater is dark except for a few lights near the front of the house. There's a grand piano, shining and sleek, sitting center stage, and the musician that's coaxing such sweet sounds from it shocks me.

It's Rizzo.

I didn't even know that he could play at all, much less anything like *this*. I ease silently into one of the seats in the last row, getting as lost in the music as he seems to be. It's nothing I recognize, angry and sad and bittersweet, and there's something about it, some twist of melody, that's so *Rizzo* that it makes me ache a little. Reminds me of the way he can be when it's just us talking about something. Despite my stealthy listening, it's not music for anyone but himself, and that makes it all the better.

Long moments of sound pass in notes and beats and nothing else before I realize that I'm not the only one listening. Jeff slipped in at some point, and is standing there, hip against a seat across the aisle from me, watching the stage. He scares the crap out of me when I see him, not expecting anyone else to be there this late, and the movement of it catches his eye. He looks at me and tilts his head toward the door behind us, an invitation for me to join him in the hallway. I know that I shouldn't be intruding on Rizzo like this anyway, so I nod and we leave the auditorium as quietly as we can.

It doesn't surprise me when we start walking toward his office, quiet for a while before he clears his throat. "Not many people get to see that. Not many people even know he plays. I think he'd appreciate if it stayed that way."

I'm not an idiot, and I nod in reply. Riz was past good enough to play for anyone, much less the people he usually hangs out with. It's something else that people would love about him, just like acting. The fact that he doesn't tell anyone means he's got a reason not to, and I'm not going to be the one that screws that up.

We make it to Jeff's office, and he gestures at one of the chairs. Being in there again brings back the hazy memories of getting kicked off the cast, but I try to forget that. It doesn't work very well, and I find myself trying to figure out what the hell I've done wrong now.

"He's in there playing a few times a week. More if he needs to. I don't ask questions - just make sure he can get in and that no one hassles him." Jeff digs through the piles on his desk, looking for something as he talks. I watch him without saying anything, waiting for something that requires me to reply.

"I think he plays more when something's bothering him. He's been in there almost every night for the past few weeks, and I knew he'd be in there after today..."

He trails off, and finally really looks at me, even though I know he's been doing his creepy people-watching thing at me the whole time. I'm not sure I'm comfortable under that sort of attention right now. "What happened today?" I force the question out, even though I'm not sure I need to, and he laughs. It takes me a second to realize that he's not really laughing at me. That it's soft and a little tired. The same sort of thing I've been noticing behind Rizzo's eyes lately at the cafe.

"We had a cast member walk off the show. He... wasn't getting along very well with the rest of the cast. So now I need to find a replacement." I wince a little. It's late February, and the show's in May. At this point, finding new cast could wreck the whole show, especially if it's a lead. He sees the look on my face and knows that I know it. Nodding again, he sits down behind his desk and gestures at me.

"Enough about our problems. Look at you! Word has it that things are getting better in your world." I can't help laughing at the way he puts it. In my world. For the first time in a long time, I'm *not* in my own world. I'm in the same goddamn crazy world as everyone else.

"It's good to have you back, Nick." There's a significant little pause, and I can predict what's coming next before he even opens his mouth again. "You're doing okay, though? Really?"

I know in that moment that Jeff knows. He knows everything that's happened, and probably even knew as it was happening. The drugs, the attempt, the hospital. Probably even the people I hooked up with. I don't know how he knows, but he does.

I nod at him, and even though I've barely said a word since

leaving the auditorium, it's hard to force them out. "Yeah, Jeff. It's... good. It's okay. Still got a ways to go, but I'm getting there." I can see the next question on his tongue, so I talk over. "And I'm sober. Have been since, well. A while, now." I laugh again to try to ease the weirdness, but Jeff just smiles at me.

"Good. Fucking great." His grin gets a little wider as I stare at him, it still being strange to hear professors curse, even if it's him. "Though if you tell me that you've given up acting in your new-found sobriety..."

"Are you kidding?" I interrupt him without even thinking. "I miss it like I'd miss my leg if someone cut it off! Hate that I couldn't even fit a class in this semester."

He laughs at me, but I don't care, because it's the truth. "What are you doing tomorrow, Nick?" The question hits me out of the blue, but I do my best to remember my schedule. Tomorrow is Wednesday, and Wednesday means:

"Class 'til 3. Why?"

He tosses a script at me and I catch it automatically, only fumbling a little. It's a battered cast copy of Hamlet, with "Horatio" written in black permanent marker on the beat-up cover. I'm so busy staring at it that I almost miss what he says next.

"Because you've got rehearsal at 5. I've found my replacement. Welcome back to the show."

* * *

I don't get stage fright. I get nervous, yeah. Who wouldn't? But it's a rush. It's never stopped me. Going to rehearsal is another matter. There's a huge part of me wishing for something to calm my nerves, and I practically twitch my way through classes. I get through, somehow, and 5 o'clock is rolling around before I'm ready for it.

I feel like a sneak, slipping back into the drama department, the sound of people gathered in the theater already filtering out into the hallway. Everyone's attention is somewhere else when I walk in the door, and it gives me a second to readjust to being here again. I see Riz right away, off to the side talking to the girl playing Ophelia, and I have no idea if he knows about me being back on the cast or not.

The surprised tilt of his eyebrows when he sees me points to "not". I drop my bag off to the side, giving him a little shrug as I slouch down into a seat.

Jeff sees me and gives me a smile and a reassuring nod before getting everyone's attention to start rehearsal. "Alright, people. I know everyone's worried about what happened yesterday, but we're going to push on, okay? I found you a new Horatio, and hopefully you all won't scare this one off." There's a buzz of awkward laughter as people look around for the new guy, and a few pairs of eyes land on me. Rizzo's are the only ones that register any recognition.

Jeff doesn't waste any time choosing a scene to start with, and within seconds actors and crew are scrambling onstage and behind the curtain to their places.

Riz comes over when I settle on a spot to stand onstage and gives me one of his little grins. "Horatio, hm?" When I look at him, I can't keep the smile off my face.

"Hope that's okay with you... Prince." He laughs and shakes his head, and I finally lose that nervous feeling in the pit of my stomach.

* * *

A week back at rehearsals, and I'm beginning to wonder how crazy I was to accept Jeff's invitation back to the show. When I'm not in rehearsal, I'm in class, and there are times when I have to run across campus to make one or the other on time. It's been close more than once, slipping into my seat just as the professor starts to lecture.

The guy who sits next to me, some jerk-off soccer playing jock, grins over at me and the way I'm practically sucking air in from my run from the drama department. Stupid cigarettes and my tiny lung capacity. He actually laughs when I glare at him, and whispers over at me: "Close call."

I don't even respond, grabbing my notebook and a pen to try to take notes in the most boring class on the planet. Like I care what some muscled-out jock thinks.

Even if he *is* less muscled and more just really in shape and sort of strong looking. And pretty attractive, for a jock. With blue eyes, and great hands, and his smile's actually *really* nice, and...

Damn. I need to get laid.

* * *

Another day, another rehearsal. Jeff seems to be pretty happy with my stuff so far, even though there are times that I forget exactly where I'm supposed to be standing. I've had the lines memorized for months, from when I didn't get the part the first time, but the on-stage blocking isn't always as easy to remember.

But he just lets me know where to be, if someone else doesn't tell me first. And even though he smiles every time, I could kick myself each time it happens. I'm supposed to be making things easier for everyone, not harder.

Jeff ends rehearsal and calls me over, and I'm certain it's going to be about the scene we just finished, and how Riz and I were practically dancing with each other with how often he had to shift me into the right spot onstage. But Jeff just smiles from his seat. "How do you feel about interviews for the paper?"

He really needs to stop with the cryptic, out of nowhere shit, because it makes me feel like an idiot every time he pulls it on me. Like I don't speak the language or something. When all I can do is look at him like I'm stupid, he laughs.

"I've got a reporter from the school paper showing up tomorrow, and I'm supposed to find people for him to talk to." No, that doesn't make any more sense than the first thing. There's no reason for him to be asking me about it.

"What about Rizzo?" I gesture over to where he's packing up his things. "Shouldn't they interview the star?"

Jeff gives me a grin and shrugs. "Thought we'd switch it up this time. So their editor's going to be here after rehearsal to talk to you." The editor? The familiar name flashes into my mind, *James Foley*, and I'm nodding before I even realize it. I wanted to meet the guy, anyway. Why not?

* * *

Rehearsal the next day is almost over, should've ended already, but Jeff's got Riz and I onstage yet, running through one of our scenes, and we're not going to stop until he's either satisfied or sick of us. I'm doing my best to focus on the scene, to give over to Horatio, which isn't hard when you're playing off Riz's Hamlet, but it means I know the second his attention falters, pulled off the stage for a split second. It makes me frown, my own eyes shifting out to the house as well, catching the figure standing by the door. It's a face I know, but the surprise of seeing it here makes me falter too, hearing Jeff sigh at the two of us.

"Fine. You two are done for today, get the hell off my stage." Jeff softens the blow with a quirk of a smile, though, the way he almost always does. "The writer from the paper's here for you anyway, Nick. Come on over."

The paper. James Foley. A familiar face at the door that puts that sort of expression on Rizzo's face.

Well, fuck me.

Riz doesn't even say anything to me as he packs up his shit at warp speed, and I watch as he heads for the far doors. I realize how much I have no idea what the hell's happening, but I can't run after him right now. Because I have an interview.

Jeff grins as I walk over, and I wonder if *he* knows what's going on. I wouldn't put it past him. "Nick, this is James, our editor-in-chief." I can't help nodding at that, looking at the guy.

"I read the paper." It sounds idiotic coming out of my mouth, but I honestly don't know how I'm supposed to be handling this.

"Congrats. That probably makes you 50% of our reader base." I get caught by his smirk, staring for a second.

Jeff laughs, breaking me out of my thoughts: "Hey, I read it too."

"Must be my lucky day," he replies dryly. He's... damn, he's actually funny. In a sarcastic sort of way. I feel myself smiling, but I don't want to like this asshole. I don't know everything that's going on, but I know the way Riz practically ran out of the theater, and I do remember some of what happened last semester. I feel Jeff watching me, though, so I force a sharp little smile onto my face.

"Must be. You get to interview me, after all." Hell, that didn't come out right, cocky in a way I'm not ready to back up. Like the way I remember Rizzo being before I got to know him. I know that Jeff's staring at me now, and that I need to pull back the attitude before he calls me on it.

The guy gives me a look. "Right. Let's get started then, big shot." He nods to Jeff with a hint of an amused smile, and leads me to the front row where it's most comfortable to sit. Jeff gives me one last look as he heads over to grab his own things, leaving me standing there with this guy and feeling like an asshole.

We sit down and he takes some stuff out of his bag to set up for the interview. Pen and notebook, plus a silver dictating machine. He tilts his head and looks at me. "You ready to start?" He looks at some scribbling on his little book. "That's Nick… Keller, right?" I nod as I try to settle myself in the seat, looking for a way to be more comfortable sitting there.

"That's me. Least last time I checked." I can still feel the asshole tone sneaking through, and I try to pull it back, knowing I'd never hear the end of it from Jeff if I screw up this interview. If this is part of what I have to do now that he's let me back on the cast, then I have to do it well.

I can tell that I'm not making the best impression so far, but he ignores my tone. "We need to cover some basics first. How old are you, Nick?" It seems like a strange question. Nothing to do with the play, but I just shrug and go with it.

"Twenty." I watch as he makes a note in his book, and before he can ask another question, I push on. "And I'm a Scorpio, blue is my favorite color, and I like rainy days and long walks on the beach." The humor's a long-shot, and I wonder if I should just drop it, but it keeps slipping out on me.

He gives me a look that's only mildly annoyed and mostly amused. "Shame. I'm not sure we're compatible then. I'm not a big beach person." He writes more into his book, not letting me see what he is writing. He continues as before, in the same professional tone, and I wonder if there's any way to crack this guy. "You're a sophomore, is that correct?"

"That's what they tell me. Though I think they're probably being generous at this point." It slips out, and I try not to wince at myself. If he *doesn't* realize who I am, and I'm pretty sure he doesn't, unless that's why he's acting like this, I don't want to be the one that clues him onto the fact that we've met before. Sort of.

He arches an eyebrow and looks at me, and he seems to really notice me for the first time now, the way he takes me in. I can see something that might be recognition in his eyes momentarily. But he doesn't seem sure. He opens his mouth to say something, shakes his head and closes it again. He takes the dictating machine in his hand and starts to record.

"So tell me, how do you feel about being in the show?"

A little laugh slips out before I reply, because that's probably the easiest question he could have asked. "It's amazing. I mean, the people. The show itself. And working with Jeff again is great." I shift in my seat, trying to face him more as we talk.

He actually smiles a little. "We've seen you in *An Ideal Husband* last year, as Sir Robert Chiltern. You were the youngest cast member then. Does it feel different to be back this year?" I know they're normal interview questions, but I can't keep the laugh in.

"You could say that. I, uh, I'm actually sort of coming to the cast late. Jeff asked me to fill in for someone who left. So that makes things different right there." I figure I'll just leave out the whole getting kicked off the cast thing. No one's going to want to read that story, even if I wanted to tell it.

He nods. "So the rumors are true." He sounds like this is off the record. But he continues the interview right away. "It's not a small part you're taking on, either. You're playing Horatio, Hamlet's confidant. Tell us how you see this character. What makes Horatio tick?"

"Loyalty." The answer slips out before I even stop to think about it. "Friendship, too, but loyalty first. I mean, here's a guy that's been in battles, is going to school at Wittenberg even though he's most likely a regular guy. And he gets pulled into all this crazy stuff because Hamlet wants him there." I lean in a little as I'm talking, getting more into it.

"Everyone else pretty much wants him to leave, but Hamlet trusts him and loves him, so he stays. And he does whatever he can to help this poor guy that's lost his dad, and had his mom marry his uncle, and who's pretty much losing his mind over everything. Oh, and who just happens to also be the prince of Denmark." I realize I'm rambling, but if there's one thing Jeff pushes, it's knowing your character, so I've put a lot of thought into this, and it's hard to stop talking.

"It's a crazy thing to think about, really. He shows up, because he really cares about his friend and wants to make sure that he's dealing with things okay. He's totally unprepared for what's happening with these insane people, so he tries to make it through with his common sense. And in return, he gets to watch as this guy he loves gets pretty much mentally torn apart by his own thoughts, and everyone around him ends up dead. And just when he's thinking that he's going to join everyone else and maybe off himself, because y'know, screw that shit, Hamlet goes and asks him to stick around a little while longer so he can tell everyone what happened. And he *does*, just because Hamlet asks." I blink, registering how much I've said, and how the guy - James - his mouth is quirked to the side in a little smile. I give him a grin and shrug. "Loyalty."

"Do you think Horatio's loyalty acts as an important counterbalance to all the lies and betrayal in the play?" I almost feel like I'm writing essays for some class on Shakespeare, but at least the question makes sense.

"Oh, yeah, definitely. I mean, you've gotta have that one good guy in there, right? Or else it's just a bunch of crazy-ass royalty running around killing each other. And yeah, that's good for tabloids and stuff, but what's a normal guy in the audience going to care? You throw Horatio in there, and it sort of... makes it hit home."

He's still smiling a little when he glances down at his notebook to find his next question, clearing his throat before he asks. "Would you say you and Horatio have something in common?" It's something I have to think about for a second, but I end up nodding as I look at him.

"I think so, yeah. I mean, I think all good actors have to find some sort of connection with their characters, you know? To really get in their heads and make it real for the audience. So I guess I do or Jeff wouldn't have let me get up there to be Horatio." I smile as I lean back in my seat to get comfortable again. "Not that I've got a friend who's going through the same stuff Hamlet goes through." Not that I have a lot of friends at all, a stupid little voice in my head throws at me. "But I like to think that I'd stand by him, if I did."

He at least looks interested in what I'm saying now, so I guess that's a good sign, even though he moves on to the next question without much of a reaction. "How did you get into acting? Is there something specific that draws you to it?"

I laugh at that one, loudly because I can't help it, and it takes me a second to stop. "You mean other than me being an attention whore?" It's something I'm willing to admit now, although I'm pretty sure Doc would be frowning at the actual term. "I actually got into it in high school, and it just carried over. I love being on stage, being able to get people to look and pay attention. To make them forget that I'm some random guy on a stage, and make them hate or fall in love with a character. It's great. Jeff gave me a chance last year, and another *huge* chance this year, and while it's been pretty crazy, I'm grateful for it." I'm still smiling, but it's serious, and I have a feeling he's going to pick up on it. "Don't know where I'd be if I didn't have acting."

He does get it. I can see it in the way he looks up at me for a minute that's just a little too long before asking the next question. "Can you tell us a little bit of what to expect from the show?"

"Orgies of death and blood. It's a Shakespearean tragedy." I try to keep a straight face, but I can feel the smile bleeding through. And then... then I can't help throwing another comment in, even though I know I probably shouldn't. "And I think costuming's been talking about putting Riz in leather pants. Though I'm not sure if that's supposed to be common knowledge yet or not, so probably don't print that." I watch to see if that gets a reaction at all.

It does, as if mentioning Rizzo finally makes the connection for him. He leans back in his chair a little and looks at me with a slight frown and a strange little smile. "Now I know where I know you from! Your hair used to be black. And all this time I've been wrecking my brains why you looked so familiar."

My hand automatically goes up to the back of my head, rubbing at my hair a little. It'd been black for so long that I still forget that it's not any more. I'm not quite sure where this is going to lead, but I decide to just throw it out there. "Yeah, a lot of people don't recognize me now." I look at him and can't quite keep the edge out of my voice. "Probably not someone you *wanted* to recognize, though, huh?"

He stops the recording and puts the dictating machine down. "Certainly not before the interview." He gives me a quick smile. "But it turns out you're not a total ass."

"Not any more, at least." I look at him, and can't quite hide the smirk. "Jury's still out on you, though." I try to hold the look as seriously as I can, but I can feel the smile pushing through more.

"What, no instant and violent loathing? Don't tell me I've lost my special touch."

"Well, you haven't special touch-ed me yet, so I don't know..." It slips out without me thinking about it, something I probably would say automatically if I was talking to Rizzo, and the fairly comfortable thing we've settled into. I know it's wrong here before I even finish saying it, and I start shaking my head. "Sorry, sorry. Ignore that... Just me being an asshole."

He eyes me somewhat amusedly. "Yeah, the thing about actual assholes? They usually don't realize that's what they are." I suppose he has a point, but I shrug and shake my head.

"Doesn't stop me from *being* one though, apparently. Old habits're hard to break, I guess." It could apply to so many more things than just flirting with the guy that had put that look on Riz's face, but I just leave it at that.

There's a short silence that could be uncomfortable, but somehow isn't. He puts his dictating machine back into his bag, and when he looks at me again there's something almost mischievous in his eyes. "You don't really like long walks on the beach, do you?"

I raise an eyebrow at him, not nearly as smooth as I'd like to be, and I swear I can feel the phantom tug of the ring that used to be there. "Are you kidding? Sand gets everywhere. And I don't exactly tan easily. It's a nightmare." I'm almost surprised that he's put away his things already, but we're not talking about the show any more, so I suppose it makes sense.

"Amen," he grins. The smile's almost contagious, and I grin in return.

"Yeah, you don't really look like one of those lucky bastards that can just tan at the drop of a hat." I smile a little more until Jeff calls over from the doors.

"Nick? I'm headed to my office. Leave one of the doors unlocked for-" He cuts himself off, glancing at James. "For later, okay?" I nod, knowing that he's talking about Rizzo.

"I got it, Jeff. Thanks." He gives me a smile and lets himself out of the auditorium with a soft hiss of the door closing behind him. I turn back to James after a second, and even though I probably shouldn't ask, I do.

"I actually don't like to hang around in here too much without anyone else around. I, uh… we could go somewhere else, if you still needed stuff for the interview?"

"Oh." He is quick to stuff his pen and notebook back into his bag. "I think I've got it covered for the most part. But if there's more you'd like to tell me about the play or maybe working with Jeff… How do you feel about coffee?"

I laugh at the question. How do I feel about coffee? "What, you mean the nectar of the gods? It's one of the only vices I've got left. I'm pretty sure my blood is about 80% caffeinated these days."

He nods as he gets up. "Guess the Plato it is then." I nod in return, getting up and grabbing my own bag, shoving a few things to the bottom so I can throw my rehearsal stuff in too. I throw it over my shoulder and look back at James.

"Ready when you are."

* * *

The cafe is just as busy as it always is in the evening, but there's a few empty tables waiting when we get there. The girl behind the counter catches my eye, and I nod, letting her know that I'm going to be ordering my usual. I glance over at James to ask if he wants anything too, but something else catches my eye before I can say anything.

Rizzo's here. Of course he is. And I would've realized that if I'd taken a second to think about it. He's sitting off to the side with Andrea, her hair still pulled up from rehearsing her Ophelia scenes earlier, and they're leaning close over a pair of still steaming mugs. And Riz is looking right at James and I, giving us a look that I can't quite place, but that I know isn't good. Even Andie's eyes are a little sad, and I feel like kicking myself.

I turn back to James and give him a little push toward one of the empty tables on the other side of the cafe. "Go. I'm getting us something to drink. And then we're going to talk." I don't even wait to listen to his reply before going to get my drink and something simple for him.

When I finally get to the table and sit down, putting his drink in front of him, I've been dealing with Rizzo's eyes on me for long, uncomfortable minutes. "Okay," I jump in, not even giving him a chance to ask about the play again, "now are you going to tell me why Riz is looking at me like I kicked his puppy, or not?"

8 ICEBREAKER

JAMES: At Nick's words, my eyes immediately want to wander over to Rizzo's table. I noticed his slender figure the moment we walked in, I always do, but I've avoided actually looking over so far. And I somehow manage to continue to do so now. Mostly by frowning at Nick. I surprise myself by answering, even though it's clearly none of his business. Although... maybe it is? "If you don't know, I can't tell you." I stare down at the coffee he brought me. But it doesn't feel right to leave it there, so I look up again. "You two are friends now?"

"The closest thing I've got to one. And he'd probably kick my ass for putting it that way. So we'll go with yes." He gives me a strange little smile as he takes a drink of his own coffee. "And I'm not used to people looking at me that way any more."

"That makes me wonder if you actually used to kick puppies." I smile grimly. "But if you need to know, Rizzo hates my guts. So I guess we can safely assume that seeing one of his friends hanging out with me is not his favorite sight in the world."

Nick returns the smile, but shakes his head a bit. "No, no puppy kicking. Plenty of other shitty things, but no puppy kicking." His smile gets a little bigger for a second. "It's a simile. I thought you'd like it." He goes serious again, though. "And okay. He hates your guts. Mind telling me why? 'Cause he sure as hell didn't use to."

I frown again. "Why do you want to know?" Like, is he really interested in this? Why would anyone be?

He leans back in his chair, cradling his coffee as he looks at me. "Because I may not remember all of last semester, but I do remember parts. I remember how much I hated you because of how he felt about you. And now things are like that." He jerks his head toward the table where Rizzo is still sitting. "So I guess I'm just curious how you go from one to the other so fast."

"Oh, that's easy," I reply a little too bitterly, too darkly. "You just do the right thing." I know to Nick that must sound more than a little cryptic, but I'm not sure I want to spill the whole story. It's too painful to think of still. "Anyway, it doesn't matter. I did something he can't forgive me. I wouldn't forgive me either if I were him. End of story."

He gives me a look that clearly conveys how much he doesn't believe me. "Right. End of story. When you're both still obviously messed up about it. You really think that's the end?" He shakes his head as he takes another drink of his coffee, making a quiet sound of disagreement into it.

I almost laugh, surprised. "What's it to you? And I'm sure he isn't... messed up about it." I can't help but glancing over at Rizzo's table after all, very briefly. "Is he?"

He raises his eyebrows at me, nearly choking on a mouthful of coffee. "Not messed up about it? Hell, I thought the editor of the newspaper was supposed to be *smart*. I knew the second he tossed me out that something was wrong, and I was on more shit than I can even list." He looks over at Rizzo's table for a second too before turning back to me. "He ran out of that theater earlier like there was anywhere in the world he'd rather be than there. And trust me, it's not because he was afraid of talking to Jeff."

I swallow. Is he serious? Is Rizzo actually still unable to cope with this situation? Can't he seem to move on, as hard as he's trying? Just like me? But he's been acting so normal, doing his Rizzo thing. From afar, he seemed exactly like he was before our paths ever crossed. I was sure that for him, this was over. The possibility that it's not makes my heart beat just a little faster. No, this is crazy.

"I guess not, but the fact remains that he hates my guts. And unless you've got any smart theories of how that could ever change, it doesn't make a difference." I shrug. I don't know Nick well enough to trust him, even though I have a feeling that I could if I wanted to. But I've already said too much anyway.

"Well I don't know. When *I* screwed up, he was the one that showed up to talk to me. If he's not doing that for you, maybe you need to try." He pauses, raising an eyebrow at me. "Have you even tried that? I mean, if you *want* to try to work shit out.

Hell, for all I know, you're fine with him hating you." He gives me a look that says that he doesn't believe that for a second.

Why do I feel like I'm getting scolded by Mom? Geez, enough with the guilt trip! Up until this moment, I had no clue that the possibility even existed that Rizzo might still somewhere, deep down, have feelings for me. Even if they consist of pure hatred. But what if Nick's right, and they don't? What if Rizzo... No, I can't even think that. It messes with me far too much.

"I'm not fine with him hating me. But that's my problem, not yours." Shit, that sounded too much like a snarl, possibly. I try to soften it with a crooked smile. "Not that I don't appreciate the insight."

"Translation: Fuck off, Nick, I don't want to talk about it." He smiles, more to himself than at me. "Fair enough I guess. And hell, maybe I'm wrong. It's happened enough in the past." He shrugs, returning his attention to his coffee.

"Ack, no. I didn't mean it like that," I'm quick to assure him. "And even if you are wrong. I guess you have a point. I should find out one of these days." If I ever work up the courage to. I can already see the door of Rizzo's dorm room closing right in my face. That should be fun.

I lean forward a little. High time to change the subject. "Off the record - tell me more about the play? What's your favorite scene in it?"

He looks up from his coffee, and as his thoughts return to the stage, the blue eyes light up. Eureka.

* * *

I get back to my room two hours later, and I'm still somewhat surprised. Things like this don't happen to me. I don't spend hours talking to perfect strangers about my life. I don't make a connection like that easily. To be honest, I don't think I ever have. But once we'd gotten the initial awkwardness out of the way, Nick and I got along surprisingly well. Rizzo's little lap dog, as I used to call him in my head, isn't anything like I'd expected. Which makes sense, since I didn't even recognize him at first. He's interesting to talk to, and I can't say that about a lot of people.

The whole thing is so weird I even mention it to Mom when I make my usual call to check on her that night. But it's so typically me in a way, meeting someone who could be a potential new buddy I could really like and open up to, mere months before I have to leave for Berlin. My first semester at the university there starts in October, but I'd like to make the move to Germany and settle in a while before that. And definitely brush up on my German long before then.

Mom used to talk to me in German when I was very little. She wanted to make sure learning my dad's first language would come easy to me later on if I wanted to. She didn't do that anymore after Simon had come into our lives. I think he must have asked her to stop. He certainly didn't like her and me having secret little conversations he couldn't understand. But I've always associated Germany with my father, which gives me strangely warm feelings for this foreign place. There's no logic to it, just a gut feeling, but I've been wanting to visit the country for as long as I can remember. The mere thought of getting to live there is exciting. A bit scary, too, but mostly exciting. The more time passes, the more real the scholarship is becoming. And the more I really want to go. And let's face it, apart from Mom, there's really not an awful lot keeping me this side of the Atlantic anymore.

* * *

I introduce Nick to Casey two weeks later. We've met up a couple of times in the meantime. Just to have coffee and talk. About anything, really. The play, stuff to do with the paper, stuff that goes on at college that we're both not happy about. We never seem to run out of conversation topics. He told me about rehab, and what it's like to be back at school for him now. It's a gesture of trust that I appreciate. Not that I can give any useful advice. But I think maybe it helps him somehow that I'm there, not judging, just listening. The whole Nick and Casey thing though… let's just say they won't become best friends anytime soon. Like, some time within this century-soon. Casey laughs at me afterwards, on the way to our dorms.

"Well, that was a little... weird."

"Not my best idea ever to bring the two of you together, huh?" I say unhappily.

"No, I'm glad you introduced us. I always want to meet your friends." Friends. Are Nick and I friends? I'm surprised by how much I like the idea. Casey continues: "I don't always have to love them, but I still want to meet them."

"Never fear, there won't be lots more to come anytime soon."

"Oh, you never know." He smiles at me. "With your looks and charms..."

"Ha ha."

"What? I'm serious. You got your own kind of charm. Not everyone gets that, sadly. But those who don't, don't deserve you anyway."

"Stop it, you're making me blush," I snarl, and he laughs out loud.

"Oh, James." His eyes are shining warmly when he looks at me. "I just want for you to be happy. You know that, don't you?"

I nod. "I do. Ditto."

Casey looks at the small buds on a tree we're walking past. "Spring is coming. Can you feel it in the air?"

"You mean the godawful cold that's making my nose freeze off?"

He rolls his eyes, smiling. "Bless your romantic little heart. Seriously, though, I can't wait for everything to be green again."

I nod, getting lost in my thoughts. Every day is taking me closer to the day I'll have to leave here. Woodhaven, my refuge. Is Berlin going to be what I expect? Am I going to love it there? What if I hate it? But something tells me I won't hate it, like that's not even a possibility. Like I already know this city somehow. Because it's such a strange place, with so much dark history, and so much amazing spirit, and just a little screwed up, just like me.

"You're going to leave in a couple of months," Casey says thoughtfully, like he's read my mind somehow. It's wonderfully familiar, him knowing what I'm thinking. He used to all the time. Not so much since our break-up, but maybe it's coming back.

Like grass growing back when the snow is gone.

"Looks like it, yeah."

"Does that mean you still haven't quite made up your mind?" he scolds me.

I shrug helplessly and kick at a small stone on the pathway. "It just doesn't feel right to leave Mom alone for so long. I won't be able to drive down on weekends sometimes to check up on her, and stuff like that. What if she needs me?"

"She'll always need you, but here's the thing: this is your life. You mom's social worker will make sure she's okay. Stop worrying so much."

"But that's me."

"I know," he laughs softly. "You're a worrier. So why not direct that worry towards more useful topics? Like how you're gonna get all your stuff to Berlin. A year's a long time."

A year's a very long time. "I have no clue. I can't take all my books, that's for sure."

He laughs. "James, what you've got is a library!"

"Apparently," I frown. "Last week Professor Weisman wanted to borrow one of my books."

"Did you give it to her?"

"Hell no. If I started with that, who knows what might come next?"

He can't stop laughing. "Only you would turn down a professor. I love you, you know that?"

I nod, smiling warmly. "Yeah. I know that." For a moment, it's almost like we were never anything but friends. Best friends. It's a surprisingly great feeling. I don't think I've been this relaxed around him since the break-up. That's a good sign, right? Maybe I'm over it at last. And maybe Nick is right. Maybe setting things right with Rizzo is the next thing I have to tackle. But as hard as the situation with Casey was at one point - it's nothing compared to what probably awaits me with Rizzo. I'm thinking protective clothing might be a good idea. I've made up my mind, though. I'm going to talk to Rizzo really soon, and try to work this out. I need to at least explain to him why I did what I did. He deserves it. And even if he hates me completely now, I need to let him know how I feel about him. That nothing's changed, as far as I'm concerned. Not that it'll do me much good. But sometimes there are things you just have to do.

9 BITTER PILL

DANNY: By March even the biggest skeptics are convinced that Keller is the best thing that could have happened to the play. I never told Keller this, but our old Horatio sucked. That guy was stiff as a puppet, and gave me little to work with. We never had a connection, let alone any chemistry on stage. With Nick, it's ridiculously easy. With his act together, he is a real talent. He's even better than last year. He's intense, and we're damn intense together, and I love all our scenes best in the entire play. I think Jeff does too. I never got why he cast the other guy in the first place, and I told him so. Jeff knows going big director on me doesn't work. It's been like this with us since my freshman year when he talked me into trying out for a part in a production of *Of Mice and Men*. I tried out for a ranch-hand. I got the part of George Milton. I seem to be firmly booked as leading man in his head ever since then. He's like a weird mixture of buddy and father figure to me. Constantly nagging me to apply for a proper drama school after Woodhaven. This is a good school with a very good reputation. It's even known for its outstanding education in performing arts. But it certainly isn't Juilliard.

But do I really see myself as an actor? It used to seem like such a great way to spend your life, doing what comes naturally and getting paid for it. But I don't feel any ambition when I think about it. Never have. I don't see myself on Broadway. I guess deep down I know what I'd really like to do. And that's got next to nothing to do with acting. I can hear the lure of music, like muses whispering sweet, tempting words into my ears at night when I can't sleep. But there's Grazzo, and his overwhelming wish for me to do exactly that, to follow in his footsteps. And that's exactly what's holding me back. I've always been so conflicted when it comes to music. I had my first piano lesson before I could walk. All through my school years, I tried out various instruments, and I've always been best at the piano and the sax. Just like Grazzo. Only I'm better on the piano, and he on the saxophone. But damn it, I don't want to be a clone of my dad. Who does? I never wanted to be "the son of". All my life I've fought to be my own person. Here at Woodhaven it was pretty easy. Out in the world, not so much. Because believe it or not, sometimes I do get recognized as his son in the streets. Everyone says I look just like him when he was young. Most would take that as a compliment. It isn't for me. Sometimes I wonder if Lilah has rubbed off on me, but I have my own reasons for not wanting to be associated with Grazzo all the time. If I went into music - not a chance.

Anyway, no matter what I do after graduation, what it all boils down to is that it looks like I've been nicely wasting opportunities at Woodhaven. It's hard to believe my time here is drawing to an end so quickly now. Only a little over two months left. It's insane. I wanna stay, and at the same time I can't wait to get out of here. Andrea and I have had this plan of traveling Europe after graduation for ages. We haven't talked about it in a long time, but if she's still up for it, I'm game.

It's past nine pm when I enter my dorm after rehearsal. The corridor leading to my room is pitch black because the light bulb went to light bulb heaven earlier, so I don't even notice that there's someone sitting beside my door until I almost step on them.

"Damn!" I curse as someone jumps up right in front of me.

"Oh god, sorry," a familiar voice replies worriedly. "I didn't mean to startle you. But the light isn't working."

"No shit, Mills." What the hell is he doing here? Trying to give me a heart attack? I've been ignoring him since before Christmas, and I thought he got the message, so what is this now? Come to think of it, I've seen him come towards me numerous times for a while now. Never gave him a chance to get close enough to get on my nerves.

I manage to unlock the door without too much fumbling around, and turn on the light inside, letting it fall into the corridor where we're standing. "Were you planning on camping out on my doorstep, or what?"

"Oh, I…"

"You got ten seconds, Mills. Spill."

"I need to talk to you. It's *really* important. I swear."

I'm bored already. I glance at my watch. "Six seconds left."

"Rizzo - oh, screw this." I'm taken by surprise when Casey Dearest has the nerve to actually push past me into my room. He sits down on the edge of my bed and crosses his arms in front of his chest. "I'm not leaving before you hear me out."

What the hell is this shit? "Who are you, Liz Taylor?" Nevertheless I close the door behind us with my body weight and lean against it. Yeah, I'm not sure why either. Maybe because the prospect of dragging Mills out by his hair after a four hour rehearsal isn't all that tempting.

Mills looks up at me a little sheepishly. "Sorry for barging in like this. I've been waiting for an opportune moment to talk to you, but it just never came. So here I am."

"I noticed that," I reply dryly. "So what brings me the displeasure of your presence?"

"James," he simply says, and a weird moment of silence follows.

I ignore the uneasy feeling that name brings about, and give Mills a look. "How about this: whatever it is, I don't care."

He tilts his head to the side and looks at me thoughtfully. "I think you do though. You'll want to hear this. Or possibly you don't want to hear this, because I guess it kinda sucks in a way, but it also doesn't, which makes it so important."

I almost smile. "Yeah… See, I get the feeling you're confusing me with someone who speaks your language."

"It's complicated, okay? I'm trying to explain it…" he trails off, and we both know he was about to say "in a way you'd understand" - and I think he doesn't begin to realize how wise a decision it was to leave that sentence unfinished. Mills sighs deeply and looks at me with his stupid big blue eyes like he's the one finding this situation less than thrilling. You've got no idea how close I am to physically kicking you out, boy.

He continues, slowly and calmly. "I just can't let this go on any longer. Because it's insane, you and James."

"It may have escaped your notice, but there is no 'Foley and me'." Why am I even talking to Mills? But deep down, I'm somewhat curious why he came here. Damn. But what on earth does he want from me?

He sighs a little. "I know. And that's what's so insane. Look, Rizzo. I know you're aware of how I... felt about you. Even when I was with James. And when I told him that, he did something amazing. Because he is a wonderful friend. And I think you really don't quite deserve him, but I know the two of you... you had something. Something James and I never had. It's like... you get him somehow. I don't know."

"Is this going somewhere?" I haven't felt the need for a smoke in a long time, but I crave one desperately right now. What is all this bullshit he's telling me about Foley and me having had a "special something"? Special my ass. The one thing that was special about it was that especially messed up break-up right out of nowhere. I can feel the anger and hurt stirring again deep inside, fiery and unforgiving, but I keep a neutral, slightly bored expression.

"Just let me finish, okay? Did James ever tell you why he ended things with you?"

I can feel a little frown on my forehead, just for a second, but Mills spots it. Asshole.

"Thought as much." He smiles a little, sympathetically. I think I may have to punch a geek after all. My fist clenches and unclenches on its own account, but at least it wipes the damn smile off of his face.

Mills finds the nerve to look into my eyes. "He did it for me. He did it because I couldn't stand seeing the two of you together. He did it because he didn't want to hurt me more."

I can feel my heart hammering madly in my chest as I'm trying to process his words. What is he saying? That J did this shit to me so that his BFF didn't get his precious feelings hurt? Does that mean he tore me apart, ripped me into pieces and trampled on me just because Casey Dearest was getting all teary-eyed when he saw us hanging out? That's the reason? Seriously? I don't believe this. All this time, I was thinking god knows what. I thought I was the one to blame somehow. That I'd done something Foley simply couldn't deal with. That, I could have understood. But this? Forget that.

My fist clenches again like it has a mind of its own, and I stare at Mills. "Time's up," I finally say quietly, but the threat is so evident that he practically jumps up from the bed. "Get out."

"Rizzo, you have to understand that this had nothing to do with the way James feels about you. It was a huge sacrifice he made for me, and I know he regrets it. And I feel awful because I suspected he might do something like that and I let him. It was selfish of me. Things were over between him and me way before you managed to come between us. We never should have been together. I realize that now. So I guess I have no right to hate you for it. Or to make both of you suffer because of how you went behind my back."

He takes a deep breath and his stupid voice trembles slightly, making me want to punch him so hard, but somehow I can't. So he rambles on as he gets closer to me and the door. "And I'm sorry, Rizzo. In the end, I was the one who messed it all up. It's my fault, and if you want to take it out on someone, it should be me, not James."

I very slowly step closer. "*Why* are you still here?"

"Okay, okay, I'm leaving. And I really am sorry. But you weren't the only one who got hurt in this. We all did."

I open the door, but he just won't stop talking.

"I just hope some day you'll understand that you and James deserve a shot. And that you'll find it in you to give him another ch…"

I don't let him finish. I grab him and virtually toss him out of the room.

* * *

One hour later I stand under the shower at the 24 hour gym next to campus, having worked off all my anger and frustration as best I could. I let the soft water run down my body soothingly, but I'm feeling strangely numb. So I turn the tap to icy cold, and I exhale harshly as the cold water hits me. But it feels good somehow, stinging my skin like needles.

I know what people think of me. They think Rizzo doesn't give a shit about anyone but himself. And yeah, for the most part, that's probably true. But those select few I do care about, I would do anything for. Just as long as they never knew. I can set the scumbag who almost raped Andrea in freshman year up so that he gets kicked out of college. I can make sure the dealer who almost got Keller killed doesn't ever come near him again. I can do that. I'm good at the revenge thing. I'm good at the intimidation thing. I have no problem treating anyone I don't care about like shit. 'Cause I also happen to be good at not having scruples.

But once I did grow to like Foley, I wouldn't have done to him what he did to me. He gave no reason, no explanation. Just "it's over, deal with it". And I thought I was over it, but god, it still hurts like hell.

Foley doesn't hurt people on purpose. He may be a snarky bastard, but he isn't heartless. And then he went and did this to me all the same. I know, who am I to talk, and I know I've done things far worse than that to people I didn't give a shit about. Maybe this is karma kicking me in the guts. But as I stand in the icy cold shower, letting the water run over my face, I just want to be who I used to be before I ever met James Foley. But hard as I may try, I'm not that same guy anymore. And then a weird little conversation with myself starts that goes something like this:

"Why can't this shit ever end? It's like the shit that keeps on shitting."

"At least now you know why. He was trying to protect his friend from getting hurt."

"By hurting me instead. I love that logic."

"Forgive him. You know you have to forgive him or this will eat you up."

"I can't. I'm not ready to."

"You need to let this go."

"What do you think I've been trying to do for months?"

"Forgive him."

"I said I can't."

"I see. But you still want him back, don't you?"

"I DON'T!"

"Don't lie to me. You know you do."

That's when I turn the water on fully, and the sound of it rushing down on me finally drowns out my thoughts. I feel like I'm turning into ice, and the needles are digging into my skin, but I clench my teeth and stand still as a rock.

* * *

When I close the lid of the grand piano at the large theatre auditorium that night, having played for over an hour, I feel even more confused than I did before. Usually the music helps me figure stuff out without having to actively think about it. But tonight it felt like with every note I played, my damn heart was breaking all over again. Images are dancing in my mind, images of us together. The memory is so vivid that I can almost smell the scent of his skin. And it makes me want to crawl right out of my own skin. Deep inside the need to hurt him back the same way he hurt me is killing me. And I realize that all these months of keeping my mouth shut, staying as far away from James Foley as I could didn't get me all that far. I'm still in the same place. Only I'm not numb from the shock or whatever it was anymore. I'm angry. It's like poison in my veins, keeping me from breaking free. And I need him to know.

I'm not sure what devil possesses me to do it, but my feet seem to walk me to his dorm room on their own account. It's a quarter to midnight, but there's light coming through the crack under his door. I raise my hand and knock.

A moment passes before I can hear a chair getting pushed back inside. Foley looks pale and tired when he opens, but the moment he sees me, he freezes in plain shock. And then his gray eyes light up.

"Rizzo!"

"You wanna tell me something? For god's sake show a little backbone and do it yourself."

"Um - what are you talking about?" He seems completely puzzled, but then it slowly dawns on him. "Oh no. Casey? Has he been talking to you? I told him not to." His eyes are not as bright now that he's seen how angry I am, but there's still an annoying shimmer of hope in them.

"With little success."

"Shit." James swallows, looking even paler now. He looks at me standing there, all my muscles tense with anger, and he seems lost, unsure what to do. He clears his throat. "Do you... do you want to come in?"

"This won't take long."

"I hope not," he tries cautiously. He takes a deep breath and adds, "Damn... It's good to see you." Since I won't come in, he steps out of the room, closer to me on the narrow corridor. My heartbeat accelerates, but I ignore it.

"Really? That's funny. Last I checked you were still pretending I didn't exist."

"Yeah. About that... I know that was messed up. I wish I could..."

"Undo it? Well, you can't."

I can see pain flickering in his eyes, and that feels pretty good to me right now. His shoulders hunched, his arms hanging at his sides, I've never seen him look so lost. He seems so fragile all of a sudden, like one strong breath of air could make him shatter into a million pieces.

"Can I at least apologize to you?" he says quietly, sincerely. "Will you allow me that?"

"Save it. All I want to know is this: Did it ever occur to your supposedly brilliant brain that you sacrificed the wrong pawn? Did you think, hey, he's Rizzo, he'll get over it?"

His expression changes to something harder, the familiar defensive wall coming up. "I thought it would be easier for you than for him, yes."

I laugh out coldly. "I don't believe this! You put me through hell, and you don't even realize!"

He shakes his head, his entire body tense now. But his eyes have softened, and are pleading with me. "I've been trying not to think of you. That's the only way I could manage to stay away."

"You managed pretty well."

He hesitates, and I can tell that there's something he isn't quite sure he should tell me. But then he does. "That's the way I work, Danny. That's the only way I can function some days. I think you know that."

Danny. He slipped back into calling me Danny. Suddenly it's summer again, and he's at my house, in my bed, having just told me about Simon, and there's an intimacy unlike anything I've ever known. Heart's beating like crazy. Every fiber of my body is craving for his touch, aches for him. But that's not how this works, and it's not why I came here. I push the feeling back violently. "Don't use that to justify what you did," I push out through clenched teeth.

James nods. "I'm not trying to justify this. I hated the possibility of hurting you. But Casey has been my friend for a long time. And let's be honest, Danny. I barely know you. Sometimes you let me in, but you keep wearing those stupid masks..."

I interrupt. "So it's my fault? That's what you're saying?"

"That's not what I'm saying. I'm trying to explain why I sacrificed the wrong pawn, as you put it." He does something quite unlike him then by stepping closer, close enough for me to feel his warm breath washing over my face. I hate myself for getting goosebumps. "I get that you don't want to hear it now, but I'm sorry as hell for what I did, and for how I've been treating you. That was not okay. That was messed up."

Momentarily I don't know what to say. He looks into my eyes, trying to read me, looking for a sign, anything. But I've got my own shield up now, so not a chance. Somehow this is what I've needed to hear. I never knew how much I needed this apology. It's like I can breathe easier now, but the hurt and the anger still remain.

James frowns painfully. "Say something?"

"If you think that's all it takes for me to forgive you, you're delusional." I didn't mean to say that aloud, but somehow it got out.

He swallows, and nods. "I understand."

I snort softly. "So that's it? That's what you're gonna do, just accept this?"

"What do you want me to do, Danny? Just say it." He looks all lost again.

Fight for me. Show me that you want me back! Because

words won't do. Words are not enough. That's what I want to say. But I can't somehow. If he doesn't get it on his own, I can't help him.

"You figure it out," I finally say and turn to leave. He lets me go, and I hate him for it. Do something! Stop me, hold me back! But he's James, so of course he doesn't. I'm already halfway down the corridor when his voice follows me, a quiet, yet determined promise.

"I will."

10 GONE

JAMES: How can I win Danny's heart back? This question has been constantly on my mind these past few days. Like it's all that matters anymore. But as hard as I wreck my brains, I come up blank. And here it is again, the realization that in truth, I know next to nothing about Danny Rizzo. What sort of music he likes, his favorite color, his favorite drink... Although I do have an inkling about the music. Because everyone knows whose son he is, right? But he's never even mentioned his dad to me, and I take that as a not so good sign. So the solution I finally come up with is this: I write Danny a letter. In the grand tradition of love letters, I'm fairly sure this one stinks. It's not very long and not very poetic, but I apologize again, in much better and more words this time. It's much easier for me to write it down than to say these things. And I finally tell him the truth. That I'm crazy about him, and that I've been wanting to be with him since last summer. I just never had the courage to take the leap of faith and let him know.

My heart's beating like it's trying to break through my chest, Alien-style, when I stop by his room. My stupid hands are sweaty as I bend down and push the letter through the crack beneath his door.

No going back now.

I wince as I briefly imagine the possibility of him reading my innermost confessions out to his entourage, everyone laughing their asses off. But he won't do that. I hope. All I can do now is wait for an answer.

A day passes, and there's no word from him. He hasn't shown up at my doorstep to punch me in the face, though. I take that as a good sign.

So I write him another letter. Little strokes fell big oaks. At least I hope that this also applies to broken hearts. And he must have had strong feelings for me at one time to still be so mad with me now, right? Oh, I hope. I start to ask him questions this time. All those little things about him I don't know, like stuff he likes and dislikes.

I don't get a reply this time either. But I'm determined not to give up before his entire room is filled up to the ceiling with my silly ramblings. I don't see Danny around on campus for days. And I miss him like crazy. The letter-writing becomes a daily routine. I even dream of those letters at night.

A week passes without the slightest reaction to my writing. I only see Danny occasionally, in the distance with his friends. He seems to be needing the space, so I try not to stalk him. It's hard.

I finally mention what I'm doing to Nick one afternoon at the Plato, out of sheer despair. I expect him to laugh his ass off, but he just grins and teases me a little. But Danny hasn't mentioned the letters to him either. This can't be good. But if he wanted me to stop, surely he would have told me so? Unless he's collecting my letters until he has enough of them to burn in a huge bonfire for everyone to see. Ack. What am I supposed to do?

* * *

I'm in a surprisingly good mood when I get back to my room, having spent the last hour with Nick, just talking. Just hanging out. I really wonder why I find myself opening up to him more quickly than I ever have to anyone. Maybe it's got something to do with us having Danny in common. Maybe it's just that he's actually a pretty cool person.

I put down my bag full of library books, take out my cheap cell phone for the daily call, and flop down on the bed. I only have this one number saved. It takes six rings before she answers, sounding tired.

"Jimmy?"

"Hey, Mom. Did I wake you up?"

"No, I was just... there was something interesting on the TV."

"You were napping, weren't you?"

She laughs softly. "How can you always tell?"

"I just know."

"I brought up a too clever know-it-all."

"You may have done."

We laugh and talk about her noisy new neighbors for a while, and she assures me that she's taken her meds. Then she demands to hear every detail of my day, as usual.

"So when do I get to meet this Nick?" she asks after a little while.

"I don't know, Mom. I'm not sure I know him well enough yet for him to stay over at the house."

"Then you'd better get to know him well enough. You know I like it when you bring friends home."

I smile. "You're making it sound like I do that all the time."

"Still, I have to do my motherly inspection."

"To make sure Nick's worthy to be my friend, or what?"

"Something along those lines."

"You're crazy, Mom."

Then out of the blue, she says: "You should have that other boy over again, too. He was gorgeous, that one. I liked him."

I swallow and wish my heart wouldn't beat so fast all of a sudden. "Who're you talking about, Casey?"

"No, silly. The tall, dark one. Quite a dish he was."

"Mom!"

She laughs softly. "But it's true. Eye candy is the big advantage of having a gay son, didn't you know that?"

I can feel myself blushing. "Oh god. Would you stop it?"

"What? Leave me my innocent little pleasures! So what happened to that boy? You never mention him anymore."

"That's because we had a falling out. I told you once before, remember?" I kind of want to tell her about my efforts to win Danny back, but then I decide against it. It's too early for that. She'd just get excited - and possibly for nothing.

"He really liked you, that one."

"Mom..." Not that this isn't nice to hear, but discussing my love life with my mother is not my favorite thing to do in the world.

She sighs. "I worry about you. I don't want you to be so alone."

"I'm not alone. Besides, I like alone."

"Trust me, sweetie, you won't say that once you're past forty."

I feel bad for her, and I wish I was there to give her a hug. "How about I come down this weekend? We could go to the fair."

"That would be nice. We could go on the Ferris wheel."

"And spit on people's heads?" We laugh. It's sort of an inside joke between us. Apparently I did that when I was four, and it had Mom in stitches. I wish I could remember. But all the memories I have of myself at that age are faded and vague. That was before she became an alcoholic. She's been sober for many years now, but the illness has left her bitterly marked. Sometimes I wish I could have known her when my father was still alive. And I often wish I could have known my dad. But all I have are a couple of bad photographs. Mom says that even though I hadn't been born yet when we lost him, he loved me. He picked my name. So I always carry a part of him with me. That's a nice thought.

"And afterwards, we'll have so much candy we'll be sick", she smiles.

"Ugh. If we really must."

"Oh, we do. Life's so short, sweetie. It all goes by so quickly. Promise me you'll always make the most of it."

I get an uneasy feeling, hearing her talk like that. "Mom, is everything okay?"

"Everything is fine, my darling. Speak to you tomorrow."

"Okay. Sleep tight."

"Sweet dreams, Jimmy."

"Bye, Mom."

I hang up with a strange feeling. She sounded so lonely that it's breaking my heart. It's making me want to hop on the next train to go see her right now. I'd be down there all the time if train fares weren't expensive and I notoriously broke. But I console myself with knowing that I'll see her in only two days. She may talk about going to the fair now, but I know it'll be a struggle to get her to leave the house. She almost never does anymore.

* * *

When I get out of my late class the next day and turn my cell phone back on, I have a voice mail from Terry, Mom's social worker. It says to call her immediately, and something about the sound of her voice has my pulse rate up in a microsecond. Whatever it is, it can't be good. Is Mom okay? Has something happened? Is she in hospital again? Wild thoughts are spinning in my head. My stomach turns into a lump of sheer panic. Terry picks up her phone, and her voice sounds even stranger than before.

"I'm so sorry, James", she starts. And I know.

My knees give way, and leaning against the nearest wall is all I can do not to fall. But I'm still falling inwardly, down, down, down into the bottomless.

"No... it can't be..."

"James, listen to me. It was an accident. The police are still investigating, but everything looks like she fell asleep smoking, and a fire broke out. I don't think she suffered. She probably suffocated in her sleep."

I can't say anything. I dig my free hand into the rough brick wall, trying to keep breathing. The world turns into a blur. Terry keeps talking, but I don't understand a word she's saying. I think I'm supposed to come down as soon as possible to arrange for the funeral and everything. I think she says she'll help me, but I'm not sure. All I know, all I *feel* is that Mom is gone.

It rips out my soul, and a feeling of panic sets in. It can't be true. No, it can't be. She can't be gone. Not now. Not like this. I was going to see her tomorrow. This can't be real. My brain refuses to acknowledge it. But my heart reacts with a pain so fierce it momentarily blocks out everything else. It feels like being stabbed, the knife twisting in the wound, brutally, mercilessly. Terry keeps on talking, asking if there's anything she can do. I'm too frozen in agony to reply. I still hold the phone in my hand long after Terry's hung up, and I let myself slide to the ground, staring into nothingness. Flicking the same old switch that protects me from feeling. Sinking into numbness, disconnected. Breathe.

I'm not sure for how long I sit painfully crouched like that, motionless and unblinking until Anna happens to find me. I'm unable to react to her at first, her words sounding so distant, strangely concerned. Eventually my eyes regain focus, and I see the shocked, scared look in her eyes.

"James, please say something."

I swallow, and suddenly a teardrop rolls down my cheek, the wetness rousing me. Anna pulls me close and takes me into her care.

11 ASHES TO ASHES

DANNY: Keller is the one who tells me that Mrs. Foley has passed away. I don't believe him at first. Then he describes what he knows of the fire. Apparently the entire house burned down. They weren't able to save much of it. I'm too shocked to really respond, but he gives me the details of the funeral tomorrow. I'm not sure why he does it. I just walk away.

I walk around aimlessly for a while as the news sinks in, and I still can't quite believe that it's true. That she's really gone. I remember our last talk vividly. I had stopped by James' house last summer after having left a couple of messages over the phone. Mrs. Foley answered the door and assured me with an all too familiar smile that James really had gone out and she didn't know when he'd be back. I was about to leave again, frustrated, when she invited me in for coffee. We'd only met once before, but I liked her enough to say yes. To be honest, I kinda jumped at the chance to maybe learn a bit more about J from her. And she seemed to like to talk about him. She was doing well that day, and we sat down in her kitchen, had a nice smoke and strong coffee, and she continued the motherly inspection of me she had begun last time. She had me tell her my major, and asked about my plans after college.

"I'm not sure," I replied with a nonchalant smile. "I haven't given it much thought."

She eyed me over her blue coffee mug. "But aren't you graduating next spring?"

"That's the plan."

"That plan won't really get you anywhere if you don't know what to do with your life afterwards, will it?"

"Guess so."

She shook her head with an amused smile. "Well, what kind of actor do you want to be? Do you want to go into theatre?

Movies?"

I took a drag on my cigarette to buy time. It was all I could do not to squirm under her gaze. This didn't exactly go as planned. "I might not do either", I finally admitted, deciding to go with the truth for once. "I mostly went into acting because it wasn't what either of my parents wanted for me."

"That's a very strange reason. What did they want for you?"

"My mother sees me as an attorney, and my dad... he would really like for me to go into music."

She studied my face with a slight frown that reminded me of James. "I suspect you could be good at either if you applied yourself."

I grimaced. "Now you sound like one of them."

She smiled fleetingly. "All parents are the same in wanting what's best for their children."

"Not mine, trust me. What they want for me is what would suit *them* best."

"Then it seems like high time to make up your own mind, doesn't it?" she smiled kindly.

I smiled back and looked away, knowing she was right. I wished I had someone like her in my life. I probably would have decided years ago.

"My Jimmy wants to be a journalist. I think he will make a great editor one day."

"Has that always been his dream?"

"Since second grade."

"Really? How come?" I was curious. I'm pretty sure I wanted to be a pilot when I was that age. As you do.

"My first husband was a journalist," she revealed. "Jimmy never really knew what that job entailed, but then we watched a documentary on Bob Woodward and Carl Bernstein one night, and Jimmy was glued to the TV. He was always exceptionally mature for his age. Even when he was very little, he would walk around with those big knowing eyes, asking questions even us grown-ups couldn't answer." She chuckled to herself, her gaze distant, almost dreamy. I could just picture little James like that, and it made me smile too. Mrs. Foley looked at me thoughtfully as if trying to read my mind. "There are old souls and young souls in this world. And I'm guessing you're not as young a soul as you let on either."

I felt strangely naked under her gaze, as if she could see through me. "I'm not sure I believe in the concept of souls," I shrugged with a smile, trying to provoke her a little.

But the gray eyes were focused on me, and she didn't buy it at all. "Bullshit."

I laughed. Some moments she was so completely like James, it was almost spooky. "That's good coffee," I changed the subject, taking a sip.

"Uh-huh. My first husband used to say my coffee made him fall in love with me."

"I think I'm falling in love with you too," I grinned at her, and she threw her head back and laughed. For a moment I could see the pretty young girl she once used to be.

"Don't you dare. My Jimmy wouldn't like that one bit."

I winked at her. "We could keep it a secret."

She laughed again, and shook her head at me. "As tempting as that may be, far be it from me to stand in the way of my son's happiness."

My heart gave a strange little jump at that. "Is that your verdict then?"

"Well," she smiled. "You and he both have a lot of learning to do first, that's for sure. There's no telling what might happen." She paused and looked at me, a little smile on her lips. "But you passed my inspection. I'm not sure why exactly," she added, laughing softly.

"Why, thank you," I bowed playfully. "I'm honored."

"As you should be."

A comfortable silence followed. We both continued to smoke, and I felt as relaxed in her presence as if I'd known her for ages. I had that feeling again, the same one I'd had the first time we'd talked. A strange kind of yearning to have what James had, a bit of family, someone who would always stand by me. You could tell just by looking at her that Mrs. Foley would do anything for her son. She was prepared to fight like a lioness for him if she only had the strength. I thought she was probably tougher than she looked, just like him.

We talked about this and that, and before I knew it I had been there for over an hour. She was getting tired, so I thanked her for the coffee and the company, and said good-bye to her. Never knowing that that was the last time I would speak to her.

My aimless walking has led me back to my dorm room, and as I let myself in, I suddenly know that I need to go to the funeral. I may not have known Mrs. Foley well, but she's left quite an impression on me. It hurts to think that she's gone, and I feel a wave of sympathy for James I never thought I'd be able to feel again in my unforgiving anger. All of that seems so silly and petty all of a sudden.

* * *

You know how it always rains at funerals in the movies? At Debbie Foley's funeral, the sky is overcast, but birds are singing happily in the trees nearby. It smells of earth and wet lawn from the light spring rain last night. I'm the last one to get there. When I enter the cemetery, a small group has already gathered around the open grave. Only two elderly women and three guys in firefighter's uniforms, the rest are James' friends. I'm surprised by the turnout. James is standing in the middle, dressed in black, his gaze pinned to the ground. Mills is there beside him, Keller, and two girls I've seen J hang out with. A lot of reporters from the Woodhaven Herald are present, showing support I'm sure James never knew he had.

I stop near a tree to watch from a distance. I'm not sure he would want me there, so I'm hoping I won't be noticed.

I can't stop staring at James, even though I know I shouldn't. He seems completely composed, but he's wearing the exact blank, cold expression he wore when he told me to stay out of his life. And suddenly I understand.

I almost can't bear it anymore then. It's like all my anger comes tumbling down, and just vanishes into thin air. Feelings I've been suppressing so hard over these last couple of months are bursting back up to the surface. No chance of holding them back, that's how strong they are. Seeing him like this does everything the many letters he wrote me couldn't. Words don't mean a thing. But this now, it shows me how hard it was for him to give me up. That exact same look on his face. It shows me that what he wrote is true, that he did care about me. That he was in love with me then. That he still feels the same way about me now.

Forgiveness. It's so sudden and strong that it feels like there never was any grudge at all. The past doesn't matter. Because nothing has changed. I feel the same way about him as I always have. I'm as crazy about him as I've ever been. My heart is beating like crazy. And it's killing me to know how much he must be hurting right now. And that I can't be there to help him through this. It's tearing me apart, the way I've been treating him. The way I let my wounded pride get in the way of being with the one person on earth I've ever really wanted to be with. I feel like the world's biggest idiot. But I can't tell him now. I need to leave him alone, because the last thing he needs right now is me barging in, trying to break through the carefully constructed composure that's shielding his pain.

So I stay where I am and watch from a distance, the wind carrying over only half of what the priest is saying. It doesn't matter; the speech is always the same. *I am the resurrection and the life.* I wonder if Mrs. Foley even believed in that. I say my silent good-byes to her, and I thank her for having been kind to me, when every other mom in the world would have surely kicked me out. In spite of her illness, she was a caring human being with a brilliant sense of humor, and she never deserved to die like this. That's when a ray of light breaks though the clouds and lights the scenery. And James suddenly looks up and right at me.

We stand completely still, just looking at each other. And the composed mask James was wearing starts to crumble almost immediately. I realize that I'm moving only when I'm almost there already. Like I'm on autopilot, and this is all that I can do. Then I'm next to him, and he's looking at me like someone losing the ground beneath his feet, and I take his hand in mine. He squeezes my hand and holds on tight.

* * *

"That's all that's left of it," James says tonelessly. We're leaning against my car that's parked in what used to be his driveway. The house is gone. Only part of the walls and a bit of the first floor is still standing, along with the porch. You can see some remains of the upstairs bedroom. Black, indefinable masses that used to be furniture. The stench of burnt wood and plastic still hangs heavy over the place, nauseating. Yellow police tape warns us not to cross, bright against the coal-black ruins.

"Are you sure you want to be here right now?" I ask softly.

James only nods, staring at the remains of his home. We stand in silence for a long while until he speaks again.

"You gotta love the irony."

I frown. "What do you mean?"

James turns his head to look at me, his expression blank. "Simon was a firefighter."

I look away, unable to hold his gaze. He's right. That's pretty damn ironic if you think about it. If Simon were still alive today, this surely wouldn't have happened. And he was the one who caused Mrs. Foley all that misery that made her ill to begin with.

J swallows, and completely out of the blue he says: "I killed him. That's what I did. I killed him, and now he's got his revenge on us."

I stare at him, not sure I heard that right. "James - what are you talking about?"

He slides down the car and sinks to the ground. Somewhat unsettled, I sit down by his side, waiting for him to explain. There's a strange expression on his face, a deep pain in his eyes that seem so distant. He doesn't even look like the James I know right now, and I admit that might freak me out if I didn't care so much about this guy.

"I'll tell you what I'm talking about," James says tonelessly, strangely calm in a way that's almost scary. "I'm talking about the day that changed my life forever." He trails off and stares at the remains of his house again, transfixed like he can see the events of the past unfold again before his eyes right now.

"I don't remember exactly when Mom started to drink. I think I was about seven. That's when things got really bad some nights. Simon couldn't stand the drinking. It made everything much worse. Everything had to be in perfect order all the time. And when we failed at that..." He trails off and just stares into the distance for a long moment.

"I was sixteen when it happened. I'd been trying to talk Mom into leaving Simon all summer, but she wouldn't. She thought he would never let us leave, no matter where we ran to, and I know now that she was right. But back then I still thought we had to try. So one weekend when he was on a fishing trip with his buddies, I packed our bags. I didn't even ask Mom, I just did." He sighs. "I bet you know how the story goes. I couldn't get Mom to leave, and Simon came home early. Saw our bags all packed by the door." James pauses, as if trying to force memories back to light that he's been suppressing for years. "I... I don't remember much of it. But he had her on the ground and he was choking her when I came downstairs. And I knew for sure he was gonna kill her this time. And... everything kind of happened really fast. I remember that I grabbed the baseball bat that was leaning by the door. I'd always hated the stupid thing, but Simon had made me join a team all the same. He loved baseball, you know. I hated it. I sucked at it. And he hated me for sucking at it. I'd been meaning to leave that damn baseball bat behind... I think I must have swung, and I'm pretty sure I hit him on the side of his head. It's... it's kinda blurry somehow. I don't remember the impact, only the swing. Then he was on the ground, and someone was screaming for him to leave... maybe it was me screaming. And then he staggered out and was gone, and we heard the car start, and he drove off."

He exhales, as if talking has taken a lot of physical effort, and I don't doubt that it must feel like that. I don't dare say a word. Shocked as I am, I need him to tell me the rest. Somehow this wants out right now, and all I can do is to witness, and listen.

It takes a long moment before James continues. "The police knocked on our door about an hour later. They said Simon was in the hospital, in a coma. He'd gone to his favorite bar. He had slipped on the stairs to the restroom and fallen all the way down. I know those stairs. They're long, steep. Cracked his neck and broke his back, they said, amongst other injuries. But I knew the truth. I knew it was my doing. The way that I'd hit him... he must have had a concussion. I know that's why he slipped and fell. He wouldn't have otherwise. He wouldn't have. He never woke up again. He died two days later. And it's all my fault."

I shake my head vehemently. "James, this is bullshit. It wasn't your fault. None of it was."

He looks at me with empty eyes that spook me. "*Everything* was my fault, Danny. If I hadn't packed our bags, if I hadn't…"

"You saved your Mom's life, James. You did the only right thing. Damn it, in my book that makes you a hero."

"No," he insists, taken aback and shaking his head. It's like he's not even really here, but in his own world, his own hell. "And Mom made me promise afterwards. That I would never tell a soul about the fight with Simon. They thought all his wounds were from the fall. Pretty convenient, right? And she didn't want anything bad on my record."

"Oh Jimmy. There wouldn't have been. Don't you see? What you did was self-defense. It's Simon's own fault he fell. You know that. Tell me you know that."

Finally he looks at me again, and his eyes are so full of pain. He shakes his head. "No. No, that's not true. That's not…"

I pull him close and the rest of his words get muffled on my shoulder. It sounds like he can't breathe, choking on the tears he can't cry. I want to give him space, but he clings to me. I hold him tight when at last a few reluctant tears fall, hot and wet on my neck, and I hold him even tighter when his body starts to tremble with an anguish I can only imagine, but never share, as much as I wish I could to make this easier. To take off some of that massive load this boy has been carrying around. I whisper soft words into his ear, soothing words, reassuring words. I don't stop for as long as it takes for him to become calmer again. All of that self-loathing suddenly makes so much sense. Everything about him makes so much sense. And I know in this moment that I couldn't love the guy more than I already do. He is everything to me now.

I'm trying my best to understand why he's so insistent that he's the one to blame for Simon's death. Especially when it's so obvious that he did the only right thing, protecting his mom and chasing that bastard out of the house. I would have done it, everyone with at least a trace of courage in their bones would have done the same thing. None of what happened after than was his responsibility. Simon was a grown man, and he should have known better. How stupid do you have to be to go straight to a bar and drink with a possible concussion? He should have gone to the emergency room instead. It's almost like he wanted this to happen, to make James believe that he had blood on his hands. To haunt him for the rest of his life. My fists clench and I almost wish that bastard weren't dead, so I could have a little heart-to-heart with him. If you ask me, what happened to Simon that day was instant karma. Payback for the life full of misery he had given to his family. Retribution. I only wish James could see it that way. Maybe some day, I'll be able to show him a different perspective. But I know it will be a long way. And maybe he never will.

I try to see myself in James' shoes, severely abused by the man who came into my family as the dad I'd been missing all my life. I try to imagine what it must have been like, trying to please Simon, but unable to keep his violent temper in check, no matter what I did. Always doing everything wrong in his eyes. I am a queer, and he hates me for that fact alone. I'm not the athlete he wants me to be. I'm not the son he expects me to be. I am a failure. I try to please him still, and deep down I just really want him to like me. I hope things will get better. I hope Mom will stop drinking. I hope we'll get some help, but there is none. People look the other way, and we're too scared to say it aloud. Simon's a hero to the community. Nobody would believe us anyway. There's no getting out of this situation. And the one day I find the courage to try, everything goes horribly wrong. I almost get my Mom killed. And I give Simon the concussion that leads to his death. I am a horrible person. I hate myself for what I've done. People should stay away from me. I'm no good. I may seem free now, yet I'll never be free. There's no-one who could love me for who I am. How could I even love myself? How could I ever forgive myself? I've been carrying this around since I was sixteen years old. I could never talk about it. Not to anyone. In all these years, it's grown and grown inside my head, slowly but steadily eating my soul.

Minutes have passed. My little trip inside James' head has left me feeling dizzy with pain. But at least now I understand. And James seems much calmer now, so eventually I haul him up, get him back into the car, and I drive to a motel I saw on my way into town. I get us a room, and he immediately lies down on the bed, and curls up into the fetal position. I lie down beside him and listen to his breathing, knowing somehow that he doesn't want to be touched right now. I wait until he's dozed off. Then I quietly leave the room and organize something to eat and some tea.

He starts to wake up when I steal back inside and sit down on the bed beside him.

"Hey," I say softly and hold out the paper cup to him.

"Hey," he replies, his voice sounding uncertain and small as he sits up and takes the cup from my hand. He won't meet my eyes.

"You hungry? I brought pizza."

He almost smiles, like he can't believe I'm here and I'm doing these things. I get him to eat a few bites, and drink some of his tea. Then he lies down again to stare at the ceiling. I join him carefully. I'm not sure what he needs me to do now, so I'll just lay here with him for a while.

I'm not sure how much time passes before he speaks. When he does, his voice sounds small and hoarse.

"You don't have to be here."

"No, I do. I want to."

He sounds confused. "But... why? Danny, don't you see that you should run from me as fast as you can?"

I almost smile at that. "You still don't get it, do you?"

He glances at me for the first time again. "Get what?"

"That I love you, you idiot." The words just slip out like that, like they've been on my tongue for months now, just waiting to be spoken.

James blinks slowly, and swallows. Repeatedly. I'm sure that's the last thing he was expecting to hear. "You're crazy," he finally says.

"About you? Why, yes I am."

"But... didn't you hear what I said? How can you..."

"Shhh. Stop that. I want you exactly the way you are. I always have. Nothing can change that."

"I pushed you away," he says, still sounding so unbelieving it's breaking my heart.

"You did. And I was angry, and stupid, and unforgiving, and I couldn't see why you did what you did. But I do now."

"Danny..." he seems to run out of words then, because he just stares at me, utterly lost. Pale, and shaken to the core, and still so very beautiful.

"Can I ask you a question?" I say softly.

He nods.

"What you told me at the house - you said you promised to keep it a secret."

He nods again.

"Why did you tell me?" Of all people, I almost add.

James looks at me with those beautiful lonely eyes and shrugs. "I don't know. I had to, somehow. Now that she's gone... I think I needed someone else to know. I needed *you* to know."

"Glad you did."

He frowns. "How can you be? Now that you know this about me. Don't you wish I hadn't said a word?"

I shake my head and roll onto my side, propping my head up on my arm. "Never in a million years. And you'll keep talking to me about these things, okay? It's obvious that you need to."

He shakes his head. "No, Danny. I can't burden you with any more of my crap."

I lean over and cup his face in my hand. "I want you to. Hell, Jimmy, I want to be with you. Let me be there. Let me be the one."

He blinks slowly. "Are you serious? But..."

"Oh, shut up. Just say that that's okay with you."

The lonely eyes light up with a shimmer of hope. "Okay? Are you nuts? That's not just okay, that's... you are... I can't believe you still..."

That's when I lean in and kiss him, and he sinks into the kiss with the softest sigh of relief. It's a careful kiss, tender, almost chaste, unlike any kiss we've had so far. But for some reason, it is the best. I know that he is everything I want. And it looks like we're finally on the same page. Hallelujah.

When we break the kiss, for the first time in ages, I see him smile. It's a weak smile, a crooked smile. But it's a start.

12 LEAP OF FAITH

JAMES: We finally get back to Woodhaven a week later. I probably should have stayed longer, but I just couldn't deal anymore with wrestling with insurances, banks, police, and about a billion other just as pleasant institutions that want something from me because of the fire. Although Danny did most of the wrestling for me. Part of me still hasn't quite processed that we're officially together now. That Danny Rizzo is suddenly my boyfriend. Damn.

I don't tell him, but I'm so glad he's around right now. Just taking on some responsibility, taking care of me, so seamlessly like that's exactly what he's always done. I'm still in doubt, because I'm not sure I can allow this to be real. I want to be with him more than anything in my life. But I can't shake the fear that he'll change his mind tomorrow, and wander off to sleep with someone else. My head's still in a bit of a funk over everything that's happened. I still reach for the phone automatically every night to call Mom, and then I realize that she isn't there to answer anymore. That she'll never be again. I'll never hear her voice or see her face again. Part of me still just can't accept this. I always feel like she's still around somehow.

I've come to learn that I do have friends, and that they're all pretty amazing. Everyone is trying to take care of me, mostly in a sneaky way, hoping I don't notice. Anna secretly does my laundry. Rhea brings me useful books from the library so I don't have to deal with *people*, and takes over as temporary editor in chief. Nick comes by almost every day, just to talk and distract me. He's a pretty good distracter. And I'm pretty sure Casey talked all my professors into going easy on me when it comes to assignments, because everyone is suddenly offering me extensions on my paper deadlines out of the blue. That's really all very sweet, but all I want is to just get on with my life. If I don't, then I'm even more miserable. Studying keeps me from thinking of Mom. Danny keeps me from thinking of Mom too, in his own special way. He has a way of sensing when I need him around, and when I want to be on my own that borders on paranormal. Sometimes I'm happy when we're together, and then I feel bad for being happy during this hard time.

"It's okay to be happy," Danny says when I finally mention it one afternoon. "That's what your mom would want."

I frown at him, knowing he's right. We're on his bed and I'm playing with his fingers, lean and beautiful. Exactly the kind of hand you'd want to touch you. "That's easy for you to say."

He smiles and shrugs. "J, you're gonna feel how you feel no matter what. You can't change that. No use feeling guilty about it."

Wise words, and I can't believe it's him of all people to say them. I can't hide a grin. "My god, you're like a talking fortune cookie."

He laughs out loud and attacks me with his pillow. "Confucius say: You get your ass kicked!"

It turns into a pillow fight that somehow turns into making out. I'm not sure how exactly, but suddenly he's on top of me, and I'm breathless from his kiss. The laughing brown eyes are looking down at me, and my heart is so full with all kinds of emotion I'm sure it will burst any moment now. Then I think of Mom again, and my smile fades. Danny rolls off of me and tugs me close. I let myself be held, and I like how that feels.

"Do me a favor?" I say after a short moment of silence.

"Let's hear it."

"Play for me."

He looks surprised. "On the sax?"

"Yeah. Show me what you got."

"I'm a little rusty on the sax."

"All the more reason to practice."

He kisses my neck and groans softly. "The things you make me do, Jimmy boy," he mumbles as he climbs out of bed, but there's a smile in his voice. He gets the saxophone from his closet and out of the expensive looking case. The instrument is shiny and elegant, not too big. I wonder if Grazzo gave it to him.

From what I've heard about Famous Dad so far, he probably did. Danny has been opening up to me a lot this past week, telling me things about his past that no-one else knows. I like that. It makes me feel like this could be a longer-term thing after all.

Danny fiddles with the mouth piece for a while, blowing on it a couple of times before he starts to play. I sit up and laugh with delight when I recognize "On the Sunny Side of the Street". The way he plays it is a bit groovier and modern than I remember the tune, but gosh, that's beautiful, masterful. And what a glorious image this is, Danny playing the sax in his boxers in the middle of the afternoon, with mild sunlight filling the room. Guess you really ain't got a thing if you ain't got that swing. Like father, like son, I guess, truly in this case. Grazzo isn't one of the great living jazz legends for nothing. You can tell that with a bit of practice and a couple of years of serious experience in music, Danny could easily be as great.

He wasn't kidding, he really does need more practice, but he's good, really good. I can just picture him on stage with a big band somewhere, just making the audience jump up and dance. He looks all loose and relaxed, and truly happy. He looks like Danny, not Rizzo when he plays. And that probably explains why he doesn't like to play for other people, always careful to keep his masquerade up. But he seems to shine with some inner light when he's making music, his eyes bright like they only ever are when he's looking at me. A case of true love, to be sure. I have to somehow make him study music. He mentioned that he's been thinking about it, but thinking is definitely not enough. So I make a little pact with myself that I'm somehow going to make this happen. Even if I have to personally drag him to music classes every day. I may not believe in destiny, but all the same - it's clear that this is his.

* * *

Two weeks later Andrea and I walk into Cafe Plato at the same time to meet up with Danny. It's still quiet here this time of day. "I won't go into the backroom," I tell her by way of greeting.

She just shrugs. "Fair enough. Keller never does either." She gestures toward the corner, where I can see Nick hunched over a stack of his school books, oblivious to everyone else in the cafe. I make a mental note to go over and say hi when he's less busy. I'd much rather join his study orgy than be faced with the ice queen on my own, thank you very much. But there's no escaping now.

Andrea and I order our coffee, then she leads me over to an empty table by the big side window. An awkward silence falls between us once we've settled down on our chairs. It's a sunny spring day, still somewhat chilly but lovely. There's a blossoming cherry tree right outside the window, branches swaying in the breeze. Little pink petals are sailing through the air, like they love to play with the wind.

I've never talked to Andrea alone. I have no clue what to talk to her about. She probably feels the same way. Because let's face it, we surely have exactly zero things in common. The play opens next Friday, and she and Danny and Nick have pretty much spent every waking hour at rehearsal during the week. But it's the weekend now, and the aloof goddess looks just a little bit tired. She and Danny are graduating next month, so I guess I could try to start a conversation about that. I'm still deciding when she looks at me and takes matters into her own hands.

"So, Foley." Somehow that opening doesn't bode too well. "It's a good thing I've caught you alone for once."

I arch an eyebrow, warily. "How so?"

"Let me make this clear: Danny is my best and oldest friend. There's nothing I wouldn't do for him. And I don't ever, ever, ever want to see him suffer again like last year when you dumped him."

I'm somewhat baffled, so I just blink and look at her. She is a bit scary, isn't she? I try to say something, but she brushes me off.

"I want to know if you're serious about him now, or if you're just messing around again."

I almost laugh, because the situation is somewhat bizarre, in the sense that I'd never expected anything like this to happen in a million years. Someone interrogating me if I'm serious about Danny. I lean forward in my seat. "I don't know if you know this, and frankly it's none of your business, but last year Danny and I weren't even together. I was seeing someone else."

This seems like old news to her, and she frowns at me as the waitress brings us our coffee. I thank the girl while Andrea ignores her, holding her tongue until she's gone.

"That's not really an excuse, is it? For the way you treated him."

"You're right, it isn't."

She eyes me suspiciously, and somehow that is almost cute. "So you're telling me things are different now?"

"Yes, Ma'am. But while we're on the subject, tell me something. Is this for real? I mean, Danny… I have no idea what I'm in for. Has he ever been in a serious relationship?" Because he still hasn't told me a lot of things, and I haven't asked. And I have this nagging worry that he is gonna get bored with me pretty soon. I don't fit into his world, do I?

Andrea takes her coffee mug and leans back in her chair. "He has. Once. Back in high school. I don't think he was even that serious about the girl, but they were together for quite some time."

"Was he…" I don't believe I'm really gonna ask her this, and clear my throat. "Was he true to her?"

Andrea snorts. "You really don't know him that well yet, do you? 'Course he was."

I'm more than a little surprised to hear this, and frown at her. "We are still talking about Danny Rizzo, right?"

Andrea rolls her eyes. "Foley, I expected more of you. But if you must know, I've never seen him this head over heels for anybody. People think he's so superficial…"

I try to say something, but she stops me by holding out her hand, and continues: "But that's all just for show. He's stuck with me through some rough times when all my other friends turned their backs on me. This lifestyle he's been leading for the past couple of years, I've always known that would end some day. Us kids of divorces, we're crazy like that, okay? I've had my times when I was out of control, too. But that's just it, isn't it? You need someone to ground you, and be your home. And for reasons beyond me, he seems to have found this in you."

Her eyes are just a little bit warmer then, and she ends her expose with a half-smile that one *might* interpret as friendly. I sit in slightly baffled silence for a while and watch my coffee getting cold. When I lift my gaze to Andrea again, she's smiling for real this time. It makes her seem like a different person, and it's suddenly clear that this lady has her own scars, and all the attitude is a protective measure.

"So we're cool?" I ask, and wonder why I even care.

Her smile widens and she nods. "Seems like, Foley. I can teach you the ropes of how to navigate his world if you want me to."

"Why would you do that?"

"Because you'd fail spectacularly otherwise. And he deserves some happiness."

I can't hide my grin. She has some serious balls, you gotta hand her that.

I wince when a thought crosses my mind. "Am I gonna have to join the entourage?"

Andrea actually laughs. "Forget the entourage. I'm the only one you need to impress."

"How am I doing so far?" I snarl, only half-joking.

"We'll see, Foley. We'll see. I don't hate you, so that's a start."

"Good to know. Surprisingly, I don't hate you either." It's really weird and unexpected, but somehow I feel like Andrea might actually turn out to be my kind of girl. When she's not all blase about her surroundings for once.

Our timing is perfect, or maybe Danny's is, because that's when he arrives and joins us. I still get those silly butterflies in my stomach, getting a welcome kiss from Danny in a public place. No more sneaking around. It's such a relief. Still almost surreal. But sure enough, everyone is watching. Guess I'm gonna have to get used to that. When you're dating the guy who's the centre of everyone's attention, the guy at least half of campus is infatuated with, you're bound to get a little attention yourself. I'm getting better at ignoring it, but it's gonna take me a while longer, getting used to this. Maybe you gotta be blase about it all, like Andrea. Maybe I'm gonna be like that some day. But today, I still get to stare back darkly at the people staring at me, until they drop their eyes. It's almost fun to do. I think maybe I'm gonna get used to this circus after all. Maybe Danny and I really have a shot.

Things are changing; I can practically feel the bits and pieces shifting all around me. Everything's in motion. As Danny and I are trying to figure out what it is we have, and what we want it to be, we're making waves that touch those around us as well. We're already building a new circle of friends. Our own circle of friends. People we both can stand. People like Nick, and Anna and Rhea, but also Andrea and Sebastian, an exchange student we kind of befriended together, which was a whole new experience in itself. Danny isn't quite cool with Casey yet, but things are getting better on that front too. It seems like we're slowly but steadily drawing more people into this funny little group of a patchwork family. And that's exactly what I need right now: family. I've been feeling so lost since Mom passed away. Some days are hard to bear, but there are more and more okay days now. Some days are even pretty good. And as Danny, Andrea and I fall into a surprisingly easy conversation about art, I think this might turn out to be one of the better days.

* * *

Danny uses the spare key to my room the next afternoon and enters quietly. I glance up from my desk briefly, not turning around. I finally managed to get my head around this cursed literature assignment from hell. I'm almost done making the important final point, and I read through a note on my little notebook before I continue to type on my computer. A smile lights up my face momentarily when a large paper cup of fresh coffee is presented to me and placed on the only free spot on my desk. The rest is covered with stacks of books. Mmm, the scent of heaven. Danny knows how I like my coffee, strong and black. He gently runs his fingertips along my neck in greeting, and walks over to the bed to get comfy, dropping his bag of school things on the way.

When I've finished typing the paragraph, I look over to him. He's settled in, shoes off, back propped against the wall, an open book on his lap. This close to graduation even Danny Rizzo has to study. He's taking it surprisingly seriously, and that's just another side of him that's completely new to me. The brown eyes scan the written lines in rapt attention. There's a small, concentrated frown on Danny's forehead. As I look at him, my heart is filled with a strange yearning, and I listen to its beating, the steady rhythm slowly accelerating. He's so beautiful. He's wearing his hair longer for the play, all soft, dark curls and sinful perfection. In moments like this, he'd make Botticelli angels wither and die with envy.

"Why me?" I blurt out without thinking, breaking the comfortable silence. I hate to spoil the moment, but I can't help it.

Danny lifts his gaze to me. His eyes are still filled with thought from reading, like he's coming back to me from another world. "Hm?"

I swallow, my throat feeling tight. "Why did you pick me? I mean, initially."

A small smile graces his lips, the dark eyes lighting up noticeably. He tilts his head a little to the side and pats the empty space beside where he's lounging. "Come here."

I roll my eyes. "Does that mean you can't tell me from where I'm sitting?"

"No, that means I intend to kiss you senseless sometime in the near future. Get your delicious ass over here right now, Jimmy Foley."

I can't help but grin at that, and sigh a little in fake protest before I haul myself up and join him on the bed. He tugs me close and kisses my forehead, his warm fingers tangled in my hair.

"Initially?" He pauses to think before he continues, then grins. "Mostly I was after aforementioned phenomenal ass."

I chuckle and kiss him. His playfulness makes way for a rare glimpse of his serious side that always makes my breath catch in my throat and leaves me a little speechless. His eyes are thoughtful as he studies my face.

"I've been in love with you for much longer than I was aware. It took me a while to realize." Danny looks and sounds the most vulnerable I've ever seen him, and it only makes me want him more, if that's even possible. "Guess it's because I never felt like this about anyone."

My voice sounds oddly hoarse. "But you're pretty sure now, right?"

"I love you, James," he replies simply. It hurts unbelievably good, in all the right places. He's only said it once before, at the motel on that black, black day. But not like this, not with such brutal honesty. No jokes, no flirting undertones. He's stripping down to truth and bone emotionally, because I'm asking him to. Because he trusts me that much. I get a strange lump in my throat.

"It's hard," I manage to get out. I know that's not what you're supposed to say back. He moves to say something, but I shake my head. "No. I want to be able to accept this. I'm trying." I look away, feeling positively crestfallen. That leap of faith he just made, I'm not sure I'm ready to follow yet. I hate myself for that, because it's not who I want to be anymore. "I wish I could just get past all theses... stupid fears, and insecurities. I hate that I can't just magic them away."

He smiles. "Who said that you have to?"

"But..."

"Look," he says, serious again. "We both don't believe in all this 'love will conquer everything' shit. So let's not pretend that we do. You've been through hell, and I have some messed up issues too. But that's just it. On some completely crazy cosmic-karmic level or whatever, you and I are perfect together."

I smile a little, sheepishly, because strangely enough, I have to agree. "On a cosmic-karmic level, is it?"

He grins. "Yeah, screw you."

I laugh and look at him, and for a moment I try to imagine us five years down the line, and the crazy thing about it is - I can. I can see this thing we have working out somehow. Even with us soon being the entire Atlantic apart. And that's something I don't even want to start thinking about, because it breaks my heart.

I smile at him, grateful for him, for everything. "If you're going to tell me to stop worrying next, forget it. Because that's just not how I roll."

He gives me a look. "Shut up now," he says, suddenly all charisma and in charge, like he can be sometimes, and god, does it ever turn me on when he does that. It might just be the sexiest thing on this planet. "If you think I'll give you a reason to chicken out again, you are so wrong, Jimmy Boy."

I punch him a little for that. "Hey, I don't chicken out."

He punches me back playfully. "You do too."

"When have I ever... oh," I say, and feel more than a little bit stupid. I make a face. "Well, that sucks. Why do you always have to be right?"

He shrugs. "I'm just that cool. Also, didn't I tell you to shut up?"

"Okay." I nod and place a gentle kiss on the special spot on his collarbone that I know when worked on properly can drive him to do unspeakable things. "Shutting up is in commencement."

There's a positively wicked grin on his lips. "You're still allowed to moan."

"Oh thank heavens," I whisper into his ear before I start to kiss a trail along his neck. I suddenly stop then, and look into his eyes. "How exactly are you so awesome?"

He blinks at me, surprised. "What, a compliment? Again?"

"Yeah, sorry. I know you prefer flattery."

He laughs, and it's the most beautiful, carefree sound in the world. Like me, he still remembers the date that wasn't supposed to be a date, when we talked about art and Europe and so much more. It seems like a lifetime ago. So much has happened since then. And look at us now. We can talk all day if we want to. We can sit in the most comfortable silence ever known. We laugh so much when we're together. He always senses when I need space, and I know when to leave him alone. It just works, somehow. Who would have ever thought it possible? It feels incredibly good. One of these days, I will come to realize it's not just a dream. This is *real*, isn't it?

"Maybe I could make an exception for you."

"For compliments?" I grin.

He winks at me. "Yeah. As long as they're not too frequent."

"You have my solemn promise."

His smile is irresistible. "Deal."

"That being established, I'll probably still try to sabotage my way out of this. Just so you know."

He chuckles softly, but his eyes are warm and full of promise. "Wiggle as much as you want, Jimmy Boy. You won't get off this hook."

"Speaking of wiggling..." I grin, and reach down to open the zipper on his fly. He laughs and covers my lips in a kiss that leaves me hot all over, and more than a little breathless. I get goosebumps when he kisses or touches me like that, all intense and focused. If there ever comes a time when I'm no longer hopelessly turned on by that amazing body of his and the things he does with it, I demand to be shot on sight. He slips his hands underneath my shirt and caresses my skin in a way that has me half-hard in no time.

"Hell, I don't want to leave you," I whisper against the skin of his chest, so softly I'm not sure he even hears. There's no real reaction to it, just him taking my shirt off, but when I look into his eyes, they are dark and thoughtful. He's back to his sexy self instantly, continuing to undress me.

"You do grasp the concept of shutting up? It means you don't talk." He pushes me onto the mattress, reaching down to expertly wrap his fingers around my now painfully hard cock.

"Gah", I reply, and follow it with something even more incoherent for good measure.

"That's the spirit", he grins, and kisses me in a way that makes me want to die from pleasure. This concept of shutting up I can buy into.

* * *

It's quiet in the large theater auditorium this time of night. Like the heavy silence from the empty corridors is pressing in through the cracks underneath the doors. The room is dark except for a few lights near the front that fill the stage with a warm, almost magical glow. I sit beside Danny on the bench of the grand piano, waiting for him to start playing. He runs his elegant fingers over the keys like a gentle caress, and I listen, transfixed, as notes begin to rise and music sweeps through the theater. It starts slowly, rises to something living and breathing, powerful and true. It's completely improvised, and the melody rises as it comes to him, drifts into something else flawlessly and touches something deep inside of me that's never been moved in such a way. His gaze is fixed on something only he can see. My heart is beating so loudly in my chest I think he must be able to hear it.

I don't know for how long he plays like this, oblivious to the world, showing me this secret side of his. Time drifts away like nothing, and when the melody slows down and exchanges its power for something tender and fragile, and finally ends, I can only sit in silence, too moved to speak.

"You okay?" he finally asks, turning to me.

I nod. I feel liberated, still swept away by his music, and at the same time scared as hell. I lean my forehead against his, and close my eyes. Only then do the words come, and I exhale with a shudder of relief. "Just so we're clear: I love you too."

He leans back a little with an amazed smile. "Hell will freeze over, he actually said it."

"Yeah well," I smile back at him. "Get used to it. I might repeat it some time."

"I could learn to live with that." He grins, only a little smug in the most endearing way.

He pulls me close, and my chuckle gets buried in his kiss. Suddenly I'm senselessly happy. I feel better than I have in... well, ever, probably. It pushes back my lingering sadness, sets me free. I'm always gonna be good old Jimmy Foley, Waldorf and Statler combined in one person. I don't change easily, and maybe I never will. I will still bite the hand that feeds me if I can. But maybe even Jimmy Foley can learn to take a leap of faith every now and then. Stranger things have happened.

13 IN SECRET PLACES

DANNY: I know it's pretty sneaky, and maybe I should have talked to James first. But the first thing I do the next day is give Markus a call. Markus is one of Grazzo's good friends, and he teaches at the JIB - the Jazz Institute Berlin. Grazzo's been telling me all kinds of good stuff about the place. It's one of the schools he's been nagging me to apply to for years.

As it turns out, applications for the next semester are already closed. Shit. My heart sinks, but then Markus starts to ramble about how Graz would probably kill him if he found out that I wanted to study at the JIB and they didn't let me in. He says he'll talk to some people. Make some calls. Looks like there might be some chance on getting in late due to being the undeniably talented offspring of one of the world's leading jazz musicians. I've never made use of Grazzo's connections, but count me in this time.

Seems stupid now, not studying music in the first place when now that I've decided that that's what I want to do, it feels so right I can't believe it. It's got nothing to do with making Grazzo happy. It's got everything to do with what *I* want to do with my life. And I think J may have more than just a little bit to do with my finally figuring this out.

So when we hang out at my room that night, and for a while I've watched him typing away on his laptop for another class assignment that apparently I made him late to finish, just feeling strangely content, I sit up straighter on the bed where we're both lounging.

"What if I came to Berlin with you?"

He freezes mid-motion and looks up at me. I can see his eyes light up at the thought momentarily, but then his expression switches to puzzled. "Come again?"

"You heard me the first time," I grin.

"This is no joking matter, Mister," he tells me sternly, with that adorable frown on his face.

"What makes you think I'm joking?"

"But..." the frown deepens, "your life is *here*."

I chuckle softly. "My life is where I want it to be."

For the split of a second, he looks heartbreakingly happy while still disbelieving. He closes his laptop with a soft click, now completely focused on me. "You serious? But... what do you want to do in Berlin?"

"I'm planning on studying music, actually. At the JIB, if they let me."

His eyes widen in surprise. "The JIB! That's a music school for jazz, isn't it?" he asks a little breathlessly. "Oh... wow. That's... Danny, that's awesome." His face lights up then, and it makes my heart beat just a little faster. "Not to sound like your dad, but music, it's your thing. You should do it. No matter if it's in Berlin or..."

"It will be in Berlin. I'll see to that."

"You're not doing this because of me, are you? Because I wouldn't want you to..."

"Oh, shut up." I pull him close and kiss him, and I can feel his smile on my lips. He gives in for a little while, but then he breaks the kiss and looks at me seriously.

"I need to know this, though. Is this really what you want to do, or is it just because it will suck balls being so far apart for so long?"

"I want this, J. I never felt better about anything in my life. I know it's the right decision."

He looks cautiously happy then, before another thought crosses his mind. "But you don't even speak German!"

I grin mischievously. "Ein bisschen schon."

He laughs. "A little bit? That sounds like more than just a little bit to me. What the hell, D? Why did you never tell me that?"

I shrug with a smile. "You never asked."

He laughs softly and shakes his head. "I'm gonna have to do a lot of asking, it seems. You," - he pokes me in the chest - "are such a mystery, Danny Rizzo."

"Is that a good thing?" I wink at him.

"It's a *you* thing. So naturally, it would be good."

We both laugh and I take his hand in mine, and I feel so happy that it's almost unreal. We fall down on the bed and just lay there, looking at each other.

"Your mind is set then, about coming to Berlin with me?" he asks quietly, looking into my eyes.

"All set, Jimmy Boy."

"That's good. Because if you change your mind about this later, I'm gonna seriously kick your ass."

I laugh. "Never gonna happen."

"You changing your mind, or me kicking your ass?"

"Neither, smartass."

There's a sparkle in his eyes as he props his head up on his hand. "You don't think I could take you, do you?"

To tell the truth, I'm not even sure. I think he could easily take me if surprise was on his side, and if there's one thing I've learned, it's that you don't underestimate J, ever. But hell if I'm gonna admit that aloud. "I'd like to see you try."

He rolls me over and has me pinned down faster than I can blink, and I get turned on.

"Screw you," I grin, far from admitting defeat.

He bends down and whispers into my ear. "I'd rather screw *you* this time, if you don't mind."

God. That's my undoing. I arch up and kiss him, and he returns it just as hungrily. It's a matter of seconds and we're panting, struggling to pull each other's clothes off. It's kinda frantic, and not all that sexy, and we both end up laughing into each other's kisses. Sex between us is still a wild, complicated creature that won't be tamed. We both like it a little rough, and it's always a dance along the edge. Nothing has ever turned me on like that. I swear I dream of him taking me at night, and there's this craving for him underneath my skin, all the time. I like to pitch as much as the next guy, don't get me wrong, but damn, I'm such a whore for James riding me hard and good. There's something almost a little desperate in it, always, and I can see something in his eyes that get so intense then. Like he still can't fully believe I'm his, and he wants to leave his mark on me *somehow*. There's this rhythm to it that goes: *Love me, love me, never be with anyone else. Want me like I want you. Burn for me like I burn for you.* And damn if that doesn't turn me on so bad. I know how much he loves to see me come completely undone at his touch, and I've learned to let it show. If that's what he needs to see to believe in us, fine by me. I'm done holding back, I'm done with all the masks, all the lies, all this circus. I'm more *me* with him now than I've ever been.

Then we're both naked, skin on skin, rubbing against each other, his hands worshipping my skin like I'm something *holy*, and I'm so hard I might die if I don't feel him inside me right this second. I kiss his neck, suck on his skin, savoring the taste of him, and he moans softly. The moan turns into a pleased little gasp when I bite down carefully, not breaking the skin, just teasing a little, like he loves it. I can see it in his eyes, something whispering: *Scar me. Leave your mark. Add it to the scars that tell my story.*

Oh, I will, Jimmy Boy. In secret places. Just wait and see.

My skin's on fire from his touch, and when he reaches for condom and lube, my last coherent thought is: I can't wait to do this on the flight to Berlin. Mile high, baby, all the way.

* * *

We're sitting in the back row at the large theater auditorium. It always smells a little dusty in here. It's early evening and the stage is abuzz with people running around, moving the props to their proper places. The first dress rehearsal is just about to start, and James flat out refuses to write the review of the play for the school paper.

"I wouldn't be able to be objective," he admits with an amused little smile.

I grin. "I'm sure you'd manage, Mr. Editor."

He gives me a look. "You have leather pants. Your argument is invalid."

Those damn trousers are far too tight. Seriously, what were the costume people thinking? That blood circulation is highly overrated? Watch me suffer for my art. "I'll still demand your honest opinion."

"Fine. I'll try to come up with something vaguely coherent."

"That's all I'm asking."

He takes me in from head to toe and smiles in a way that makes my pulse race. His eyes seem to say, proudly: Mine. That's right, Jimmy Boy. About time you realized.

"Would anyone notice if you took the costume home tonight?" he grins.

I laugh softly. "Kinky. I like."

"Well, will they?"

"I'm afraid they're sworn to guard it with their lives."

J sighs deeply. "Damn. My life, so hard."

"You'll have to wait for opening night. Everyone will be too distracted to notice then."

"That sounds like you have some experience in the costume smuggling business, Mr. Rizzo."

I wink at him. "Possibly."

"You dirty dog," he says fondly, and I shut him up with a kiss.

When we finally manage to part, we sit in comfortable silence for a while, just watching the comings and goings in the room. Jeff is bellowing orders from backstage that appear to be mostly ignored. I like the little rush of excitement that always sets in before a show, even if it's just a full run-through rehearsal. But James will be watching.

"Will you tell Nick?" he asks quietly, and we both look over to Keller who's standing to the side of the stage. Rhea is fiddling with the collar of his shirt that won't stay down properly, and he's trying in vain to evade her hands. He looks good in his costume.

I know immediately that J's talking about Berlin, and nod. "Yeah. Let me do it."

"Don't wait too long. If he hears from somebody else, he'll be so pissed."

"I haven't even told Andie yet."

"Well, you should then." James glances at me uneasily. "Unless there's a reason why you..."

"James." I shake my head. "I want to go with you, more than anything. I just suck at good-byes."

He smiles a little, knowingly. "Or we could just skip that part and elope in the middle of the night."

"Tempting. Far too tempting."

That's when Jeff calls everyone to the stage for some final instructions, and I smile at J as I get up.

"Break a leg, sweet Prince," he calls after me.

I turn around, and wink at him, slipping into character. "Beggar that I am, I am even poor in thanks."

I give him my best small Hamlet bow. James pretends to swoon, and I'm on my way, laughing to myself. I'm gonna miss the theater, no doubt. But with a little luck, I'll be back on stage some day with my music. A thought a million times more terrifying, and about three gazillion times more exciting. The possibility of my most secret dream coming true with time makes my eyes shine with anticipation. Damn, I cannot wait.

14 BREAK A LEG

NICK: I know I should've been paying more attention to the calendar, or the syllabuses for my classes or something, but I've been so focused on getting shit done and working on the show that I completely forgot about this group project that we've been assigned in one of my classes. I can't ignore it any more though, when I rush into class and the professor's there early and already started reading off pairs of names and the topic of their project assignment.

Great. Just what I needed at this point in the semester. It's not like I can really complain about it though, so I just wait to hear my name and hope that I get a partner that will at least pull their own weight. I'm still actually doing pretty well this semester. I know, I'm pretty surprised by it too. I'm not going to be winning any academic awards or anything like that, but I think I might be able to swing a pretty solid B average this semester. It's not going to help much with the disaster of my cumulative GPA from my first three semesters, but it might help a little at least.

"Keller." The professor finally calls my name, and I wait to find out my partner. I haven't been paying attention, so I don't even know who's left. "And... McKenna. Let's see if you can maybe keep us from losing one of our better soccer players." It takes me a minute - a really confusing minute - to realize that the prof's talking to *me*. And that *I'm* supposedly the smart one of this pair? Seriously?

I don't think that's ever happened to me before.

We must've been the last pair called, because people are turning to one another, exchanging the information and shit and talking about meeting up to work. I look around, waiting for someone else to come to me, because yeah, I admit that I don't really know anyone's name in this class. Hell, I don't even know if this McKenna is a guy or a girl.

"So I guess I should at least get your number or something, right?" I turn to look a who's talking to me, and of course. Of course. Because it's super jock of the blue eyes and big smile that's got his phone out and is waiting for me.

So much for getting a partner that'll pull their own weight. Now I have to keep a jock from getting kicked out of school for being an idiot. Like I didn't have anything better to do with my time.

* * *

We decided to meet at the cafe the next day because it's really my only day off from rehearsals this week. Which is great, but I've been at the cafe for over an hour now, and he still hasn't shown up. And when I tried to call him at the number he left in my phone, it went right to voicemail. If I wouldn't have already been here working on other shit, I'd probably be even more pissed off. Not that I'm happy about waiting around for someone to show up.

So I've been here for about an hour when Mister Big Shot Jock decides to finally show up. He doesn't even look like he's that sorry, not that I'm that surprised, really. What else should I expect from a jock like that. It's a good thing I *don't* have rehearsal today though, or we'd never get anything done before I'd have to run off again.

SuperJock (sorry, Mac, as he put himself into my phone) gives me a smile as he sits across from me, and I swear that I can see just about all of his very straight white teeth. I'm not falling for that sort of shit though. I've been dealing with Rizzo's brand of smiles for over a year now, and Mac's got nothing on Riz. I mean, it's a nice enough smile, I guess. If you like teeth.

He drops a bag next to the table, and it actually sounds like it might have books in it. I don't think I've ever once seen him carrying a bookbag. But he starts pulling shit out of it - books, papers, a highlighter - as he angles another smile over at me. "Sorry. I lost track of time starting on some of the research."

And damn. The books have pages marked by little flags of paper like he's actually gone through them already looking for shit. So much for being too dumb to stay in school. What the hell is up with this guy? By the time he pulls out a stack of typed notes, I can't stop the "what the hell?" that slips out.

He smiles at me again (white teeth blue eyes) and shrugs, like this shit happens every day. "Spring's my off-season, and I know that something's got you running around, so I figured I'd get a head start for us." And yeah, that explains absolutely nothing, but I guess I shouldn't complain, right?

Maybe this project won't be so awful after all.

* * *

Another hour into our meeting, and I'm convinced that there's been some huge mistake. Mac actually knows what he's talking about, keeps pulling books over to make some point, and is writing down things we both are coming up with so that we can use them in our project. There's no way that this is the same guy that needs someone to save his ass from failing.

He's reading over a few paragraphs when I finally decide to call his ass on it. He looks up when I clear my throat (blue eyes smile without teeth). "So what's the deal with you needing help? You know this shit just as well as I do." If not better. In fact, his only problem seems to be that he looks up every time the front door opens, like he expects someone to come in and catch him doing some actual homework or something.

"I dunno." And there's that smile again. The 'you want to like me' smile. "I like the project, I guess." It's a lame-ass, cop-out answer, and it doesn't sound even vaguely true. What I don't get is why he'd lie about something like being as stupid as all the other jocks.

The door opens again, and right on cue Mac glances over toward it. "And why do you keep doing that? You waiting for someone? One of your jock friends? Or maybe the paper wanting to interview you about doing an actual school project?" A strange look crosses his face, and it finally hits me that he doesn't want his teammates knowing that he's smart. Which is ridiculous, but I guess it makes sense, too. In a twisted way. "Relax. The paper's not going to print your sordid academic secrets or anything."

I shove another book across the table at him and he takes it with a wary look, like he's not sure whether or not he should. It's one that discusses a point he was making earlier, though, so he takes it and finally starts to read again. It gives me a chance to look over at the last person that had walked into the cafe. And I see Riz standing about halfway across the room, coffee in hand, like every other time he's joined me at my usual table. He's smiling too (and this is one of the annoying ones), looking between Mac and I and the mountain of books between us. It's enough of a smirk that I know I'll hear about this later, and I flip him off as he changes direction and heads for the back room. It isn't loud, but I hear his laugh from across the cafe.

* * *

Riz never really gets the chance to give me a hard time about it though, because the next few weeks of the semester are pretty much hell for both of us, I think. Jeff's got everyone doing rehearsals pretty much every day now, and for as easygoing of a guy as he usually is, rehearsals running up to a show are serious business for him. Get caught dicking around, and there's hell to pay. Not that he can kick anyone out of the show at this point, but there's public humiliation in store, at the very least.

And when we're not rehearsing, I've still got papers and projects and normal shit like trying to keep my life together. I'm doing alright, I think, but that doesn't mean that it's easy. Especially when one project still requires me to deal with secret-smart Super Jock. Mac. The little time I have to be at the cafe, he's usually there too, stealing part of my table with his books and stacks of notes on our topic. He's actually got me feeling a little guilty about not pulling more of my own weight, but when I offer to take more, he gives me that smile and says that I've got enough on my plate and that he's got it taken care of. I really have no clue how he knows what's 'on my plate', but I suppose it's good that he's taking care of so much.

I know I'm going to owe him for doing so much on this project. I tried to bring it up once, but he just laughed at me and told me to grab him a coffee. I know it's messed up, and just asking for a beating from the entire soccer team, but I actually caught myself thinking about us getting coffee sometime when we're *not* studying.

Because thinking about dating a straight jock is exactly what I need in my life right now.

* * *

Dress rehearsal hits before anyone is ready for it. That's the way it always goes, but it seems even worse this time for some reason. Jeff had planned for us to start our last run-through at 3, but by 2:30, people are still running around, half in costume, makeup only partially done, and Jeff is looking like he's about to lose his mind. It'll all come together in the end, but it's hard to be positive when the theater looks like a brightly costumed war zone.

Strangely enough, dress rehearsal doesn't hit me as hard this time as it sometimes does. My costume's not nearly as complicated as most people's, so while they're being laced in and made up, it leaves me sitting in the auditorium, watching everyone scurry around on stage, and listening to Jeff shout that we're starting in 10 minutes, whether people are ready or not. And that he expects people to hit their cues even if they're naked.

That'd be quite the show. I know it won't happen though. Even for dress rehearsal, we'll all be ready for the curtain to go up in a few minutes.

Riz finally emerges from backstage, looking like he's ready for opening night instead of just a rehearsal, and finds me sitting a few rows back. He comes up, looking every bit the prince that Jeff's wanted him to be, and takes the seat next to mine. While everyone else is done up in crazy colors and make up and even some masks, Riz and I get the luxury of pretty normal clothes - him in black and me in gray. Jeff had worked a long time with costuming to get that right, saying he wanted Hamlet and Horatio to be this sane sort of contrast to all the craziness and posturing in the court. I have to say that I'm not at all jealous of some of the things the other cast has to wear. I'll take normal gray clothes any day.

I'm not lucky enough to get a pair of the leather pants that costuming has practically poured Riz into though. I guess that's part of a princely wardrobe.

We sit, like an island in the chaos that's starting to sort itself out, just like I knew it would. I never would have thought half a year ago that the silence between us could actually be comfortable. I finally told Doc the other day that I'm pretty sure that Rizzo and I are friends now, and she looked at me like I was an idiot for taking this long to notice.

I just wasn't expecting it, okay?

"I'm going with James." The words slip into the quiet like they're supposed to make sense, but they don't. Of course he's 'going with' James. Not quite how I'd expect him to put it, or why it needs to be said. I was pretty aware of their reconciliation after Riz stopped being so stubborn and let James talk to him.

"Going with?" I can't keep the smirk off my face or out of my voice. "You can say 'screwing'. I'm a big boy. I can handle it." I glance over, teasing. "Or you can call him your *boyfriend* if you want." A stupid smile crosses his face before he shakes his head. He looks at me for a second and then back toward the stage, where Jeff is frantically trying to wrangle people up. Andrea runs by in just her under-dress, a costumer chasing after her with an armful of colorful fabric. I nearly miss Rizzo's next words in the commotion.

"No, I mean I'm going *with* him. When he leaves for Berlin. They've got a music school there, and because of Grazzo they've pulled some strings for me..."

It hits me like a ton of bricks, and I don't even know what to say. He keeps watching the stage, and I stare at his profile until Jeff finally notices us sitting there and yells at us to get backstage in our places. Riz pushes himself up and heads up the aisle, not looking back once, like he knows I'll be watching him.

* * *

Rehearsal doesn't go nearly as smoothly for me as it should. I try to put Riz's bombshell out of my mind, try to think about

Hamlet and Horatio, but it keeps sneaking back into my brain at the most inconvenient points.

The ridiculous part is that I don't even know what I'm feeling. It's not good, but I'm not sure why. And I can't even be all that surprised, because it's obvious that neither Riz nor James wants to be apart for very long now that they're finally getting their shit together. I've even teased them about how disgustingly couple-y they've gotten. And it was always obvious that Riz wasn't going to hang around at Woodhaven after graduating. But Berlin is *so* far.

It's as Hamlet's dying in my arms that I finally realize: I don't want to be alone again.

* * *

Opening night.
I'm dressed and as close to ready as I suppose I'm going to get. I'm lurking backstage, waiting for curtain, and it takes Jeff running into me three times before he tells me to fuck off and find Rizzo because no one's seen him for close to 15 minutes.

He's doing his pre-show warm-up in a quiet corner when I find him. He's in costume and his eyes are closed, and I know I shouldn't interrupt him, so I lean against the wall and watch until his eyes open again and focus on me.

"Ten minutes, they're saying." He nods. "They're also saying that there isn't an empty seat in the house." I don't know how to tell him that I'm not sure I can do this.

Because I'm terrified. Of the show and of everything that's going to come after. Summer, next year, when James and Riz are gone, and I'm left on this campus not knowing anyone other than Mac, and I'm not even sure if we really count as friends yet, and Marc, who I still see from time to time, running away from me if he notices me. My own graduation in a few years, and everything after that. And in this moment, the sheer terror of getting on the stage and finishing out this year is more important than Riz taking off. I can't be angry when I'm this scared.

He knows it, too. Anyone that looked at me right now would know it. And I think he's going to say something about doing some breathing or some other shit that they teach us in classes, but he doesn't. He comes over to me, standing close, and he puts his hand on my shoulder. And in a low voice, he says one thing.

"Horatio..."

And I don't know why, but it grounds me. It takes away the part of me that's making my hands sweat and my stomach clench. I close my eyes and take a breath, smelling the dusty makeup scent of backstage laid over that scent that my brain recognizes as Rizzo. And when I open my eyes again, Rizzo's still there, Hamlet behind his eyes, smiling at me. I smile too and reach a hand up to lay over his. I can be mad at him again later.

"The same, my lord, and your poor servant always."

* * *

When the final curtain goes down about 3 hours later, we get a standing ovation, and not a single person is left in their seat.

The post-show rush hits fast and intense once the curtain's down, with people hugging each other and congratulating each other on a good opening night. All the little glitches that Jeff will have us working on in the days to come are forgotten in the high of a job well-done.

Backstage, it seems that the number of people that should be there has grown almost exponentially. I'm certain that there's people back there that shouldn't be - friends and family - but no one's getting kicked out, so I just smile at everyone that congratulates me, no matter if I recognize them or not.

There is one familiar face though, Mac is somehow backstage and grinning his bright smile at me as people jostle around us. He throws a quick glance around, like he's expecting someone to call him out for being backstage, and smiles at me again when he realizes no one's going to. "Good show!" He nearly has to shout to be heard over the other commotion, and I lean in to hear him better, but before I can get close, he lifts his hand to hold out a cheap bouquet of daisies to me.

It takes me too long to register that they're for me. But I reach out to take them, and Mac gives me a wide, bright grin.

Maybe he *could* give Riz a run for his money in the smile

department.

15 LONG WAY HOME

DANNY: It's early evening and the sun hangs low in the sky when Nick and I leave the theater department together. There's no performance tonight, but Jeff made us go over some of our scenes again. It's not unusual. A show's never really finished. It grows and evolves from performance to performance. My mind is still with Hamlet, and Nick's quiet too as we walk along towards the dorms. He hasn't really been talking to me since I told him that I'm going with James. We pretend nothing's wrong backstage, polite to each other in a way we normally never would be. Jeff has noticed that something's off in our chemistry. Hence the run-through.

"So, you and Mac, huh?" I finally break the silence.

Nick blinks, then he gives me a wary look. "Mac and I what?"

"That's what I'd like to know." Keller and Sam "the Mac" McKenna, goalie of our soccer team and acclaimed school hero. Now that's an odd couple if there ever was one. I arch an eyebrow. "You seem to hang out a lot."

"None of your business." He scowls over at me, shaking his head. "Because there's nothing going on."

I shrug and grin. "Shame. He likes you."

"Will you stop it already," he groans, actually blushing for once. "And he doesn't *like* me."

"Trust me on this. He just doesn't know it yet."

Nick gives me a death glare, and I punch him lightly on the shoulder, just because. He punches me back and we let the pretend-fight continue a little. He looks away to hide an unwilling smile. It suddenly hits me that I'm gonna miss him. I never really thought about what graduating would mean for our friendship. Let alone moving to another continent. I hate the thought of leaving him on his own again. So here's hoping Mac will get over his supposed (but doubtful) straight self and provide some sexy distraction in my absence.

"Promise you'll come to visit," I say when we're back to walking along again like proper grown-ups.

There's something I can't read in the blue eyes when they glance at me. He kicks at a small stone on the pathway. "Yeah, okay."

I roll my eyes. "How about we try that again, and this time you make it sound like you mean it?"

He suddenly stops and stares at me darkly, his jaw all tight. "Next you'll ask me to be happy about you leaving, too."

Okay, maybe that breaks my heart a little, but I don't let it show, more out of habit than anything else. I bury my hands in my pockets and look at him, tilting my head slightly to the side. "Nick…"

"Forget it," he snarls and walks on.

I'm quick to catch up. "I'm sorry," I say quietly. "It sucks for me too."

He throws me an unbelieving glance and actually laughs, quiet and bitter under his breath. "Right. Sucks so much for you and James to be starting a whole new life together in a great new place. I'm *stuck* here."

Alone. He doesn't say it, but it's there, underneath the words. I don't know what to say, so eventually I opt for: "I'm just a phone call away."

He shakes his head, refusing to look at me. "That's not the same thing."

"I know. So what can I do? Just tell me."

Nick stares into the distance. "You can't do anything. And you can't make me not angry with you by looking at me like that. Not a chance."

"You sure?" I give him my best lost puppy look. This is a serious weapon I only use in dire need.

He manages to stare at me darkly for a couple of moments more, then he has to smile and looks away. "Screw you."

I allow myself a mental high five, but then I get serious. Apparently, this needs to be said. "It's not as easy as you think, leaving here. I'd stay if I could. But that doesn't mean we have to lose touch, you and I. Unless that's what you want."

He laughs dryly in reply. "Like it matters what I want."

I shrug. "Matters to me."

He looks at me as if to say: since when? And ouch, that hits home. I wonder if he'll ever forgive me for the shitty way I treated him last semester. I've been trying my best to make amends, but those wounds appear too deep to heal in such a short period of time. I realize how much I'm hurting him again now, just when I'd finally established that I'd be a part of his life. I wish there was something I could do, but I'm at a loss when it comes to making things right with him. It seems there's nothing I can say.

We stand there for an uncomfortable moment, not looking at each other. If words are futile, there has to be another way to convince him that I care about him. I step closer and pull him into a hug. Nick tries to push me back, but only half-heartedly, and when I don't let go, he gives in. He sinks against me, ducks enough to press his face against my neck, and I pull him closer. We stand like this for a long time, neither of us saying a word. It's getting darker now, and the streetlamps along the path come to life, shining their light on us. I close my eyes briefly and inhale the familiar scent of his skin. I think we'll be okay some day. It's neither today, nor tomorrow. There's still a long way to go. I'm not even sure what I mean to him now, or what I ever meant to him. But standing here with him, the thought of leaving makes me sad for the first time.

* * *

On the day of the graduation ceremony, I get a delivery of flowers and a ridiculously fat guilt-trip cheque from Lilah. I already knew she wouldn't be able to make it. She's in Spain, probably looking for her next potential husband. What I don't expect is for Grazzo to show up at my dorm room unannounced. I'm in my black graduation gown, silly cap and all, and I'm more than a little surprised. This is the first time he's ever shown up to anything like this.

"Damn," he says when he's given me one of his bear hugs. "I'm proud of you, son."

He never calls me "son", so I guess I'm allowed to be baffled. I don't know what to say. It's good to see him, the scent of his familiar aftershave filling the room.

"They were impressed with the recording you sent in to the JIB," he continues. Ah, that's the way the wind blows. "Congratulations, Dan. You should get your acceptance letter any day."

Wow, that was quick. I'm happy to hear it, really, I am. But the way he's acting is pissing me off too much to let it show.

"Listen, Graz. I'm not doing this for you. I'm doing this because I love music. And I'm grateful that you've helped pave my way in this time. But for god's sake, back off now. Let me do my own thing. I don't want your help. I want to make it on my own."

He looks at me and a broad, impressed smile appears on his face. "Okay," he says. Just like that. "I respect that."

"I mean it."

"So do I."

I'm still a little wary. "So you promise you won't interfere in any way?"

He laughs softly. "It's a deal. Just don't come a-knocking later, big boy."

I grin. "Never happen."

"I'll drink to that," he grins. "Once you show me the way to the good stuff."

"You'll have to make due with cheap champagne. But you're coming with me first." I grab him by the arms and shove him out of my room.

"Where to?"

"There's someone I want you to meet. And be kind, because once he sees you, he might be a little in shock."

"And who is this mysterious someone?"

"My boyfriend," I say simply. Grazzo arches his eyebrows in surprise. But then he grins and puts his arm around me as we walk along. It's actually a nice feeling, though I'd never admit that to him.

"I'll be on my best behavior then."

I glance at him with a small grin. "Let's hope that for once, that'll do."

* * *

It's my last day at Woodhaven, and the last time I'm in my dorm to get one remaining bag. The room is stripped bare of everything that made it mine for the past four years of my life. I look around, feeling a sad little sting. These four walls sure have seen a lot! It's not like me to grow attached to a place, but the fact that this room witnessed an important phase of my life gives it some strange significance. It's witnessed me growing up, or at least growing up a little more. Woodhaven and its inhabitants have changed me, shaped me into someone different. Someone more myself. I'm not quite *me* yet, but I'm getting there. I'm not the same person that waltzed in here four years ago with an ego so big it almost didn't fit through the door. Okay, screw you, so most of that ego is still alive and kicking. So what? I hope I'm at least a bit less of a dick now than I used to be. But in the end, all I can say is: no regrets.

I let my gaze sweep through the room one last time, then I grab my bag of books and head out. I close the door quietly behind me. Other people on my floor are leaving as well, and everyone promises to stay in touch, knowing that's not likely to happen. I get hugs from overly emotional people I've never even talked to, but somehow I don't mind. With a wink I promise them to forget them as soon as I'm out the front door. They seem to think I'm kidding, which makes me grin.

I head downstairs quickly, avoiding more hugs from more half-strangers. James is waiting for me outside. I already said good-bye to everyone else I care about the other night at our little improvised farewell party. I'm sure most of them are still asleep and hung-over. Some of them may have left here already.

James doesn't notice me right away. He looks aloof and lonely, leaning against the banister of the stairs leading to the front door. He also looks incredibly handsome in his dark blue shirt that makes his eyes look bluer. He turns his head and sees me when I come closer. He tries to smile, but it looks heartbreakingly sad.

"Wish you could stay until the semester's over for me," he greets me.

"Wish I could too." I place a kiss on his temple. "But I'll be back to kidnap you for the weekend. It's only four days." I deliberately don't add that four days have never seemed like such an unfathomably long time.

He manages a crooked smile, and sounds amused. "Look what you've done to me. I can't even imagine this place without you!"

"What can I say, I'm hard to forget."

His smile widens. "No. You are *impossible* to forget, Mr. Rizzo."

"I'll let you in on a secret: So are you, Jimmy Boy."

I nonchalantly put my arm around him and we walk the short distance to my car. How is it so hard to even think of having to go four days without seeing him? We make it quick and painless, just a tight hug and a kiss. Then I'm in the car, and moments later he's just a small figure in the rearview mirror, turning around to walk away. It doesn't hurt to leave Woodhaven, but it hurts to leave him, if only for a short time. I find a jazz station on the radio. Benny Goodman provides a cheerful soundtrack to me leaving school, and I feel much better as the tall neoclassical buildings disappear from view. The drive home is only two hours, and it's a warm, sunny day. All around spring is in full bloom. Lilah is still in Europe, so I'll have the luxury of being by myself. There's nothing to do but enjoy life and practice music. And possible be a little pathetic, pining for James. The thought makes me laugh to myself. I turn up the radio as I head out of town. It suddenly hits me how ironic it is that I never wanted to be in a relationship for fear of feeling trapped. And now that I've found someone I'd be happily enslaved to for the rest of my life, I'm feeling absolutely free.

16 BLUE SKIES

JAMES: Months have passed in what seems like the blink of an eye. Suddenly it's late August, and all our things are packed, some have already been shipped to Germany. There's no denying it: we're officially ready to go.

I'm nervous and ridiculously excited. This isn't just a holiday. Danny and I are moving to a different country, a different continent. The next time I'll come back to the States is probably for graduating at Woodhaven. Until then, the entire Atlantic is going to be between me and the burnt down ruin that used to be my home. And that is a very good thought. I don't ever want to go back there. I hear they're already tearing the remains of my house down, now that I've sold the place. It feels good to not have any strings attached to it anymore. A new family can build a home free of ghosts there. Maybe from now on, it will be a happy place. Mom would have liked that.

Sometimes, when I'm not just sad thinking about her, I like to imagine that there is some sort of heaven after all. That she's there now, reunited with my dad. And that Simon can't touch her there. I don't really believe in heaven, or god, or any kind of afterlife, but she did, and it's a nice thought. I get why people need to believe in this sort of thing. It makes things a hell of a lot easier.

I drove back down the other day to visit her grave one last time before I leave for Berlin. Danny lent me his Porsche. I felt like a perfect snapshot for "what is wrong with this picture?" the entire time I was driving, but it made me grin. I don't think I'll ever get used to the standard of living Danny has grown up with. And that's a good thing.

The sun was low in the sky, throwing long shadows of gravestones across the lawn when I entered the cemetery. There was no-one else there, just a couple of crows staring down at me from the trees. For a moment I thought I could smell a trace of fall on the wind, rustling the leaves.

I don't believe in talking to dead people. How are they supposed to hear? But Danny suggested I try. Just because. I felt silly, crouching down before Mom's grave. I didn't know what to say. I felt lonely and miserable.

"I miss you, Mom," I finally said hoarsely. "I miss you so much." A warm wind tousled my hair, and I got goosebumps all of a sudden. It felt like a loving touch. Before I knew it, I was blurting it all out, all the things I couldn't tell her when she was still alive. "I'm sorry I hit Simon that day," I heard myself saying. "But I'm also not sorry at all. Because I love you, and you were the only thing that mattered to me." I took a deep breath and ran my fingers along the rough, cold gravestone. "I'm sorry I wasn't there to stop the fire and protect you. I'm so sorry."

I don't really know what happened, I can't explain it. But once the words were out, I felt an immediate change in me. Like forgiveness had somehow, miraculously come. Or maybe there had never been anything to forgive to begin with. Mom would have said so for sure. She wouldn't have wanted me to live in the past, but to let go off my shame and turn my life into something to be proud of. Maybe with time I can learn to accept myself with all my faults and insecurities. Maybe I can even learn to be proud of myself, like she had been. I suddenly understood that she would have wanted me to let her go, and be happy. I felt like a weight had been lifted off my shoulders. I could breathe so much easier. And there was the most amazing feeling of peace. I'd never felt like that before.

"Bye, Mom," I said as I finally got up. I touched her gravestone one more time, and I left the graveyard, never looking back.

* * *

Our itty bitty farewell committee accompanies us to the airport. There's Casey, Andrea, and Nick. Anna and Rhea gave me a call last night from their holiday in Mexico to wish us a save flight. Danny is in an infectiously good mood. He can't wait to get away. Now that the big day is here, I don't really know what I want anymore. Only that I want to be with him, and that I'm the luckiest bastard on the planet to have this amazing human being for my boyfriend. The thought helps take my mind off the possibility of a plane crash into the icy waters of the Atlantic. I have about a million disturbingly detailed plane crash scenarios in my head. Did I mention that I hate flying?

Then there's hugs and good-byes all around, and more promises of everyone coming to visit us in Berlin as soon as we've settled in. I watch Danny and Nick hug tightly for a long moment. It's a bit heartbreaking to see. I wish we could just kidnap Nick and take him along. For the third time Casey tells me to call when we get there, or he'll worry himself sick. I'm a bit shocked when Andrea wipes a tear out of the corner of her eye and attacks me with a hug that's so quick she probably hopes no-one saw. Then it's time to leave.

Our friends are still there as we get in line for Security Check to soon be absorbed in the usual degrading pre-flight rituals. I look back once we're through, at this motley crew that has nothing at all in common but us, and I wonder what new things will await them once we're gone. They wave at us again, laughing and shouting for us to be naughty, and have the time of our lives. I have every intention to.

Danny casually takes my hand in his as we stroll along, past a long line of duty free shops. There's plenty of time to waste those last dollars in our pockets on things we really don't need. But we're gonna be paying in euros in the very near future. My god, it's actually happening.

* * *

Three hours and one not so unexpectedly crappy paperback novel later we've finally boarded the plane. We quietly make fun of the flight attendant's little safety instruction dance, and I feel silly for laughing so hard about it. My fingers dig into the armrests as we take off. I get that alarming squirm in my stomach that makes me remember why not having wings should be a clue for mankind to just stay on the ground.

Danny laughs at my frozen face, and I frown at him. "What? I told you I don't like planes."

"I love take-off. The speed, the rush…"

"…the feeling of sheer terror," I finish his sentence dryly.

The laughing brown eyes are looking at me. "I'm gonna find the biggest roller-coaster in Europe and take you on it."

"Keep the roller-coaster. Living with *you* is gonna be challenge enough."

"Look who's talking," he grins. "Why am I doing this again?"

"Because you're crazy about me. Or so I hear."

His grin broadens as he shakes his head. "You got that wrong, Jimmy Boy. You're crazy about *me*. That's what *I* hear."

"Oh, is that right?" I grin back at him. "If I remember correctly, you were after me first."

Danny laughs. "Fine, you got me. Guilty as charged."

I chuckle to myself. "I always thought you were incredibly hot. Since I first saw you."

He arches an eyebrow. "Did you now? You were pretty good at hiding it."

"I did my best. And look where it got me."

He looks at me, all pretend-smug, but his eyes are shining brightly. "We could have saved ourselves a lot of trouble if you'd shown me."

"But then again, that wouldn't have been as much fun."

He laughs. "Fun? More like torture."

"That's fun, the Foley way." I grin.

Danny looks at me fondly. "Never change, Jimmy."

"Ditto." I lean over and kiss him. He pulls me closer, and I lose my train of thought. When I very carefully glance at the small plane window next to him again, I have a big, goofy grin on my face, my fear of flying almost forgotten. The plane breaks through the misty clouds, and then there's the endless sky all around, and the sun is on my face. Beacon-bright. I close my eyes for a moment, and a happy little smile steals onto my lips when Danny sings close to my ear: "Blue skies, smiling at me, nothing but blue skies do I see…"

Excitement stirs in my stomach again, the best kind. This is my one shot at a new beginning, a clean slate. New country, new city, and maybe even a new me. A me that finally allows itself to be loved. And even if I stay the old me, that's okay. It's not that bad, being me. Took me quite a long while and the world's most gorgeous boyfriend to see that, but there you go. So there. The realization comes as a surprise, but I have faith, I do. Faith in myself, faith in us, and for this one moment, even faith in this planets' sad population. Oh, this is gonna be good. Brace yourself, world, here we come.

EPILOGUE

A Letter, 2 Months Later

Hey Nick,
How are things on the other side of the Atlantic? Is Woodhaven treating you well?
Sorry it's taken me so ridiculously long to write an actual letter, but life's been kinda crazy around here. Like I mentioned on the phone, I guess you don't know how well you speak a language until you actually move to the country. Gulp. I have come to learn that I don't know shit about German; at least it feels like that more often than not. It's either that, or the dear people of Berlin just have a *really* weird dialect that seems to have never heard of that thing called grammar. It contains absurd words that don't even exist in actual German. Did you know that they say "icke" instead of "ich" around here, and crazy stuff like that? When I'm not utterly confused, it amuses me way too much. At least my profs at uni (mostly) speak the language I have been studying for so long.

Danny handles the language problems pretty well, though, the bastard - as was to be expected. You get pretty far here with a wink and that damn gorgeous smile.

Speaking of Danny, damn, you really should see our place! I promised details, so here goes. The "tiny Berlin hideaway" Grazzo is so graciously letting us stay at is a *gigantic* loft with marble floors, housekeeping, and a view of the Brandenburg Gate. Four bedrooms! Pictures included, so you can pick one in advance for when you're coming to visit. (When *are* you coming to visit?) I thought it was a practical joke when Danny let us in after an 8 hour flight with no sleep and a jetlag from hell on my part. I have vague memories of making him call Grazzo on the phone and demanding to speak to him in order to believe it. I may have called the great Graziano Rizzo insane. Wah. He may have laughed at me and said I was "perfect" ...whatever that means... But really, this place is so huge I managed to get lost on my way to the bathroom on the first night. I had to send up smoke signals for Danny to come get me.

I'm not sure what I expected of life with Danny Rizzo. Not this, to be sure. I remember being mildly terrified when I looked around our place and thought "Perfect party hub" - I swear I foresaw sleepless nights with crowds of people totally trashing our place to painfully loud music so vividly I may have sobbed. But it turns out - there's none of that. What can I say, living (hell, *being*) with Danny is surprisingly... normal. No, it's more than that, it's kinda zen. He makes it so, somehow. Sigh. It's like nothing can faze him, so when I break into a panic about super important things (that may appear trivial to anyone not inhabiting my brain), he just makes it go away. I will keep this PG-rated, so no details on how. But you know what that guy can do to us mere mortals.

I know, I know, you say I think too much. But sometimes I still worry that it's too good to be true. Because I'm like that. But seriously, how on earth did I get this lucky? That's not even *real*.

And it's not even like everything is sunshine and roses *all the time*. We still have Our Daily Quarrel - which comes so punctually that it's almost getting too funny to go through with anymore. Because he gives me that damn grin every time I start. He says I should stop trying to make life miserable when it's not. I'm not sure I'm quite ready yet, but I may have to succumb some time in the foreseeable future. Dear god, what's happening to me?

We've made some great friends. Okay, so Danny made them, and I don't hate them, which is a huge plus. I already told you about Silvia, the petite jazz singer with the deep, raspy voice (who smokes like a chimney, and drinks us all under the table). There's also Anton, this cool artist Danny met at a supermarket (how does one make friends with artists at supermarkets, for crying out loud?), Gabriel the gorgeous singer-songwriter, and Marie the Lesbian, who's an amusingly foul-mouthed cab-driver and reminds me way too much of Anna, but kinda in a good way. There's tons more people and I don't yet remember everyone's names (D suggests that's something I could work on - bah!), but we hang out on a regular basis, and they try to teach us Berlin speak.

We go out a lot now, mostly to all those little jazz clubs and awesome cabarets they have here. I may have started to like going out. What's wrong with me? Am I turning into a *normal* person?!

Danny is putting together a band, did he tell you? I actually look forward to future jamming sessions at our place. I did mention the piano, right? (We need to talk more often, time-zones and international call fares be damned!) Anyway, there's a black Steinway grand piano in the concert hall Grazzo calls living room. I may be making Danny practice on it way more than he needs. But damn, I love watching him play and get lost in the music. It gives me funny feelings inside, if you know what I mean.

On that shockingly mushy note, I'll leave you because class starts in half an hour and I gotta hit the road. Do tell me more about your adventures at good ol' Woodhaven, would you? I never would have thought so, but I may just be missing the place a tiny little. Go figure.

I almost forgot - Danny says to say hi and tell you to "go get the jock" - whatever that might mean. I'll let you two have your little secrets.

…Okay, spill. Who is this mysterious jock? Is it Mac? I hope it is. He seems nice enough from how you talk about him. Bring him along when you come to visit! After all, I have to make sure he's good enough for you.

Take care for now, you crazy dog,
James

ABOUT SUSANN JULIEVA

Susann Julieva writes bittersweet LGBT fiction, some light and charming, some with a slightly darker edge - but always with a happy ending. She writes in different genres including romance and paranormal. Susann publishes books in English and German.

She lives in Germany, is owned by a crazy cat, and believes chocolate is the answer to all questions.

Find out more and get in touch with Susann on
www.susannjulieva.com

Printed in Great Britain
by Amazon.co.uk, Ltd.,
Marston Gate.